The Dreamstone

She woke knowing the bed was empty. The candlelight, coming from the window-ledge, seemed very bright. It lapped at the pillows and ringed the armchair with a yellow radiance.

In the middle of it sat Gwyn, naked except for a large blue sweater. He was hunched over a notepad on his knees, writing. His face was exhausted but vibrant with concentration, his downcast eyes two dark scoops of lashes, his lower lip pushed out, his cheeks hollowed. The tiny movements of his writing hand made the bunched muscles of his shoulders quiver.

'It's finished.'

Gwyn laid his pen on his notepad. He lifted his face to hers; his eyelids were drooping but his eyes shone triumphantly. His face was rosy in the candlelight. 'Shall I read it to you?'

'Go on.'

Jane's voice was painful but he didn't stop to wonder about it. He bowed his head to the notepad and began to read.

Jane saw the harbour and the ten ships gathered in the water, heard the shouting and banging and music, and the cry of the gulls and the swish of the waves, looked into the eyes of the man beside her and lifted her face to the open sea.

In the shadowed bedroom the unknown woman was back.

The Dreamstone

LIANE JONES

A Mandarin Paperback

THE DREAMSTONE

First published in Great Britain 1992
by William Heinemann Ltd
This edition published 1993
by Mandarin Paperbacks
an imprints of Reed Consumer Books Ltd
Michelin House, 81 Fulham Road, London SW3 6RB
and Auckland, Melbourne, Singapore and Toronto

Reprinted 1993 (four times), 1994

Copyright © Liane Jones 1992

A CIP catalogue record for this title
is available from the British Library

ISBN 0 7493 1206 8

Printed and bound in Great Britain
by HarperCollins Manufacturing, Glasgow

For Jamie

PRONUNCIATION OF WELSH NAMES

Ceinwen	Kíne-wen
Madoc	Mád-uck
Glesig	Gléss-ig
Buddug	Bíthig
Dafydd	Dáv-ith
Meilyr	Mý-leer
Yns Wair	Uńn-iss Ware
Yns Llyr	Uńn-iss Leer
Marared	Murrár-ed
Gwydion	Gẃidi-un
Rhys	Rees
Goff	Goff
Eirlys	Íŕe-liss
Graig	Grige (both gs hard)
Pengroed	Pen-gróid

´ *indicates the stressed syllable.*

The best way to reproduce the Welsh 'll' sound is not as 'cl' but as 'hl'. Ynys Llyr becomes not 'Unn-iss Cleer' but 'Unn-iss Hleer'.

The Welsh 'r' is rolled.

ACKNOWLEDGEME|

I should like to thank Professor Gwyn
enthralling books on Welsh history and th|
rarely left my side for eighteen months. I al|
and Frank Norman for sharing with me t|
books. The learning is all theirs; the inaccura|

With thanks also to my family and friends |
ment; to Jamie Buxton for reading the wo|
helping to shape it; to Sara Fisher my agent fo|
one, and to all at William Heinemann who ha|
on the book. Finally, my special thanks to L|
imaginative and inspirational editor.

Part One

I

The plane flew west, through the blue sky. Staring out of the window, Gwyn could no longer see ground – only banks of white cloud far beneath. They were fifteen minutes out of Heathrow, heading north-west: they would soon be passing over Wales. He had left there early this morning while it was still dark; the houses and fields had looked unreal in the orange glow of the streetlamps.

He had been unable to feel anything, then. Now, though, he felt excited and anxious. Sitting in this metal tube, being carried through the air, he was suspended between two lives. Behind him were all the familiar things – Wales and London, friends, the pubs and parties and the gradual progress he was making with his work. And ahead lay what he hoped was his big break: a year in New York. A year as resident poet at Brockham University. No more juggling day jobs and time to write: now the two would be combined and they were going to pay him forty thousand dollars for the privilege. Forty thousand!

So here he was, wearing his new tweed jacket (maybe he should sew some poetic leather patches on the elbows), straining to catch a last glimpse of home. But he was too late for that. He lifted his eyes from the clouds and caught sight of his own reflection in the glass: a square Welsh face, curly dark hair, broad hands drumming on the sides of his miniature bottle of scotch. Gwyn wished he could look or feel like a seasoned international traveller but he knew that he looked exactly what he was – a boy from the valleys, going west: nervous, keyed up and uncertain what to expect.

His eyes were surprisingly heavy. He leaned back in his seat and let the steady vibration of the engines lull him.

It was a doze rather than a sleep; a half-consciousness into which the noises of the aircraft impinged. The rustling of other passengers, the clanking of a trolley moving down the aisle still sounded in Gwyn's outer ear as the dream overtook him.

The blue water lapped the sides of the ship. The bodies of the men who crowded the deck were burned brown and red; Gwyn saw their muscles strain as they hauled at the ropes to bring down the sails. There were women on deck too: they lined the edges of the ship, leaning over the sides and staring towards land. And there were children, clinging to the women and running about shouting.

All the people were thin and looked sick. Their eyes were sunken and some of them had bald patches where their hair had fallen out. Even on the open deck, with the warm, fragrant air blowing, Gwyn could smell the stench of human dirt. But he was not thinking of that, nor of the excited company around him. His gaze was fixed on the prow of the ship and the man who stood there. He could hear the man's name being spoken repeatedly as people called to him and relayed his orders: Madoc. Prince Madoc.

Madoc was turning towards him. Gwyn noticed how short he was, but then they all were: every adult on this ship was at least a hand-span shorter than he. The cloak the prince wore over this tunic was stained and torn: it fluttered away from his bare shoulders. Gwyn saw that Madoc's left hand clutched the gunwale; his right hand was lifting in a beckoning gesture to Gwyn.

It was a strong, weathered face. It had years of experience marked on it, yet the eyes were young. Madoc was no older than Gwyn.

Gwyn felt the pull of the young prince as a physical force, tugging at his vitals. He moved down the deck, weaving through the sweating men and clamouring women, craning his neck to keep Madoc in sight. He was very near him now; close enough to see the white scars on Madoc's shoulders and the passion in his eyes.

Then he was next to Madoc at the prow. With a quickening

4

of all his pulses, he looked out over the clear blue water to the shore. Before him curved a pale yellow strand and behind that, dark green vegetation rose twice the height of a man. There were no people, but in the far elbow of the strand strange birds stood on tall, thin legs, uncoiling swan-like necks and dipping their beaks into the water.

The hunger and the ruthless desire were things Gwyn had always believed possible. But now he tasted them.

Because he was no longer standing next to the prince. In these closing moments of the dream, as it grew thinner yet remained searingly, intoxicatingly clear, Gwyn had become Madoc.

'No further in,' he shouted. 'No further! Mother of God's blood, throw stones!'

He turned to watch the men lift up the heavy boulders, netted and tied to ropes, and heave them over the side. The women and children scattered excitedly.

By the main mast, where the sails were half-furled, stood Ceinwen. Her hair had come loose under her grubby white head-dress and her face, thin and roughened by the wind now, was flushed with a wild triumph. He held his hands out to her and the command in the gesture aroused him still more.

'My lord,' Ceinwen's high, clear voice cut through the noise. 'It's seven twenty-five am in New York.'

Gwyn's exultation changed to fury. He threw his head back to order her out of his sight, off the foredeck. How dare she speak such things? Didn't she know that to shout those reckless words would destroy the ship, banish the sea, return him to the mundane world . . .

Gwyn opened his eyes to see the stewardess bending over him. She was holding a plastic-covered tray, with packaged food arranged in compartments. As he looked from it to the woman's made-up face, he felt a bundle of sensations whirl past him: colours and warmth and the taste of salt, the echo of shouts . . . and then it was gone.

Disoriented, he smiled up at the stewardess and accepted his airline lunch. So it was only seven twenty-five in New York: before breakfast, even. It was funny to think that he was actually flying backwards, to land at an earlier time.

Gwyn began to ease the plastic covering off his food tray. His short doze must have invigorated him; he felt suddenly very hungry. He ate his meal quickly, gazing out of the window at the endless, featureless blue.

2

'What are you doing?'

Harry's voice startled her. She had been concentrating so fiercely she hadn't heard the door open. She blinked at him: standing in the doorway he looked fresh and vigorous, aggravatingly so.

'I'm working,' Jane said.

'You're attacking that sheet of paper as if you hate it.'

'I do.'

'Sssh.' Harry shut the door and walked across to his own desk. 'Blasphemy. Isn't everything that Professor Jewell writes a joy to read?'

Jane rubbed her forehead to ease her headache.

'He certainly thinks so. I'm going to go crazy before I finish editing this – it's seven thousand words long!'

Harry set his books down and stretched lazily.

'Ease up,' he said.

Jane's eyes flickered over his handsome face. She was tired and frustrated and the easy flippancy of his tone piqued her. It was all right for Harry. He was a junior professor, a respected member of the university, and his post on the *West Side Review* was yet another feather in his cap. Jane was just a salaried employee, assistant editor in name and performer of all the hard slog in reality. She was the one responsible for getting the magazine out every month, and doing all the unglamorous, behind-the-scenes work.

By contrast Harry, lounging in his chair, looked every bit the golden boy from the privileged background. He might be relaxing on the pillared porch of his family's Virginia home.

'Professors don't get rich, son. They don't get to Washington either.' That had been Harry's father's verdict on academia. It had taken Harry's winning of the Cornell Dargener Fellowship to reconcile George Crown to his son's choice. Harry might not add to the Crown fortune, but he would be eminent. He might still get high office. Look at Kissinger.

And look at me, thought Jane. Harry and many others at Brockham might measure themselves against the politicians and lawyers and corporate emperors; she still measured her distance from welfare. Sometimes, her colleagues' arrogant complaints made her smile; at others they filled her with a desperate sense of insecurity. However well she did, she would never have that assurance with which Harry had been born: the assurance of belonging, of being gifted, of taking it for granted that the world was there for you, laying all its promise and opportunities before you like a feast.

Harry told Jane that she had all the more reason to be proud and she knew he was right. Renoxia, her small home town in North Dakota, had not exactly given her a good start in life. She had fled from it at sixteen, alone on the Greyhound bus with no qualifications and no references and nobody predicting much of a future for her. She had come to New York and stayed in that grim, nineteenth-century Mission, queuing up to use the bathroom, cooking one-pot meals in the shared kitchenettes, ironing her clothes for the next day's work in the series of boring shop and office jobs.

After two years, she had moved into a shared apartment; after another year she had started to attend night school. It took her three more years to get her qualifications. Finally, when she was twenty-four, she had become a student of film studies and literature at Brockham University, on the Upper West Side.

And now here she was, with a degree to her name and the kind of job that many people were queuing up for. Professor Jewell himself, head of Brockham's English Department, had hand-picked her for the post while she was still a student.

'It will be a big, bold, brawling arts paper!' he had said to her, sweeping his hands in her face. 'A publication with guts, not

8

afraid to be confrontational. None of your nit-picking, lily-livered pamphlets. We'll review books and plays, of course, and publish essays and poems, but we'll do good red-blooded interviews and film and TV write-ups as well. You can run it day to day. We'll give you an office. You have office experience, don't you?'

He had known very well that she had office experience – more than enough to run a small university-funded magazine. Jane had had her doubts taking the job: she had hoped to get away from office work once she had her degree, and she didn't look forward to coping with Professor Jewell's ego every day, but there had been no real possibility of refusing. One simply couldn't pass up such a chance.

Jane's editorial office was eighteen months' old now and the *West Side Review* was doing well. It was sold by subscription and on some bookstalls, locally and in Soho and Greenwich Village, and in recent months Jane had managed to increase the advertising revenue. It was known as Duane Jewell's magazine, of course, with the names of the associate editors, almost all of them younger academics like Harry, coming next in the readers' consciousness. Jane doubted if anyone noticed her name, appearing in modest-sized print on the mast-head. But she knew that she was doing a good job.

However, that did not alleviate the task of editing down the more pompous articles, like this month's contribution from Professor Jewell.

'Oh *shit*,' she muttered through clenched teeth. Her jaw was aching now to match her head. She realised that Harry was watching her sympathetically.

'Do you want me to leave you alone?' he asked.

Jane shook her head.

'No. I'm sorry. I'll give it a rest now and we can go to lunch.'

Jane began to put her papers away, stuffing them into the overflowing trays which made a border round her desk-top. Her corner of the shared office was drab; her gesture towards decoration consisted of two posters and a plastic bunch of grapes hanging from her reading lamp. It was left to Harry to provide the colour and life in the room. Even though he was only at his desk a few hours a week, the two walls behind it were vibrant with a display of postcards, prints and posters. Even his bookshelves were pleasing. Course books and volumes of Jacobean drama nestled with lurid paperback thrillers; handsome first edition sports books stood alongside contemporary novels.

Jane like to look out from the mess of her corner to the brightness of Harry's. Sometimes she wondered what Harry thought of his own view. He had never complained – although three weeks earlier he had struggled in carrying a large palm in an earthenware pot and had placed it carefully on her side of the room, in his line of vision.

Jane looked at him now, his fair head haloed by the vivid colours on the walls behind. Harry was exactly the same age as her – twenty-eight – but he seemed so far ahead of her. He belonged in this world of old buildings and endowed libraries; she knew that she did not. By comparison with Harry she was an upstart and she often felt like it. Moreover, she often felt the upstart's restless energy. It was in her bones today.

'What's the matter now?'

Jane realised that she was staring at him. In the dark glass of the bookstand next to the door, she saw herself reflected: her pale, oval face was tense, her shoulders raised; her dark hair leapt away from her forehead where her hands had been tugging at it. She looked like some angular insect, about to spring at Harry. Jane was often embarrassed to catch herself in poses like this. She wished she could have composure but she was too impatient.

She opened her mouth to deny that there was anything wrong, when she was pre-empted by a sudden babble of noise.

'What in God's name is that?'

A commotion had begun outside, in the campus square. Voices were raised, a din of male tones yelling over one another in what seemed to be furious protest.

They went to the window. Down in the square was Professor Jewell. Florid of face and impressively large, he stood with his corduroy-clad legs apart and his check-shirted chest thrown forward. He was in uproarious conversation with the new resident poet.

Jane saw at a glance that the professor was well aware of everyone's eyes on him. He remained an unnecessary ten feet away from Gwyn Thomas, his grey head thrown back in full-throated cry. He was brandishing a book in his right hand.

'Do not say I bring you no inspiration,' he was bellowing. 'Do not assert that never do I make you offerings. This, dear boy, is book three of Homer's *Odyssey*, which, if you bend your too-little exercised mind to it, might spur you to emulation of a real poet. What do you say to that, you squanderer of talent?'

Gwyn Thomas looked surprisingly unembarrassed, caught in this blast of exhibitionism. He shrugged and grinned.

'There's no place like Homer,' he shouted back. 'Which way is Kansas?'

'Hah! Tacky wordsmith, shitting on your own civilisation.'

'Civilisation is the worm in my turd,' Thomas countered.

'Dylan bloody Thomas. He paraphrases Dylan lick-spittle Thomas and thinks it gains him points.'

Jewell was now openly playing to the spectators. He waved his book at them and spread his arms so that he looked like a huge and bizarre traffic policeman, book in one hand, briefcase in the other. His beige cardigan flapped slightly in the breeze.

'Jesus, it's embarrassing,' muttered Harry. 'Gwyn Thomas has to be the world's biggest brown-nose to go along with that.'

But Jane, watching Gwyn Thomas, wasn't sure. He didn't look uneasy or self-conscious. He seemed to be taking the whole display in his stride.

'Oh hell, give us a look then,' he said. He walked towards Jewell, holding out his hand for the book. While they had remained some yards apart, there had been a certain resemblance between the two: they were both thickset men with short necks and curly hair; Thomas's dark brown, the older man's grey. But now that Thomas was moving close up to the professor, the similarity vanished. Gwyn Thomas was much shorter than Professor Jewell and compact where Duane Jewell was bulky. His movements were direct and dogged, and entirely devoid of Jewell's extravagance. The poet was altogether a denser, darker figure. Reaching the professor, he plucked the book from his hand and in the same movement dropped it into the canvas bag he wore over his shoulder. Then he swayed and stepped back.

'He's drunk,' said Jane.

'You're drunk! shouted Jewell, and for an instant real disgust mingled with the fake version on his face.

Gwyn Thomas said something they couldn't hear. His broad

face, with its wide-set eyes and long nose – a typical Welsh face, so Jewell had informed campus on another occasion – wore a beatific expression.

'Oh of course, if you've written a *poem*!' Jewell had lowered his voice but it still carried easily up to the window. Its bombast was now heavy with sarcasm and edged with a clear warning note. 'Then there can be no more to be said. Let's all hope that the result is worth the physical abuse. I recommend that you take yourself to the refectory and get some food inside you. We'll be seeing you tonight, of course. Please come disguised as a serious poet.'

Professor Jewell turned and strode up the faculty steps, vanishing beneath them. Gwyn Thomas smiled, turned a ragged circle and walked away across the square, in the opposite direction from the refectory.

'Shit,' said Harry, watching him go. 'He's pushing his luck, Duane's protégé or not. That's the third time he's been drunk on campus, but at least the other times have been at night.'

'Is he an alcoholic?' Jane was interested now. She had seen Gwyn Thomas around campus since the start of semester, but knew very little about him.

'I don't think so. Just an asshole. A sub-Dylan Thomas type who thinks that wenching and puking into beer cans goes with the territory.'

'You're very tough on him. How has he crossed you?'

'He hasn't. He just ain't my kind of guy.'

Jane examined Harry's profile, still turned to the window as he followed Gwyn's departure. His expression was too complicated to interpret, compounded of disapproval, pensiveness and a careful reserve. Was Gwyn Thomas rather more his type than he admitted? Or was he brooding over Professor Jewell's championing of Thomas and antipathy to himself?

Neither Harry nor anyone else could work out why Duane Jewell had recently turned against him. There were a number of possibilities: Harry was beginning to be acclaimed in Jewell's own field of Jacobean studies, and Jewell was renowned for his intense competitiveness. Then again, there was the fact that Harry was gay. Professor Jewell had been active in getting Harry to leave Cornell for Brockham, offering him excellent terms as a junior professor and the editorial position on the *Review*. For the first year they had got along well and Jewell had seemed to beam on the growing friendship between Jane and Harry, his two protégés, and to take a sunny view of all Harry did.

But during the last semester, the senior professor had done a rapid about-turn. Many people felt the chill of Jewell's hostility in their time, but he was now being especially vituperative to Harry. Harry steered his course at Brockham skilfully and would probably outlast the vendetta, but he was not disposed to like the professor's favourites.

And Gwyn Thomas was very much a favourite; even Jane, who was not well informed on faculty politics, knew that. You only had to see Jewell hailing Thomas in the lobby, or hear him shouting friendly insults across the library, to see that he was this semester's choice. The professor like to play the good ol' boy libertarian with him, the fellow red-blooded son of toil. But the poet was evidently giving Jewell a run for his money. Jane found herself smiling at the back of Gwyn Thomas's head as it disappeared, somewhat lurchingly, behind the austere grey stone of the history faculty.

'Tonight's party might be more fun than we expect.'

'Gail will be mortified if Thomas is still drunk. She's wearing him like a badge these days.'

'Really? She's serious about him?'

'Extremely. She lights up like Times Square whenever he appears. Her students think it's hilarious.'

So did Harry, evidently.

'Gloating, Harry?' asked Jane.

'And after all, why not? The abbess finds true love. She'll be giving up her Madonna-blue frocks next. If she can hold him, of course.'

'Of course she can, if she wants to.'

'You reckon?'

'Yes,' said Jane contemptuously. 'Men like that who fuck around and get drunk always want some tough, prim little bunny to come along and sort them out.'

'Thinking of getting in line?'

'I'm not prim, you bastard.'

'No, but you're certainly tough.'

Jane laughed.

'What are his poems like?' she asked, as they turned away from the window.

'Quite good. Not what you'd expect. You mean to say you haven't read them yet? But you've got a copy in your apartment.'

'It's just for show.' said Jane, pulling on her jacket. 'In case Duane drops by. Harry, you look shocked.'

He did. Beneath his flippant manner, Harry was an extremely serious scholar. He had a rather princely, Renaissance idea of what it was to learn and understand. Sometimes Jane longed to send him out into the real world for a while, to be a short-order cook, say, or a taxi driver, and see how pure he found the joys of learning after a twelve-hour shift. Now, the expression on his face nettled her.

'Look, I haven't had time. I have so much to do getting the *Review* out every month, chasing up all the contributors and editing everything down to a bearable length. Some drunken Welsh poet is hardly essential reading for me just now.'

Harry raised his hands.

'I submit. I submit. Let's get some lunch. You're in an angry mood today.'

They walked down the stairs together. The corridors were populous with faculty staff and students all making their way towards the refectory or off campus for lunch. As they wove a path through the crowded lobby, Harry linked his arm through Jane's. She felt him big and powerful next to her; he was one of the few men who made her feel small. She took pleasure in the athleticism of his movements and adjusted her stride to his long one. They pushed open the double glass doors and stepped on to the stone terrace; the crisp fall air rushed into Jane's lungs.

'Can you remember what they say about holly berries?'

'No. Are they poisonous? Aphrodisiac? Hallucinogenic?'

'Isn't there something about the weather and holly berries? If they come early and stay, it's going to be a hard winter.'

'Is it? Sounds very Renoxian to me. What brought on this attack of folklore?'

'I noticed those berries down there this morning. They're so red, and yet the trees have hardly started turning. I've never noticed them so ripe, so early.'

Jane waved her free hand in the direction of the holly bush. The drops of red were vivid in the gentle sunlight. They looked oddly unseasonal. With a shiver, she thought ahead to January. Then there would be a grubby snow-sky and her fingers would be pinched pink and blue with cold. She imagined the way the bushes would look encrusted in white, the darkened red berries and leathery green of the leaves showing through in patches where the birds had pecked the snow away.

Winters in New York could be bitter, but they were nothing compared to the long fierce hardness that a bad year brought to Renoxia. The thought of it laid a chill, soft and inexorable, on her mind.

She gave her head a quick little shake. What had they been talking about before? Ah yes, Gwyn Thomas and the party tonight. The Welsh boy wonder; no doubt Jewell would want to publish him in the *Review* soon. She wondered idly if he wrote about Wales and reflected that it would mean little to her anyway: she knew absolutely nothing about the place.

3

Professor Jewell's drawing room was full of people. Holding glasses, they stood in groups, sat on the arms of chairs and drifted across yards of Indian carpet in search of new conversation. Before one of the windows, set fetchingly against the floor-length drapes of heavy blue silk, research student Amanda-Lee Chadburgh and linguistics professor Liam Connolly were getting to know one another. Around a small sofa, four of the cleverer and more pretentious third-year students were poised in attitudes of casual intimacy. Dressed every one in Left Bank black, they were chatting to Ambika Thalo, Brockham's new resident novelist.

Harry, Jane saw, was having an amiable conversation with Molly Jewell, the professor's wife. Molly's elegant dark head was inclined up towards him, bracelets glittering on her wrists as she gesticulated. Harry and Molly had always liked one another; Jane supposed that Harry could not resist bearding Duane in his lair.

The Jewells' apartment was well suited to parties. The rooms were large and square, the polished wood floors scattered with richly coloured Indian and Turkish carpets, the walls bright with silks, scrolls and contemporary paintings. This was the side of Duane Jewell with which he liked to surprise people: the good ol' boy act was merely a foil to his aestheticism.

It was a good party. The buzz of conversation was constant and rising. Professor Jewell was sweeping round the room with two bottles of wine, joining in conversations as they took his fancy. Hand-painted pottery bowls were piled high with clementines, nuts, little envelopes of pastry with spicy fillings, Turkish marzipan candies. A range of the delicacies was laid out on the long table by her side, beneath the bookshelves. She picked up a pastry and bit into it – creamed avocado and hot sauce – and nodded her head at Gail.

'I don't really know what to say to them about it,' Gail said.

Gail looked happy and relaxed, Jane thought. She had always found it easy to talk to Gail, unlike some of her colleagues, even though there was usually a formality between them. It was Gail's formality. Gail, serious-minded, committed and a junior professor at only twenty-seven, often seemed to talk to people as if she were following a conversation manual. Now I compliment her on her dress; now I laugh. Now I chat inconsequentially.

Gail was in Madonna blue tonight. Her face, framed by bouncing copper hair, was very smooth, lacking the marks of experience you would expect in a twenty-seven-year-old. Harry was right: she did have the air of an abbess. But this evening it was an abbess who had received a holy vision.

How long had Gail been glowing like this? A couple of weeks, Jane thought. She had not been paying much attention to couplings in the faculty recently; she had been too wrapped up in work. Perhaps it was time to raise her head. The fastidious Gail Hunter in love was a novel sight; Gail in partnership with the hard-drinking poet would be a sight well worth seeing.

In the ten minutes that Gail had been chatting to Jane, Gwyn's name had been spoken at least half a dozen times. When Jane had confessed she didn't know Gwyn, Gail had suggested they go out to dinner together – she, Gwyn, Jane and Harry – later that week. Gail was now discursing on the problems of teaching medieval sexual history (work was still a big preoccupation), but she had even managed to bring Gwyn Thomas into that.

'Gwyn pointed out that in the Middle Ages the Welsh were believed to have lost their country as a punishment for buggery, bestiality and incest. But as I was explaining to my class, those practices were considered sins but not sins which set you apart from a so-called normative. There was no normative. It was difficult for a chapel-raised person like Gwyn to accept that.'

She laughed, showing very small white teeth, and looked eagerly across the room to where Gwyn Thomas stood in a group of people. He was not quite standing though: he was leaning against a polished walnut cabinet, his elbow propping him up. His face wore an expression of great concentration, dark eyebrows drawn down over his nose.

He was drinking too much for safety, thought Jane. Would he be making an exhibition of himself later on? She half hoped so.

'I was chapel-raised too,' she said to Gail. 'The hooks go deep.'

'Professor Jewell,' said Gail, as he suddenly loomed between them, a bottle in each hand. 'This is a lovely party.'

'Do you think?' Jewell said. He tipped the two bottles into the two women's glasses in perfect synchronisation. 'Given the number of fine brains and good bodies in the room, I hope it will turn a damn sight more Dionysian before it's over. Perhaps we and our close friends shall see what we can do, eh?'

He turned his head from Gail to Jane, his bushy eyebrows working. Jane smiled cautiously. Was he referring to Gail and Gwyn, or to her and Harry? All of them, probably; managing to exert his power over four people in one go and make everyone uneasy.

'How are your labours going this month?' he asked her.

'Hectic, as usual,' she said.

'You got the piece I left on your desk? "The Decline of the Art Market"?'

'Yes,' said Jane quickly. 'It's very interesting indeed, but I'll have to edit it down a little.'

'Of course,' said Jewell, smiling expansively. 'You don't have to ask me, you know that. You are the 'hands on' assistant editor, as the revolting phrase is. You know how tight space is and who must be cut.'

Jane nodded, wondering if she would now have to drop her own article about the new women film directors. She had been hoping to squeeze it in.

'You know I shan't complain,' said Jewell. 'Have you brought a mask, or will you be wanting one of mine?' he swept on, changing the subject yet still on the attack.

'I've brought my own,' said Jane.

'Really? Good, good. Something you happened to have lying around? It's fascinating what people have in their bottom drawers, isn't it Gail?'

'Well, I don't have a mask, Professor Jewell, actually. I'll be needing to borrow one from you.'

'Perhaps you have something else in your bottom drawers that the rest of us – that is, most of the rest of us – don't know about.' Jewell's floridly handsome, middle-aged face smiled down at Gail.

A ripple of comprehension and embarrassment went over Gail's face. But she continued to stare politely up at him.

Jane didn't try to hide the distaste on her own face. A second later she wished that she had done, for Jewell had glanced at her and she saw him register her reaction.

'I see my wife is talking to your friend,' he said. 'How charming he is. Excuse me.'

'Oh shit,' muttered Jane. 'Now he's going to take it out on Harry.'

Gail was silent for a second. Then she smiled past Jane. 'I'm just going to have a word with Andrew.'

Jane turned her back on the party in an attempt to shut out Jewell's voice. It didn't work: from across the room she could hear him baiting Harry. It was a crude kind of baiting – insinuations that Harry was spoon fed, that he lacked originality, that he was effete – but Jewell had good comic timing. There was a horrible fascination in listening to it.

Jane poured herself a long glass of wine.

'How the bloody hell can he put up with that?'

She hadn't heard Gwyn Thomas approach. He was standing very close to her, almost shoulder to shoulder. Close to he looked fresh-faced, despite his scowl. The scowl was briefly transformed by a smile as she passed him the bottle.

'Thanks,' he said. 'Jesus, listen to him. Should we go and interrupt?'

'Harry can handle it.'

'Shouldn't have to. God alive, why does everyone take it from the vicious old bugger?'

His voice was very deep and the Welsh accent made the hard consonants – the ts and the ds – very emphatic. He was not very tall, only a centimetre or two bigger than Jane, and so she was looking directly into his face. It was a solid, open face, with eyes set wide apart. Up till tonight, Jane had assumed he had a broken nose, but now she saw that this was an illusion. She understood how she'd been misled: his head was round and covered in short, curly hair like a boxer's. He stood like someone prepared for a fight too, defensively squared.

'I thought you liked him,' she said curtly.

'When he's nice, I like him. Not when he's being a vicious old bugger. Anyhow, why did you think that?'

'I saw you in the square today.'

Gwyn winced.

'Oh damn. Do you want me to crawl away and be ashamed of myself?'

Jane examined his face. It was relaxed and full of a rough charm, but she resisted the impulse to smile back. The implied criticism of Harry still rankled.

'Are you going to do it again tonight?' she asked.

'What?'

'Whatever it is you do when you drink too much.'

Gwyn's face changed. He went on smiling but within the laughter wrinkles his eyes were quite level. His face and his body seemed to have gone very still. Holding the gaze, Jane felt conscious of Thomas's closeness, and of the squareness of his body inside the red jumper and black trousers, and even of the clean washing-powder smell of the clothes themselves. She found she was searching his face with her eyes and with a flurry of discomfort she realised that she was attracted to him. She was extremely attracted to him.

'I don't drink too much,' Gwyn said, slowly and with exaggerated clearness. 'I just get drunk. And I don't do anything. Well, I do – I spill things and fall over, mainly. I can't help it, I think I'm in the rugby club back home, see.'

Jane willed the flush back down from her face. She guessed that Thomas would now turn and walk away. Insufferable boor; what did Harry call him – the wenching wordsmith? She reached out a dismissive arm and took a clementine from the bowl on the table. She began to peel it and glanced up. Gwyn was still there, staring at her, half smiling. She recognised the look in his eyes and was seized with a mixture of excitement and triumph and dismay.

'It's going to be a long night,' she said.

'Yes,' said Gwyn after a pause. 'This masking-up fidaddle, you mean.'

'Mmm.' Subliminal messages were shooting from her to him, back, out again, returned – without either of them being able to interrupt the process or take control of it.

On the edge of her vision, Jane could discern a mass of shining copper. She struggled to tear her eyes from Gwyn's face and failed. Gail had already come to a stop beside them, and was smiling, when Jane wrenched her attention away from Gail's lover.

'Hi Gail,' she said in confusion. 'Would you like a clementine?'

Gwyn began to laugh.

It was a few minutes before midnight and the guests were shifting around the room like flotsam or 1 wind-roughened sea. Duane Jewell had just ushered out a stream of guests . . . 'Out, people, out along the hall and into the second room on the left. The masks await you on the bed!' and was now lighting long white candles, some held in branched candelabra and others in roughly worked, free-standing iron candlesticks, bought by Duane and Molly at enormous expense from the Mexican and Native American Craft shop in Soho.

Even with the lights still on, the effect of the naked flames flickering into life was unsettling.

Jane, having rummaged in her bag for the mask she had brought with her, now carried it suspended by the elastic around her wrist. Like everyone else holding half-concealed disguises of sequins and beads and coloured paper, she felt self-conscious. The non-mask-owning guests were beginning to trickle back into the room now, wearing expressions which ranged from the agonised to the amused. Duane Jewell insisted on subjecting them all to this elaborate Hallowe'en charade, and there was no help for any of them but to take part.

Jane saw Harry come in from the hall, faint contempt on his face. He carried a scrap of blue fabric in his hand; he had probably opted for the most nondescript item in Jewell's collection. He rolled his eyes at her as he wandered to the other side of the room. She saw him speak to Ambika Thalo, who was looking furiously embarrassed.

There was an almost palpable awkwardness in the room now, which teetered on the edge of excitement. Jane looked from one face to another and saw her own tension mirrored in her colleagues' eyes. But it was not for the same reason. No one else raked the room for the figure of Gwyn Thomas. No one else was tuned in as she was to the frequency of his voice, hearing it however low and distant in the babble of party noise.

Since that first conversation, which had become three-way with Gail's arrival and which had stretched out and out until Gail, growing wary, had borne Gwyn off, they had been playing a soft cat-and-mouse game. For the last hour they had watched one another move around the party. Sometimes they belonged briefly to the same group; sometimes they broke away from different groups at the same time, so that they could pass one another and exchange words and smiles. It was utterly decorous and wildly exciting. Even Gail, her face growing stiller and blanker as the evening wore on, seemed a part of it.

Jane knew that Gwyn was standing by the long vertical wall hanging, and that Gail was beside him. A murmur of anticipation rose and died on the lips of the guests as Professor Jewell held up his hands.

'Every person at last being in possession of a mask, I mean to turn off the lights. We will mask up. From this moment, no one is permitted to address any other person by name, nor to unmask himself nor any fellow reveller. Now.'

As Jewell switched of the lights, the radiance of the candles flared lengthways into the dark and made cones of shadow and half-light. For a second Jane stared confused at the figures surrounding her and wondered why each person's head was bowed, as if in some act of shared religious observance. Then she realised that they were putting on their masks and she slipped hers on too, adjusting it so that the feathers stroked her forehead and cheekbones and she looked out through two long, slanting apertures at the strange scene before her.

All around, people were raising their heads to look at one another. Ripples of chatter and short laughs were breaking out. Directly in front of Jane, Amanda-Lee Chadburgh turned the face of a Dutch doll up to Liam Connolly, who stared down at her through a scarlet half-mask. Someone – who? It was hard to discern clothes and hair in the candlelight – stood alone, his or her face a nightmare of swirling colours and elongated, curling gashes. A metallic sheen glittered on the forehead of Professor Myers, who was wearing something that looked like strips of chain-mail, swagged beneath the eyes. Harry was easily distinguishable because of his height and the pale gleam of his hair: most of his face was still visible, only his eyes were changed by the small dark band which shaded them. Perhaps because the rest of him was so recognisable, the altered eyes looked sinister.

People were turning this way and that, trying to catch glimpses of themselves in the mirrors and glass cabinets. Most of them moved differently, Jane noticed: slowly, with actorly grace.

'More wine?' a voice said. A totem pole face appeared before her and Robert Wendell's eyes shone at her through the holes.

'God, Robert! You look terrifying.'

'Please, no names. You heard Duane's orders. Hold your glass out, bird person.'

Jane watched the dark wine flow into her glass. She nodded her feathered head and moved away. She was beginning to feel unreal. A chimney-sweep stared at her as she passed; two sets of eyes regarded her from behind traditional ball masks. Someone had drawn back a curtain from the long window and in the glass she saw herself dimly reflected, a tall, thin figure with the head of a crow, picking her way purposefully through the crowd.

Where was Gwyn? Suddenly she wanted very badly to see him. She looked to her right and to her left, but couldn't find him. She had to turn her head widely, like a bird, because her sideways vision was hampered by the edges of her mask. There was Gail: even in the dim light, her small frame and that mass of hair were distinctive. Gail wore a mask of roses: they grew all over the mask, and the effect was at once beautiful and grotesque.

Jane turned away and her heart seized with terror: in her path stood a man wearing an executioner's hood. Before she could flinch, the executioner's hands shot forward and grabbed hers.

'Got you.'

'No!' The word shrilled out harshly, even as she realised that it was Gwyn. The surrounding strange heads flicked in her direction and then she heard laughter and exclamations start up.

'Gwyn Thomas . . .'

'He frightened Jane . . .'

'The axeman . . . who screamed?'

'No names! No names, by order!' The last was Jewell's voice, bullying and pleased. The conversations resumed around them, louder and more buoyantly than before, now that she was still standing with her wrists in Gwyn's grip.

'Ssh. Hell, I'm sorry. Are you all right?' he was saying. 'Hush, you're shaking.'

'Jesus, that thing. Let me go.'

Gwyn released her. He shook his head; the motion of the hood was mesmerisingly horrible.

'Sorry. I thought you knew it was me.'

'I did. All the same.'

'Sorry, it was just a joke. Look, you've spilt your drink. Let me get you another one.' He took her dripping glass from her and put it down on a bookshelf. He put his hand gently on her back, between her shoulder blades, and guided her across to an armchair.

It was a very different touch from his grasp on her wrists. It was soft and suggestive; nerves across her back prickled in response to it. She could feel the exact shape of his palm and the varying pressure of his fingers. She looked at the mask again: this time it didn't alarm her; her glance went straight past the black fabric to the faint outline of his face beneath, and ended up at the two holes where his eyes were looking at her. Gwyn raised his free hand and touched the tips of her feathers.

'That's an amazing bird mask. Where did you get it?'

'Harry brought it back from New Orleans last Mardi Gras.'

'That was clever of him. Is it a crow or a raven?'

'I guess it's a crow. It's not blue-black enough for a raven.'

'You can tell?'

She could see from his eyes that he was smiling.

'Between crows and ravens, yes. I was raised a country girl.'

Jane sat down on the squashy arm of the chair, not because she needed to, but because with Gwyn standing in front of her it made them a private corner. He twisted round to find them each a glass. They had been drinking for hours and Gwyn, at least, had seemed drunk when they had first spoken, but now everything seemed sharp-edged and clear. Jane reached out to

24

take the newly filled glass of wine from him, and he settled himself on the opposite arm of the chair. Beyond them outlandish silhouettes moved against the candlelight. The heavy black executioner's hood no longer seemed sinister; together with her own black feathers, it afforded them the little bit of protection they needed to take the next step.

'Do you have to be so blatant?'

'What do you mean?'

'You and the wenching wordsmith, that's what I mean. You've been down each other's throats for the last hour. Everyone's noticed and Gail is not happy.'

Harry was standing firmly in front of her. Jane tilted to the right, trying to see past him to where Gwyn had just been distracted by Ambika and Gail.

'Jane!'

'We were just talking, that's all.'

'Yes. Of course. Would you stop acting like a metronome and leave him alone for a second?'

Harry had dropped his voice very low; nevertheless it had an unpleasantly hard edge to it. Jane darted him an angry look.

'All right, all right. What the fuck is it to do with you anyway?'

'Show some decorum if you can't show any compassion, for God's sake. Good manners. Enlightened self-interest. Don't move in on Gail's pitch in front of all her colleagues and yours.'

Jane glanced around. The party had thinned out considerably. There were about twenty people left and they were moving into departure configurations, staring to take their leave.

'I don't see anyone watching.'

'Take it from me, everyone has noticed. Now let's go, shall we?'

'Well, just a minute, aren't we going to say goodbye?'

'Yes, to Duane and Molly over there by the door. Come along.'

Jane didn't move. She was quite incapable of walking away from Gwyn; it was unthinkable that the evening should end so. She turned to look for him but Harry took her hand and squeezed it uncompromisingly and then they were walking across the room to the Jewells. Duane reclined against the door jamb, grey hair fluffing up around the exquisite plaster-and-bead dragon mask.

Molly's simple gold opera mask was an effective contrast, perfect for the perfect hostess. They both looked at Jane rather pointedly, she thought, although it was of course hard to tell their expressions.

'Thank you for a splendid party,' Harry said to Professor Jewell in his most courteous voice. 'It was lovely, Molly, thank you.'

'Yes, thank you so much,' said Jane. Her voice rang out clearly; suddenly she was glad of her crow mask.

'You were the event of the evening, my dear,' Professor Jewell boomed. 'Your reaction at the touch of the poet was a star turn.'

Jane stared at him.

'Your shriek,' Molly said. 'That's what Duane means.' She smiled at Jane, the complicitous, slightly impatient smile of an accomplished woman married to a difficult man.

Jane rallied her forces.

'Sorry about that,' she said. She looked from Molly to Duane and felt a smile grow across her face. 'I confess, I didn't realise I still knew how to do it.'

Rather pleased with herself, she allowed Harry to steer her out into the hall.

Harry paused two doors down, took off his mask and flung it in on the bed.

'Don't say a word,' she hissed as he returned.

'I won't,' he said, lips hardly moving. 'Not yet.'

Arm in arm they left the apartment, Jane fighting off the desire to cast one last look backwards for Gwyn.

Jane padded round the apartment in bare feet, touching things. The metal shade of her reading lamp, the wooden desk, the rough fabric of her discount store armchair, the cold glass of the window. Outside, the darkness was full of shadows. Two lights still burned across the well of the apartment building, oblongs of brightness. What were people doing behind the blinds: working, reading away insomnia, making love?

Jane had on two sweaters against the cold and she longed to go to bed and to sleep but she could not stay still. She passed out of the living room and into her tiny bedroom, edging round the few inches' space between bed and walls. The clock on the bedside shelf said three forty-five. She picked up the book next to it and put it down again.

Back in the living room, she sat down at her desk. It was stacked with back copies of the *Review*, listings magazines and faculty circulars: the physical evidence of her life here at Brockham. In the low light of the reading lamp they looked insubstantial, like props on a stage. She ran her fingers over the different sheets of paper, feeling their textures, and her hand closed on an envelope: it was the letter which had arrived that morning. One of the regular three-monthly missives from Miss Archer, one-time librarian at Jane's old school back in Renoxia.

Jane picked up the envelopes and took out the two folded sheets of paper. Miss Archer had been kind to her twelve years ago; it was thanks to her that Jane had had somewhere to go in New York. Jane had never forgotten; she was a bad correspondent but she had kept Miss Archer informed of her progress and every season a letter would arrive from Renoxia, bearing local news and good wishes. Jane had not written since Christmas; maybe she would write back now and tell her that she had met a poet. Jane found a sheet of blank paper and a pen, but when she had written the date she came to a stop. Her mind was elsewhere, somewhere between here and what had happened in Professor Jewell's apartment this evening, somewhere between here and wherever Gwyn was now.

Jane was curled in the armchair, watching the sky turn to robin's-egg green, when sleep finally came.

4

Steam from the coffee machines had misted up the windows of Dora's, so that it was hard to see who passed outside. Jane crumbled her second croissant into the remaining froth on her coffee. She was speeding. Maybe if she ate enough she would still the whirring in her stomach and along the nerves of her arms and legs.

She'd told Harry she might feel ashamed of herself this morning but she didn't. She felt excited and jumpy. She felt afraid too, which was why she was still sitting in Dora's having breakfast when she should be on campus.

She was afraid of what Gail would say to her, afraid of what would happen when she saw Gwyn, afraid of the determination growing inside her. It grew silently, like a pale green shoot nudging its way through the dark earth, around obstacles, finally splitting open the concrete slabs to reach sunlight. She was no stranger to desire.

Gwyn was not on the sidewalk outside, nor was Gail. Jane raked the morning crowds with her eyes as she strode up the two blocks to Brockham campus. Moisture had crept into the air today and as she turned right into the main campus avenue of trees, she smelled the sweet, decaying scent of earth and humus. Ahead, in the campus square, the clock began to strike nine. Jane broke into a run, looking eagerly about her.

Gwyn planted his feet on first one slab, then another, and so crossed the campus square with awkward, heavy strides. Treading in the squares, not on the cracks; it took his mind off his hangover and gave him something simple on which to concentrate. Otherwise, he kept flagellating himself with memories of last night's scene with Gail and undergoing terrible rushes of doubt and loss of nerve over Jane.

He didn't know who she was; not the first thing about her. He hadn't even known her surname until Gail had given it to him, through frozen lips. Pridden: an unexpected name for a woman like Jane. It sounded so buttoned up and Boston prim.

Images of Jane had been with him ever since she had left the party – and she had left so suddenly he hadn't noticed her go. Why had she done that? Second thoughts? He saw her looking angrily at him over the bottle of red wine, the anger transforming to something else, something akin to recognition. He saw her standing across the room, her dark eyes, set slightly askew under the winged eyebrows, restlessly seeking him out. The direct gaze of those eyes was with him now, as he reached the south end of the campus square and looked up at the Brockham University Library.

He did know the first thing about her. The first thing was that they desired each other. The other first things were all those they had talked about last night, intimate and disconnected chunks of experience they had bitten off at random and offered to one another. He couldn't remember them. He had been drunk.

Jesus, he must have been drunk to say what he'd said to Gail. 'She's not nearly as pretty as you.' No wonder her face had turned to stone. At the time – around three thirty this morning – he had thought that quite a reasonable consolation prize. He groaned. The sound came out small and pathetic.

Like me, thought Gwyn. Like me. Remorse and self-loathing coursed through him, a thin, sludgy stream. But even that couldn't take away the other feeling: the heady, foolish excitement at the thought of seeing Jane again.

The library was the most imposing building on campus: a large, oblong construction of grey stone, it had ornate carvings round the windows and pilasters entwined with stone ivy on either side of the main door. Gwyn went round inside the revolving door, opened his bag to be checked at the security desk and put his magnetic card through the machine. The barrier clicked open to let him into Square Hall (as it was idiotically known), the reference area.

The daylight poured through the glass ceiling, four storeys up, and disorientated Gwyn. It seemed brighter inside than out. He meandered through the banks of catalogues and card-index chests, squinting at the other library users. They were dewy-faced undergraduates mainly, most of them in far better clothes than he could afford. Jane was not among them. He hadn't expected her to be. He knew she would be in her office first thing, wrestling with Jewell's wordy prose – that was one thing he did remember from last night. But he also knew she would have to come in here later today, because he had seen the stack of new posters on the faculty reception desk this morning. They had been wrapped in brown paper and plastic, but stuck on the top was one copy of the poster: it advertised a new subscription deal on the *Review*. Gwyn had seen similar posters up in the library before. At some time today Jane would have to go round the campus sticking up the new posters.

He would ambush her. Incapacitated as he was by a hangover and exhaustion, a cunning efficiency seemed to be operating in his brain. He did not wish to meet Jane in the faculty where Gail and Jewell and Harry and God knew who else could observe them. He preferred to meet her here. Apart from one writing class – and how the hell was he going to cope with that, today? – he was free to stay here. And he would.

Gwyn walked to the iron staircase at the back, right-hand corner of Square Hall and hauled himself up, holding on to the rail to steady himself round the spirals. On the second floor, the edge of the poetry stacks, he stopped. In the corner formed by the staircase and the first stack was his favourite table, and his place on it was spread with someone else's books. Aggressively he swept the books and papers on to the other side of the table, moved the bag from the back of the outward-facing chair on to the inward one and sat down. He could tell from the notes that it was a student's place he was taking; the student would just have to lump it and think he was a pig. From this position Gwyn could look out over the whole of Square Hall and watch all the people coming in to the library. He opened the books he had half thought of using in his class and settled down to his vigil.

It was nearly midday when he saw her. He glanced up from the letter he was writing to Roy and saw Jane's miniaturised figure below, standing at the magnetic-card machine. Her head was bent, as she was feeding the card into the slot, but he recognised her instantly from the fall of her dark hair. She retrieved her card from the machine and walked through the barrier and he recognised her walk too, arms and legs swinging slightly. All that information about her was already burned into his mind, after just one evening.

She walked into the middle of Square Hall and stopped at the notice board. She unpinned an existing poster from it and replaced it with a new one, from her case. She seemed distracted: instead of moving on, she stood looking vaguely round the hall, perusing the people around her as if she searched for someone. Him; surely, it must be for him. Gwyn was already on his feet: he began to climb down the iron staircase, growing dizzy by the time he reached the bottom. It was a few seconds before he could locate Jane again and then he was nudging people aside, working his way towards her across the wood-block floor.

He approached her from the side and had to step in front of her to get her attention.

Jane turned, saw Gwyn in front of her and suddenly felt happy. After all the feverish emotions of the morning – when would she see him? How would she speak to him? Did she even want to? – he was in front of her, very real and solid. He wore a dark green jumper which made his eyes look green-grey rather than charcoal. He looked tired.

'Hallo there,' he said.

'Hallo.' Jane knew that her smile was lighting up her face. She pushed her hair back from her temple and waited.

Gwyn had planted his legs apart, like someone determined to make a stand. He was barring her way, she realised.

'Are you busy?' he asked.

'No.'

'I've got twenty minutes before my class. Come for a walk.'

While Gwyn went back up the stairs to collect his books, Jane's mind floated. She couldn't catch it. She was without thought. She watched him reach the second floor, hunch over a table for thirty seconds and then reappear on the staircase. Together they left the library.

Once out through the doors they turned left, leaving the campus square behind. The air had grown damper and warmer and the sun shone mildly on the fallen yellow leaves which lined the paths and lay in patches on Brockham's lawns. They turned right, following the path behind the philosophy building. There were quite a few people out here, dawdling in the sun.

'What's your class?' asked Jane.

'How to write poetry,' said Gwyn. 'Want to come? It's quite an experience.'

'Do you like doing that?'

'Yes. I didn't think I would but I do. Mind you, I don't know what I'm saying half the time, but I do enjoy myself.'

'Good,' said Jane, listening to his voice and not his words.

'Look,' said Gwyn, 'shall we go to my office?'

As they walked along the path they kept passing students, singly and in groups. Some of them greeted Gwyn or Jane or, occasionally, both.

Once or twice Gwyn's arm knocked against Jane. They weren't saying much, just enough to keep the sound of their voices in one another's ears. They climbed the faculty steps and walked into the lobby, across the tiled floor, up a flight of stairs and along a corridor. There were many people about but no one gave them a second glance. Half-way along the corridor Gwyn paused outside a varnished wood door with his name on it. He felt in his pocket for the key, unlocked the door and stepped back for Jane to enter. Her immediate, confused impression of his office was that it was no bigger than hers but looked north, over lawns.

As soon as the door closed behind Gwyn, they began kissing. Jane let her bag slip from her arms on to Gwyn's desk; he just dropped his books on the floor. They clung together, mouth to mouth, holding each other tightly. Jane felt her skin hot with longing; Gwyn's arms strained her against him, his face moved fiercely against hers but his mouth was very soft.

Jane could not let go of Gwyn. A part of her mind told her to pull away but instead she raised frantic fingers to his face and felt Gwyn's hands moving down her sides, over her buttocks, to pull importunately at the folds of her skirt. Her flesh was leaping and she pressed herself against him, wanting his hands to reach between her legs yet not able to bear losing his touch for a second.

Clumsily Gwyn had dragged her skirt up and now she felt one hand touch her inner thigh and close on her vulva. She was burning beneath his palm; the desire so intense it felt like pain. She struggled to undo his zipper, suddenly desperate to feel his penis erect in her hand. She could imagine it clearly: as if the nerves in her hand were already responding to it, her fingers curled.

She was through his trousers and his shorts and she grasped his penis. They both gasped, a gasp which turned into a groan and then, on Gwyn's part, into an exclamation.

'Dear God, the door. Wait – ' He staggered backwards a step, drawing Jane with him, and shot home the lock on the door. His face was alive with laughter and Jane seized it with her hands and kissed him furiously, moaning deep inside herself as she felt his hands come back on to her. In a tangle they slid down the wooden door. Gwyn rucked her skirt up round her waist and tugged off her panties. She lifted her legs round him as he bent over her, kissing her and murmuring. Then she felt his groin hot against her pelvis, and the floor tiles cold against her bottom, and all her sensations rushed to a point as he parted her labia and pushed his penis into her, gently at first, then harder as she opened up to receive him.

'Oh Jane – '

'Jesus – '

'The bloody clock's striking! My writing class – '

'I know. I know. Ohh!'

'Ssh. Oh Jane.' Gently laying his hand over her mouth, Gwyn stifled his gasps and kissed her lightly, again and again, and thrust into her again and again. Jane moaned into his hand, half hearing the footsteps in the corridor outside, not caring, burrowing her hands under his jumper against his bare skin, pulling him further into her on waves of wild, extreme pleasure.

They climaxed one after another, in violent shudders. Tears spilled from Jane's eyes and ran into her hair. A second later, the first knock came on the door.

Jane gazed up at Gwyn, feeling horror rise inside her and drain the colour from her face. He shook his head at her. Putting a finger on her lips, he called out:

'I'll be with you in a minute. Just finishing a meeting.'

Gwyn got quickly to his feet, tucking in his clothes and silently picking up the fallen books. He was grinning but Jane's hands trembled as she clambered back into her panties and straightened her skirt. She felt in shock, from the love making and the realisation that there were people outside. She watched Gwyn open a window and quietly draw a second chair up by the desk. He beckoned her into it.

Oh my God, she thought in a panic, we'll never get away with it. We must have been crazy. What's going to happen to us? Gwyn leaned over her, licked his finger and stroked away some mascara smudges from under her eyes.

'Smooth your hair, cariad,' he whispered, opening a file at random on the desk. 'Do I look decent?'

Jane nodded. Gwyn went to the door, eased the lock back and opened it.

'Come in,' he said. 'Sorry about this. We won't be a minute, we're just finishing off something very complicated. Grab some chairs and I'll be right with you.' He stepped back and eight students came into the room. Jane knew several of them. 'Hallo,' she smiled, one hand propping her chin, the other holding a pen (did she look convincing? Please God), 'Hallo.'

Gwyn came back to the desk, rubbing a distracted hand through his hair. 'Sorry, Jane. We'll have to do the final stage later. But you think this, this and this – ' he had reached the desk again and was pointing to different words in the open file before her, 'are OK?'

'Oh absolutely,' she said. 'Fine for the January issue. So long as we're clear about which sources we're using.'

Gwyn flashed her a sceptical look under cover of closing the file.

'Oh yes. No doubt about that. Well thank you. See you later today?'

'It'll have to be after six now.'

The students were pulling chairs forward from a line around the wall and settling themselves into a circle. Gwyn pulled out one for himself. Jane watched him as she gathered her books and crossed the room. The students were chattering to one another or idly watching Gwyn. No one seemed to suspect. Gwyn's eyes met hers as she opened the door and she almost stopped dead. If people really noticed nothing different, they must be blind.

5

Gwyn lay on his side, watching Jane sleep. Her face had a bloom on it; her hair, tangled from their love making, lay across her cheek, shielding it. He felt the funny little twist in his chest that often came when he watched Jane; half pain, half pleasure.

He inched his hand towards her face, thinking of stroking it, then stopped. It wouldn't be fair: she needed her sleep.

But he was wide awake now, and thinking. It was an uncivilised hour to find your brain working so clearly, but he could tell that there would be no more sleep for him for a while, and he slipped gently out of bed, taking care not to disturb Jane. He pulled on a jumper and a pair of jeans and left the bedroom.

Through the sitting room blinds he saw the first glimmerings of daylight. He pulled the cord to raise the blinds and sat in the armchair, bathed in the pale grey morning light. He heard urban noises: the growl of traffic, more subdued than usual; the distant rattle of a crate being unloaded; a car radio. He thought that such noises would always now remind him of Jane and these early weeks of their love.

Gwyn was unsure of what was happening to him, but he realised that this was love, as he had never known it before. Oh, he had loved Eirlys in an unspoken, teenage sort of way, and he'd had a couple of intense affairs at university. Then there had been the relationship with Catherine, in London. But nothing like this thing with Jane.

Gwyn felt an overwhelming physical passion for her. He loved her tall body and her pale, wary face. When he woke in the morning he found himself kissing her eyes and her mouth so that she woke in a flurry of confusion and half-protest. During the day, when he was giving his creative-writing classes or roaming the campus gardens trying to write, he yearned for the touch of her skin.

Whenever they met at the end of the day, they were making love within minutes – in her tiny, box-like flat, or in his, or in his office, if she had come straight up from the *Review* – or in less convenient places. Once, meeting in the Arts Bar for a drink in the early evening, they had slipped down the corridor to the women's toilet, locked themselves into a stall and fucked desperately standing up, Jane's legs wrapped around his, his tongue sucking at hers and his hands tangled between her thighs, sticky with her wetness.

He felt sexual desire for her like a thirst: he would have liked to drink her all up. When they were making love, he sometimes had strange fantasies about unzipping his skin and dissolving into her in the ultimate consummation.

But it wasn't just a sexual passion. It was a passion for all of her: her voice, her thoughts, her attitudes, her impatient, self-doubting ambition – even her past.

It tantalised Gwyn that Jane's life up till now was so very different from his own. He still felt imaginatively anchored to his home country, for instance, yet she was an independent rootless sort of American. She said her home state, North Dakota, had nothing to draw her back; she described it as empty, with wide sweeps of unfarmed, unpopulated land. It all sounded so utterly different from Gwyn's own country of damp green hills and jostling terraces.

He found it hard to imagine what her childhood had been like, and although she patiently answered his questions – what kind of house had she lived in? What games did she and her friends play? Did they fish? Swim? Climb trees? Go on school trips? – he always had the impression that she didn't really care about the answers. She didn't seem to have the same sense of her own past as Gwyn had of his. Oddly enough, Gwyn found that now he was in love with Jane, he thought more and not less about the valley, with its shallow river and rows of red-brick houses, and the bluebell woods half-way up Graig Mountain, and Goff's packed bookshelves.

Goff. Gwyn had been thinking of him too; meaning to write and let the old man know how his new life was going. Gwyn locked his hands and stared at them, feeling the homesickness steal over him. *Hiraeth*, Goff would call it; the longing a Welshman feels for the land and people he's left behind.

Gwyn glanced at the telephone. What time was it in Wales? They were five hours ahead or was it six? It must be about ten in the morning there: a good time for a phone call. After all, whatever troubles he and Goff had been through, Gwyn still owed him a lot.

Mr Jenkins; Goff the verse. Gwyn owed him everything really.

Gwyn could still remember with absolute clarity that first English lesson with Goff at Pengroed Comprehensive School. He could remember the grimy interior of the classroom and the smell of hot eleven-year-olds and chalk dust. They sat wearily at their desks, twenty-four new boys and girls, their heads buzzing with all the information that had been flung at them during this first day at 'big school'. Gwyn was sitting next to Roy Stephens from his own village; they had been given neighbouring desks because their surnames followed one another in the alphabet, and Roy was busy doing a filthy drawing of Miss Morgan, their class teacher. Gwyn's eyes felt gritty with tiredness as he contemplated the last lesson of the day. So far he had been bewildered in maths, bored sick in history and had already run foul of the teacher in chemistry. He didn't think he was going to do very well in big school. And now there was English, which he had always been bad at in junior school, because he didn't like using the posh English words and phrases the teacher insisted on for their boring old stories and 'news' essays.

He watched sullenly as the door opened and a small, wiry middle-aged man came in. He had a head shaped like a fox and a bald forehead. His nose was joined to the corners of his mouth by two deep wrinkles and he wore spectacles. Mr Jenkins; he lived in Gwyn's village too, up the other side of the valley. He had sometimes shouted at Gwyn for throwing stones at cats and had once cuffed him round the ear for being rude to old Mrs Bevan. Just Gwyn's luck to have him as a teacher.

Gwyn barely bothered to struggle to his feet with the rest of the class and didn't even pretend to drone 'Good Afternoon Mr Jenkins' along with them. He slumped back into his seat with a thud and gazed longingly at the window where the September sun was picking out the dust on the pane.

He groaned under his breath when Mr Jenkins said they were going to read a poem by Taliesin. Roy heard him and giggled, and Gwyn made a tough, leering face at him. Unfortunately Mr Jenkins saw it. The foxy face looked straight down the classroom at him, the eyes unexpectedly bright behind the spectacle lenses.

'Gwyn Thomas, isn't it?'

'Yes,' mumbled Gwyn.

'Yes sir,' said Mr Jenkins' surprisingly deep voice.

Gwyn leaned back in his chair and thrust his hands deep into his pockets.

'Yes – sir,' he said tonelessly. Dumb insolence was his strong suit.

'Tell the class what you know about the poet Taliesin, then, lad.'

Gwyn held Mr Jenkins' sharp stare and said nothing.

'What do you know?' Mr Jenkins prompted.

'Nothing,' said Gwyn. 'Sir.'

He smirked as the snigger travelled round the room.

'That's enough,' Mr Jenkins snapped, and got silence immediately. 'Stand up, Thomas.'

Slowly, Gwyn shuffled to his feet. Here it was; this was what he was used to. Old Jenkins must have been tipped off by one of the junior school teachers – he was wasting no time in picking on Gwyn. He waited for the announcement of his punishment and concentrated on keeping his face blank. He was aware of every eye in the room being on him.

'Your attention, class,' said Mr Jenkins, looking round, and then began to talk, completely ignoring Gwyn as he stood uncomfortably behind his desk, towering over Roy.

'Taliesin,' said Mr Jenkins, 'worked for a Celtic king, King Urien of Rheged, back in the sixth century – the time we call the Dark Ages. Taliesin was a bard – he celebrated his king's battles in song and verse. In the king's castle, while the king and his men feasted, Taliesin would sing his songs. His language was the old

British language – which some of us still speak today. It is called Welsh . . .'

'Pig, pig, pig,' thought Gwyn, staring stonily at the blackboard. 'Bastard,' he thought secretly, relishing the dirty word. 'Bloody bugger. Arse.'

He stayed standing while Mr Jenkins completed his little introductory talk, distributed the books and told them to find page eight. Gwyn glanced round the room: every head was bent; every hand was busy riffling pages. He considered not opening his but at that moment Mr Jenkins calmly met his eyes and something in the teacher's level expression made him reach down and pick up his book from the desk, and turn to page eight.

On one side of the open book were lines of English writing; on the opposite page, were lines of Welsh.

'The Welsh is poetry,' said Goff, 'and the English isn't, even though the words say the same things and the lines rhyme. The English words translate the meaning of the Welsh words but they can't translate the sounds of those words and the rhythm of them. They can't give you the same feeling when you listen to them. And do you know what that feeling is? The feeling you get from hearing the sound and rhythm of words is poetry. Poetry's got nothing to do with sticking a rhyme on the end of a line; poetry is when the words excite you. Now shut your books and listen.'

If Gwyn had been sitting down, he wouldn't have listened, he would have doodled or cracked his knuckles or gouged lines in the underside of his desk with his penknife. But standing up with his hands in view, there was no distraction from Goff's voice.

He listened, scornful and bored, as Goff read the English translation of the poem. It was a stupid, boring story about a prince who went off to kill some Saxons. A bloody fairy story. Gwyn stared contemptuously past Mr Jenkins' head, hoping everyone could see his expression.

But then Mr Jenkins began reading the Welsh version. Gwyn couldn't understand a word of it – like many families in the mining valleys, his hadn't spoken Welsh for generations. But he could hear. Mr Jenkins' voice was deep, soft and sing-song and the sounds he made were like music, lulling Gwyn's mind and bringing pictures with them, like a film on telly. He could hear the wind blowing in the trees, and the river rushing along the valley and horses' hooves thudding. He could feel the prince's heart-beat getting faster and faster as he went towards the battle. He could hear the clashing noise of swords and then the long wails of the grieving women and the crying of the birds overhead.

When Mr Jenkins stopped talking and looked up, he found Gwyn's gaze on him. Immediately, Gwyn wiped the life from his face and resumed his sullen, don't-give-a-monkey's expression. But he could tell, from the sudden gleam of interest in Mr Jenkins' eyes, that the teacher had seen.

At the age of eleven, Gwyn had discovered that he was a poet. Gwyn smiled as he remembered it. He had been so excited and yet so wary, almost resentful of the idea that he could enjoy anything to do with books and school. His mother had found him sneaking the *Daffodil Book of Friendship Poems* off her bedside table and had shouted at him, assuming he was going to deface it in some way. He had skulked around the village general store, looking for poetry on the paperback books stand, until Mrs Evans had ordered him to turn out his pockets. In the end it had been Goff who had stepped in to help him, beckoning him over at the end of a lesson and taking a couple of books out of his scratched brown leather case. 'Do you want to have a look at these, boy?' was all he'd said. 'Keep them as long as you want, but look after them, won't you?'

Goff had handled Gwyn's waking talent so carefully, never embarrassing Gwyn by focusing his classmates' attention on him, never lavishing praise on him, but always being there with a quick, sharp look, a nod of interest, a casual word when Gwyn's friends were out of earshot. Gwyn had never become a swot, a teacher's pet; in most subjects he was an above average trouble-maker, but in Goff's English lessons he was special. As term after term, year after year, rolled gradually out, Gwyn's passion for poetry, and especially for the old Welsh poetry, blossomed and grew strong under Goff's tutelage.

By the time he was fourteen, Gwyn was taking three extra lessons a week at Goff's house, learning new and old Welsh and all the history and mythology that went with it.

They would sit at the formica-topped kitchen table, each with a glass of beer in front of him, and talk about the old stories, and read the old poets. It wasn't like school-work for Gwyn; it was like being a man, out in the world, arguing about the things that old princes had argued over, fighting their blood-thirsty battles over again with the broad, muscly Welsh words on his tongue. In the summer, the kitchen door would stand open, letting in the rich, warm air, scented with grass and daisies and – coming from the colliery over the mountain – the faint, acrid top-note of coal. In the winter, the curtains would be drawn and the boiler set into the old hearth would steam and rumble, and they would be shut into the little room like the old lords and their bards shut themselves into their crude stone castles.

It was good to have somewhere to go, where he could concentrate on the things he was good at, things which he understood, things which touched him. Gwyn had been writing his own poems almost as long as he had been reading other people's; now, awkwardly, he began showing them to Goff. 'Interesting,' Goff said. 'You've got a way with you. Try to find your own voice, though, boy. It's the twentieth century we're living in now, not the ninth.'

Goff was an exacting critic. He drove Gwyn to be ambitious with his poems, developing internal rhymes and manipulating rhythms. He taught him never to be sloppy. He goaded him into being a perfectionist. And then he bullied him into breaking cover: he nagged and urged and argued until Gwyn submitted some of his poems to a South Wales school competition. He won.

Gwyn smiled at the memory, a chuckle rising in his throat. He had been so proud inside, and so outwardly dismissive. He could remember seeking out Goff in the school corridor and telling him, so casually, that the letter had come. He could still see Goff's face – the straight, thoughtful look he gave Gwyn, and the way he had said: 'Of course you won. I knew you would.' That look had caught at Gwyn's lungs and made his pulse race; for the first time, he saw how much Goff admired his talent.

He'd often thought about that moment since. It had been a turning point; it had been the moment at which he decided that his future lay with Goff. Even Goff had not known, then, the extent of Gwyn's troubles at home. Most people in the village knew that his father had another woman somewhere in Cardiff, and that his mother was doing more and more overtime for the floor manager at the factory. Their neighbours heard the house reverberate several times a week to their raging, hysterical rows. But Gwyn had not told Goff about the way his parents forced the children to take sides – his mother claiming the two little ones; his father trying to co-opt Gwyn into a manly alliance.

When he came home from school one day to find his mother packing up the china, he wasn't surprised. He went upstairs and locked his records, books and stereo into his wardrobe, pocketing the key. Then he pulled his old suitcase from beneath his bed, packed his clothes and wash things, kissed his little brother and sister goodbye and walked out of the house. He lugged his heavy case along the street, past all the twitching front curtains, and over the bridge. He paused to look down at the shallow water, running peacefully over the large stones. Then he picked up his bag again and trudged on up the main village street and round the corner to Goff's house. 'Can I stay?' was all he asked when Goff opened the door. And Goff just said, 'Yes lad.'

It was impossible to know whether it had been a good thing or a bad, moving in with Goff. If he hadn't moved in, he would not have spent the next two years surrounded by Goff's books and notes, his strange old paintings and drawings, his incredible wealth of knowledge that was almost an obsession. He would never have become as intimate as he did with the old stories and the old verse forms. They wouldn't have entered his dreams and coloured his adolescent emotions with the same intensity. He would have missed that – but might it not have been better in the long run?

If he hadn't moved in with Goff, then he would not have come to resent his control so much. He wouldn't have felt that gradual sense of Goff taking him over, forcing him to think and write and imagine in a certain way.

But then, where would he have lived? His mother had moved to a flat in Newport with the floor manager, Ceridwen and Tom. His father had moved his fancy woman into the family house – Gwyn couldn't have stayed there. If he had been closer to Roy at the time, he might have been able to move in with him from the start – if, if, if . . .

Well, there had been advantages and disadvantages. Goff had never tried to act as a parent or uncle, and Gwyn had had a lot more freedom than many of his friends. He could go out drinking

43

as often as he liked, stay out all night, wear what he liked, look how he liked – so long as the old stories and the old poetry kept their hold on his mind.

That mind control had been what came between them in the end. The first sign had been when Gwyn wrote a poem about Roy's Dad's new car. There was nothing unusual in that – he wrote on all sorts of subjects, with Goff's blessing – but Gwyn had known, when he finished this poem, that he had done something special: he had brought Roy's father, and his bashful attachment to the new car, vividly, eccentrically alive. He had found the beginnings of his own voice and his own technique.

When he'd shown the poem to Goff, Goff had read it once, then again. Then he had looked up, too casually.

'It's technically good,' he said. 'But it's something and nothing, isn't it?'

And he had left the room.

When he came back in, half an hour later, he was carrying his annotated copy of the *Black Book of Camarthen*. He put it down on the arm of Gwyn's chair, where Gwyn was sprawled, watching television.

'Have a look at the verses of Geraint. They lend themselves to reworking, they do. I think you're ready for them now.'

Gwyn twitched his head lazily towards the book.

'No thanks,' he said, and turned back to the screen.

'No thanks?' He could feel Goff watching him. 'What do you mean?'

'No thanks. I don't want to rewrite Geraint. Or the *Death of Gwen*, or *Heledd's Lament*. No thanks.'

'Don't be dull, boy. It's what your gift is for.'

Gwyn went on lolling in his chair, staring at the screen. He felt raw inside from Goff's dismissal of his car poem.

'Oh well. I'll leave it by here, anyhow.'

'Don't bother,' said Gwyn, getting up. 'I'm going out.'

That had been the beginning. Gwyn had embarked on more poems in the same vein, writing about mundane objects and situations and searching for the spark of anger or hope or courage which lay at their heart. He knew these poems were good, but when he showed them to Goff it was always the same: Goff

44

nodded and dismissed them, and tried to persuade him to write about the old legends again, like he used to when he was a kid.

Every casual dismissal of his new poems cut Gwyn to the core. He came to dread the evenings he used to enjoy, when he and Goff would read together. He came to resent the weight of Goff's interest in him and his eagerness for him to learn. He even began to fear it. Yet it was so hard to put into words what it was he feared. Even Eirlys – intelligent, practical Eirlys, his girlfriend – didn't understand. But Gwyn felt that he was beginning to suffocate in the rich mysteries of Goff's scholarship.

The struggle went on for months. He should have moved out sooner, of course. But he was young and didn't know where to go, and so it dragged on, without Gwyn being able to explain it to Goff or anyone, until everyone in the village and the school knew that something was wrong. He was still ashamed of the way he had left: one autumn evening, eighteen months after he had moved in, he had simply packed his bags again and gone. He would always remember the silence in the little house as he carried his possessions down the stairs and through the back room with Goff sitting like a statue in his armchair, staring at the mantelpiece.

Was the memory of that leaving as strong for Goff as it was for him? He had done his best over the years to make amends, asking Goff to visit him in his college at Oxford, going back to stay with him for several days, sometimes several weeks, in the vacations, writing, telephoning. And he had stood by Goff when the valley was rife with rumours against him, evil-minded people speculating as to why young Gwyn Thomas had moved out.

But Gwyn had never returned to the old stories in his poetry, and he knew that Goff saw that as the greatest betrayal. Goff had encouraged him to find his own voice so that he could deal with the old themes – the legends, the blood lines, the magic – in a way that that would make them live again.

But Gwyn had turned his voice to new themes and made them his own. During his last six months at school, and once he had gone to Oxford, Gwyn concentrated on writing about the things he knew: the broken bonds of love in his family; the twisted sinews of his relationship with his teacher; the enclosing, encroaching reality of day-to-day life.

They were tough, unflinching poems, enriched by his knowledge of the old Welsh bards whose images he sometimes borrowed. These poems had brought him success. When Gwyn left Oxford he was already publishing in small literary magazines and getting a name for himself as a boisterous, hard-drinking poet. He had spent three years teaching English at a polytechnic in London and another three years back in South Wales, working for an arts programme on Welsh television. He had published two books of poems. Both books contained a sequence of knotty, cathartic poems about him and Goff, and those were universally considered his best.

It was those poems which had got him his break. Professor Jewell had said as much to him; yes, if it wasn't for Goff, in more ways than one, Gwyn wouldn't be here now.

Gwyn went across to the door and closed it, so that his voice wouldn't wake Jane. Then, before he could change his mind, he reached for the telephone and punched out the number he knew by heart. He had to wait several seconds, listening to clicks on the line, and then he heard the distinctive double ring and at once he was back in Goff's narrow hall. He saw the knobbly brass-look mirror and the swirled pattern carpet and the coats hanging in a bulge from the hook. He could smell the hairy smell of Goff's tweed overcoat, filtered through the hall's other smells of furniture polish and sun-warmed dust and – always, everywhere, inside and out in the valley – the trace of coal.

'Graig 463.' It was the familiar voice, dropping low on the registerlike the voices of so many Welsh men, like Gwyn's own. These days, Goff's was crackly with laboured breathing.

'Hallo Goff. It's me, Gwyn.'

There was a pause.

'Well. Hallo then. Are you in America?'

Gwyn laughed.

'You know I am.'

'What time is it there?'

'About five in the morning. I couldn't sleep, so I thought I'd ring you.'

'How's it going then, lad? What's the work like?'

Typical Goff: not 'How's New York?' or 'Have you made any

friends?' but 'What's the work like?'. Gwyn smiled wryly at the mouthpiece.

'It's good. I take poetry classes, give the odd reading. I have a "writer's surgery", would you believe?'

'Do you, now? Do you kill or cure?'

'God knows. But I get plenty of time for my own work, which is great. How are things with you, Goff?'

'Not bad, thank you, boy, I saw Roy the other day. After news of you, he was; I told him you'd write when you got round to it.'

'Yes, I will. Say hello to him and Eirlys for me, in the meantime.'

'Busy, are you? Have you read the book I sent?'

'*Madoc, Poems To A Prince*? I've had a look at it.'

'And you don't think much of it.'

'It's not my style, Goff. But it's vivid, I'll give you that.'

'I didn't send it to you for the poetry, boy. It's muck, that doggerel. I sent it for the legend. You're in Madoc's continent now; you should get to know the story. You might want to use it.'

'We're not going to have this argument again, are we? You know I'm not that kind of poet.'

'Oh I know what sort of poems you like to write. We all know those very well.'

The old voice was sharp suddenly. Gwyn kept silent.

There was a spasm of coughing at the other end of the line and then Goff's harsh breathing. It was painful even to hear. Gwyn could so easily visualise his old teacher's bony face, with its faint shadow of stubble now that Goff could no longer see to shave properly.

'That sounds bad.'

'Just a cough, a bit of Welsh winter. I dare say you spend your time down the health club now, or what do they call it? – the gym.'

Gwyn chuckled.

'Hardly. I spend my time with – some good people. They're a nice crowd here.'

He shifted the mouthpiece in his hand, opened his mouth and

47

shut it again. At the last moment, he found himself unable to speak of Jane. It was Goff who spoke first.

'Oh aye?' he said wheezily and with a touch of amusement. 'That's good, lad. I'm glad to hear that. Now hadn't you better go? This is costing you.'

'It's all right, Goff. I get paid well now.'

'All the same. Save your money for getting to know the country. Listen lad, do something for me, will you?' Goff spoke slowly, as he did when he wanted Gwyn to take notice.

'Yes. All right. Go on, then.'

'I know you don't want to follow the legends. But if you get a chance to go to Madoc's country, to the part of America where he made his Welsh settlement, go on my behalf.'

'Hmm. Where is it?'

There was a pause.

'No,' said Goff, as if he was talking to himself. 'No, leave it at that. If you're going to go, you'll find your way.'

Gwyn listened hard but nothing followed.

'Well Goff, I think I'll go back to bed now. See if I can catch a few more hours' sleep.'

'You do that. Thanks for calling me, lad. God bless.'

Gwyn put the phone down and sat quietly for a while. Talking to Goff had stirred unexpected feelings. An emotion was growing within him; no, it was more than an emotion – it was a peculiar, atavistic urge to do with Jane and Wales. He wanted, he realised in surprise, to take her there. He wanted to set her feet on Welsh earth, walk with her in the shadow of the mountain, feel the soft rain fall on to their faces. He had given his heart away in a strange country and now he wanted to take his woman home.

6

They are coming. Can you hear them coming? Look – here, look. Through the tangle of hazel branches, beyond this sheltering thicket, over the slope of grass, can you see the tops of the trees shake? Their young green leaves tremble against the sky. They are coming up the hill. Their footsteps make the earth rumble, can't you feel it?

Ah, listen, – now you can hear their voices. They are carried up over the brow of the hill on the wind. They could be mistaken for the rustling of grasses or the tumble of waves. But they are not the sounds of the island; they belong to people.

Now move, just a little, to your left. That's it. Move away from the opening of hazel branches and find this nest of leaves, down here. Crouch down. Kneel. Now do you see, through the gap in the bushes, down the other side of the hill, its steeper slope, to the harbour? The land curves round, lush and green, in the shape of a horseshoe and at the foot of the rocky slopes is the inlet: blue as the flower of a speedwell today, and lapping gently against the sides of the ships.

There are ten ships in the harbour, their masts soaring to the sky. And the decks and the quay are thronged. The foals are being led aboard: one foal and its mare for every second ship. The horsemen are carrying bags of hay and the mouse-ear herb to quiet the horses when they fret. And stretching from the quay to every deck is a line of people, passing great baskets full of salted meat, roots and grain. They are making stores so we will not starve on our long journey.

On the far side of the harbour, women are carrying the last of the chickens on to the tenth ship.

And his men are swarming over the decks, checking the furled sails, scrambling up the masts, hanging upside down over the sides. That one near the top of the mast has found something amiss: he is taking the belt from his tunic to bind a loose piece of wood, and he is calling down to those on deck. See their faces turned up to him? Anxious, they are, and frightened of getting the blame. One makes a trumpet with his hands and calls up a question.

Those men on the edges of the ships, doubled over, and the others climbing the side ropes, they're counting the ship's nails. Forty stags have died for the nails already in the ships and the meat, rolled in salt and stored in linen, will keep good for months in the hold.

He takes no chances, my Madoc. Or thinks he takes none.

There he is, his tunic and cloak fluttering round him like the standard held by his men. He is turning his head towards the right: everyone is turning. The new arrivals must be coming into view. Listen! I hear music and so does he. My man is giving orders, clearing the people from round him. He is preparing to receive the newcomers.

Now, gently. Creep forward a little. Feel the earth under your feet, the bark beneath your fingers. You can see him, can't you; there on the edge of your vision you can see him stepping forward to greet them.

But you can also see something else: you can see that they are not what he expects. You can hear the music notes changing to other noises: harsh, dangerous noises. The newcomers are sweeping around the hill in a mass of iron and hooves and confusion and look, look over to the far side of the harbour. There, on the spit of land which guards the harbour entrance, a man is kneeling and doing something with his hands. He is building a fire; he is lighting it: its flames burn a fierce, small heat in the spring day. Now Madoc is pointing at him, his mouth opening in a cry, because a huge bird is rising from the flames. It is black and the size of a man. As it rises straight up into the air, it grows larger, twice, three times the size of a man. Its wings spread wider and now it hangs in the sky and a cry breaks from Madoc's throat, for all that is gathered in the harbour – the people and the ships, the sailors, the herdsmen, the cattle, the butchered stags, the bowsmen and the musicians, and Madoc himself amidst them all – are tipping over, tumbling into the water, sinking among the splintering masts and planks. The green hills shudder and slide into one another; the white rocks crumble and the sand flies up and showers down on the drowning people as everything goes falling, falling into the blue.

And above it all, its great eyes unwinking, hovers the bird.

Harry looked over the top of the *Village Voice* and around the recreation room. It was a cheerful scene: all the armchairs were occupied and there was a good sprinkling of people at the tables here in the middle of the room. Outside, early darkness pressed against the windows. As Harry looked, people seemed to materialise from out of the darkness, pass by the lighted window and vanish. Jane was late.

Harry turned the pages of the *Voice*, trying to ignore Gwyn Thomas, who was sitting in his line of vision at the bar. Gwyn had come in fifteen minutes ago with Jermaine Wuncliffe, the professor who was organising tonight's reading, and a man Harry had never seen before, who was probably the other invited reader. Harry did not want to talk to them; correction, he would have liked to talk with Jermaine and the other reader but not with Gwyn.

Harry was dubious about Gwyn Thomas. That don't-you-love-me-rough-as-I-am style irritated him and he found Thomas's success with women, and intelligent women too, truly amazing. The man had spent his first month at Brockham drinking and fucking as if there was no tomorrow. Then he had taken up with Gail. And now, for God's sake, with Jane.

Not for the first time, Harry found himself wishing Jane luck. The love affair had now lasted six weeks; there were only ten days to go till the end of the semester. Perhaps the Christmas vacation would cool their passions.

Here she was. Jane was passing in front of the lighted window; she looked in. Yes, wouldn't you know it, her glance flew straight to Gwyn like a homing device. She went out of view for a second and Harry lifted the paper again, as camouflage. Perhaps he could remain hidden behind it until Jane had finished her greetings to Gwyn.

'Good evening.' Jane stood by the table, blinking at him. 'I need a drink. Would you like another?'

Harry put down the paper and pointed to his tequila.

'I have one.'

'I'll be two seconds then. I have to get alcohol inside me right now.'

She looked very pale this evening, without the bloom that Harry had noticed on her cheeks recently. She looked ruffled as well, her hair blown about by the wind and her jacket on awry. She crossed to the bar in long strides, and bought a Stolichnaya on the rocks. She was drinking more since she had met Gwyn. As she was served, Harry saw her raise her hand to Gwyn and Jermaine Wuncliffe, then she was bringing the drink back to his table.

'You look splendid and formidable,' Harry said as she sat down. 'Has someone been aggravating you?'

'No. It's just been a long, full day.'

'And about to be a longer one.'

'You said it. Gwyn's nervous as hell about having to read.'

'Is he? He doesn't look it.' The words came out more caustically than Harry had intended. Jane slid him a curious, long look.

'Harry,' she said after a pause. 'You do – ' she stopped, and then resumed. 'Don't you like Gwyn?' she asked mildly.

The vibrations in her voice, the stillness of her arms on the table, alerted Harry. She wasn't really asking him that; she was preparing the way for something else. Negotiations were being opened, and he might reply in any number of ways.

'It's not so much that I don't like him. I'm inclined to be cautious on your behalf, I suppose.'

Jane was watching Harry carefully, her eyes very dark in her tense face.

'What's to be cautious about?'

'Well, don't you think the way he writes about that old man is somewhat invidious? After all, the old man is real, everyone knows who he is. And Gwyn's made his reputation by writing poems against him.'

Jane tapped her long fingers against her glass; she looked extremely uncomfortable.

'He's a poet, for Christ's sakes. When he feels something strongly, he writes a poem about it. What else would you have a poet do? And in any case, the poems aren't *against* Goff, they're about Gwyn's relationship with him.'

'Yes, well. A fine distinction.'

'You're being pompous, Harry.' She smiled at him. Aha. She was going for a lighter tone, steering the conversation away from choppy waters. He shrugged slightly and waited. She was observing him across the top of her glass.

'I want you to like him,' she said deliberately.

'Yes, I can see.'

'I'm in love with him.'

Harry sighed. He picked up his glass and put it down again. Then he stretched out his hand and touched Jane's arm.

'Hey, I'm sorry. I didn't realise. Well, yes I did, but I thought it might be just one of those things.' He looked sideways at her. 'Are you sure it's not just one of those things?'

Jane nodded. Her gaze went to Harry, then down to the table, then back to him. Her lips were working but no sound came out. Harry watched half in amusement.

'I love him. We're going to be married. In ten days' time.'

Harry stretched out his long legs. He could scarcely believe what he had just heard. Eventually he said, 'Congratulations.'

A blush was sweeping over Jane's throat and cheeks, making her face glow deep red. She struggled to control it but was powerless; she just sat there, her eyes flickering from Harry to the floor and back again, a wide grin of embarrassment and happiness bending her mouth.

Harry smiled. Some selfless impulse – or perhaps an irresponsible one – was asserting itself and making him happy for her, against his will and his judgement. He gave into it and surrendered to a spurt of laughter.

'Your face. You look like Scarlet O'Hara having a menopausal flush.'

Jane, covered in confusion, bent down and pretended to search for something on the floor. When she sat back upright, only two spots of red remained on her cheekbones. She looked seriously at Harry. He looked seriously back.

'I do love him, Harry. And he loves me. I've got to be with him. I've got to,' she repeated slightly desperately.

'I just want you to be happy,' Harry answered. He was leaning towards her, lowering his voice. 'I'll be happy if you're happy. But I don't want to lose you and I don't want you to get hurt. Promise me you'll be careful.'

'About what?'

'About him. Do you have to rush it like this? What's so urgent?'

'I feel urgent. I can't explain.'

'You felt urgent once before.'

'I was a child then, for God's sake. I'm an adult now. I've earned this.'

Out of the corner of his eye, Harry could see Gwyn moving away from the bar, and coming towards the door with the other two men. They passed within a foot of the table and Jane must have seen them too for she began to turn towards them, but Harry reached out for both her hands and held them tight.

'Look at me,' he said, his face close to hers. He saw the conflict in her eyes as she struggled to focus on him. It was as if her mind couldn't stay with him, but was irresistibly drawn to the man now almost within touching distance. But she held his gaze, just. 'I'm your friend. I know more about you than anyone. Last time you fell in love you got yourself thrown out of school. Yes, yes, I know that was all kids' stuff and this is the real thing. But don't take it too fast. You seem so obsessed with him – I feel like I haven't really spoken with you in weeks.'

Gwyn had moved away again, without interrupting them. The tension went out of Jane and she smiled at Harry. It occurred to him that her love for Gwyn – or whatever it was – had changed her face. Despite the glow and the readier smile, she looked older.

The reading was in the Russell Room, a tactfully-sized space which could hold eighty people but looked respectably full with twenty. At one end it had a low podium: this sometimes held a table but tonight it was furnished with just three chairs. The body of the room was already quite well populated. Scanning it, Jane recognised students, research students and a good sprinkling of faculty in the loosely arranged rows of seats. In the front row, on the right, sat Duane Jewell, flanked by Margaret Micheson and Carlos Daneda, both on the resident appointments committee. Well, they would naturally be interested. Jane felt a knot of anxiety pull tight in her stomach; she had not spoken to Gwyn since this morning and she had no idea how bad his nerves were now. How long had he been in the bar this evening? He was standing in a group with Jermaine Wuncliffe and some of the members of his third-year writing class. He seemed to be talking enthusiastically.

'Shall we go to the front?' Harry said. 'Oh I guess not. Duane's down there.'

'Preparing to glare at Gwyn all the way through, I bet,' said Jane.

'Has it come to that?' Harry sounded amused.

'You know Duane, he likes to keep people unsure of themselves. Some days he's all over Gwyn, others he's telling him he's a no-talent bum.'

'I wouldn't have thought it bothered Gwyn much.'

'It doesn't, but it should. Duane's a powerful man.'

'God you sound tough. You're cut out for realpolitik, did you know that?'

'I'm learning,' said Jane shortly. She was beginning to feel on edge. It must be overspill from her conversation with Harry. That and tiredness catching up with her. For some reason, she had slept badly last night.

She had no reason to feel anxious about the reading. She had heard Gwyn read a month ago, in the first frantic days of their affair, and he'd handled it well. Yet looking round the Russell Room, at the posters advertising exhibitions and arts festivals and at the small-talking audience, all waiting to hear what Gwyn had to say, she felt uneasy. As she moved towards an anonymous, middle row of chairs she found herself staring at the floor, frowning.

'Jane. Jane, love.' Gwyn was at her shoulder. She had not seen him cross the room but other people had and she was aware of faces turned towards them. She looked in surprise at Gwyn: he was charged up with energy, his narrow eyes gleaming.

'Listen, I wanted to tell you.' Gwyn plucked at Jane's sleeve and smiled from her to Harry. 'I've had a marvellous day, fantastic. I've been working like a dog, on an idea I had this morning. I tell you, it's the best feeling I've ever had. I've done something completely new for me. Wait and see.'

He winked at her and walked back across the room. The buzz of excitement in his voice stayed with her, vibrating in her ears.

Faintly embarrassed, Jane met Harry's quizzical stare and shrugged.

'For God's sake, let's sit down,' she said, and slid quickly into a seat.

'Oh muse,' murmured Harry in her ear.

'Oh shut up,' said Jane.

She looked away from Harry, around the room. About as far away from her as it was possible to be, Gail was taking a seat next to Robert Wendell.

'Gail's here,' she whispered.

'Why shouldn't she be?' Harry said. 'You're all on civilised terms aren't you?'

'Gail and I, yes. But things are very po-lite between her and Gwyn.'

'He's still resident poet. Gail wouldn't let a ruined romance get in the way of her work. And circulating at events like this is part of her work. The woman is an extremely serious academic.'

All the same, Gail did not look particularly happy. Jane covertly watched her and felt a twinge of guilty pleasure. It was she, Jane Pridden, whom Gwyn loved.

Jermaine Wuncliffe was asking the person nearest the door to close it, and the spatters of conversation died away. Gwyn had sat down on one of the podium chairs and the other reader, whose name Jane now recalled, was Stephen Prost, was next to him. Jermaine was introducing them both and explaining that Prost would read first. Gwyn was advancing in the pecking order, thought Jane. She tried to empty her mind and listen to the short story which Prost now stood up and prepared to read.

But Jane could not concentrate. She found herself staring at Prost, who was in his mid-twenties, thin-faced with a neat brown beard. It was a mild face but disciplined: very different from Gwyn's. Prost's voice matched his face: it was light and soothing and Jane found herself lulled into what was almost a day-dream.

She jerked out of it as she realised that Prost had finished reading. There were the usual questions, to which she didn't attend. Then it was Gwyn's turn.

Jane watched Gwyn arrange his papers on the stand and square up to the room. After Prost he looked stocky and earth-bound. Deep in her viscera, Jane felt a fierce twist of desire. It was intensely physical, so strong that it alarmed her. She had him now. It wasn't necessary to feel like this. But she did.

Gwyn began to speak and with the part of her mind that still functioned, Jane was relieved to hear that he spoke clearly and confidently, and that there was no hint of drunkenness about him.

'Since I've been in New York,' he was saying, 'I've begun to see new patterns in things. Different things seem important over here,' his deep voice held on to the vowel sound for a few seconds, 'and I've done some new work these last two months. I want to read some before and after poems.'

First came two of the Goff poems. Jane didn't look at Harry while Gwyn read them. She knew the poems, of course, but when Gwyn read them they seemed to gain another dimension. He knew how to get his voice inside the rhythms, swinging from one phrase to another, dropping low into the vowels. She'd had such misconceptions about the kind of poetry he wrote that the first time she read his work on the page, she'd been dumbfounded. Expecting image-laden, plangent verse in the Dylan Thomas style, she hadn't known how to respond to these tight, rebarbative poems. They dealt in the minutiae of life: objects, unwanted letters, silent meals. They were unyielding and frequently bitter – especially the poems about Goff, in which the language grew dense and knotty with frustration. She thought they were his best but listening to Gwyn's voice clamping down on the consonants of the last line, Jane understood why these poems made Harry uneasy: they were so intimate and unforgiving.

Jane looked up and saw Gwyn shuffling among his papers. He picked out a single sheet, took a step back and, to her astonishment, recited a bawdy little limerick. It sent a ripple of laughter round the room. Jane had never heard it before; she didn't know he wrote such things.

'Juvenilia,' said Gwyn, with a sly smile. Jane stared at him

57

curiously. His eyes gleamed in the bright overhead light and he seemed exhilarated. She hadn't known he could play the show-man so well.

'This is one I wrote a few weeks ago,' Gwyn said. 'It's a New York poem.' His glance moved across the room and rested briefly on Jane's face. 'Called "Box".'

Jane sat very still, as Gwyn's voice flowed into her mind. Would anyone else know this was about her? Anyone could tell that it was a love poem. The central image was inanimate – a cuff-link box which Jane had given him as a gift, and in which, having no cuff-links, Gwyn kept paper clips – but the passion with which he described the details of the box and the sensuousness of the language made the poem a celebration of love and desire.

Jane looked past other people's shoulders and heads to the far corner of the stage, listening. He was speaking directly to her. Inside the words she could hear his voice caressing her, saying the things he said when they were alone but in code now, in a secret language which the other people in the room might guess at but could not decipher.

With the end of the poem, Jane bent her head. She was punch-drunk and while she knew she should have been elated, she simply felt exhausted, emotionally and physically. Beside her Harry sat with legs stretched out and arms folded, glaring at Gwyn.

Gwyn was now introducing his last poem. Jane hoped it would be a short one; she was looking forward to the end of the reading and getting out of this room.

It was a while before the meaning of the poem penetrated her mind. At first she was aware of a different, more complicated rhythm, with internal rhymes. The rhythm was insistent, like an old chant. Then the words themselves came; spoken softly by Gwyn in a voice which she knew, but did not recognise.

They are coming, said Gwyn's voice. Can you hear them coming? Look – through the tangle of hazel branches, beyond this sheltering thicket, over the slope of grass, can you see the tops of the trees shake? Can you feel how the earth rumbles beneath their feet?

Ah, listen; said Gwyn. Here come their voices. They are rising over the brow of the hill on the wind. They sound so distant, don't they; they could be the rustling of grass or the murmur of waves. But they are not.

These are no sounds of the island, Gwyn said. This is not water on rock, nor the cry of seabirds. These are the voices of people, and they are coming. And what is that down there, to the east? Turn your head, look down this steep slope which curves round the lapping waters, and what do you see gathered in the harbour?

Jane saw nothing; nothing save the pictures made by Gwyn's words. She felt the compartments of her mind being ravished by these sights and sounds. She was helpless. Inside the thicket, looking out through the pale branches, she felt the buffeting wind and the vibration of the earth slip into the marrow of her bones. The short, lush grass of the slope ran dizzyingly down to the water and filled her eyes. And in the water? She lifted her eyes longingly.

Gwyn stopped talking and raised his head. There was a pause and people began a smattering of clapping.

Slowly, Jane unclenched her fingers from the sides of the chair. She heard Harry's voice coming through a fog.

'Jane, are you all right?'

She was going to pass out.

'I'm *so* embarrassed,' said Jane. She was sitting on Gwyn's two-seater sofa, pulling at the corner of a cushion. 'God, it's humiliating. Everyone thinks I passed out because you read me a love poem.'

Gwyn handed her a second glass of water.

'No they don't,' he said unconvincingly. 'Anyway, you didn't pass out. You just came over all strange. Are you sure you don't want to go to the doctor?'

'Absolutely sure.'

'You're not pregnant or anything, are you?'

'God, no.'

'And you're not going to be sick?'

'No. Look, I'm really sorry. I've fouled up your evening.'

Gwyn waved his hand.

'Don't be ridiculous. I just want to know you're all right.'

But he was sitting on the very edge of his chair, and although he looked solicitously at her, his knees were jiggling restlessly.

'I'm fine now, just a bit shaky. It must have been too hot in there, that's all. Why don't you go back to the bar? I'll just stay here and relax.'

'Trying to get rid of me?'

'Of course not.'

'Well, you looked horrified enough when I came up to you in there.'

Jane sipped the water; it wasn't quite cold enough. It felt unpleasant on her tongue.

'I was having a black-out, sweetheart. I wasn't feeling too well.'

'You're telling me. There I was, rushing over to do my Florence Nightingale act, and the look on your face when you saw me – !'

Jane laughed. 'Gwyn, I think you're offended.'

He shrugged. 'Well, it was a bit disconcerting. You cringed away from me, love. Everyone noticed it.'

'It was probably the effect of hearing Jewell call you "dear lad".'

Gwyn grinned.

'Oh you heard that, did you? I've obviously pushed the right button with the old sod, at last. He takes it as a personal compliment that I've started writing in bardic metre. Mind you, you've got to hand it to him, he knows his stuff. He recognised the verse form as twelfth-century, which was more than I could do without looking it up.'

'It was pretty good, that poem.' Jane spoke casually but she was watching Gwyn. She half closed her eyes, to disguise her interest. 'What's it about, by the way?'

'Well it's funny, that, because I don't know.' Through her lashes, Jane saw Gwyn think. He tilted his head slightly, as if he were listening for something, then smiled to himself.

'What is it?' she asked.

'Mmm?' Gwyn looked up. His eyes were bright, as they had been under the lights of the Russell Room. 'Oh, nothing. I was just wondering about it, that's all. I haven't really thought until now – I was so excited about the verse form, you see. I was feeling all restless this morning – you know how I do when I've got something I want to start – and then I found myself thinking, out of nowhere, "I know, why don't I try something in bardic?"'

Re-living it, a flash of pure excitement lit up Gwyn's face. Jane noticed that, unconsciously, he was rubbing his hands.

'I was just experimenting with different metres and forms and the next thing I knew, it came out. Internal rhymes on the fifth and ninth syllables – Goff would be in heaven.'

He was exhilarated. More than that, he was truly happy. It troubled Jane. She couldn't remember exactly what had happened in the Russell Room but the one thing she did know, and which stayed uncomfortably real even now that they were sitting alone together, discussing it, was that she recognised his poem. She had heard it before.

Was it possible that Gwyn had plagiarised it, without realising?

Jane put a hand up to massage her forehead, bewildered. Where could she have heard or read anything like that before? She wasn't a great poetry reader. Where could she have come across it? She couldn't ask Gwyn: he was gazing at her with love and pride, so pleased with his new work. It would be cruel to hint that maybe it wasn't all his.

It was an extremely good piece of work. Even through this distracting nausea, Jane could remember the poem's beauty and power. It must be wonderful to be able to write like that.

The poem was so simple; it had described so little and yet had seemed to hint at so much. Once again, she saw the hillside and the wide, pale sky, and felt the sea air on her skin. A rush of emotion seized her: fear and excitement and something deeper and darker than both.

She took a slow breath. This was no poem. Of course it wasn't: this was some long lost memory of her own that had been stirred to life by Gwyn's words. That would be it. She was overwrought, thanks to the emotional peaks she had been riding all semester, and Gwyn's poem had inadvertently touched off a reaction in her.

She took her hand from her face and smiled at Gwyn.

'Honey, why don't you go over to the bar now?' she said. 'Everyone'll be there. I think I just need to sleep.'

'Perhaps I will, then,' Gwyn said. 'If you're sure.' He got to his feet and paused, looking down at her. 'Did you tell Harry, you know, about us?'

'Yes. I did.' Jane was touched to see the delighted smile which spread over Gwyn's face.

'So now you can tell Jewell and I can go ahead and arrange it? There's nothing to stop us getting married?'

'Not that I can think of.'

Gwyn bent over her and kissed her forehead.

'Bloody marvellous.'

At that moment, a shiver ran along Jane's body. It rippled from her toes and fingertips up to her scalp.

'What's up?'

She sat very still. What was that? A fleeting thought? But it was gone. She reached up and kissed him back and this time everything felt normal.

7

Gwyn put the mug of coffee down carefully on his desk and used his sleeve to wipe up the drops he had spilt. Where the liquid had dropped on to his notes, translucent circles appeared in the paper. He watched the words fuzz slightly, tiny tendrils of ink spreading through the damp fibres.

He willed the letters to disintegrate but although the lines thickened and blurred they held; the words were still legible. The poem was still there.

It wasn't that he wanted to destroy the poem. He couldn't anyway; it was lodged firmly in his mind now. He could feel it in there, hard and sweet; he treasured it as, when he was a boy, he used to treasure the first conker of the year, picking it lovingly from its prickly pod among the leaves and carrying it in his hand, feeling its smooth shininess inside his palm.

There was no destroying something which felt like that. But he had been thinking about the damn thing too much, trying vainly to analyse it and understand where it had come from. He had made himself dizzy and frustrated, and now he felt horribly blocked. It was his own fault. Why had he gone poring over something he had already written, when the instinct had been on him all morning to write something new?

It was gone now, or rather, the instinct was still there but the ability had diminished. The sheets in front of him were covered in heavy doodles, block after block of geometrical shapes, relentlessly filled in as each attempt to write failed beneath his pen.

He was blocked, claustrophobically so. The worst of it was

that he felt the possibilities all around him; there was something he wanted to write about, but he couldn't quite see it. There were words calling to him but he couldn't hear them. He was standing in a wood, abundant with ripe conkers and falling leaves and squirrels, but his eyes looked on to a blank wall and whenever he turned, the wall turned with him.

Gwyn cradled the mug of hot coffee in his hands and inhaled the steam. The light was failing. He looked at his watch: the afternoon was further advanced than he had realised; a quarter to four already.

He got up and went to the window. The trees were amassing shadows around the edges of the lawns. The lights of the city studded the early dusk, exotic and alien to his eyes. He had been glad, this morning, that Jane would be working all day and then out this evening, seeing an old friend. He had wanted the time to himself, to think and write. But now he felt unsettled and oddly anxious; he picked up the telephone and punched out the extension number of her office. There was no answer.

The Bloomingdale's lights dazzled Jane, glinting off mirrors and glass shelves and large, bevelled bottles of perfume. From the various counters, immaculately groomed women looked out at the shoppers like duchesses from the royal box.

Jane received a squirt of a new scent on her wrist, and, rubbing it in, walked on through the perfume counters to the costume jewellery.

Jane had awarded herself a few hours away from work. She deserved it: she had spent most of the day in Brockham library, checking facts for someone else's article on French movies. The article was deadly dull and pretentious – even she could hardly read it and she loved French movies. She had earned her time off.

Besides, she wasn't fit for work today. She still felt strange after last night's fainting episode. The aftermath was more mental than physical: a brooding unease, and a sense that there was something she was failing to recall.

She had been unable to place the memory set off by Gwyn's poem. She had searched in vain for a clue last night, until she had fallen asleep. She had slept heavily, not stirring when Gwyn returned from the bar, not roused by the alarm clock this morning. Gwyn had finally woken her at twenty to nine. And then he had seemed eager to get rid of her, anxious to press on with his writing.

It was the first time Jane had ever felt shut out by Gwyn. And she was surprised by how much she minded. Although she tried to concentrate on her work, her mind kept flickering to Gwyn's. How was it going? Was he now, this very minute, writing more about that hillside place? Had he raised his eyes, as yesterday she had done so longingly, to the shore? Was he now able to see, unlike her, what lay there?

Jane recognised the emotion stirring inside her: envy. It was curious: she had never before begrudged Gwyn his talent or his success. On the contrary, she had delighted in it. But since the reading last night, she had felt the unmistakable pulse of jealousy. And it was not the usual wistful envy of another person's achievements: this was a fierce, possessive jealousy, directed at the poem itself.

Jane had shrugged and tried to ignore the feeling. But she couldn't; it kept getting in the way and tangling up her work.

Now, after an hour in Bloomingdale's, she was sated with objects, smells and sounds. And the unease was still with her.

She hesitated by a rack of ear-rings, shaped like bunches of fruit. Behind the counter, a young sales assistant wearing a purple feathered hair clasp asked if she could show Jane anything.

'I'll let you know,' said Jane, moving on to the necklaces. She picked one off the stand and fastened it experimentally round her neck: it was a heavy black-sprayed chain strung with varnished acorns and oak leaves. It was bold and unapologetic and it looked rather good on her. On top of her red jumper, it struck a farouche note.

She peered at her reflection in the mirror: the circle of forest symbols at her throat gave her an unexpected dignity. As she looked at herself, another woman – less self-doubting, stronger and enigmatic – seemed to come to the fore.

It was Jane and not Jane. She stared into the mirror, fascinated.

'Oh, that's so cute,' said the sales assistant. 'It suits you so well.'

'Yes,' said Jane. 'I like it.'

She couldn't take her eyes off the mirror. In it she saw a woman with white skin, dark, dark eyes like a peat pool, and a mouth which curved red. She was harsh and beautiful. Jane felt a sharp twist of longing as she gazed at her, and her mouth opened in a sigh.

The red mouth, the colour of crushed berries, opened too.

Jane reached out a hand towards the woman. In the corner of the mirror, white fingers appeared, reaching for Jane.

The gleaming props of Bloomingdale's – the counters, the gliding escalators, the racks of sales goods – were moving on the edge of her vision. They rose up, buckled and snapped into a million shards, exploding around the mirror so that nothing was left of the world but dancing splinters in a great darkness and at the centre of it, constant in the vortex, the face of this beautiful, savage woman.

The image seemed to flicker. Jane felt a terrible loss contract her heart, then she was looking back into her own face, pale and askew with shock.

She was struggling to undo the clasp when she heard a precise voice say, 'I think it's based on a Native American design. It suits you, actually.'

'Gail!'

Jane heard her own voice hit the air, sounding high and unnatural. She looked down at Gail – from a great height it seemed to her, and very slowly. Gail stood beside her at the counter, wearing a smart blue coat, her face turned up to Jane's with a pleasant expression.

'Gail, I didn't see you,' Jane's voice was saying, and her fingers fumbled and tugged at the clasp. 'I don't know, I'm not sure about it.'

There was a click beneath her fingertips and the necklace fell limply into her hands. She placed it back on the stand, awry. 'I expect it costs a fortune,' she said.

She slid her gaze sideways to the mirror. The shining oval reflected both her and Gail now, very prosaic and unexceptional. Gail's lips were moving; she was saying something about the *Review*. It seemed that they were having a conversation, for now they were walking away from the counter together and Jane was nodding competently at Gail.

She was at the mercy of a strange vertigo and it was necessary to measure her steps carefully to Gail's. Her thoughts began to return to her, as if they were birds gliding in from a long way off.

What had happened? What had she seen? Suddenly desire and panic hit her in the stomach, the conflicting urges tearing at her like a pain. She bent forwards, crossing her arms over herself.

'Jane? Are you all right? Jane?'

Jane looked up to see Gail peering anxiously at her.

'I don't feel so good.'

'You're white as a sheet. Would you like to sit down? Shall we go to the juice bar?'

'Yes. I'm rather hot, that's a good idea. Thank you.' Jane straightened up and allowed Gail to take her arm. She was trembling violently.

People jostled on the sidewalk of Forty-Fourth Street. Jane shouldered her way through coats and suits, heading towards the blaze of tawdry neon at the Times Square end. She needed to get away from Bloomingdale's and its brightness, from Gail and her well-meant concern, from this street and its glaring, flashing lights.

She groped her way through the doors of the Algonquin and into the lobby. In here the lights, in yellow and amber shades, were low; they cast peaceful shadows on the sofas and carpets and the people standing at the reception desk. Jane turned right, under the lintel where the blue sign burned, and into the tiny Blue Bar. It was dim and comforting, and half-full.

Jane ordered a margarita and watched the bartender pour, shake, pour. The glass came to her rimmed with cloudy crystals. The sour liquid flowed over her tongue, steadying her, and she lifted her eyes to the wall mirror. Now.

Her reflection looked tired, with faint bruises beneath the eyes. Her skin was ghostly pale in the blue light of the bar. But it was just her own reflection. The other woman, the Jane who was not Jane, was no longer there.

Where are you? She asked silently. She listened but no answer came. I'm ready for you, she said. I was frightened before. I'm ready now. Come back.

But her reflection remained only her reflection.

She stared at it until she saw hope fade from her mirrored eyes. She glanced around the bar: two men were watching her with amused interest. She began to feel self-conscious.

Disappointment hollowed her throat and made her greedy: she finished her margarita in three gulps. Oh well, what the fuck was she playing at? Wandering round Bloomingdale's having psychic experiences; perhaps she was sick, after all.

If Dina didn't get here soon, she'd have to have another drink without her. Jane wondered how Gwyn's writing was going. Her disappointment was edged with an irrational anger.

8

It was nearly one o'clock when Jane closed the door softly behind her and shot the bolt home. The apartment was silent, the hall a cube of unrelieved blackness. She padded to the right and pushed gently at the living room door; it swung open and the darkness diminished. The living room was empty: its two chairs, table, bookshelves and television looked remote in the grey-orange half-light which spread in from the street.

Jane moved down the short corridor, brushing against the wall. Gwyn was in the bedroom; she could smell him. His scent — heavy, warm, sherberty — filled her nostrils and made her fingers fumble on the door knob. She paused and pulled herself away from the bedroom door to the bathroom. Wash first; wash and drink some water to cool her brain, and then she could go to Gwyn.

The fierce fluorescent light bounced back at her from the white tiles. She ran hot water into the basin and stripped off first her coat and then the rest of her clothes. She rubbed the soap into a lather, splashed water on herself with her hands and began washing. She smeared the suds over her face and neck and breasts, creamed them into her armpits, smoothed them between her legs. Her eyes shut, she let out the frothy water and ran some more. Her hands trembled and she rinsed herself hurriedly, pouring rivulets on to the floor.

The erotic charge had been building in her all evening, as she sat with Dina in the Blue Bar, as they ate in the restaurant, then during the final hours while they had talked and drunk in the fashionable clutter of Dina's latest preferred venue, the Nevsky Prospect. She could still taste the bison grass vodka: an oily liquid, freezing and acrid. In the club, with her senses sharpened and her intellect lulled, the taste had conjured up a vision: the vodka had rolled across her tongue and made her think of wide, empty plains stretching out in every direction and as far as the eye could see. The picture slipped back into her mind now, replacing the smooth white hollow of the basin.

It was a puzzlingly familiar landscape. The colours of the earth, the grass, the yellow-red dust were those of Renoxia, and yet this country was too flat. There was a suggestion of hills in the distance; yes, a series of bluffs towards the horizon, rising one after another like the bluffs south of Renoxia. But on either side, ahead and behind, was flatness: too much of it. She could recognise it but it was changed, as if someone had taken the contours and was playing games with the proportions and perspective.

Jane reached for the towel and pressed it to her face. Here was Gwyn's scent again – his soap and washing powder, mingled with a trace of his cologne.

Fleetingly, through the tangle of her hair, she glimpsed in the mirror the pale outline of her face and a bright glitter of eyes.

Had Dina found her silence strange? For the last hour they were together, Jane had been unable to talk; she could feel herself taking longer and longer to answer her friend's questions. There was a stillness in her head and from it no words came, only this shocking desire.

Her arms ached to hold Gwyn. She brushed her teeth fast, gazing at the chrome and enamel basin, longing to press her skin against his. Through the minty foam she could already taste the soft wetness of his mouth.

The need was fierce in her: her nerve ends were burning and leaping all along her arms and legs, in her breasts, down the length of her back.

A tug on the light cord brought the grateful darkness back down on her as she slipped across the passage and eased open the bedroom door. Gwyn did not wake when first she crawled under the sheets and wound her cold bare limbs around him. A second passed; her lips were brushing his chest. Then his hands closed on her, an instinctive, strong grip which made her shudder.

'Jane?' he murmured. She moaned, raised her head and stopped his questions with her mouth.

It's peaceful here in the wood, and so quiet you can hear the season dying. The gentle sun is travelling on down through the trees, lighting up the webs the spiders have thrown between the trunks. The spiders have been working since morning, spinning for the turning weather.

This evening the sun will sink behind the ridge of the valley a few minutes earlier than it did yesterday; tomorrow it'll reach its rest earlier still. The season is changing and already there are new fallen leaves on the ground to scratch and tickle my feet.

And I could scream with wanting it to be different. I'm not a fool. I know there's some things you can't change and one of those is the coming of autumn. But the sight of that dying sun and the copper shades creeping into the bracken fills me with impatience. Even the stream runs over the stones with a slower splash.

I tighten the twine knot with my teeth and put the bundle of sticks in the hollow between the tree roots, with the others. I have four good bundles now. I don't want to work too fast, mind: it's better to be up here in the woods than down in the valley, where Mam and Buddug and the other women are picking over the oats and separating them into piles for grinding. My hands are rough with oats dust and my ears are ringing with the noise of chatter and rustle and the bang of stones. There's all the fun of the harvest down there and I ought to be enjoying it, but this year I feel different.

I feel restless. I keep looking at all the faces that I know so well and love – yes, I do love them – Mam's strong face, broad at the temples, and Buddug's pretty heart-shape with her teasing eyes, and little Dafydd making a nuisance of himself clinging to Mam's waist, and Nest my friend who purses her lips kissy-fashion whenever she sees Meilyr come near. Meilyr: all harvest, he has been courting me. He's been doing it quietly, but all the same, when I look up from the winnowing, he's watching me; in the morning, when I walk to the river to draw water, he's along the bank, splashing his face. Last night when he came in from the hunt, he walked to our house and gave my mother a cut of shoulder from the stag. He wanted me to know that he helped kill it, that he's now a man.

When I see Mei watching me, the shape of his shoulders pleases me. I've noticed that he has a long stride. And his upper lip is darkening: soon, he'll be wearing hair on it and I think it will be thick and handsome.

I could do worse than marry Mei, of course. His father Bran ap Iolo is one of our most important men. Bran and Teilo Gruffydd lead the kindred in this valley, and are first cousins to Llywelyn, the pencenedl of the whole kindred, who keeps his home two valleys away. Bran and Teilo and their families get the first share of the crops and the livestock and they have judgement over the rest of the kindred in Cynfael in disputes. Mei is not only one of Bran's sons, he's well in with Hywel Drwyn. If I squint through the trees I can just see Hywel Drwyn's new house, built with stones as well as earth, like a lord's castle. Hywel's even built the sides forward so he's got a courtyard. Very clever is Hywel, with his new status as musterer of arms to our overlord, Elydyr Tewdr. Hwyel is below Teilo Gruffydd and Bran in the kindred, but he got in there with Elydyr fast and this new house is a sign of it.

Mei's already ridden out on a muster with Elydyr Tewdr and Llywelyn. He'll do more in the future. If I marry Mei, then he might become musterer like Hwyel. Even if he doesn't, he'll be important in Cynfael. One day we could build ourselves a house like Hwyel's, further up from the valley floor. I could receive Elydyr in my house and feed him and afterwards play to him and his men – and Mei – on a harp. Mind you, we'd have to be doing well to feed Elydyr and his men. Hywel's still grumbling about the last time they passed through the village and ate him out of house and home.

I can see such a future, almost. So can Mam. Last night, after I'd been giggling with Nest, she said to me: 'You keep your wits about you. There's moments when things come, and then they're gone. You be ready to take it while it's there.' We were standing outside the house and I could hear beetles rustling in the roof-thatch, just above my eyes. Mam was using the sharp voice that makes my stomach run hot. She was closer to me than I wanted her to be and I could see her eyes, bright and probing. 'I was married by the time I was fourteen,' she said. 'I was married and carrying you.' She paused and stared at me and when I didn't answer, she sighed out the air in a hiss. 'Ceinwen Maelgwyn,' she said, and I heard the anger leap into her voice – I make her angry so quickly nowadays – 'don't you go setting yourself above Meilyr. Don't you damn well dare.'

I said nothing still. She was watching me very closely but I didn't flinch or look away. For a second I thought she might hit me – her hand made a sudden movement and then she turned and went inside the house, all elbows and shoulders and sharp movements, snapping down her head to avoid the low branches of the thatch.

I stood outside, looking down the hill, at the cluster of the kindred's houses and sheds on this side of the river. I wondered about marrying Meilyr. I'm fourteen now, well into marrying age. If we marry, I'll leave our house and go across the valley to his and live with his father and mother and his three brothers and two sisters. Dear God, what a thought.

I might do it. I know I might. When the harvest is done and the leaves are all turned and ready to fall, we might walk up through these woods in a procession and lay our hands on the ladyrock, to ask her blessing. The ladyrock, our lovely cold grey stone who stands beside the track, guards the valley and protects it. I've followed enough other girls there and sung and chanted and cat-called them, and then splashed the ladyrock with marriage wine. She's brought enough children to this village – children of marriage and children of the brake and brush. Will I get one or the other by Meilyr, under her gaze?

Oh there's bored I am of this sleepy warm haze. And bored of these thoughts too, if I'm honest. Bored of teasing myself with Will I? If? Shall I? What if?

All summer this strength has been growing inside me. I don't know what it is. It murmurs at me when other people are talking; it laughs when they want me to be serious. It strokes my limbs when I'm working and tickles and fidgets them when I'm asleep. Sometimes it grows very fierce and takes on a colour – deep orange-red in the evening, or intense blue in the middle of the day, or rich, rich yellow in the early morning when the fields are dewy and the sun's pale and it should be impossible to feel warm.

Some days I feel so strong I think I'll burst out of myself. I'm surprised the others can't see it, as we're working in the fields bending over the rows of oats; when we're walking, chatting, to the river to rinse our hands of the choking dust. Sometimes I hear myself speak and I'm afraid I've given myself away and that everyone will know that my head is filled with thoughts of the world outside our valley, and people outside our village, the people who sometimes ride through . . .

I haven't even told Nest that I think these thoughts. We used to make stories about leaving, when we were little. When we went with our fathers, taking the sheep to the summer pasture on the hills, we'd see the tracks leading across the hills and the sea gleaming in the south and we'd say that one day we'd go off and make new lives there. We'd talk about the great castle at Cardiff – though we'd never seen it – and about the castle at Abercwm, which we passed right in front of. But in the last year or so, our own valley here has become more important to us now, and the valleys on either side, and the people in them – and the young lads, especially the lads.

But men still ride through here, along the track above these woods. Men with spears as well as bows; men with fine coloured cloaks over their tunics, going to meet the Lord Rhys, the great overlord of all the southern kindreds, in his western stronghold of Dinefwr.

I've never been to any town except for Abercwm, but I listen to the stories of Hwyel and Teilo and Bran and imagine the bigger, further places, where the overlords meet.

Men ride through and I watch them go.

Mam knows. She hates it. Duw, she hates it.

Bugger the sticks and the oats and Mam, I'm going to the Lady-rock. It's a slog up the slope, the mossy soil springy and dry under my feet, tiny hazel and birch branches whipping back on my bare legs. Bundle my skirts up and lift them up, so I've got more room to stride and scramble. Plunge through the bracken, climb the fallen tree and round the roots and up on to the track. And now I'm running, running, holding my skirts clear, feeling the air on my legs. I'm running with my head lifted back and my eyes on the sky, running past the stream and its feeders, past the damp rock face where the caves are, past the holly bushes and the lush grass where the horses graze, straight along the track. My legs are leaping and pounding. Run, run. My chest is growing tight. Run. Breathe. My throat is rough where I'm gasping now and my spit is pooling in my mouth, bitter, running into the corners of my smiling mouth. I feel my energy flow out through my muscles and into the air, down into the earth and the earth sprays under my feet and the slight wind lifts my hair and the flies and birds scatter.

Oh it's so good. And there she is – the ladyrock. In the afternoon sun, by the track, her quiet greyness blessing it.

She's cool to touch. It's lovely to stand here, pressed against her, feeling the damp cold soothe my cheeks and my forehead. Beneath the surface warmth, where the sun has shone on her, she's always cold. You can feel it deep down inside her, working its way out towards you, the cold from the heart of the stone, being drawn up from the depths of the ground.

I can feel something else too. Tremors, a distant rhythm of beats travelling up through the stone. No, I'm not imagining it; it's there and growing stronger. Now I can hear it as well as feel it. Hoof-beats, thudding along the track. People; men on horses, coming this way. I don't know if I'm frightened or excited; I still have one hand on the Ladyrock as the noise breaks out of the trees and, cantering round the corner into the sunlight, they come.

There are four of them – no, five. They're wearing dark cloaks and pale tunics; the horses are saddled quite plainly, except for one which seems to have a blue insignia on its headband. Every time its forelock lifts, the dark blue flashes. Well, isn't dark blue a royal colour?

Even across this distance I can see that these men are young; they're riding boisterously and shouting to one another. They're wearing their knives but carrying their bows behind them – they're not looking for trouble, then.

Now they've seen me. One has put his hand out – I didn't see which – and they're reining in their horses. Their pace slows to a trot and now they draw near, staring. Is it excited I am, or afraid? I'm looking at them hard, trying to gather my wits, but these young men mean nothing to me.

Four of them are dark, there's one of them has red hair; my

eyes go from face to face and at first it's just a jumble of eyes
and noses. Then gradually they begin to make sense and I can
see that one of them is round-cheeked and heavy; that the red-
haired one is the tallest; there is one with a long nose and another
who's as pretty as a girl.

But all of these details I'm seeing out of the corners of my eyes,
because there's one man who has all my attention. I feel like a
hawk when the jesses have closed round her; I'm caught. He's
looking down at me from his chestnut horse and I can't look
away.

He's square-faced with eyebrows far apart like two black
smudges and beneath them his eyes are a blue-green colour that's
strange in a man. But he's not quite a man. I can see clearly that
he's still a lad. He has a manly way of sitting on his horse,
though. He's wearing a cloak of fine-woven linen, dyed dark blue
like the tassel on his horse's bridle. His tunic is longer than people
wear round here, and there's a pattern embroidered into the
weave on his breast. He looks proud and powerful, but his legs
and feet are bare, like mine. Behind him and the others now,
there are more people riding into view. There's four of them, on
horses laden down with bags and baskets: they're the servants,
trotting behind the masters. The young man's hand on the dark
copper mane is lifting to forestall the others.

He's staring at me.

'Good day. Are you from the village?'

His voice is young and throaty. And it's not a local voice either;
it's from the north, from the inhospitable country of mountains
and the old, blood-thirsty clans.

I don't know if I can speak, but I open my mouth and hear
myself replying courteously. My voice sounds oddly clear to me;
how does it sound to this stranger?

'Good day sir,' I reply. 'I'm from Cynfael, beyond these woods.'

'Cynfael.' It sounds like a very small place when he says it so
imperiously. I shouldn't be looking at him really; it's ill manners
to stare at a lord. But I can't look away and after all, he's looking
at me. His blue-green eyes are gazing at me. Eyes to eyes, we
look, and eyes to eyes I don't think we are lord and servant.

'Whose land is that?' he says in his guttural, northern voice.

Whose land indeed? I know he doesn't mean us, the kindred

who live on it, any more than I'd mean the half-free if I asked the question.

'Elydyr ap Tewdr's, my lord.'

'And who are you?'

'Ceinwen, Maelgwyn's daughter.'

'Will you take us to Elydyr ap Tewdr's house? We'll be asking hospitality.'

His men are surprised at this: they're exchanging quick glances. This young man has only just decided to break his journey here – only now, in this instant, since he's seen me. Yes. Yes. Yes.

I reach out my hand behind my back and press my fingers against the ladyrock, feeling her secret strength.

'Elydyr ap Tewdr doesn't live with us, my lord. But his man at arms keeps a house for guests and will be honoured to have you.'

Now Mr Pretty is opening his mouth to protest. His long eyelashes sweep down and shadow his cheeks.

'But prince,' he says, and loud his voice is, and carrying. 'We were going to go on to Llantrisant tonight. If we hurry we can make it by sundown and it's only a day's ride from there to Caer Llion.'

Prince: what prince is he? The prince looks over his shoulder.

'I'm tired of riding,' he says. 'There's good countryside here, a friendly village and Elydyr's man at arms longing for the honour of our company.'

'It's only mid-afternoon,' says the man with the fat face. 'Who'll see to us? Every woman and girl round here is at oats harvest.'

'Ceinwen Maelgwyn isn't,' my prince replies and suddenly he turns and smiles at me.

He has spoken my name. I can see the knowledge of me in his eyes. And what should I be doing if not smiling back?

He has dismounted from his horse and is walking beside me. He isn't much taller than me and his skin is fresh and young. It looks odd for a lad so young to be so sure of himself; a real prince, this one is.

At first I could hear the silence behind us apart from the clop of hooves and the flappings of the men's cloaks but now they've started to talk to one another again, idle talk in deep voices. It has a different tone from the chatter of valley men; it's full of the sound of power and ownership.

The prince has just told me his name and his blood.

'I am Madoc ap Owain ap Gruffydd,' he said. 'My father is Owain, Prince of Gwynedd.'

I didn't know what to say. Gwynedd: there's power even in the name of it. The territory spreads from the north of the Dyfi river across scores of miles. It has mountains in the heart of it, the English border on the east and the north and west beyond the mountains, the seas. The blood-line of the Gwynedd princes is the longest and the princes and lords are the fiercest and most ambitious. In the nights, the cyfarwyddion often tell us stories of the old battles of Gwynedd and news keeps coming in of new ones. The battles are among the prince's sons: greedy, they are. We hear that they raise whole cantrefi of armed men to carry out raids and snatch each other's territories. It's a harsh place to live, is what we tell one another down here, and are glad to be under the Lord Rhys's protection.

Now, I hear the name of Gwynedd on Madoc's tongue and I see another side to it.

Prince Madoc's looking at me as if he wants to suck me into those strange sea-blue-green eyes of his. I've forgotten to kiss his hand, but then he's forgotten to hold it out for kissing.

I'm out of breath when I speak.

'You're very welcome in Cynfael, my lord.'

Now we are talking like any lad and girl, except that looking at his face I can almost see the great hall of his father's house up there in Gwynedd, and the wall hangings and the torches burning on the sconces and the bards telling their stories of battle and glory and, at the head of the long table, his father the prince with all his sons and men around him.

Madoc is teasing me, wanting to know why I'm not at oats harvest. He's accusing me of laziness and I'm laughing and pretending to protest.

'I did. I came to collect firewood. We've been that busy at the harvest for the last few days that we've run out.'

'That's a good lot you've got there, too. What a heavy bundle; shall I carry it for you?'

'I have some, really. I was down in the coppices gathering bundles, and I've left them there.'

'To come and look for more on the track.'

'Yes.'

'There's no wood on this track.'

'No, but there's sun.'

Madon's eyes run over my face curiously. I feel his gaze like a touch, like a prickle on the skin. The sun is warm on my back and under my skirt my legs rub against each other, smooth.

'So that's what you were doing on that stone? Guzzling the sun like a wall lizard?'

The blush creeps into my face. Me and the Ladyrock. I remember her touch beneath my fingers.

'Ceinwen Maelgwyn? What?'

'Nothing, my lord. That's our Ladyrock. She guards our valley.'

I am embarrassed and flustered. My eyelids drop.

'Oh, I see. You were meeting a lover.'

I look up at him, startled. Madoc's smiling and he's cocking his eyebrows but he looks huffy.

'No,' I say.

'Who is he? A lad from your village?'

'There isn't a lover, my lord,' I reply.

'He had to dive into the bushes then, when he heard our horses? He won't thank me for that.'

I'm not sure if Madoc is still joking. I'm not smiling any more. I don't want him to think I have a lover: an admirer, yes, lover no.

'I've interrupted your stolen meeting. I'm sorry.'

On he goes, eyes watching me, chuckling, and it's not nice.

'You'll have to point him out to me this evening, so I can make amends.'

I can't bear having him talk to me like this, as if I'm his serf. After the way he spoke to me first, no I can't stand it. I whisk my head up and say without thinking:

'And if I did have a lover, what would you do to make amends? Would you give him a button off your cloak? A ride on your horse?'

My voice is scornful and I give him my look, the one I get from Mam, which burns cold. Most people drop their eyes.

Madoc doesn't, though. He looks back at me and suddenly I wish I hadn't said it.

For a second all kinds of things crowd my mind. Madoc striking me. Madoc calling his men to deal with me. Madoc swinging back up on his chesnut horse and galloping away.

But no, he's not angry. There's something else moving in the dark centre of his eyes. After a while he says, deliberately and slightly breathless, 'I'd fight him.'

We've walked on quite a way. We're being quieter now and more polite. The sound of those words hangs in my mind: in my gut, my blood and muscles vibrate in response.

Madoc is asking about the valley and I'm telling him who is who and what is what. A few minutes ago we reached the part of the wood where I left my sticks and I went off the path to collect them. When I came back up the slope, Madoc smiled at me, a deep, intimate smile. Then he told Wenlyn and Longnose, whose name is Bredmor, to take the bundles from me. So now they've strapped them to the backs of their saddles and Wenlyn's horse, already fed up with having Madoc's mare on his rein, is kicking his hooves in annoyance. I walk beside Madoc empty-handed, my burden carried by these young men who came from noble blood-lines and whose horses alone are worth half our village.

So now Madoc knows about Hywel Drwyn being Elydyr's steward and about Elydyr finding favour with the Lord Rhys. He's discovered that our two chief families are those of Teilo Gruffydd and Bran, Mei's father – though I haven't mentioned Mei to him – and he's surprised to hear that our village hasn't been raided in four years. That was when the raiders of Abercwm got away with all our swine. He listens carefully when I tell him how our men went out after them and four were killed, including my Da.

'And what happened then? Galanas?'

'Yes. They paid us in sheep and horses. They were good horses and we breed from them. You'll see when we get to the village.'

'It's a good system, the galanas. More's the pity they're doing away with it. The English law just makes more trouble than it solves.'

'We don't know much about the English law,' I said. 'Elydyr comes here now and then with a justiciar from Aber and he tells us that we can't use the galanas any more and we must send all our quarrels to him. We say yes and then we just go on as usual.'

'We still have the galanas too,' says Madoc proudly. 'We won't take the English law, never.' He walks a few steps with his head lifted and his mouth set. Then he shrugs. 'It doesn't work any more with us, though.'

'Why not?'

'One kindred raids another, and then they pay galanas for the dead. But then they raid them again. Or the second kindred takes the galanas in recompense, then takes revenge on the first kindred anyway. Or they get together and attack a third kindred. So galanas gets paid but it doesn't end the blood feuds.'

He sounds very worldly but he's scowling.

'I'm sick of it,' he mutters.

He might be talking about a family quarrel. My stomach tugs and twists as I think about his princely family up there in the stark hills, raising armed cantrefi to ride down on one another, settling their arguments in blood.

I want to touch him. I want to lay my hands on his arms and feel the warmth of his skin through the linen cloak. There's strange, how I feel — I want to protect him but I want to see him in danger, too.

'Are you on galanas business now?' I ask. I know he can't be — he's much too far from home.

'No. I'm going to Caer Llion to see two lords of Ireland about a ship.'

He's said this defiantly, as if he's daring me to comment.

'A ship for you?'

'For me and my men. Gwynedd must be strong on the seas as well as on the land. My father, Owain, agrees. I've made two voyages already, with our cousin Bledyr. Have you heard of him?'

'No, my lord.' Suddenly it seems a good idea to call him my lord again.

'He's a great seaman. As great as any Norseman or Irish seafarer. I've sailed to the Southern Isles of the Norsemen with him and I was with him when he raided them on the Isle of Flocks last year. We taught Vorten's men a lesson! Now I'm going to build my own ship and take it to the northern and western lands. Where the English and their Norman masters don't dare go, but where we've always gone.'

'And the Irish lords will go with you?'

'Perhaps. But it's not likely. It's their goodwill I'm after. I need to know they won't attack my ship.'

'Are they your enemies?'

'No. No Ceinwen Maelgwyn, the Irish love me. I was brought up in Ireland, and Rhiryd of Clochran is my foster brother. I first went on a ship with him. My warband is his and his is mine.'

He grew up in Ireland, across the sea. Great men send their sons to fosterage, to link the families and help them build their own warbands. And this one went to Ireland: I try to see it in his face, this country that's as wild as Gwynedd and more.

'It's that dangerous on the seas? Your foster brother would attack you?'

'He'd have to, if he thought I was challenging him.' Madoc looks sideways at me. His cheeks have a faint flush of excitement on them and as I think about his danger, out there in the huge borderless seas, I can feel my heart beating in my throat. I have a peculiar feeling that I want to laugh.

'Well, God be with you,' I say.

I must be smiling, because he is.

'You'd like to see me come back, would you, Ceinwen Maelgwyn?'

He's said the last words lightly but his hand is moving towards me. His bare forearm and wrist is stretching across the small distance between us; I seem to have swallowed my tongue.

His hand brushes just lightly against my arm and then it's too late: we're round the last corner of trees and the valley opens up before us, with the track forking down to the village and as we hesitate, faces – in the crop fields, around the houses, from the pasture – are turning up to look at us.

There's a great fuss being made now. One of Teilo's boys is about to ride off to fetch Hywel Drwyn, who is on his way back from Aber; meanwhile Teilo and Bran Meilyr's Da, are shoving each other aside to play host. Duw, you should have seem them rushing up the track. They stared at me as if they'd never seen me before, as if I was standing on my head or doing something incredible.

Madoc got back on his horse when he saw them coming and moved it slightly ahead of his men and me. Our people came within a few yards, just above the line of houses, and then they stopped. They stood back and bowed, looking wary. I couldn't understand what was going on but Madoc gave a quick glance down at me as if we were sharing a joke and turned to speak to them.

'Good day, kindred of Cynfael,' he said. He made his voice deeper and gruffer than it had been when we'd talked. 'I am Madoc ap Owain ap Gruffydd, son of the Prince of Gwynedd. We ask hospitality.'

Teilo and Bran both started saying how welcome he was and explaining that Elydyr had no house here and his man at arms was away but would be back soon. Still, their eyes kept sliding from Madoc and his men, to me, standing beside Madoc's chestnut mare.

Suddenly I saw Mam in the cluster of people behind Teilo and Bran. She was staring at me, her face completely blank.

Teilo and Bran had finished inviting the strangers in and there was an odd pause. Madoc turned to me.

'Ceinwen Maelgwyn brought us here,' he said as if he'd only just remembered it. 'She's a good pathfinder.'

Our villagers all laughed a bit too hard and I saw relief and colour flow into Mam's face. And then I realised: they thought I'd been raped by Madoc and his men!

The next thing I knew, Madoc had walked his mare on and the others had followed and I'd somehow moved away from them into the crowd.

And now we're all walking down the slope, and Teilo's boy is fetching his horse, and Mam's fought her way through the people to reach me. She catches my arm and grips it so tightly I wince.

'What were you doing up by there?' she says. 'What were you doing up on the track? Did they touch you?'

'Ow! No Mam, they didn't touch me.'

Yes Mam, *he* did. But only just, only very very lightly. And I'm not telling you about it.

Mam's eyes are raking up and down me; she can see my skirts

are untorn. Still holding me too tight, she starts to walk me down the hill with the rest of the people. The heads around us are turning this way and that, not sure if they want to concentrate on the strangers or listen in on me.

'You were up on the track, weren't you?' Mam says, low.

'Yes, but only for a minute. I went to ask the Ladyrock for the fine weather to hold.'

Mam's not fooled for a second. Her fingers dig so deep into my arm that I can feel the jagged edges of her nails.

'He was off his horse when you came out of the trees. He was on the track with you, I saw.'

'He was tired of riding Mam. He wanted to hear about the village.'

'You haven't got any sticks. You haven't got any wood. You've been up by there nearly two hours and you haven't got any wood. Don't you damn well lie to me, my girl. What have you done?'

The crowd jostles me and I poke my elbow hard into Mam trying to hurt her. Where's Madoc? The bitch is clutching me next to her and he's got so far ahead I can't even see him.

'I have got sticks,' I say to her, furious. 'I collected six bundles. Madoc got his men to tie them on their horses.'

Her free hand flashes up and slaps me hard and quick on the cheek.

'Don't tell me stories.'

Mam's eyes are bright and hard. Ever since Da died it's been like this with her, watching me. My cheek stings and I bite my teeth together.

'Look,' I say, through their hard, closed edges. 'It's the truth Mam. Look.'

She gazes across the heads of the people to the horses, whose haunches are rolling gently from side to side as they walk down the track. There, fastened awkwardly behind the saddles of Pretty and Longnose, are the bundles of wood.

There's foolish she looks now. I hardly feel the last squeeze as she drops her hand and turns jerkily away.

Meilyr has been hovering round me all evening. Duw, if only he'd go away. I know that whenever Madoc looks over to me, he sees Mei here, easing his weight from leg to leg, flexing his fine big shoulders. Mei isn't speaking to me very much – he can't, because I'm keeping with Nest – but he's making it clear to everyone that I belong to him.

The whole village is crammed into Hywel Drwyn's courtyard. Now Madoc and his men have finished their dinner, we have all come to join in the after-feast. There's been a lot of wine drunk, and a lot of songs sung. Everyone seems to be excited in the same way: the night looks bigger than usual, lit by the two generous fires in the courtyard, and there's an atmosphere of adventure. We are usually in bed an hour from now, but I don't think we will be tonight.

I have barely spoken to Madoc since we came into the village. First he and his men saw their horses rubbed down and fed, and then they took off their weapons and left them at Hywel's door, and vanished into his house. Hwyel's wife got into a terrible stew, and Teilo Gruffydd and Bran were busy bossing her about. Her daughters came rushing out of the house to beg extra food and wine for the guests and then every household in the village was trying to give enough to get it a place at the feast, and hold back enough for its own dinner.

Then word went round for the girls to go and play to the guests. So we went: me, Buddug, Nest, Mariad, Cigfa and Branwen. Madoc and his men were waiting by the pasture, where their horses had been tethered. They were looking at the Cynfael horses and as we arrived, I heard Madoc say to Wenlyn: 'They got these horses as galanas for six dead.' He said it casually and I knew he was saying it for no reason except that I'd told it to him.

We didn't get a chance to talk then. Bran was with us, settling us all and telling us to play our best and fussing. Madoc's eyes went to me, then round the other girls, then back to me.

'Who are your friends, Ceinwen Maelgwyn?' He said, but before I could speak Bran was in there, gabbling names. When he came to Branwen he put both hands on her shoulders and pushed the poor girl forward, nearly making her lose her balance. 'My eldest daughter Branwen,' he said. 'She'll play the harp for you, my lords. A fine harp player, she is, the best in the village, besides being so pretty and such a good girl. A very good girl.'

And what did that make me, I wondered? Madoc smiled at

blushing Branwen and my stomach tightened but the next moment his eyes were back on me.

But that was all we had this afternoon – looks. We played our instruments – Branwen and Cigfa on their harps, me and Nest on our smaller crwths and Maried and my Buddug on their little pipes. We played nicely, though I wished it was me with the harp, making those notes run up and down like shivers on the skin.

And we talked and laughed and flirted with the guests. But I didn't really flirt with Madoc and he didn't favour me. Our eyes kept meeting and fixing on each other, and whenever he spoke, however low in the general chatter, I heard him. And when I spoke, his head would lift and I knew he heard me too. At first it was enjoyable, but somehow it changed and for a long time now it's been like an ache which stretches my chest and throat taut.

In the early evening, when the guests ate dinner in Hywel Drwyn's, I was with Mam and Buddug and little Dafy in our house. I kept dropping the dough that I was trying to make into bread. I kept spilling the water from its cup. The fire was burning hot with the good sticks I collected, and which Teilo's boy Bryn had untied from the visitors' horses and brought over to our house. I watched them burn and crackle, making the flames bright.

And now we're here, with everyone else, and thank God the evening has turned into a feast. The firelight is flickering on the faces of our kindred, and over by the alder the cyfarwyddion are telling some long story. There's singing in the big group, where the Gwynedd servants are sitting with the next kindred down from Bran and Teilo – as servants in the royal court, they are important people here. Prince Madoc himself is sitting with his men and Hywel, Bran and Teilo, on low benches a few yards back from the fire. They stopped eating long ago, now they're drinking and toasting and swapping stories of north and south. Bran's got his own children close to the royal visitors: Branwen is up there, playing her harp to long-nosed Bredmor, who's heavily taken.

There's excited I am. Madoc's eyes are on me again and something in the restless turn of his head tells me that this is it – he won't be kept apart from me any longer. At last, at last it's going to happen. He smiles at me, the same deep smile he gave me when I brought the firewood up on to the track. And then he raises his head, very prince-like, and calls to me.

'Ceinwen Maelgwyn.' It's like an announcement or a command. The people on our side of the fire stop their talking and the next minute the singing from behind me has trailed off. All around me people are turning their heads; I sit still on the ground, listening to Madoc. 'Ceinwen, I want you next to me.'

It's hard to get to my feet without scrambling, but I manage. Mei's standing near but I don't look at him; it wouldn't be kind. People move out of the way as I walk through them to Madoc. He sits, looking up at me, then he whispers to Wenlyn, and Wenlyn and red-haired Owain get up. Then Hwyel Drwyn and Teilo and Bran get up as well and then Madoc himself is on his feet amidst the other men. He holds out his hands, pulls me towards him and gives me the traditional greeting kiss on the mouth.

He might be in his castle, welcoming me. I might be not a village girl but some daughter of a neighbouring prince, come to meet him as an equal. Madoc's men are taking no notice; they are talking to our men, arranging a game of skill sticks. But the kindred are fascinated. While he's clearing a space for the game, Teilo Gruffydd is staring at me; and there's Hwyel's wife's face, and Olwen Manawg's, and – curious round the side of her harp – pretty Branwen's.

Madoc has let go of my hands, but I can feel his touch on them still. And now his hand's on my shoulder, turning me toward the men who are squatting on the ground, making a circle. There's Cadell, Madoc's fat-cheeked man, sitting on his haunches examining two forked sticks.

'Cadell's been challenged to a game,' Madoc says. 'What's he got to do?'

'It's skill sticks. The other man puts his sticks leaning together on the ground and Cadell uses his two sticks to flick them up in the air. He musn't touch them with his hands and he wants to make them jump around higher and higher till they go out of the circle of people. If the other man catches his sticks in the air he can flick Cadell's, and Cadell has to catch his again and take over.'

It's hard to concentrate on what I'm saying. My voice is talking on its own.

'Well, Cadell's got a good wrist. You'll cheer for us, won't you?' he says.

'Yes, of course, my lord. You'll lose, mind,' I add.

Madoc pushes me.

'You say. You haven't even seen what Cadell can do.'

'Yes, but he's playing Gwion and Gwion's our champion.'

He's Mei's younger brother too, and Mei's appeared at the other side of the circle, behind him. He's bending forward, his hands on his knees, scowling at Cadell.

Madoc takes my hand again and draws me back to him. His fingers are twined through mine and it's very hot where our palms touch. He's pulled me so close now that we're pressed side to side and I can feel his hip-bone and the ridges of his belt digging in to me and in trying to keep my balance I've stepped one foot on top of his. I can feel the outline of his tendons under my sole.

'Look,' says Madoc eagerly. 'Cadell's learning.'

Cadell is a fast learner. He's got the knack of tapping and levering one stick with the other to make it jump. He got the stick to turn on all of its branches that time. He's played some form of skill sticks before.

'See? Now are you so sure?'

'Well, I said I'd cheer for you anyway.'

'Politics. Perhaps I should take you to Caer Llion.'

'You should.'

Everyone's crowding round to see the skill sticks now. Wenlyn and the red-haired Owain are giving Cadell advice and shouting their clan cries. Madoc and I are squatting behind them: it's very comfortable having them as steadying blocks, to lean our hands and elbows on their shoulders. Madoc can do what he wants, of course, but they don't seem to mind me doing it too.

Cadell starts off well, twirling his sticks down on Gwion's and twice flicking them high in the air. But each time Gwion's back, quick as anything, to save it and then the game turns and Gwion's sticks are flashing all over Cadell's. The lads and some of the girls are all supporting Gwion, cheering and clapping and yelling. The guests have got all our important people – Hywel Drwyn and Teilo and his whole family and a good lot of the girls. They'd have Bran too, if he could desert his son and still keep face. I heard him whisper to Branwen that he had to be for Gwion, but she should make sure she cheered loud for the royal guests.

Gwion's won the first game. But Cadell plays the second fast and daringly and wins. We're laughing and cheering: Madoc keeps grabbing my hand and beating out tunes on Owain's back. When Cadell wins the second game, Madoc turns and kisses me hard on the mouth again. My lips burn and I can feel the roughness of his unshaved skin. When I look back into the crowd, I can see Mei's face, orange and black in the firelight, staring at us.

I drop my eyes. I don't want to hurt Mei; I don't want to embarrass him. But I'm that happy, and I feel that strong. You can't stop me, Mei; you can't hold me. And nor can you, Mam. For an instant I see her face among the others, but she's not looking at me, she's looking at Madoc.

And Madoc — he's looking at Meilyr. He must have followed the movement of my head just now. His face is lifted and still and he's smiling, but his eyes — they're violet in this light — are angry. He reaches out his left hand and closes it hard on my arm, but he hasn't looked away from Meilyr.

'Who's going to win, Ceinwen?' he says. His voice is so loud that people hear it through the noise and start to turn.

'Cadell, my lord.' I say it as proud and carrying as I can. Cadell hears; he looks over his shoulder and mimes me a bow and a kiss.

Madoc glances from Meilyr to Cadell, then back to Mei. Then finally, almost reluctantly, his eyes come to me.

'Well said.' His voice is easy and full of strength, but he's flushed. I'm not sure if he really sees me. He loosens his fingers from my arm and doesn't apologise for the marks they've left. 'Come on then Cadell, what are you waiting for, man?'

Cadell must win. He must. Madoc is leaning forward, his shoulder wedged against mine. I can hear his excited breathing. The play's even. At first it looked as though Gwion had the better of it, but now Cadell is making the sticks hop. But he can't get them out of the circle, and he's not making them snap. Instead, suddenly, Gwion's taken an inch off one of Cadell's sticks — off one of the forks, which is the worst bit to lose.

Cadell's having trouble getting his rhythm back now he's got a lame stick. Madoc has shifted away from me and is digging his elbows into Owain's back, peering over his shoulder. Gwion's got all the ground to himself and he's building up a momentum with his two whole sticks, catching and flicking Cadell's sticks higher and higher. Don't let them leave the circle. Don't. Mei's straightened up at the far end, and his arms are crossed. I can see his mouth moving non-stop as he calls out encouragement and advice to Gwion.

Everyone's roaring now. Cadell's found his balance and he's catching his sticks more nimbly, snatching them out of the air quicker and getting better hits in at Gwion's.

I can't see Madoc's face. He's turned away and all I can see is his tumble of dark brown curly hair and his hand, resting completely still on Owain's shoulder. He's not moving; he's not moving at all.

The game is coming to a furious climax. Gwion and Cadell are playing so fast now it's hard to see whose sticks are which. There seem to be six or eight sticks jumping, not four, and fragments of bark are spinning away into people's faces.

There's a crack which cuts through the noise and a pair of sticks flies out of the circle, skimming people's heads. There's an uproar of cheering and groaning and laughter, and Hywel is hopping round Cadell, lifting a cup of wine to his mouth and crying congratulations.

Madoc and I look at each other. I can just see the violet irises of his eyes round the black centres.

'You said we'd win.'

'Yes my lord.'

'Come to bed.'

'Yes.'

I'm trembling. I'll remember this moment for ever. The house is cold after the courtyard, and dark. The embers of the fire give just enough light for me to see – but then, I've got good eyesight.

Madoc has my hand in his, and his hand is shaking too. We walked through the kindred without speaking; now we're here, alone.

Madoc's left hand is unsteady as he lifts it to my face. I know what to do – of course I know. But why are we both trembling so much?

Madoc's hand is on my cheek, burning, and now his mouth presses into mine and I can feel the warm wet of his tongue and his hard teeth. His hands are in my hair, struggling with my head-dress and I'm clinging to his body. Down there, our groins are pushing together and through his tunic his prick is hard. It presses against me, through my skirts, and one of his legs comes between mine and parts them.

He has got my head-dress off now and with one hand he's shaking out my hair. His other hand is unfastening my dress and stroking my breasts. His touch on them sends a long thin heat through me. Madoc breaks off kissing me and bends his head to my breasts, placing his mouth on them and stroking them with his tongue.

I am clinging to him, clutching him. If I don't, I'll fall over. I'm longing for the feel of his skin under his tunic and my hands grapple with the linen, trying to find a way in. I'm moaning, soft little whimpering moans.

Madoc cups my breast in his hand and lifts his head.

'Touch me,' he says.

I drop my hands to the folds of his tunic and pull them up. I feel the heat of his flesh before I touch it. His prick is swollen and hard and as my fingers close round it, he groans. There's a trace of wetness beneath my palm. It's secret down here and so strong. The heat and hardness fills my palms and down where it joins his body I feel his muscly abdomen and wiry curly hair.

My knees are bending and suddenly Madoc's hands are under my skirts and pressed against my buttocks, supporting me. His fingers slip inside my cunt.

'Let's go to the bed,' he says. His voice is so husky I can hardly hear him. 'I've got to lie down on you. On you. In you.'

I don't know how we find Hywel's bed. I've forgotten where it is – or rather, I don't know where we are in the room. Clasped together, we stumble across the floor. Then Madoc pulls my robe off my shoulders and strokes my free breasts, and then the robe is stuck, pinning my arms to my sides. He tugs and gives a frustrated gasp.

'It's the other way,' I say. 'It has to come off the other way.'

I'm not sure if we're laughing or not as I lift my arms and he pulls the robe back up over my breasts and shoulders and head, baring my legs and my groin and stomach. For an instant, with my head muffled in the dark rough cloth, I hear him draw breath, and then I feel his hands on my naked skin, slowly stroking up from my thighs to my breasts, then back down again.

Then he lifts off the robe and I can see him gazing at me, his lips parted. He kisses my breasts and my neck and pushes me gently down on Hywel's bed. My thighs have fallen apart and my arms are reaching for him as he fumbles with his cloak, tears off his tunic and drops kneeling on to the bed.

He crawls on to me and at the weight of him and the touch of his warm salty skin, every inch of me burns.

'Dear God, I want you,' he mumbles. 'Ceinwen, Ceinwen.' He has spread my legs further with his hand and now he's pushing his prick against my cunt and I arch my back to help him. All I want is him inside me. All I want is the feel of him filling me up.

It hurts but I love it. It's a funny kind of pain, a hurt that's a vicious, delicious pleasure. Now his arms are around me and his fingers are twined in my hair and we're kissing and rubbing our faces together and his prick is drawing out and thrusting, drawing and thrusting, and there's no pain at all, only Madoc, my lord, fucking me.

It has been a long, sweet night. I don't know when the others came to bed. They stayed out for hours, but we weren't sleeping when they came. Hywel put more dried turf on the fire at the foot of the bed and blew its embers back to a small flame; the muddy flare lit the house dark red and green and in the shadows I saw Madoc's men yawning together. Madoc rolled over me, putting me next to the wall, and wrapped the brychan around us like a cocoon. We stayed secret in there all night, fucking and loving. Some of the time our bed was shared by Madoc's men; at other times we heard them wake and go and sit next to the fire, rubbing their cold limbs and telling each other sleepy stories. I don't know where Hywel and his family slept – on the ground, I suppose.

I woke like a princess this morning. I wasn't embarrassed or coy. We were still naked under the brychan so Madoc sent everyone out while I dressed. Cadell pretended to plead for just a little peep.

'There's cruel you are, Ceinwen Maelgwyn. You put those roses in our prince's cheeks but you don't give us so much as a look to help us keep up with him today. It'll be your fault if he rides away from us all and falls into a bog, with no one to pull him out.'

'Get out, arse-face,' said Madoc.

Cadell's face does look like a soft, baby's dimpled arse. I like him.

Madoc held out my clothes to me and watched me dress. His face was still and serene, like a man dreaming on a warm day.

I smiled at him.

'Will you help me with my head-dress, my lord?'

He got up, still naked, and held my head-dress while I smoothed back my hair, then he fitted it, a bit clumsily, over my head.

'Thank you, my lord,' I said. He was looking at me very seriously.

'Angel wings,' he said, tracing the stiff folds with his fingers. 'You're very beautiful, my lady.'

And he leaned forward and kissed me softly on the mouth before he turned and got dressed himself.

They're on the other side of the valley, trying out the Cynfael horses now. I'm sitting here with Nest and Buddug and Mam, straining cheese. I'm not doing the oats harvest today and Mam hasn't tried to make me. Even Mam can see that wouldn't be right.

Nest and Buddug have already asked me what happened and what it was like. I shook my head and didn't answer but then I began giggling and giggling and couldn't stop. Mam is looking at me with funny blank eyes, and I don't know what she's thinking. Whenever she moves far enough away, Nest and Buddug start asking me questions again.

I don't feel so lovely any more. Bit by bit, this coldness has crept into me. I'm warm in so many parts, but right at the centre there's this little cold dread and it's spreading.

I don't know what to think. I've given my virginity away and I could be fined and disgraced. But surely, no one's going to suggest that, when I gave it to such a great man. It would be an insult to Madoc and his father, the Prince of Gwynedd. But what will happen to me now? Madoc's still here but the morning's wearing on and I know they should be on their way. As I left Hywel Drwyn's I saw Owain, the older, red-headed lord, speak to Madoc. He nodded up at the sun and Madoc shrugged his shoulders irritably, and twitched his cloak round him.

When I saw that, I was pleased and felt strong, but now the feeling's trickling away. Yet, they're still here.

Madoc and his men have been trying the horses for over an hour now. Madoc has remounted the second one he tried, Elfan the bay, and this time instead of exercising him on the far side of the valley, he's turning his head in our direction, splashing through the ford and now he's riding him at a gallop all the way round the western head of the valley towards us.

He sits differently from the way we ride down here, leaning further over the horse's neck. Is that the way the men of Gwynedd ride in battle – urging their horses up and down the mountainsides? The horse thunders up the hillside and is almost on us.

Madoc pulls Elfan up, just a few feet away, and looks down at us.

'Angharad Fach,' he says to Mam. He must have asked someone her name. Two faint red spots appear on Mam's cheeks and she inclines her head, her neck very stiff. 'Are your daughter's eyes as fine for judging horses as they are for looking into?'

'It's two daughter's I have, my lord,' says Mam. 'Ceinwen and Buddug.'

Madoc smiles at Buddug.

'Congratulations, Angharad Fach,' he says. His eyes are already sliding to me, and they glow with the speed he's been riding and the wind in his face.

The memory of his touch last night makes me catch my breath.

'Can you pick a good horse, Ceinwen?' he asks. He's using his prince's voice.

'Yes, my lord. I should hope so, after Da died to get them for us.'

'I should hope so too. I want you to watch me and the others and see which horses go the best with us. We want to take some to Caer Llion with us, as gifts. Your kindred will be well rewarded.'

Cynfael will be honoured, my lord,' I say, gazing up at him. There is a laugh hidden in his face and it makes my heart beat fast.

'Good. Watch carefully now, won't you? I'll need your opinion.'

He canters off and I look down at my work, not wanting the other girls to see my face. What did he mean by that? Why should he want my opinion? I've been watching them across the meadows and I've seen that between rides, Madoc and Owain keep talking. Owain talks with his head bent down, earnestly, and occasionally he seems to be gesturing at the village, at the horses, in my direction. Madoc sometimes slaps the older man's shoulder's, sometimes tosses his head.

Madoc has tried all the horses now, more than once. He likes Elfan best, I can see that by he way he rides him, urging him to jump the streams and the little banks, turning him easily through the rocks. Last night he took and turned and gripped me like that.

Across the valley now, they're talking to Teilo and Bran and deciding. And I'm watching – watching closely. They're not taking one each – good, says my sweet sister Buddug, otherwise the kindred would have hardly any left. Mam often asks how my sister can be so gentle and me so difficult. We all watch as Bredmor Longnose leads three horses to one side: they've got Elfan, Cynog the grey and the bad-tempered black mare, Penca.

'Well,' says Nest, her high voice gusty and bewildered. 'I don't see how your opinion's going to come in useful now, Ceinwen. They've made their minds up already.'

I don't answer her. I'm watching Madoc as he mounts Elfan again and starts off once more towards the river, crossing it at the ford. Now he's riding up towards us again, not galloping this time, but cantering steadily. I turn to watch him draw near along the hillside and out of the corner of my eye I can see Mam, also watching. Is she thinking what I'm thinking? Is she hoping it will happen or that it won't? Everything is in the balance now. Across in the meadow I can see Owain turned away, examining the horses.

Elfan walks up to us and Madoc nods courteously to Mam. But he speaks directly to me. He isn't able to keep a hoarse note of triumph out of his voice.

'Well, Ceinwen Maelgwyn? Do you approve of my choice?'

'He's the best for you, my lord, as you know.'

'Yes, I know. But what about for you?'

Buddug gasps. I stay very still. I hardly dare breathe.

'Siani's the best for me.'

'Siani? The little dark brown mare who kicks?'

'Yes, my lord.'

Madoc's strange eyes are the colour of lake-water, and they're shining. It's an odd shine — not joy but defiance, almost anger. It's the way he looked at Meilyr last night.

He holds out his hand. I rise and take it, standing close against his leg and Elfan's warm side. Madoc's dark blue cloak falls over my shoulder.

'Angharad Fach,' Madoc says to Mam. He's speaking a bit too loud. There's something about Mam's tight-lipped stare that's making him shout. 'I ask you to let me take your daughter to Caer Llion. She'll be honourably treated.'

It is, it's happening. Prince Madoc ap Owain ap Gruffydd is taking me with him.

'What?' Gwyn rubbed the water drops from his hair and smoothed the last flecks of shaving soap from his face. 'What is it?'

'Hmm?'

'You're staring at me. Again.'

'Sorry.'

There was something about Gwyn that was different this morning. Jane turned to the mirror and went on brushing her hair. In the glass she could watch Gwyn, his bathrobe flapping open, as he sorted thoughtfully through his shirt drawer. In the mirror frame, diminished by the added distance of the reflection, he looked like a figure in an old painting. The bathrobe could be a cloak, his dark curls wet with rain, his face bent down towards a compass . . .

'Jane, for Christ's sake!'

Gwyn's abrupt movement shattered the picture. In a flurry of navy blue, the bathrobe fell away from his shoulders and he was buttoning himself into a plain white shirt, his eyes intercepting her gaze.

A compass? Where had that come from?

'Jesus, this meeting with Jewell is really getting to you, isn't it?'

Jane put down the hairbrush.

'Yes, I suppose so. Yes, I guess that's what it is.'

'Why don't you let me speak to him first? Ask for your hand in marriage. Assure him I've got good prospects.'

'It's not you marrying me that he'll object to – it's me marrying you.'

'Bollocks. Anyhow, who cares? Let me tell him, for God's sake. It's not worth getting so worked up about.'

'No, I've fixed to see him now, he's expecting me. Anyway, you said you wanted to get straight down to work today.'

'Yes, well, that's true. I didn't write a word yesterday.'

Jane leaned against the bedroom door and watched Gwyn pull on his jeans. He always got dressed quickly and stolidly, as if he were strapping himself into the day's harness. She looked at his hands, square and pale brown, with a shadow of dark hair on their fingers, as they fastened his fly.

Perhaps this peculiar sharpened sense was the aftermath of last night's sex. It had been incredibly fierce and explosive. Her appetite was now sated but she could still remember its force.

She could remember the hallucination which had visited her in Bloomingdale's.

And there was something else which she could almost, but not quite, remember: something which hovered irritatingly just behind her conscious mind. Was it something someone had said? Was it a dream, now obscured by the day?

Yes, she thought, it must have been. She felt that if she could only bring it to mind, she would be in possession of something rich, exciting and lovely. But it continued to elude her.

'I hate having dreams I can't remember,' she said.

'Perhaps it wasn't a dream.'

Jane frowned and looked slowly up at Gwyn.

'What do you mean?'

'Well, something interesting happened to me last night. About one o'clock in the morning, in that bed.'

'Ah, that.'

'Yes, that.' Gwyn's voice was muffled by his jumper; after a few seconds his face emerged from the woolly folds, slightly flushed. 'Very vivid, that dream was. Very convincing.'

Jane smiled, amused at the speculative gleam in his eyes. 'You have a problem with that?'

Gwyn shook his head.

'Oh no, no. On the contrary, my lovely.' But he continued to wear a curious expression. Jane shrugged mentally.

'Gwyn, have you ever had a hallucination?'

'Only acid-induced ones, when I was a wildish young thing. They were usually horrible. Why?'

'I had one yesterday, in Bloomingdale's.'

'Go on. I'm listening.'

'I tried on a necklace – an Indian Nation-type design, varnished acorns and beads – and when I looked in the glass there was another person in there.'

'Yes? Who?'

'A woman. I don't know who she was.'

'Hmm. What did she look like?'

'Me. She looked exactly like me. But she wasn't. She was like something out of a folk tale, or someone in a poem. You know, skin like snow and hair like ebony and lips like blood.'

'Ugh, bloody bad poem.'

Jane looked at Gwyn in surprise. He was chuckling as he tied his shoelaces. He glanced up at her.

'Oops, sorry, have I said something wrong?'

Jane was silent.

'Oh hell, I can see I have.' Gwyn bent over his other shoe and Jane could see that he was grinning. It both puzzled and irritated her.

'What's funny?' she asked.

'Well, sweetheart, you must admit – you look in the mirror in Bloomie's and see Cruella de Ville . . . "Cruella de Ville, Cruella de Ville!" ' He began singing the Walt Disney song, ' " – if she doesn't scare you, nobody will!" '

Remembering what she had seen in the mirror, Jane was revisited by a pang of loss.

'Why are your poems serious and my hallucinations funny?' she said mildly.

Gwyn's humming trailed off.

'Fair enough,' he said. He straightened up. 'So, what was it like, seeing this alter ego? How long did it last?'

'It lasted several seconds. Long enough for it not to be a trick of the light. Long enough for her to look back at me.'

Gwyn was standing in front of Jane now, watching her closely.

'Was it frightening?'

'No,' Jane said slowly. 'Not at the time. It was exciting. It was very exciting.'

Gwyn raised one eyebrow.

'Aha. I think I begin to see a connection.'

'What?' As his arms came round her, Jane laughed. 'Oh, I see what you mean. Well, maybe she had something to do with that.'

'Good for her,' murmured Gwyn, nuzzling her ear. 'She can come again, even if she does make you a bit violent.'

'Violent?'

'You bit my lip last night, made it bleed. Look. Just here.'

There, on Gwyn's lower lip was a small cut, sealed with a tiny scab of dried blood.

'Jesus, I'm sorry. Did I do that?'

Jane kissed the wound very softly.

'Baby, I'm really sorry. Look, I'd better go and announce our marriage. Jewell's always tied up after nine thirty.'

'Good luck with the old bugger.'

'Good luck with the writing.'

Jane walked quickly down the stairs, not waiting for the elevator. Her heart was beating fast and she couldn't have said why.

Part Two

9

Wales: this was it. Jane leaned out of the upstairs window and breathed in the moisture-laden air. It smelt green; the grass in Roy and Eirlys's backyard was deep green; the meadow which ran from their gate to the line of trees was a brighter green; the valley side which rose up beyond the trees was another green still, a dark mossy green.

Jane had never been anywhere like this. She had always associated this kind of lushness with heat and humidity, a Mississippi delta kind of climate, but the air here was cool and fresh.

She felt free and exhilarated, which was strange because it was all so unexpectedly small. Her view was stopped short by the valley side rising ahead; when she leaned to the left she could see a hill shutting in the perspective over there, and even to the right, where the line of trees led away, marking the river bed, the land rose after about a mile.

And there were many houses clustered in this little valley. Roy and Eirlys's house was one of a terrace; there were one, two, three – five other houses joined on to it. To the left there were more houses on either side of the bridge, and through the bare winter trees Jane could see that on the other side of the river, three separate lines of houses were cut into different levels of the hillside. Yet that was the empty side of the valley. The populated side was hidden from Jane at the moment but they had driven down through it last night: it had seemed to Jane that they zigzagged down row after row of identical red-brick houses, joined in pairs.

When Gwyn was out of the bathroom and they'd had some coffee, maybe they could go out and explore. She could hear him singing in the small bathroom next door – his tenor voice relishing a somewhat dirgy tune. It was the first time he'd sung for weeks.

He was home. He was happy. Last night he'd led her out into the small backyard, and stood with her in the darkness under the black, faintly star-strewn sky. He'd pointed out to her the river, the shadowy bridge, some indeterminate point on the hillside where he used to go as a child, and then he'd gathered her to him and kissed her very gently. Roy and Eirlys, peeking through the kitchen window, had been amused.

It had been good to come here. They both needed to get away from Brockham and the upper west side and campus politics. Perhaps now they were here, Gwyn's writing would come back.

Three weeks was a long time for him to be blocked, he'd told her, almost yelling at her in frustration one night last week. Then he'd apologised and slumped down in a chair, digging his fingers into his hair. He'd been blocked before, he'd said, yes, true, he'd been blocked for several weeks at a time. But not like this. It hadn't felt like this. As though it was all there, just beyond him, ready for plucking down, but he couldn't get his hand through the wall to it.

But maybe now that they were away, the problem would solve itself. Already, Gwyn was so much more relaxed and happy; it reminded Jane of the way he'd been when they met, back at the beginning of semester.

Gwyn appeared in the doorway, his hair wet and his face newly shaved and boyish. 'Bread of hea-ea-ven,' he was singing, very deep. 'What are you doing, cariad? Getting some Welsh air?'

'Getting my bearings.'

'Mrs Davis is in the first white house by the bridge. Dilys Williams is two houses along from this one. Bill Carter's in the bookie's – '

'Idiot.'

'Fee-eed me till I want no mo – oer,' sang Gwyn expansively. He pulled a grey jumper out of his suitcase and put it on. 'Shit, it's all crumpled. Never mind, I can't be bothered to unpack now. What do you feel like doing today? Shall we have some breakfast and go for a stroll round the village? I can show you the sights. Maybe I can borrow Roy's car.'

'Sure. That'd be great.' Jane watched him strapping on his watch, ducking his head to glance out of the window. 'Feels good to be back, huh?'

Gwyn paused. Jane looked tired, the skin pulled tight beneath her eyes.

'Didn't you sleep, again?'

'Not really. Jet lag I guess. Everyone said it would be bad, coming this way.'

'We've got to do something about you. You haven't had a good night's sleep for weeks.'

'It's just one of those things. They say getting married is one of life's most stressful events.'

Gwyn looked at Jane, silhouetted against the sash window. The room suited her: the thick stone walls and the fireplace, nicely done up by Roy and Eirlys, and the pot of African violets on the deep window-ledge. It brought out an earthiness in her which he'd never noticed before. He saw that she was resting her hand against the corner of the window embrasure, unconsciously exploring it with her fingers.

'Is it coming here?' he said. 'Is it horrible for you?'

Jane laughed at him.

'No, stupid. Why should it be horrible? I was just thinking, while you were in the bathroom, how liberated I feel to be away from Brockham.'

'Perhaps you'll sleep tonight.'

'I know I will.'

'Because it's been too long, you know. Weeks.'

'I know. Let's forget it. Thinking about not sleeping is the worst thing. Can we go downstairs?'

'Kiss me first. We've only got a few days left to be lovers. After that we'll be married and it'll feel different.'

Cupping Jane's face, Gwyn kissed her, then he slid his arms round her and held her close to him, pressing the length of her body against him. She felt pliant and sinuous. His erection stirred. And that wasn't all that stirred: ever since he'd handed Jane down off the bus last night, watching her step on to Welsh soil – well, all right then, tarmac – he'd felt better in his mind. He'd been stupid to get so het up about a little block, but then that was campus life for you: everything got out of proportion. He'd only been back here twelve hours and already the lovely, insinuating feeling that marked a new piece of work was stealing over him.

'Tell you what,' he said to Jane. 'Tonight I'll fuck you to sleep.'

Jane felt unexpectedly at ease with Gwyn's friends. Roy was large and talkative; Eirlys was quieter but by no means in the background. At Cardiff Bus Station Roy had hugged both Gwyn and Jane and punctuated the journey back to Graig with excited male bonding punches to Gwyn's arm. Eirlys had greeted Gwyn affectionately, squeezing him for an instant as they kissed, and then turned on Jane a friendly curiosity.

It was Eirlys who, at one am local time, three hours after their arrival, had insisted that Gwyn and Jane go to bed. Roy would have liked to keep them up all night, asking them questions and feeding them an unstinting flow of local news.

Now when Jane entered the kitchen Roy's large, round-shouldered bulk was bent over the kettle. He smiled broadly at her from under his thinning hair.

'Morning Jane. Is it tea or coffee for you?'

'Good morning Roy. Coffee, please.'

'Is Gwyn up yet? Oh there you are, Gwyn mon. Coffee for you is it, as well? I'm making Eirlys's third cup for her. She's in the living room, hogging the Sundays. You weren't woken up by that little bugger from next door, were you?'

'What little bugger?' asked Jane.

'They've got a four-year-old who has tantrums. Regular as clockwork he has 'em, every weekend. Sometimes it's both Saturdays and Sundays, just when we're having a lie-in.'

'No, I didn't hear a thing,' said Jane. She didn't tell Roy that, after a night of fitful dozing, she'd just fallen asleep when the child's screams had jerked her awake again.

Her eyes grew heavy just thinking about it.

'What's that?' she asked, listening to a faint, soothing melody coming through the wall.

'Oh that's Eirlys, that is, playing records. Hey Gwyn,' Roy went on. 'You know Tommy Yorath? Did I tell you about him last night – I can't remember. Well, do you know where he's working now, mon?'

Jane wandered into the living room. It ran from the front of the house to the back and was painted a pastel blue, with white-painted bookshelves lining the chimney breast and bright floral and bird-patterned cushions scattered on the slate-grey sofa and chairs. Eirlys was sitting on the sofa with a pile of newspapers. Classical music which Jane couldn't identify came out of the discreet black music centre.

'Morning,' said Eirlys. 'Did you sleep well?'

'Hi,' said Jane. 'Ah – I'm a little jet lagged.'

'Poor thing,' said Eirlys. She pronounced it 'poow-er', and said it on two notes, down and up, like a little tune. Jane found Eirlys's voice very restful. 'Why don't you sit down here and have a look at these papers? You'll be drifting away in no time at all. I can't guarantee you sweet dreams, though.'

Jane smiled and took Eirlys's advice, curling up among the pretty cushions in the crook of the sofa arm. She picked up the nearest newspaper and settled down to read the main article. Eirlys was right; her eyes kept slipping over the words and trying to close. She really was so tired.

Sweet dreams: it would be nice to dream again – good, enriching dreams, not the frustrating little snatches, like jammed radio broadcasts, which had been disturbing her sleep for weeks now.

Jane wondered if what she'd said to Gwyn was true: perhaps it really was getting married that was stressing her out. There had been plenty of minor aggravations piling up recently. Her interview with Professor Jewell, when she told him the news, had been difficult, just as she'd expected. He must have known what she'd come to say, but he pretended to be astonished, and then pretended to be delighted, in a way that implied she was really very lucky indeed to land a catch like Gwyn Thomas. Working with him had been tiring ever since; he'd been especially picky about the last issue of the magazine and Jane was sick to death of his probing little comments and quips about her and Gwyn.

Then there were the people she actually liked – friends and colleagues, all of whom had to be told and who all asked so many questions.

And there was the trip over here to organise. Gwyn had done

107

most of that, and he had got bad-tempered too with the difficulty of booking a marriage licence and arranging dates with Roy and Eirlys and Goff, and telling friends so that they could come to the party he wanted to have, all on the telephone.

Booking a flight in what Gwyn called 'the holiday period' had been almost impossible. Who were all these people who took flights to the UK for Christmas, and all their friends who followed for the New Year, taking up all the airplane seats? So they'd had to change their plans and travel on January the second, leaving them less time to spend in Wales before they had to return for the new semester.

Perhaps it was all that, and the strain of Gwyn's writing drying up. Gwyn hadn't handled that well at all: Jane had been shocked by his rage and despair. And for as long as Gwyn hadn't been writing, she hadn't been sleeping – only dozing, to be jerked awake every few hours by intermittent, garbled dreams. It was very disturbing: she didn't know what the dreams were supposed to be, as she could scarcely ever identify anything in them. It felt like having disparate objects hurled at a large white screen: she glimpsed their outline briefly and then lost them in the general chaos.

There was a door opening and closing, somewhere in Gwyn's flat; there were loops that were sometimes necklaces, sometimes garlands, sometimes snakes with their tails in their mouths. And there were dizzying little flashes of light that burst on the inside of her eyelids and told her she'd woken up again.

But nothing coherent. And nothing enjoyable, nothing lovely or strong or seductive, nothing like that since . . .

'Jane. Darling. Sleepy-head. Come on, you've been asleep two hours.'

'Oh, leave her alone mon. Let the poor girl sleep.' That was Roy's voice.

'No, he should wake her, Roy. Otherwise she won't be able to sleep tonight and then she'll be in a pattern. That's the way jet lag works.' That was Eirlys.

'Hey, Missis. Wifelet. Eirlys the experienced traveller says you've got to wake up.'

Jane opened her eyes.

'Mm. OK. Have I really been out for two hours? Sorry.'

'You needed it,' said Eirlys. 'You look better now. You've got some colour.'

'Yes, I feel better.'

She did. She stretched tentatively; yes, she did feel better. She actually felt refreshed. Gwyn was watching her with an indulgent expression.

'You were smiling in your sleep,' he said.

'Sweet, it was,' said Roy.

Jane blinked at the three faces staring down at her. Coming straight out of sleep, it struck her how alike they were. She hadn't noticed it last night, but today she could see that they all shared a native cast of feature. It was difficult to work out exactly where it lay – Roy's nose was really quite different from Gwyn's and his eyes tipped up where Gwyn's tipped down; Eirlys's face was delicate and certainly not broad like the men's. Yet all three faces were composed of straight lines. A wide jaw here, a long nose there, level brows there: each face gave the impression of rectitude.

For a second Jane saw the three of them as foreigners. It was only a flash, but it gave her a powerful, tantalising sense that she was on the outside, looking in.

'I'm going to have a walkabout,' said Gwyn. 'The man in the footsteps of the boy, and all that. D'you fancy coming?'

'Yes,' said Jane quickly. 'I'd like that.'

There was the school, with the lane running alongside the wall, so that the children could go from the quiet streets in the valley bottom to the school entrance without having to make the long circuit along the main road. There was the main road itself, running horizontally along the valley side half-way up, with the older side roads hanging down from it and the newer ones wriggling up to get lost in council-built closes. The older part of the village, below the main road, was red-brick. Houses were joined in pairs: they had raised front gardens, with steps leading to front doors that were seldom used, and funny one-brick-high walls separating them. Above the main road, the newer streets were grey-white and pebble-dashed.

'Where does Goff live?'

'Up there,' said Gwyn, pointing to a street parallel to the one they stood in.

'Shall we go and see him?'

'Oh, not today. To be honest, I don't really feel like it today.'

'But won't he be waiting for you to call?'

'No. He knows I'll get round to seeing him.' Gwyn put his hands in his pockets and shifted uncomfortably. Jane didn't know what to say; all along, he'd been adamant they shouldn't stay with Goff. Yet sometimes he talked about him so affectionately.

'Look.' Gwyn nodded to the southern side of the valley, whose upper slopes were clothed in trees.

'Up through there is a track in the woods that becomes a road and leads over the hill to Pengroed. It's where we used to go when we were kids, to the caves. Then when we were teenagers we used to go to the Pengroed Arms.'

'Isn't there a pub in Graig?'

'Of course, but we couldn't go there. We were local boys, everyone knew how old we were to the day. The Pengroed was in the next valley, so no one cared, and we could get there through the woods with no one seeing us.'

Jane quite wanted to go up to the caves and the illicit Pengroed road, but Gwyn said it was too far. Instead he took her to the main road and showed her its tiny grocery store, its butcher, its hairdresser, its video and flower shop and its petrol station. The petrol station looked like the oldest, most rustic part of the place: two hundred yards down the road from the other shops it was a dirt forecourt with two pumps, backed by a low, humped white cottage with small windows all crammed with merchandise. On the wooden door, stick-on letters said 'The Old Post'.

'It used to be the post office,' Gwyn explained.

It was shut. Jane peered through the windows: she could see a poky interior, with shelves and stands that held food, soaps, shampoos, clothes, books, electrical goods, toys – she stopped counting.

'Mrs Evans still runs it,' said Gwyn, reading the name painted on a wooden strip above the lintel. 'The old cow was always throwing me out for trying to pinch things, even when I wasn't.'

Above the Old Post, up a metalled lane, was the church. And a hundred yards back up the main road was the pub. From the forecourt Jane looked across the road to the broadening valley floor, marked out as a playing field. The white rugby posts poked up towards the overcast sky, and beyond them rose the Pengroed side of the valley, closing in again. She found something very pleasing in the shape of the land here.

On Monday, with Roy and Eirlys gone to work, the little house was quiet. Jane came out of the bathroom towelling her wet hair, and immediately heard that Gwyn was talking to someone. She paused: there was only one voice, Gwyn's and it was downstairs in the hall. He was on the telephone.

His voice was deeper than usual, and louder. Goff was slightly deaf. Jane gave Gwyn a quick half-smile as she reached the bottom of the stairs, and walked past him into the kitchen. She had decided to be very careful when they were in Wales: Gwyn's relationship with Goff was tangled enough, for whatever reason. She didn't want to complicate it further by taking sides.

She was curious, though, she acknowledged as she searched for the horrible instant coffee Roy and Eirlys kept. She was very curious to meet Goff Jenkins.

The houses in Garth Place were like almost all the others Jane had so far seen in Graig: red-brick and clinging to the hillside. She was beginning to realise why Roy and Eirlys were so pleased with their little whitewashed terrace, which looked over the meadow. The Garth Place houses looked across the tarmac road to the backs and roofs of the street below.

Gwyn led her to number twenty-three, last but two in the street. Like all the other houses, it was joined to its neighbour on one side, and had a path leading up on the other. Gwyn ignored the steps into the front garden and took her up the path, between the high red-brick walls of twenty-three and twenty-five.

She glimpsed an elderly head through the kitchen window and then Gwyn was opening the back door.

'Well. Hallo then. Hallo, lad.'

'Goff. How are you?'

'It's good to see you, boy.' There was a second's hesitation, then Goff and Gwyn shook hands, their big hands clasping round each other and holding on. 'Good to see you.'

The thin, patchily stubbled face turned to Jane.

'Jane, is it?'

'I'm pleased to meet you, Mr Jenkins.' She hadn't meant to call him that, but there was something in the wiry old man, in his austere face and creased eyes, that stopped her calling him Goff.

'Croeso i Gymru, Jane. Welcome to Wales.'

'Thank you.'

His handshake was as strong as she'd anticipated. His eyes, behind the spectacle lenses, went from her to Gwyn.

'So how's America treating you Gwyn? You look well.'

'I am, Goff.'

'The teaching is all right? You enjoy it, do you?'

'Yes, actually, I do. Wouldn't have thought it, would you?'

'Oh aye, I would. I always knew you'd be able to teach. Would you like some coffee, Jane, or a cup of tea? Put the kettle on Gwyn, there's a good lad. Come through by here, and let's all sit down.'

Goff took Jane through the doorway into the middle room, leaving Gwyn alone in the kitchen.

Gwyn blinked. He watched Jane walk slowly behind Goff and pause as Goff steadied himself on the corner of the Welsh dresser. He saw her glance at the plates arranged on the dresser, and then up at the walls, where rows of framed prints covered the wallpaper. Gwyn hadn't realised how he'd feel, seeing Jane in this house: it was so familiar to him and yet he could see her staring at it, not knowing what to think.

He wanted to go and take her hand and lead her round the house, impressing his vision of it on her before she could form her own. He wanted her to know what all these things meant to him — the shape of the kitchen, the smell of the boiler in the hearth, the way the light fell through the side windows.

Slowly, feeling rather dazed, Gwyn carried the kettle to the kitchen sink. Could he ever really have been half-way across the world from this? He touched the formica surface of the kitchen table, and remembered it. He looked out of the kitchen window and saw the yard, and the garage, and the side wall of number twenty-five.

The familiarity of it was pulling at him, making him forget exactly why he was here now. The water was boiling for coffee.

He opened the cupboard above the sink for the cups and saucers, but it felt wrong. What he should really be doing was pouring himself a beer from the bottle in the larder and wandering through into the front room, singing a pop song to himself as he decided which book to take down from the shelf.

Later Goff would put his head round the door and peer at the book, and ask if he wanted a sandwich.

'All right, lad?'

Goff's voice, calling from the middle room, broke the dream.

'Yes thanks. Nearly ready.'

Good God, boy, get a grip on yourself, thought Gwyn. He began to clatter cups and saucers and teaspoons.

'So you haven't had it all easy, then,' Goff was saying as Gwyn carried in the coffees. 'No, I can see that.'

Gwyn shot Jane an anxious, wary look over the cups. What in God's name had Goff been asking her? He was relieved when Jane, sitting back in the ugly but comfortable winged armchair, gave him a reassuring smile.

In fact, Jane was enjoying herself. Usually she hated giving résumés about her past. And Goff was certainly trying to find out, but he didn't seem to be doing it with the intention of judging her, or even building up a picture of her. His questions were all to do with work: what was her job? How did she get into it? What had she studied? How had she come to study that? Had she specialised?

'Well. You must be very determined. And you must have wanted to study very badly.'

'Quizzing Jane about her academic record already, Goff? Let the girl have a coffee before you enrol her, for God's sake.'

'Oh, I know you don't care for scholarship. I know that all right. Too much like hard work for you, isn't it boy?'

The deep voice was good-humoured enough.

'What's it like in Manhattan, then? Is it a faster pace than in Cardiff?'

While Goff and Gwyn talked, Jane watched. Goff's face was deeply lined from nose to mouth and the cheeks, patched with rusty stubble, were sunken. His expression never wavered from calm, intelligent interest but she saw how his eyes held steady on

Gwyn's face, and how he leaned forward in his chair when Gwyn spoke. There was passion in the old man's feelings for Gwyn.

Gwyn was sitting the wrong way round on a hard chair, resting his hands on the wooden back. It wasn't a pose she'd ever seen him in before, but it suited him here. He and Goff were talking in a combative, almost quarrelsome way, but she could hear the sly affection beneath their words. They insulted each other cheerfully, broke off to laugh (and for Goff to cough), and then cast around for another subject on which they could wrangle.

When she'd read the Goff poems, and on the few occasions Gwyn had spoken of his life with Goff, she'd imagined the house as if it had been a typical mid-American small-town home, with books added. But of course it was quite different. This room was taller than it was wide or long, and the walls had all kinds of funny corners and niches in them. The beige-tiled hearth was very small and topped with ornaments; there were rows of etchings on the walls, dark black-and-white scenes and castle-scapes mounted on yellowing surrounds; the large, tall dresser was made from highly varnished wood and the plates on it were glazed in old-fashioned colours and scrupulously dusted.

There were large, thin, red and orange cushions on the chairs and in one corner was a low stool with a blue fabric seat, which had 'Workbasket' embroidered on it swirling letters. Next to that, opposite the chair Goff sat in, was a medium-sized TV. There was only one small bookcase with a selection of hard- and soft-cover books on its shelves: none of them looked like Celtic poetry.

'Looking at the books?' Goff said, following her glance. 'You won't find much to impress you there. That's Gwyn's bookcase, that is, to give him something nice and easy to read when he comes by.'

'Oh aye,' said Gwyn – Jane controlled the impulse to smile at the sound of his unconscious Goffism – 'I've always been a Jeffrey Archer fan, I have. You going soft in the head, Goff, reading that stuff?'

'Megan Landers brought it for me last autumn, when I had the flu and couldn't get out. Very thoughtful of her, it was.'

'Did you like it?'

'I didn't have to read it. They serialised it on the wireless a year back, and I heard it then. Well, enough to discuss it with her and sound grateful, anyhow. Now, this one I did read.' Goff leaned over laboriously, and pulled from the shelf a fat, cheap-looking book with an illustration of a prairie and an Indian chief on the front.

'Why, for God's sake?'

'Because it's about a part of America I'm interested in. The plains, where your ancestors went, boy.'

Gwyn thrust out his lower lip and shook his head.

'Oh yes. How could I forget. You'd better ask Jane about that, she comes from that part of the world. Ask her if she remembers any Red Indians with Welsh accents.'

Goff turned slowly from Gwyn to Jane, his eyes suddenly beady behind the spectacles.

'The plains, is it? Is that where you come from, then?'

Jane nodded, wondering at his interest.

'Yes. That's right Mr Jenkins. The state of North Dakota.'

'You know, Goff,' said Gwyn. 'It's just to the north of South Dakota.'

'I do know it Gwyn, thank you. I should know it. It's Madoc's country.'

'Oh, bloody 'ell. Here we go.' Gwyn's voice had gone broad Welsh, and he grinned at Jane. 'I didn't think we'd get away without having Madoc dragged out and dusted down.'

'Who's Madoc?'

Jane looked from Gwyn, who raised his eyes at the ceiling, to Goff. The old man was sitting upright in his chair watching her, his head on one side. It made him look like a very alert, very inquisitive fox.

'You haven't heard of Madoc, Jane?'

'No, I don't think so, Mr Jenkins. Who was he?'

'Oh Goff, call me Goff. He was a prince of Gwynedd, in north Wales, in the twelfth century. He was a great sailor; we believe his grandfather was a Viking, and the Vikings were the greatest mariners of all, mind. This Madoc, now, he went off on a long voyage in the late 1160s. He was looking for the lodestone, see – the magnetic pole. Every sailor looked for the lodestone then.

'Well, Madoc didn't find the lodestone. But he came back talking of a great country he'd found, beyond the sea where treacherous plants grew.

'In 1170 the old prince was dying and the princedom of Gwynedd fell into the hands of the sons. They had never lived in peace, and they plunged their country into wars of greed and ambition. It was the old story of Gwlad.

'Madoc was a very young son with no power base; some say he was a bastard son, though that wouldn't have stopped him inheriting under the old law. But he chose not to stay and join the fraternal wars. He built ten ships and filled them with his country-people, and he sailed these ships back across the ocean to the great country he'd found before.

'He landed his ships on the southern shores of the country and led his people north, up a magnificent river, bigger than anything anyone had seen before. They travelled for months, some say years, and many of them died, from sickness and in battles, when the indigenous people attacked them.

'But some survived, to reach the source of the river and the heart of the country. They settled on a wide plain, where buffalo grazed in herds, and bears lived. They made peace with the people living there. They inter-married, and had children and gradually, generation by generation, you see, the Welsh and the Mandan Indians became one.'

Jane's heart hit her collar-bone. She saw Goff and Gwyn staring at her and knew they had seen her jump.

'Oh. Hey, I'm sorry.' Jane's hand was on her chest, her other hand raised in a placatory gesture. 'I was startled. I guess I was listening so hard, I – I don't know. You tell such a good story.'

'Oh yes,' said Gwyn softly, looking sideways at Goff. His expression had turned to irritation. 'A regular star of the cyfarwyddion, Goff is.'

'You know the Mandans, then?' Goff said, smiling encouragingly.

'Yes, sure. In a vague kind of way. They don't exist any more as a nation, you know. There was an epidemic back in the Frontier days that killed almost all of them. I don't think there are any pure blood Mandans left. But in our town, in Renoxia, there were some native Americans with Mandan blood in them. They don't have a language any more; they speak Sioux. There were some kids at school . . .'

Jane was aware that she was chattering unnecessarily. She

trailed off, smiled at Goff and glanced quickly at Gwyn. He was looking at her with faint surprise.

'You see, Gwyn?' Goff said. 'You see, mon? I'll bet you didn't know any of that. I'll bet you've never asked her. I don't know, you're a marvel to me, boy. The way you practise wilful ignorance, it's an art.'

'Oh belt up, Goff. Jane didn't come here to buy the Goff Jenkins version of world history. Look at her, poor woman, she doesn't know what you're going on about. Let's change the subject.'

Gwyn had seen that she was rattled. Though he didn't understand why, he was moving automatically to help her. Jane felt a trickle of gratitude warm her veins: this unquestioning protectiveness was one of the things she loved him for.

Goff was peering at her.

'Well, Jane. I can't believe you've never heard of Madoc. Are you sure, bach?'

'Well, it does sound a little familiar,' Jane said, feeling inadequate. 'But to tell you the truth, I wasn't a very good student of history.'

'I've read there are monuments to him in your country.'

Jane laughed. 'There certainly aren't any in Renoxia.'

'No? Is that so? But there must be some mention of him in the reconstructed Mandan village in Bismarck, surely?'

'I only went there once, with school when I was little. I don't remember it well.'

'Well, good God. Just think of it, there's myself here, reading and writing and studying, learning about these small traces of Madoc so far away across the world, and there you are, growing up within – what is it then? A hundred miles of Bismarck? – and never felt an interest in it. There's irony for you, isn't it Gwyn?'

'Leave off, Goff.'

Goff looked beadily at Gwyn, then an unexpectedly mischievous smile transformed his face.

'Well, well,' he said. He winked at Jane as if they shared some joke together. 'Gwyn never had much of a sense of irony. So how are the wedding arrangements going?'

'We're a bit behind,' admitted Gwyn, grinning. 'I'm taking Jane into Cardiff this afternoon, to have a look at the catering firm.'

'It's a bit late to change your order, isn't it?'

'Yes. But Eirlys and Roy told me I had to do it and you know how bossy they are.'

'Good God, it'll cost you an arm and a leg, boy, taking their advice. Regular gourmets they are.'

'Don't worry, I vetoed all their first-choice companies.'

'Oh well, you know your business. While I think about it, I've got a drawer full of congratulations cards for you. From people you've already invited and some more who no doubt want to be invited. Hold on.'

Goff pushed himself out of the chair and went out into the hall. Gwyn came to sit on the arm of Jane's chair.

'Are you all right cariad? He doesn't mean to pry. He's just besotted with his old legends.'

'I'm fine.'

'You seemed upset.'

'No, just startled. It feels so weird to be here, talking about Renoxia, that's all.' Jane paused. 'That was an interesting story about Prince Madoc though. You never mentioned it before.'

Gwyn grimaced.

'Are you surprised? I get enough of the bloody bards and princes when I see Goff, without going on about them myself.'

'I see what you mean.' She did. Goff certainly had a powerful way of telling a story. She could almost see the twelfth-century prince, escaping his warring brothers and setting sail in his ships, landing on the vast, unknown shores of her own country.

'The problem is,' she said to Gwyn in a low voice, 'it can't be true about the prince and the Mandans. One thing I do remember from history class is that the Mandans weren't indigenous to North Dakota. They were migrants from some other part of America – I can't remember when they settled on the Missouri but it was much later than the twelfth century. Our teachers were hot on that – you know, proving that the Native Americans weren't that native after all.'

'Bloody hell,' said Gwyn, staring, 'you'd better tell Goff.'

'Should I? No,' said Jane uneasily. 'I don't want to. It would feel arrogant.'

'But it's an historical fact, for God's sake.'

'It's just out of line. Let's leave it, OK?'

Jane looked at Gwyn anxiously. She didn't want to come into Goff's house and start correcting him, being an American smart-ass. But it wasn't only that: when she thought of meddling in the Madoc story, a prickle ran over her skin. She couldn't have said why but it made her feel edgy, like an animal that senses thunder in the air.

'If you're sure,' Gwyn said, after a pause. 'For now.'

10

All evening Jane was plagued by memories. They first began to
tug at the edges of her mind while she and Gwyn were waiting
at the bus stop in Cardiff. The crowded streets, with their lighted
shop windows, arcade entrances, elaborate window-sills and
parapets, gave way to visions of Renoxia in winter. She saw the
snow blowing through the commercial district, and the loose
shutters and doors banging up on Toller.

Once they were in the warmth of the bus, on the top deck,
Jane looked at the elegant walls and towers of Cardiff castle, and
its park, and saw instead the emptiness of the lake-shore, with
the line of trailers taking the force of the wind.

And there were the people too. The other passengers on the
bus became faces and figures she knew from her past – Jock
Bruger, Miss Archer, her sister Rose; other people she couldn't
put a name to, yet whom she recognised: the long-faced girl from
sophomore year, the old woman with the plaid coat, someone's
grandfather.

Why? Why after all this time were they coming back so vividly
and pointlessly?

As the bus carried them past row after row of small, semi-
detached houses, Cardiff's outskirts, Jane decided that it must be
a sympathetic reaction to Gwyn. She was helping him revisit his
past and rediscover old faces and places, and it had stirred memories of her own. It was that, and the unexpected conversation
with Goff this morning.

But at least, when she looked at Gwyn and squeezed his hand, she saw him and no one else. His broad face and curly hair and solid shoulders filled her eyes.

Roy had turned the lights down low on the dimmer switch and the food was robbed of its colour. It tasted good, though: Jane had never had goat's cheese lightly fried with apple slices before. Nor julienne of veal in paprika sauce, on saffron rice. It hadn't taken Eirlys very long to prepare, either, and as for shopping, Roy and Eirlys had assured her there was a very good delicatessen in Cardiff, near Eirlys's office.

Jane thought of the many years she had lived on bagels and salads and pasta. She liked it; it had never occurred to her to spend more time or imagination on her diet. Gwyn's favourite food was chilli. If Gwyn had stayed with Eirlys, the sweetheart of his teens, then he might now have a double wine rack, an educated palate and a pastel-decorated house.

Jane caught her mind floating away again just in time. She must concentrate: she forced her attention back to the table talk. It was more robust than the food would suggest: both Roy and Eirlys enjoyed a good gossip and seemed to know a lot about the sex lives of their and Gwyn's old school-fellows and neighbours.

'Honest to God, Gwyn, they were all there in the garden shed. Racks of 'em,' Roy was saying.

'Sergeant Davis nearly had a coronary when he saw them,' added Eirlys. 'And do you know what?'

She looked from Gwyn to Jane, playing her audience like the good raconteur she was.

'Marion swears that when she got them back, there were a couple missing.'

'And people who saw Bethan Davis in the next few days swore she was walking very peculiar!'

Jane laughed with everyone else. She found Eirlys's muffled nasal giggle very infectious. But she wasn't really paying attention, and she didn't think Gwyn was either. He had a rapt look on his face which she recognised.

'Sweetheart, what are you at?'

Jane sat up against the pale yellow pillows and stared at Gwyn's back. He was sitting on the end of the bed, head bent.

'Mmm? Just a sec, cariad.'

Jane knew what he was doing. She was glad. But she wished he wasn't doing it right now. Now, she needed him to climb into bed with her and make love to her.

The bed trembled as Gwyn's writing hand moved. Jane drew up her knees and rested her chin on them, stroking the soft cotton of the duvet down the length of her calves.

Gwyn scribbled, holding his breath. There was just a line or two, not there in full yet – there were words missing, but the rhythm was there and the images were beginning to come back. He'd been right to wait; not that he'd had any choice, but he'd been right not to try anything else. The visitor was back.

'What do you mean, "the visitor"?' Jane put her hands to Gwyn's face, partly to caress him, partly to let him suckle gently on her fingers, which she loved: it sent long spiny tickles of desire through her.

'That's what it feels like,' said Gwyn. He licked her fingers gently in a line from little finger to thumb, his tongue circling each tip. His hand was already between her thighs, spreading them and stroking her vulva. 'It feels like someone's come to see me and is showing me things.'

'What things.'

'Places. Feelings. I don't know. Wait and see.'

The sensation came swift and unstoppable, like darkness. For a split second, it filled her mind. Jane sighed with desire and turned her head in the soft pillow.

'What was that?' said Gwyn.

'I don't know.'

'Well, wait for me.'

But she couldn't. Here it was coming back again, this engulfing, overwhelming tide. Gwyn thought it was his touch on her, but it wasn't. It was happening inside her mind.

Let Madoc come back. Please, grey lady. Sweet stone mother.

Madoc's ship is out on the seas, sailing home to me. I've got no time for anyone who says otherwise.

I haven't spoken his name aloud in sixteen months. Five seasons of sowing and ripening and harvesting, of gathering in the oats and moving the sheep to new pasture, and I haven't said his name. Others have said it – asking me nosy questions, tattling as I walk by – but me, no.

They're all mad with curiosity, they are. They want to know why I can wait without fretting. They want to know why he brought me back. They want to know what happened last year when Cadell and Wenlyn rode into the village, harnessed Siani for me, and took me off with them. Oh, they found out fast enough where we went: they followed our tracks to Dreugyllt and saw the camp and the foundations of the castle going up. They've been gathering news about the progress of the building ever since, as the stone walls climb higher and the wooden fence rings it round. They tell me about it, and peer at me to see my reaction. 'That's good,' I say.

But I don't tell them what happened, why should I?

I still see Caer Llion, the huge broken walls with the houses built into them; the stalls selling meat and cheese and cloth, medicines, hides, threads, oils; the Norman lords and gentlemen, wearing swords, and the women, with cloaks high around their throats. I can still hear the noise and smell the dust and dirt.

I can see the ships sailing up the river at high tide, and riding at anchor outside the walls.

The torches still burn in their sconces, inside the hall where Madoc feasted with the Irish lords. There's nervous I was, walking into the hall with him.

I hadn't been nervous on the journey, you see. Oh, the journey – me and Madoc and his men, riding off together. It was easy to pretend that I was not me but someone grander. A mysterious lady in gold silks on a pale grey horse, like in the story of Pwll and Rhiannon. We left Cynfael when the sun was past noon, and as we reached the track and turned east along it, I looked back down the hill. There were the thirty or so houses of the kindred, and the oat fields, filling up with women again now that the kindred had been thanked and dismissed by Madoc and were returning to work. Teilo and Bran stood where we had left them, thirty yards further down, with their sons. Meilyr wasn't there though. The half-free were working the land as usual, and there were people in the meadow with the remaining Cynfael horses. I could see Buddug and Dafydd looking up from the cheese-making to watch me leave. Mam was busy straining the curds and didn't raise her head. Below them I could see the fire burning in the forge and across the distance the sound of Dai hammering a new ploughshare came chink chink chink. I felt like a traveller looking down on something she had no part of; I knew then that it was no longer my home.

We rode east, along the track I had run in the other direction yesterday. At the monastery, the prior came out to greet us and ask us in, but Madoc didn't want to stop. He paused just long enough to let the prior bless our journey and we rode on, Madoc and me and the men in the front, the servants with the baggage and the Cynfael horses behind.

We rode like that for two days, stopping for the night in a tref on the Rhymney river. I loved every mile of that journey, with Madoc riding at my side, Wenlyn and Cadell flirting with me and even Owain being grave and courteous.

But at the end of the second day's ride, when I saw the jagged walls of Caer Llion, and the roofs and the tower rising beyond them, I remembered who I was. Ceinwen, a village girl, that's who – a nobody even in our own kindred, with secret half-free blood still in my veins. Madoc and the others were all sitting that bit straighter on their mounts, and Madoc was looking round him with proud, bright eyes. I sat straight too, but as we rode through the crowd of traders into the town, I saw that even the girls selling grain had bits of trim on their cloaks, and inside the walls many people wore shoes and the women wore small, rounded head-dresses and stared at the white wings rising from my forehead.

I sat up there, on Siani, and wished there were more people mounted, so I didn't stick out so much. Faces were turning everywhere – all these people, Normans and Welsh, some with official badges on, some in tatters, some fine – they were all gawping at each other. You'd think they were all afraid something was going on without them and were hunting for it with hard, curious eyes. I saw the dark blue tassel on Elfan's bridle, and told myself that I was with the prince.

'Which way is it to the Red House?' Owain asked a man with a brooch on his cloak. Owain is the one of Madoc's men who seems to take charge of the practical things.

'The Red House?' said the man, looking us up and down, eagerly. 'You'll be wanting the seamen from Ireland, will you? They arrived last night, you know. Brought a hold full of stores with them in their ship too, as if we didn't have food and drink here for them. The traders aren't happy.'

'That'll be wedding gifts,' said Owain. 'Rhiryd the Irish lord is marrying his sister to Cuhelyn of Ystrad Tywi. Didn't you know that?'

'Cuhelyn, is it? That's Rhys's cousin's boy. Well, he's not here yet. Straight up this road, you want, then right by the old baths down the hill and you'll find it by the saddlemaker's.'

The man went on – chewing over the information Owain had given him and muttering, 'So. Cuhelyn. Marriage.' He might have been one of the new officers the Normans have in the towns now, but I didn't want to ask. I didn't want to show up all the things I didn't know.

The Red House stood behind a patch of trampled, muddy grass. A dozen horses were tethered there, with twice as many men and boys standing round them, guarding them. The building was high and narrow, with thick walls of red-brown stone.

Madoc went ahead, inside, with Owain and Wenlyn. Then came Bredmor and Cadell and between them, and slightly behind them, me. I blinked in the smokiness: there were high windows with glass set into them, but the light came mainly from the torches which burned as if it was feast-time, and the air was heavy with their smoke. The hall was crammed with people, all bunched in groups and collected round one spot – a high table where men were clustered, talking and shouting, and at one end of this table sat a party of women.

When they saw us, the men at high table stopped talking and one of them came forward.

'Madoc!' he said. 'My foster brother. We've been waiting for you. You're very welcome.'

'Rhiryd!' said Madoc. There was warmth and emotion in his voice: I could see he loved this man with the yellow-brown beard and the thick gold bands on his arms. Loved him yet still had to settle with him before he sailed the same waters. 'I saw your ship at anchor. She's very splendid – and they tell me she's stuffed full of food and wine and livestock.'

'Yes, we've brought some small considerations for Rhys ap Gruffydd,' said Rhiryd, grinning. 'Your father should learn some politics from us, Madoc.'

'My father's too busy provoking the English king,' said Madoc. He shrugged, and he and Rhiryd embraced again. 'By God, it's good to see you again. And Mulhaoch and Bren, and the lady Pryste. Is her husband here yet?'

'My lord Cuhelyn? No, man. He should be here tonight though. I don't know, I think Pryste should be going to someone of more account, even if his uncle Rhys is the coming man. Ah – ' he stopped, catching sight of me. 'You've brought women with you too?' Then, looking, he realised that there was only one of me, and stared harder. He had a muscular face with hooded eyes; he was several years older than Madoc.

Madoc flushed as he turned from Rhiryd to me.

'She's Ceinwen Maelgwyn, from the kindred of Cynfael,' he said. 'My lady, this is Rhiryd of Clochran, my foster brother. I hope you two will love each other for my sake.'

My lady. I walked forward, as steady as I could, and tried to pretend that my rough cloak, spattered with mud, was made of the same dark silk as Rhiryd's sister was wearing. There was nervousness in Madoc's face, and a fierce, excited pride. I looked from his to Rhiryd: his eyes were bright with interest and speculation. Beyond him, I could see other faces turned towards me – all the men and women at high table were looking.

I don't have the birth or blood or fine silks on my flesh. But I am beautiful.

The five steps I took to Rhiryd lasted forever. I forced myself not to look at his hands, or bow my head to suggest that I might kiss them. When I came in front of him, I smiled.

He reached forward and kissed me on the mouth.

'Welcome, beautiful lady,' he said. 'You're welcome at my table as long as you're Madoc's lady. And as long as you're so lovely.'

'Thank you, my lord,' I said. 'And I'm your friend for love of Madoc and your own bravery.'

Should I have said I was honoured to be his guest? For a second, I thought I'd done the wrong thing, but then his face creased into a wide smile.

'God Madoc, she's lovely,' he said. 'Lady, we'll sit you with my sister.' He took my arm with a graceful, heavy turn and led me to the women's end of the table.

So for three nights and two days I, Ceinwen Maelgwyn of Cynfael, got to be a great lady. Strange it is, how quickly you get used to new things.

That first night, I sat with Pryste and her women and listened to them talk about their lives in Ireland and Cuhelyn, this nephew of the lord Rhys who was due to arrive soon. They weren't all friendly to me: they could see very well that I was in simple clothes, but because they were from Ireland they weren't sure what it meant. After all, Madoc and his men were less splendidly dressed than the Irish, and they knew that Madoc was the son of the most powerful king in Wales. So they treated me politely, and I was able to tell them some of the things I knew about Lord Rhys and his court, and I made it sound as if it wasn't all hearsay but that I'd been there too.

I guessed from some of the things they said that Pryste was in love with an Irish lord. She didn't look happy: her face was set and although she smiled, her eyes kept shining with tears. Then, when Cuhelyn arrived, she went forward to meet him with a face white like a lamb's. I wasn't surprised: he was at least five years younger than her – he looked about twelve or thirteen, the same age as Buddug. I felt sorry for her – especially when she went to sit next to Cuhelyn at the centre of the table, and Madoc called me to sit next to him. Madoc and I were lovers, strong and happy and well matched; poor Pryste had to bend her head down to listen to her boy husband.

Soon after Cuhelyn and his people arrived, Rhiryd made me a gesture of friendship. Cuhelyn had brought a wedding party of his kin with him, and they were many of them dressed in cloaks and tunics of coloured silk. Though they weren't as fine as the Irish silks, they showed me for what I was. Madoc and his men were in simple warband clothes, but I – I was just poor. I saw some of Cuhelyn's party staring at me – and Cuhelyn did himself, but with something more like delight in his young eyes – and I saw Rhiryd notice. A while later, when we were settling ourselves for the wedding feast, he carried a length of silk up to me.

'A gift to do honour to your beauty, my lady Ceinwen,' he said. His face was serious but his eyes were amused and knowing. He handed the silk to Cadell, who was standing beside me, and told him to help me on with it. It was a cloak, in dark green silk, sewn with red thread. When Cadell fastened it round my shoulders it slithered cool and heavy against my skin.

The feast lasted hours into the night, with Cuhelyn's harper – sent by the Lord Rhys himself, from his court – playing songs in honour of the bride and husband and of the Irish lords and the Welsh lords, and the women. And the talk – it ranged from love to war and politics, to the sea, to war and politics, and circled round and round two figures who weren't there but whose names were in everyone's mouths – Owain Gwynedd, Madoc's father, and the Lord Rhys.

'Rhys ap Gruffydd is clever,' Rhiryd said to Madoc. 'While your father's pushing his land to the Dee and making an enemy of King Henry, Rhys is marrying his kin to everyone in the Marches and taking bits of Ceredigion and Dyfed for himself, with no one to stop him.'

'Still,' said one of the other Irish lords, leaning in, 'Madoc ap Owain's taken a nice piece of Morgannwg for himself from under Rhys's nose. He won't be pleased, Madoc, if he finds out that you've stolen from his territory.' He lifted his cup to me.

'He's got too much territory, then, if he doesn't know what's to be found in it,' said Madoc. 'A man gets complacent on land. That's why I'm putting to sea.' And he lifted his cup to me too, and drank.

Back and forth the talk went like that, with puns and word plays, and everyone watching everyone and listening hard.

At the end of the first night, Pryste and Cuhelyn had the marriage bed, of course, but Madoc spoke to Rhiryd and after a while some servants brought in two goat-skins sewn together and nailed it like a curtain to the wall, and put a mattress and a brychan behind it for us. It was very, very dark in there: completely black, and the smell of the hides mingled with the smell of Madoc's skin and sweat in my nostrils. From outside the curtain I could hear the clamour of everyone else in the hall settling down, and it excited me.

'Take it off carefully, my lord,' I couldn't resist saying, as I felt him fumbling to remove my new silk cloak.

Every minute of it I remember, every minute. Because I was with Madoc, I was the equal of anyone there. Oh there were moments that were horrible. I didn't always know the right thing to do or say, and when I went out with Cadell to buy a new head-dress, the kind the Norman women wore, I didn't know how to put it on and the stall-holder laughed at me. But Cadell stopped her by saying, 'Watch your mouth you insolent bitch. This is Prince Madoc ap Owain ap Gruffydd's lady.' I wouldn't have thought Cadell would use such rough words. I can still hear him now, the way he said it, and the way the woman apologised. Cadell didn't see her grin as we left, but it didn't matter. There, I was Prince Madoc ap Owain ap Gruffydd's lady.

Yes, I remember every minute of those days in Caer Llion. And I remember how I listened to the talk, and what I learned from it. I remember how the knowledge grew in me and what it showed me. I'm not stupid. I could see that there was no place in Madoc's life for me.

Madoc is a prince, and his father was the greatest king in the country a few years ago. All my life I've heard stories about him and his power and it's always been growing. When I was a baby, it was a bad time: the Normans had come and taken the richest lands and overpowered Lord Rhys, who's prince of the southern cantrefi, and Owain Gwynedd who had become prince of the cantrefi in the north. Just as we paid tribute to our overlord and he paid it to Rhys, so Rhys had to pay the Normans. And the same in Gwynedd.

But all the years of my life, the Welsh have been growing stronger. Owain and Rhys have been calling on their lords and men at arms, mustering men from the kindreds and attacking the Normans and the English king's garrisons. Every kindred has lost some men in these battles but they've been good battles, which we've won. Our Lord Rhys and Owain Gwynedd of the north are allies, now.

And I sat in the hall in Caer Llion with Owain Gwynedd's son, and knew I couldn't hold him.

The knowledge was there from the first night, and as the feast went on it grew stronger. At first, the delight of being Madoc's lady was greater. But then, every bit of that delight was eaten into by knowing that it couldn't last.

When I remember that feeling – just remember it, mind – I get a pain knotting and hollowing inside me.

I didn't ask Madoc, I knew better than that. He was a prince, I was a no-one, a girl from low down in a kindred; why remind him of it? When he told me how much he loved me, I said I loved him back and nothing more.

But on the last night of the feast I couldn't sleep. I lay in Madoc's arms behind the stifling curtain and stared and stared at the goat's hide.

Just before dawn Madoc stirred. He lay still for a while, facing away from me, then he spoke.

'Ceinwen.' His voice was hoarse and strained. 'Ceinwen, get dressed and come outside with me. Hurry, please.'

It was hard getting dressed in the dark and when I stumbled out of the recess into the hall, I had to pull the silk cloak around me to hide my misfastened dress. Madoc was walking fast through the sleeping men and women: I had to hurry to keep up. We passed the sentries at the doorway and stepped out into the city. The air was blueing with the first signs of the day.

The horses were still asleep but there were people about in the streets: horsemen and sentries outside the big houses, traders carrying their stuff down to their stalls and other people, huddling in groups. Madoc took my hand and almost pulled me through them, all the way down the hill to the old walls and the river. In the blue light his face was smooth and empty, but it was a desperate sort of emptiness, like a fear. We stopped on the bank and he took my other hand in his too. He was trembling, not like he'd done on our first night in Hywel's, but a cold trembling, taut like a harp string.

'Ceinwen,' he said, in that hoarse voice. 'Do you believe I'm going to be a great man?'

'Yes my lord.'

'Why?'

I looked at him. What did he want me to say, this prince of Gwynedd? What did he mean? He was born into the greatest blood-line there was.

'I mean – oh, will people talk about me the way they talk about Rhys and my father and Hywel Da? Will the bards tell stories about me in the halls?'

'It depends what you do,' I said. There's painful it was, talking to him about the things that would make him great, and how future generations would remember him. Talking about his future with no room for me.

'You don't know what it's like, Ceinwen,' Madoc said. His grip tightened on my hands and there was a sweat glistening on his cheeks and neck. 'I'm only a young son, and not by an important woman. My father always loved Cristin the best and he's always favoured Dafydd and Rhodri, her sons. I've always been below them – always.'

He shook his head, as if to brush tears from his eyes. And when he looked at me again, his lashes were wet.

'I've been speaking to Owain,' he said. 'He advises me. He's my father's man, you know. My father sent him to watch over me.'

I nodded. I'd guessed.

'He won't have you, you know. My father won't recognise you. He won't and no-one in Gwynedd will, and Owain says that if I try to take you there, they'll ignore us, laugh at us.'

Here it was, and the pain was too much to bear. I opened my mouth to say: I don't care, we'll still be together. But something stopped me.

Was it pride, after all? Or was it some deeper, clever instinct? I don't know.

But I didn't speak. I looked into his eyes as he stood there, gazing angrily at me, and then, swiftly and sharply, like a shooting star falling through the night sky, I saw it. I couldn't believe it, but there, true it was. He was helpless. Madoc, this young prince was helpless and in pain. He wanted me so badly. He wanted greatness so badly, and he didn't know how to get either. He needed me to tell him.

Moments come and go, Mam said. Well, this was our moment.

When I spoke, it was carefully.

'How do you want to be great, Madoc my lord? On the seas?'

'Yes. On the seas. I've got to make my own name. I must be my own man, I must.'

'You've made your agreement with Rhiryd?'

His head went up.

'Rhiryd's my foster brother. He's bound to me, and I to him.'

He was haughty but his eyes were the eyes of a lad in anguish. My head went up too and I looked into those eyes.

'Make your voyage, Madoc,' I said. My voice was low and passionate. 'Gather a sea-going warband and make your voyage. Cast your net over the seas.'

He stood very still, watching me. He didn't know it but he was squeezing my hands so cruelly that I had to grit my teeth not to flinch or moan.

I breathed out, long and gently, and spoke again.

'Cast your net over the seas, my love. And come back in triumph.'

Gradually, his face changed. Colour came back into his cheeks and his eyes lost their wildness and became darker. He went on looking at me, but his grip on my hands slackened. I saw his chest begin to rise and fall rhythmically.

Then he smiled, a smile which made me gasp.

He lifted my bruised hands to his lips, bent his head and kissed them.

'I will, my lady.' His voice was throaty, as it had been on the track, the first day. But it had something hard and powerful in it now, too. 'I will. I'll cast my net over the seas. I'll bring you home islands and peoples.'

'I'll wait for them, my lord.'

Madoc uncurled his fingers. He moved his hands to my face and stroked my temples, smoothing back my tumbled, uncovered hair.

'I will be great. I'll be a great man for you, Ceinwen. Our children will be princes of Gwynedd.'

He put his mouth on mine to seal the vow. I felt we had taken a step out of our old world already. I wasn't sure who this was who kissed me, nor what I'd become in the last few minutes, but I knew I was his lover.

'My lover,' said Madoc. 'My lady and my lover. I've got to start now. At once.'

'Yes.'

'I don't want to take you back, but I must.'

'I know.' I lifted my head and bared my neck, like a roe deer to the knife. 'I'm yours.'

'And I'm yours. My lady, I'm yours. Forever, until honour dies. Until Gwynedd and Morgannwg and Deheubarth die.'

'And longer,' I said, low and passionate, as the darkness came and closed up my eyes. 'And longer.'

So we came back here. I didn't want to come back, of course I didn't. Every step our horses took dragged my heart down into my body until in the end it was so heavy it felt like a lump of lead, buried deep in the secret core of me and weighting me down. We talked — we talked love at first, and plans; then we just talked anything; then we couldn't think of anything and our voices had no resonance. When we entered the woods above the valley, Madoc was pale like whey.

We stopped when we came to the ladyrock. In front of Cadell and Wenlyn, Bredmor and Owain, we made our marriage. We knelt down: I unfastened the front of my dress and pressed my breasts against the stone. Madoc took his sword from his belt and whetted it against the stone's edge. Then he laid it, gently, on its cold, cold flat, across my naked breasts. We pledged.

In the village, of course, they talked gossip and told-you-so till they were tired. They decided I must have done something shameful in Caer Llion. They decided Madoc had taken me to see his father and been ordered to return me. They decided I'd been offered to Madoc's Irish lords and rejected. They could never work out why he'd brought me back, though. Why didn't he just abandon me?

I told them nothing. I didn't belong to them any more. I just lived with them for the time being. I lived, and waited. In my head the torches of Caer Llion burned and the ships sailed up the Usk, and Madoc was walking through the great stone halls of Gwynedd, and riding south to the Lord Rhys, and clearing our way.

It was the middle of winter when they came. Cadell and Wenlyn, it was; riding through the bare trees to the village. They claimed food and drink of Hywel Drwyn, then they came to me. They got Siani from the meadow and harnessed her.

'Where are you going?' Mam said and for the first time since Da died, there were tears in her eyes.

'I don't know,' I said. There's hard I was, and distant.

I didn't know, either, not exactly. Not until we were on the horses and rising back up the track, when they began telling me, chattering and interrupting each other because they were in a party mood.

Dreugyllt: it took us four days to reach it. I remember the moment of crossing into Owain Gwynedd's territory: it was when we crossed a river, the rain boiling down on its surface, its drumming filling our ears. We went due west after that, until through the endless rain, the horizon opened and we were drawing near the coast, the southern-most shore of the kingdom of Gwynedd.

It was a mountainous shore, with a cleft hill standing guard over the river inlet. The camp was on the hill, a cluster of knocked-up shacks and shelters in a semicircle. The hall's foundations had been dug down fifteen feet into the turf and the grey blocks of stone were being cut and joined under the hands of the workmen. People were heaving, shifting, carrying, measuring, shouting orders, resting, watching. I saw Madoc, his arms wrapped in a winter cloak, his hair drenched and torn by the wind on the clifftop, talking to some men by an anvil. Behind him and beyond him was the iron grey sea.

Two whole weeks I spent there with my husband, watching the walls of his stronghold rise. I ate side by side with him in our shack. I rode with him to see the stone being quarried. With him, I visited his brother Rhodri and stayed in his house as Madoc's lady. I rode with Madoc the day he attended the sharing out of the land of one of the elders of the neighbouring bro. And when the gale came, we didn't leave but stayed there as guests of the new elder.

And just like the torches still burn in Caer Llion, Madoc's lips are still on mine in Dreugyllt. He's still hurrying to me across the torn-up grass of the hilltop. He's still racing his horse down the cliff path and along the shore, in a contest with Wenlyn and Rhodri. Madoc and his races.

And we're still standing in the cold, looking north up the coast to where he says Conwy is, and he's telling me about his father's stronghold there, and that one day, when he's made his place on the sea and is a power in his own right, he'll take me there.

I'm not a fool. I know that there's marrying and marrying. Madoc's a prince and princes have to make useful marriages. Especially these brothers of Gwynedd. When they all start fighting again, he might have to run to his Irish sealords or to one of the Marcher houses, or our own Lord Rhys, and marry some daughter or sister or cousin.

But I'm his lover and his first wife, and I'll be his last.

But there's long it is since I've seen him. Thirteen months since I left him in Dreugyllt. Ten months since the news came that his ship had sailed. And here I am, waiting, waiting, and never speaking his name.

Him a prince and me a village girl, only just one of Elydyr Tewdr's kindred, the most distant branch. But Madoc is closing the gap: he paid Elydyr my amobr, my virginity price. Cadell and Wenlyn didn't tell me at the time, but when they came to fetch me they brought the amobr from Madoc. They gave it to Hywel, for Elydyr: it was a written pledge that Madoc would give Elydyr four cows and a stallion, to release me. If things had gone different, I might have had to bare my breasts as punishment for sleeping with a man. But as it was Madoc, no-one dared call for punishment, and Madoc showed them all by paying a princess's price.

When Madoc told me what he'd done, when we were together in his tent at Dreugyllt, I couldn't speak. I could only cry.

I haven't stopped thinking of him for one hour since I left him; I haven't got the sweet taste of him out of my mouth or the touch of him from my skin.

At night, under the brychan, I remember how he touched me.

At night. At night. Each night is so long. Like this one.

Sweet God, what's that? Oh dear God, Mam, why aren't you waking? Oh!

Oh. Oh. Oh. It's a bird. Flapping so violently, thrashing round. The air seems full of its wings. Now it's still. It's perched on the ground now, near the fire, looking at me. Its head is cocked towards me, its eyes are small, round and black in the firelight.

It's a sign, that's what it is. No one else has woken, despite our scuffle. Mam's still sleeping under the brychan, curled round Dafy. There's just me awake, me and the bird. And Madoc.

I can feel him near. I can feel his closeness. Almost I could put out my hand and touch him.

After a while I crawl out of bed and roll a piece of old dough towards the door. The bird – it's a crow, black and sleek – hops after it, then jumps into the air, hovers for a moment and flies off.

I must talk to Marared. I must ask her what it means. She said to me once, when I first came back from Caer Llion, that she could see for me. She said I'd need her one day; that she knew I'd be coming to ask.

I've slipped away; I don't think Mam saw me go. Nest did, though: I saw her lift her head from feeding her new baby and watch me slide behind the houses, into the trees. I've walked a round-about path above the village and now I've come back down to the alder grove again, and Marared's house.

I slip round the side of the house, keeping close to the wall. There's filth underfoot – that's what you get for coming the back way. Achyfy. Lift my skirts; tread carefully. Damn! I'm so busy looking down, the thatch branches scratch my face.

There's nothing wrong with coming to Marared, but if people see me here, they'll wonder what's happened. They'll start tongue-wagging again.

I call low, through the wall.

'Marared Ifor. It's Ceinwen, Maelgwyn's daughter. I want your help.'

There are rustlings inside. Oh Duw, don't let it be that husband of hers. He's so nosy and such a talker.

'Ceinwen Maelgwyn.' Marared's voice. 'Come in girl.'

I bend down and plunge through the doorway. No Bryn; good. And no other women – just Marared and her two young children. Marared's sitting on one side of the fire, which is burning too fiercely for the walls. Behind her a patch of clay is cracking and, directly above the flames, sap's oozing out of a green branch in the roof thatch. It's hot like a forge in here.

Marared waves at the two children and they crawl off under the brychan, out of sight.

Marared's gazing eagerly at me; she knows what I've come for all right. She's so nearly beautiful – her skin's wet and smooth and her forehead's even higher than mine. But she's too strange: her eyes go through yours and into the dark space within.

She leans towards me.

'Sit down. Get close, you don't know who's outside listening. Give me your hands. I know what you want. I know.' Her voice is thrilling me like the plucking of a harp. 'Whisper,' she says, very low. 'Ask about your man.'

I speak as quietly as I can. I don't trust the children; they're lying still beneath the brychan but they've got ears.

'I had a sign last night. A bird flew in my house and got tangled in my hair. Marared Ifor, when I woke and looked at it, I felt him.' I pause. 'I felt my Madoc.'

There, I've said it. His name has come off my lips. I listen to my voice saying it at last, low and strong, through the crackles and hisses of the fire.

Marared starts her rocking – I don't take my eyes off hers. She's not like the older seers: they whirl and scream, foam at the mouth and fall in dead faints. Marared rocks, back and forth, back and forth, and keeps hold of your hands. Her eyes stay open and you can look in them. It's a pleasing, blank stillness you see there.

And now Marared opens her mouth and begins the secret speaking. I can't understand her. I can't. Be patient. Concentrate on the rocking. Rock, rock, rock. All these words. No sense.

No sense . . . just the words pouring . . . close my eyes. There's tired I am. Close my eyes, look away Marared and let me close them, they can't see you any more, they can't see . . .

Madoc, on his ship. Look at the spray blowing in his face and soaking his hair. The water's running down his skin. He's screwing up his eyes, the blue-green eyes blinking the water away and searching for me – or someone . . .

The calm green shallows lap Madoc's legs. He raises his hand to the shore and to a man standing there, a dark-skinned man with long hair like a horse's tail that hangs straight down.

Madoc is on the shore now. He gazes at me, searching. The other man is kneeling beside him now, holding up his hands in prayer. Madoc is reaching out his hands to me; he's calling me nearer. So close to me now, his face and the dark man's face; my hands are reaching out to theirs, and something caresses my palm.

Madoc lifts his head and opens his mouth and out of it comes a beautiful, shivering song . . .

Dear God, what's happening to Marared? Her face is creased and her eyes are bulging like a dying squirrel. Why is her throat heaving like that?

No, no, no. I'm screaming. Oh stone mother, listen to my terrible low noise, like moaning, like Marared's retching. My hands are spattered with her vomit because she won't let them go.

Now, at last, in the silence Marared chokes, shudders and presses her hand to her mouth. I hear the noise of my own teeth chattering.

We do our best now to clean her up. And we send the children out to fetch water and see if anyone heard. I look at her and to ask her, I have to lick my lips. My voice is uneven and too high.

'Marared Ifor, what did you see?'

Marared's scooped the last of the vomit-covered earth on to the fire and now she's staring down into the leather purses slung round her belt, picking out herbs to sweeten the soil and the air.

'Your man's coming,' she says. 'Your man's coming back for you.'

She pulls out a pinch of fennel leaves and sprinkles them on the fire; the sharp scent catches at my nostrils.

'He's bringing you something,' she says. Then she shuts her mouth and the silence spreads.

My heart's beating uncomfortably slow, dragging in my chest. I can hardly bear to ask. Remember though – no coward, me.

I repeat it again, the question the seer must answer.

'What did you see, Marared Ifor?'

Marared turns her moon face to mine. Her high, rounded forehead glows with moisture and her eyes are blank.

'I saw nothing to be able to tell, Ceinwen Maelgwyn. If you saw something, you saw it.'

So that was the end of it, with Marared. I left her house without knowing. She won't tell, see. Perhaps she truly can't.

I don't know what happened there, and what the signs mean. I'm afraid. Duw, grey mother, I'm afraid. But happy too, and proud.

Madoc, my lord. I can feel you coming closer.

It was half a gallery, half a shop. There were stacks of prints in the two windows, prints and paintings hung on every inch of wall, and unwieldy cabinets took up too much floor space. Behind their glass doors the cabinets displayed the tools of art – brushes, spatulas, palettes, tubes of paint and pots of pigment, odd-shaped knives and brackets.

Jane opened the door and stepped inside. The doormat pinged as she trod on it. The man at the counter gave her a smile and went back to the picture he was measuring.

She was the only customer in the shop. It was warm and smelt of paper and wood. She didn't plan to buy anything, but the place had looked so welcoming from the street that she'd been drawn into it, pushing the door open before she'd thought it through.

She walked to the wall opposite the counter and began casually looking at the pictures hanging there. They were jumbled together without any regard to medium or style: etchings, watercolours, sombre landscapes in oils, jolly contemporary silk screen prints. Most were small and there was a lot of detail. An etching of a castle on a river bank – no, it was an old town within broken walls – invited the eye into its perspective and shadows. 'Caer Llion, the old city' read the inscription in scratchy copperplate.

Goff would like that. Though he might already have a copy; it could well be one of the prints on the walls of his middle room. She could maybe get it for Gwyn then. He was certainly receptive to old Welsh things right now.

The past two days, he'd been full of the vigour of writing again. He wouldn't tell her much about what it was, only saying 'More of the same. Goff's guff', but he kept singing so she knew it was going well. He didn't write all the time – just in snatched half hours here and there. The rest of the time he was being energetic about their wedding party, for which he'd hired the village hall.

Jane had looked doubtfully at the oblong building, stuck all over with ornamental grit on the outside and bare as a barn inside. But Gwyn had insisted that he'd been to some bloody good parties there and she should trust him and wait and see. Since then he'd been spending his time on the phone to the caterers and the wine merchants (wine merchants? The name conjured up visions of hogsheads and flagons of mead, and Jane was disappointed when it turned out to be a very ordinary liquor store), and taking Jane into Cardiff to look at decorations and candles and sprigs of holly.

This wedding party meant something very important to Gwyn. He refused to invite his parents or even to contact them but, as if in compensation, he seemed determined to turn the wedding into a major production. Jane held her tongue. It was disconcerting to be swept along like this, but quite exciting. Gwyn had been a fantastic lover since they'd been here: the sex was as explosive now as it had been in the very first weeks, and somehow more stirring.

Gwyn seemed high with energy, in bed and out. At this moment, he was at the town hall sorting out some last-minute problems with the marriage licence. He'd sent her off to go home ahead of him, saying that she looked tired. Jane suspected that he wanted her out of the way so he could settle some accounts: she was sure this wedding must be costing more than he'd told her. But she was tired, it was true. She was still being bothered by memories of Renoxia; they bobbed along at the edge of her mind throughout the days, distracting her, and then they invaded her dreams at night. Was it the memories themselves that made her tired or the fact that she was keeping them from Gwyn?

There was no reason to be secretive about these nostalgia attacks. There was just no reason to mention them, either. Maybe she'd get some sleep before they went out tonight. She wasn't at all sure about these separate evenings Roy and Eirlys had arranged for them. A stag night for Gwyn and – for God's sakes – a *hen* night for her, with a bunch of women she'd never met? 'I know, I know,' Gwyn had said last night. 'It's not my sort of thing either. But they've arranged everything now. I can't really get us out of it, can I, not when we're guests in their house.'

Funny, screwed-up Gwyn. She'd buy him something from this shop, a gift, a private marriage token. The Caer Llion etching was sixty pounds with the frame. That was possible, for a start.

Jane wandered slowly towards the back of the shop, browsing among the pictures. The soft lighting and red painted walls were soothing. Outside, the rush hour was beginning: two buses lumbered down the narrow street, their windows brightly lit in the dark, and pulled in at the bus stop opposite, blocking the traffic. Passengers getting off clattered busily into the road, weaving between the halted cars. It was so different here from home: the shapes, the colours, the noises people made – everything.

It was the last picture on the wall, tucked into the corner. It was small, about twelve inches square, mounted on dull grey card and set into a black frame. The painting was crude at first sight, and pictorial: the figures lacked depth and their colours burned fiercely on the surface of the canvas.

It was an apocalyptic scene: the ships lay at crazy angles, masts broken and hulls splintering in the waves. Oxen and sheep were drowning. A line of chickens, tethered together, slipped beneath the sea, clawing one another and vainly thrashing their wings. People – scores of tiny people were being tossed into the spray and sucked under the wreckage. They were upside down, horizontal, falling with arms flung out. Their tunics and cloaks made tongues of colour against the white-blue of the angry sea.

The headland to the right of the harbour was sliding into the water, shards of rock and lumps of turf disintegrating. The only still part of the scene was the green spit of land on the left of the bay. It stuck out peacefully into the sea and on it a figure knelt, coaxing a fire to life. His hair hung straight down his back to his heels and his face was in profile, turned upwards to the dark shape in the sky.

The bird, twice as big as any of the ships and painted in inexorable detail, with every feather showing, hung at the very top of the painting, far above the scene of the wreck, and its spread wings and bent head were a strange benediction.

Jane was out on the street, breathing the smoky winter air. She was walking fast, heading for the floodlit castle. She didn't hesitate at the kerb of the main road, but strode across, dodging the traffic. Now she was on the same side as the castle itself. It spread its long wall out behind the landscaped grass, looking cared for and civilised. It was a very twentieth-century castle, well and truly tamed. Through the gateways in the wall the park breathed quietly in the darkness, untouched by streetlamps.

Jane went up and down the line of bus shelters, trying to understand the route maps. Why wasn't Graig on any of them? If you didn't already know the route you wanted, how the hell were you supposed to find out?

'That's the number seventy-one, dear,' said the woman with the hat. 'You want two stops along – there, by the lamppost.'

Of course, there was no mention of Graig on the shelter.

'Yes, this is the Graig bus,' said the man at the head of the line.

Jane pressed herself against the bus shelter wall and stared into the invisible depths of the park.

Haydn Phillips. A painter who had died nearly twenty years ago. The man in the shop hadn't been able to tell her much else, although he was perfectly willing to go and look it up in the catalogue for her. He was already turning to the wall shelf and reaching for the heavy ledger when she said she had to go.

He'd looked surprised and she knew she was behaving oddly, backing towards the door, but she couldn't help it. She kept glancing down the room at the picture and the more she glanced at it, the more it frightened her. At that distance it was only a square of colours, but she could make out the shape of the bird, and its image was so clear in her mind that she felt at any moment it might raise its head and look at her.

So she had stumbled backwards on to the door mat, set off a series of pings, and found her way out on to the street.

Where did she know that picture from? She did know it. She must know it. This was just like the poetry reading last semester, when she'd recognised Gwyn's poem. She had exactly the same feeling of fear and exhilaration, an excitement so intense she didn't know where it stopped and the terror began.

The bus engine roared, loud and smelly. Jane climbed up the steps behind the other passengers and had trouble finding the right money for her ticket. The lights inside the bus were glaringly bright. Silently she made up her mind. She knew where to go.

Goff didn't look surprised when he saw her standing alone on his doorstep. He glanced over her shoulder into the yard, but it was more a confirming look than an enquiring one. He opened the door wide.

'Hallo Jane, love. Come in out of the cold, there's a good girl.'

Jane followed him into the kitchen which was warm and steamy from the boiler.

'Would you like a cup of tea? You look frozen.'

'Yes please.'

'Gwyn rushing round, is he? I passed Roy in the village this morning, driving to work. He said Gwyn left all the arrangements to the last minute, as usual. Thrives on it, he does.'

'Yes. Well, I didn't foresee any of this either.'

Goff looked at her over the top of the tea caddy, a shrewd, assessing look.

'It's all come as a bit of a surprise to you, has it? Gwyn's a traditionalist at heart. He's a lad from the valleys and families are very important here. Gwyn's own family was no good for him. You're his family now.'

'And you. You brought him up. You gave him a home. I know he cares for you.'

'Good God, of course he does. I know that. Don't you worry about that now.'

Goff smiled and his face was suddenly transformed. Jane realised that he was very attractive; what had he been like when he was young?

'That's not why you're here, though, is it?' Goff filled the teapot and placed it on the small, formica-topped table by the boiler. Jane helped him carry the cups and saucers and milk, and sat down opposite him. 'What do you want to know?'

Jane didn't speak for a moment. She was tasting the flavour of complicity that was suddenly in the room. She had expected Goff to be taken aback by her visit, but instead he almost seemed to have been waiting for her.

She remembered what Gwyn had said about Goff's obsessive theories and interests, and how he had tried to use Gwyn's talents to his own ends. Be careful, she thought.

'We went into Cardiff this afternoon,' she said. 'And I went into an art gallery. I saw a picture there that really interested me and the man in the gallery said it was by a local artist. He couldn't tell me very much about him and I wondered if you knew him.'

Goff's gaze was level behind his glasses. Her conversational tone was totally unconvincing and she gave a half-smile to match. Goff lifted the teapot and poured with a gnarled, rock-steady hand.

'I might know him. But you'll have to tell me his name.'

'Oh, yes. Haydn Phillips.'

'Yes, I know him. That is, I knew him; he died, oh, fifteen, twenty years ago. Did Caradoc tell you that?'

'Caradoc? The man in the shop? Yes he did.'

'Well. I'm glad to hear it. Caradoc could tell you plenty about Haydn Phillips if he wanted to. But I suppose he wasn't sure who he was talking to.'

'Why? Is it confidential?'

'Not exactly. But it's important to those who are interested in it, and you don't go round broadcasting important things, do you? It's a shame to waste them on people who haven't got ears to hear.'

'Do I have to say a password?'

Goff's amused look niggled Jane. She wished she hadn't shown that she was offended. She shouldn't be offended anyway; there was nothing to get emotional about. Nothing.

'Oh don't be touchy, now. There's no need for that. If there was a password, I think you could guess it, anyway.'

Nothing.

'What was the name of this picture that interested you?'

'*Madoc's Dream*.'

'*Madoc's Dream*. Yes, I know it. The wreck in the harbour and the Mandan making his prayer-fire. You recognised the Mandan figure, did you?'

'I could see it was supposed to be a Native American.'

'Oh God, girl! Poor old Haydn wouldn't be thrilled to hear that. He thought he'd captured the very essence of the Mandan race, did Haydn. He went there you know, to your part of the world.'

'He went to North Dakota?'

'That hard to credit, is it? Well, I must admit, he didn't intend to go there. He went to Chicago first, won an art scholarship there in the late fifties. When his year was up he didn't come straight back but went off on a walkabout into the rural Mid-West. It was the Beat era, and Haydn Phillips was always up for anything like that. He and a couple of fellow artists from the Institute bought themselves a battered old car and drove round from state to state. They were taking a fair amount of drugs, and not the Jack Kerouac and Neal Cassady soft stuff either – cocaine. Well, they ended up in North Dakota.'

Goff looked intently down at the table, as if he were seeing the young men's route winding through the cups and saucers, stretching out over the fawn and white checks of the formica.

'Haydn knew about Madoc of course, and must have gone to Bismarck and whatever there was to see back in those days. Of course, they weren't interested in conserving the Indian heritage then. No, mon, the clearances were still going on.'

He leaned forward on his elbows, hunching his shoulders so that the dark red cardigan lapped his neck. It was a young man's gesture and sat oddly with the speckled, bristled skin and the hollow cheeks.

'Well, Haydn started painting in North Dakota. Very excited, he was, apparently; he believed that he had found a new technique, had an artistic breakthrough. He said it was all to do with the Mandan Indians but his friends thought it was more likely the cocaine. And they thought what he produced was a load of old rubbish and told him so. They had a falling out, whereupon the friends took the car back to Chicago and Haydn stayed in North Dakota.

'He came home three months later. He'd been deported for possessing drugs. He was in a terrible state, terrible. Thin as a stick, he was, and talking wildly, telling stories. There'd been a woman – well, you'd expect that with Haydn. He was a good-looking man and he always had a taste for the women – more than a taste, in fact, what you might call a healthy appetite.

'We got him into hospital and cleaned up. But he was never his old self again. He used to have black fits of rage – mind you, he'd always had a temper – and he was tortured by dreams and delusions. He had a spate of creativity in the months after he came out of hospital. He did, oh, about thirty paintings, all in the style of the one you saw. Well, it wasn't fashionable, you see. He couldn't get anyone to show them.'

Goff fell silent. Jane waited but he showed no sign of continuing.

'So what happened?'

'What happened? Nothing. He did one small show – guess where? Yes, at Huw's, the place you visited today. Huw was Caradoc's father, died last year. Well, Huw agreed to mount the show because, as a matter of fact, some of the paintings were very good. And they were all – interesting. But we knew very well that people wouldn't like them. Oh, we tried to prepare Haydn for it, but he wouldn't have it, would he?'

'The show was a failure?'

'Oh aye, a failure all right. The press sent people to cover it – a couple of the big boys from London came down, even. Haydn being deported had been in the papers, so there was a bit of notoriety to interest their readers. Well, first of all Haydn disappointed them by being relatively sober. And then when they asked him about the story behind the paintings, he wouldn't talk. He just clammed up, telling them to use their eyes. Finally, when the man from *Artsworld* magazine gave Haydn his honest opinion of them, Haydn started to cry. And that was the end of the show – Haydn crouched in a corner weeping his heart out and everyone shuffling out embarrassed.

'No one wrote about it, of course. And Haydn never painted again. And that was the end of *him*. Not being able to paint killed him. That, and the drink, and the cocaine when he could get it. He died in 1963.'

'What happened to his paintings?'

'He destroyed them just before he died. He must have known he was going. He burned the lot, except for *Madoc's Dream*. He left that to Huw.'

'Just that one. I wonder why?'

Goff laced his fingers on the table top and looked at Jane. It was a friendly, slightly sardonic look.

'Come off it, Jane. None of us really wants to vanish without trace. He left a clue.'

'A clue.' Jane wished Goff wouldn't look at her like that. An idea pressed into her mind, big and frightening. 'A clue to what? His past, in America?

'Oh aye. That's it. The past.'

Jane leaned her head against the wall. Goff had been doing all the talking but she felt as if she had given something away. The picture still hung in her mind, dwindled to a manageable size but very clear still. It was soothing, sitting here; she knew she should get up and leave, go back to the cottage and get ready for tonight, but she didn't want to.

'Tired, is it?' said Goff.

'Yes, a little. I have to go soon. Eirlys is taking me out on a hen night.'

Goff grimaced.

'Dear God, they are giving you the works, aren't they?' He paused, looked closely at her, then began to fidget. He unlaced his hands, picked up his empty cup and put it down again. When he spoke there were two spots of colour on his cheekbones. 'Look now, I'd like to give you and Gwyn a little present for your wedding,' he said. 'I hope you'll accept it. You're both going to need some time to yourselves after Saturday, and I'd like to give you a honeymoon. I know you haven't got much time, but a few days away from it all would do you good. There's a little island in the Bristol Channel, midway between the coasts of Wales and England, called Lundy. It's beautiful and quiet. Will you let me book you a few days there?'

Jane dressed carefully, trying to still the knocking of her heart against her chest. The fear and excitement were still with her, chasing the blood around her veins and making her eyes shine. Her hand trembled as she smoothed creases out of her black leggings.

She tried to keep her eyes focused on the objects to hand: the hairbrush, the mascara, her silver bracelet. Because when she lost concentration she would see it again in her mind's eye: the bird, every black feather distinct, hanging with its wings outspread and its head bent. And when she saw it, the terror and the exhilaration intensified.

Gwyn was in a fluster, bare chested and hunting for deodorant, cologne and a shirt. He was also complaining about their honeymoon-to-be on Lundy. He'd looked it up on a map and wasn't impressed: it was miles from anywhere; a dotted line showed that the only way of getting there was a ferry from North Devon, and Roy's *Good Holiday Guide* showed that the whole island was a bird reserve. Why in God's name did Goff want to send them there?

Jane kept quiet. 'A lovely, quiet place,' Goff had said. 'And interesting historically. It's where Madoc and his ten ships set off from, to seek out America.' Goff had spoken casually and their eyes had met briefly, much too briefly, before flickering away.

'I more or less accepted already,' she told Gwyn.

'Oh Jesus. Why?' Gwyn shook the bottle too vigorously and splashed cologne all over his bare chest. 'Oh shit, now I'm going to smell like a tart's breakfast.'

'Here,' said Jane, handing him a wet towel. 'Sponge it. Sweetheart, I'd really quite appreciate a few days quiet.'

'Mmm? What? You want to go to bird watcher's paradise?'

Gwyn looked up from his sponging. Jane, dressed in a black jumper and black leggings stood against the bedroom door. She looked stunning, all dark limbs and hair and pale skin. But she looked tired, too: her eyes had an insomniac glitter.

'Cariad, are you all right?'

'A little stressed out. I really wouldn't mind going to this island. You could write. I could relax.'

'True. That's true. But Lundy, for Christ's sake? Why not the Brecons or St David's? Oh all right, I give in. We'd better not seem ungrateful. I just hope you won't be disappointed. I'll ring him up, shall I, and say go ahead?'

'I already did.'

Gwyn put the towel down, slowly. 'That was a bit pre-emptive, wasn't it?'

Jane shrugged. 'Sorry. I didn't realise it would be an issue.'

'Cariad, is anything wrong? You do like it here, don't you?'

'Yes. I do. But it's a lot for me to take in — it's your home, not mine. I just think it would be good to get away after the wedding, just a day or two.'

She carefully suppressed the persuasive note in her voice.

Gwyn looked crestfallen.

'I see. Hell. I've been really selfish, haven't I? I'm sorry, lovely. Are you completely dreading tonight?'

'No.' Jane shook her head. 'I'm not. I really like Eirlys. I'm sure I'll like her friends too.'

Gwyn smiled and kissed her shoulder. 'Thank you.'

Jane turned away to hide her jubilation. They were going to Lundy. She didn't know why it pleased her so much. She didn't know, either, why she hadn't told Gwyn about the picture. Instead, she had simply said she'd dropped in on Goff in passing. Gwyn didn't seem to notice, or mind.

They were sitting at a long table, set in an alcove off the main bar. The walls were built of big, uneven chunks of stone and carved wooden spoons and iron stirrups hung on them, suspended on dark blue ribbons. The bar itself was low-ceilinged and white-plastered and warm with pink-shaded lights. Beneath the large crossbeam, decorated with a long line of plates, were several tables of young people. Over by the windows and the hanging brasses were older customers, the men in tweed jackets or wind-cheaters, the women in patterned jumpers and slacks. At the bar leaned more men.

Jane had been determined not to get drunk but she was, very. Eirlys and her six friends had made sure of that, lining up the drinks demurely but relentlessly in front of her and inventing toasts. They were an interesting group — Megan, Kate, Suzanne, what was the blonde's name? Janice, Dilys and whatsit. Ceri. Very different from Jane's friends at Brockham. Different from her pre-Brockham friends like Dina too, though they had more in common with Dina. They did all sorts of things, these women; Kate was at the Welsh Office in Cardiff, with Eirlys; Janice had a clothes shop — they called it a boutique — Suzanne and Dilys were at home with small children . . . they got on with life.

Jane's head was awash with alcohol and stories of Gwyn's childhood and teenage years. These were all old school-friends of his – that was why Eirlys had invited them – and all evening they had been reliving past events for her, regaling her with stories and explaining names, dates, places. It was a weird feeling, sitting here being the centre of attention. She felt like a queen, being fed with amusements by a court.

The court was raucous now. In the main bar, heads were turning to look at them. No one seemed to mind: people who peered into the alcove smiled and nodded and said hallo. Now a middle-aged woman in a green and blue tracksuit, worn with high heels and ear-rings, had come in and was chatting with Eirlys and Suzanne.

'Congratulations,' she said to Jane. She said it 'Con-grat-oo-lations', like everyone else had tonight. It sounded incongruously like a tidied up Chicago accent: Tom Jones meets the Sears Building. Each time she heard it, she found it harder not to laugh.

Something very odd was happening to her mind. It was slipping all over the place. From Wales to Chicago to Renoxia, to New York and Brockham. Scenes from her life, places she'd been recently and long ago were coming back and free associating. Her old school in Renoxia, the oblong building of brick and glass with the car-park in front. Herself eating lunch in the salad bar on Third and Twenty-seventh, when she had the job in the shipping office. The snow falling on the East River. The moving staircases in Bloomingdale's.

Bloomingdale's. That was the last time she'd felt like this: was it the bright lights and the bustle that made the connection? Maybe. But that wasn't all. Jane looked at the flushed, chattering faces around the long table and saw how far away from her they were. There was someone else, much closer, someone she couldn't see but whose presence she could feel like the light stroking of a hand.

I've missed you, she thought. Behind her eyes, deep in her mind, she felt someone smile.

It was too late for explanations, Jane thought. She was too drunk to bother about them. If she hadn't spent so much energy trying to rationalise it in the first place, she wouldn't be so tired now. She'd tried to forget what had happened at that reading and in that mirror; she'd tried and for a time she'd almost succeeded. But now it was back again. Caressing her, smiling into her mind. Hallo.

The barman was at the head of the table with a tray of drinks.

'The gentlemen at the bar would like to drink to the bride,' he said.

Jane's hen party cheered. Jane smiled and blushed and called thank you. They all raised their glasses to her – at the table, at the bar – shit, everyone at all the other tables too – and a thickset man with a v-necked sweater said 'To the bride. What's your name darling? Jane? To Jane from America, with the best of bloody luck!' Everyone laughed and drank and then someone started singing 'Here comes the bride'. They all joined in, and then at their table Ceri began singing, rather sardonically, 'We'll keep a welcome in the hillside.' They all joined in with that too, even Jane in the chorus.

My God, she felt happy; languorously, voluptuously happy, sitting here with her secret friend.

Eirlys had placed a walkman on the table and was asking Jane for a speech. She couldn't speak. Instead she knelt up on her chair and, to the laughing and clapping of the other women, sang a song. It was an old childhood song she hadn't even known she remembered, a folk song someone had taught her years ago. The unremembered words flowed off her tongue and filled her with happiness.

She didn't notice the smiles of the listening people stick, then fade, then finally give way to embarrassed, uneasy glances.

12

We've stopped for one last time before we reached Dreugyllt. It's only a mile away. The hills are behind us and the land has begun to slope down to the sea. You can feel it, even though the trees and the hillocks and ridges keep the coast from view.

All day we've been catching glimpses of the mountains ahead of us, great swells of land to the north, the heart of Owain Gwynedd's country. But after our midday meal we turned our horses west and since then we've been heading towards the sea.

Cadell is talking to Idris, his second in command. They are still mounted on their horses, with their spear carriers only a few feet away. Mounted men with toughened leather hauberks over their tunics are positioned in a circle, watching every opening from this glade. The green buds that sprinkle the tree branches are still tightly curled and it's easy to look through the latticework of branches and twigs and see if anyone's coming. Things have grown more dangerous in this country since last time I was here.

The woman Cadell brought with him, Eiluned, is holding out her cloak to shield me. She keeps darting her head over the top of it to look at me.

'Can I help you, Madam? I can get Marged to hold the cloak.'

'No, Eiluned, I'm nearly done.'

Madam. If only she knew how strange that sounds. This Eiluned is now my woman. She's the same age as me, probably a bit older, but you'd think she'd never seen anything like me before. She's been like this ever since Cadell first gave her to me in Cynfael. It makes me realise that there are stories about me;

while I've been waiting and longing in Cynfael, people in Madoc's court have been talking about me. Well, I mustn't let them down.

I've already snapped off some of the new green shoots from the coppice of hazel trees and rubbed and polished my teeth. I've combed out my hair and put it up again, under the head-dress. I was going to wear the head-dress Madoc bought me in Caer Llion but then I thought no, that's a Norman coif and I am a Welsh lady going to welcome home a Welsh prince. So I put on one of my normal head-dresses, the one Madoc once called 'angel wings'. Under it my hair is smooth and coiled: last night, when we stopped in the little tref in Dyfi, I bathed in the water of a spring pool.

There it was that the woman of the kindred gave me these nets. She approached while I bathed: I saw her before Eiluned or little Marged did, and I was opening my mouth to shout when she put a finger to her lips and raised her other hand. She was holding something dark and soft. As she came closer round the grassy rocks I saw that it was netting, made with fine twine and dyed grey-black, the same colour as the water in the pool. Silently, she shook out the nets: there were two small ones, the size you use for salmon.

Just then, Marged saw the woman and jumped up, shouting to shoo her away. But I called for her to be quiet and beckoned the woman closer. She wasn't old – about the age of my Mam – and her face was rosy and plump. She squatted at the side of the pool. The icy cold water was chilling me, but I stayed low in it, so my breasts were hidden from anyone else who might be spying, and reached my hands for her nets.

'What are these, mistress?'

'Salmon nets, they are, girl. You can see.'

Girl. As Madoc's lady, I should have told her not to call me that but I didn't.

'Why have you brought them here?'

'You can use them. The nets that catch the salmon in the deep pools catch the man.'

'I've caught my man,' I said, very low, so Eiluned and Marged couldn't hear.

'Keep him caught, girl. Tangle him closer and closer to you.

You've got a long way to go with him, you a girl from the kindred and him a prince.'

'What do I do with them?' I asked. The cold of the water was soaking into my bones and my teeth, playing tunes on them.

> ' "When you clothe your legs in nets
> Your man on you a son begets
> And all his other debts, forgets." '

She chanted it sing-song and quiet, her hands, red and dimpled, stroking the webbing.

'What can I give you for them?' I asked her.

She nodded her head and smiled.

'Remember us, girl, that's all. Here in this bro. There's bad times starting. Remember us.'

And now, screened by Eiluned's cloak, I've nearly finished. It's not easy, winding fishing nets round your legs, but now I've managed. The fine dark web is wrapped around each leg and fastened with tiny lengths of twine the woman gave me. The nets cling from my thighs all the way down over my knees and my calves, encasing my feet like soft slippers. They feel harsh and silky at once on my skin. I straighten up and look down at them, holding my dress high in front. My back is turned to Eiluned and she can't see what I'm doing, no matter how much she strains her neck. I drop my skirts back down to cover the nets and turn to her.

'I'm ready. You can put your cloak back on.'

She glances up and down me, trying to see what it is I've done, and her eyes halt on my feet. She stares and blushes. Then she hurries Marged away back on to her stocky little horse. She doesn't know what to make of me, Eiluned.

We're out of the trees now, riding across hillocks covered with long grasses. The armed men are riding ahead of us and behind us, and there are two bowmen several hundred yards out on either side of us, where they can keep an eye on the land around.

It's usual now, Cadell says. Madoc's got no quarrel with anyone yet, but for months there's been raiding going on between his brothers, vicious, unpredictable raiding with no quarter given. Before, Owain has always interfered, sooner or later, in his sons' quarrels. But now he has his own problems with the English king and they say he's sick. Madoc's men at arms put a guard on Dreugyllt even before his ship returned.

The sky and the land are opening out. We are very near the coast. And there it is: suddenly appearing over the next rise in the land, less than half a mile from us, the stronghold stands grey on its mound, and around it is what looks like a temporary camp, with huts and tents, horses and groups of men, prickly with spears.

I stare wordlessly at Cadell and my heart is thudding, shaking my ribs. Dreugyllt has been attacked. But Cadell shows no alarm. Hasn't he seen?

'Cadell – those soldiers! Those men. Is Dreugyllt under attack?'

I've reined in Siani, without thinking. Cadell has to pull his horse up too, as he turns to look again, sharply this time, at Dreugyllt. He smiles and shakes his head.

'No my lady,' he says, his round face creasing with amusement. 'They're Madoc's men and Rhiryd's. Rhiryd has sent over some of his warband by ship, to help Madoc defend his base if need be.'

So much protection. When we were raided in Cynfael for the swine we just had our own kindred. We were hidden in the houses, but we could hear the fighting – the yelling and the scraping noises of the swords, the rolling noise of the horses and men meeting, and the angry, angry screams of pain.

Yet these defences are on a bigger scale than anything I've imagined. The danger must be so much more terrible, that Madoc has to muster all these men.

'What are they doing?' I say, squinting at the activity: there's so much of it, people are carrying things, digging, measuring, heaving, and now I can see that the things I thought were slings and war engines are something else – large frames of wood, on wheels.

'They're digging a moat,' says Cadell. He glances at me then, and his lashes fall over his brown eyes. 'And they're working on a new ship.'

'A new one? Already?'

'Madoc is a great seafarer now.'

156

I know. I heard it from other people, Cadell, before you came to the valley five nights ago. The news has been travelling through the cantrefi. Madoc sailed his ship far, far west and raided a great island, bringing back spoils and prisoners.

Cast your nets over the seas, I told him. That was sixteen months ago, and now, on this cold sunny afternoon, with the green only just creeping through the bare clifftop coppices and primroses edging the track, I'm riding to meet him again.

As we approach across the meadows a detachment of men rides up. Our front riders trot forward to meet them, their spears held out to show the token tied to them: holly leaves twined in a circlet on a dark blue background, and studded with scarlet berries. This is Madoc's mark, his standard. It's been invented since his return, Cadell told me, in answer to the marks which his warring brothers have chosen – a fighting lizard, a wolf, an eagle. Cadell says that his brothers' marks are fearsome. Madoc's is terrible too: the holly leaves have sharp edges and the berries are like drops of blood.

The guards recognise their own men and part to ride alongside as escort. They're all gazing at me as I ride up by Cadell's side. Their eyes are avid and interested, staring at my face, glancing fascinated and sidelong at my feet. I return their looks, ready to meet any challenge, but there's something odd and sheepish about this curiosity. For a minute I can't understand it and then I realise what it is – they're being careful not to offend me. These men at arms are showing me respect.

We are close to the castle now, underneath the thick wooden walls, built in a circle to enclose the two open spaces, the baileys. Now we're so close it's no longer possible to see the ramparts of the stone hall rising from the centre. The noise of the men digging the moat is deafening. Cadell tries to shout above it but I can't hear him, so he gestures with his hand, round to the entrance of the castle. There is a wide ramp still undug in front of the entrance and the huge wooden doors stand open, with armed men on either side. They salute Cadell as we ride past them, under the walls and into the outer bailey.

The wooden walls soar above my head, making the sky a far-off blue thing. There he is. Across the bailey, in front of the entrance to the hall, with three men around him. My lord; my husband. Madoc.

His skin is brown from the sea winds and he's grown broader and deeper in the chest. He's listening to the man in the dark red cloak with the beard; he's standing very straight, his head tipped back and his right hand is playing with his sword, a restless, repetitive movement.

He's wearing a cloak of dark green with a blue pattern woven over the shoulders and a short woollen tunic.

He glances away from the bearded man and sees us. For a long moment he doesn't move a muscle. Cadell is swinging down from his horse and reaching up to help me down from mine, and the men are coming forward to lead our mounts away. There's a fuss of motion around and in front of us but I'm looking through it, to the young man who swore himself to me in Caer Llion, who held me in his arms on the banks of the Usk and said he was mine.

He's moved away from the other three men now and is standing directly ahead of me, waiting. What is he thinking? It's been so long; am I the way he remembered me? I'm too far away to see the expression in his eyes.

Cadell is walking me forward. The first few steps are terrible, but then the fear falls away and all I want is to reach him, to be with him. I step carefully across the bailey, feeling the nets press into my soles.

Madoc watches me come and his eyes are wide, like a boy's.

I stop in front of him and slowly sink on to my knees. I don't take my eyes off his.

I don't speak, nor does Cadell. Madoc and I are holding each other's eyes, not able to break the gaze.

'Madam,' he says finally. There's familiar his voice is, that guttural resonance. 'Your lord welcomes you.'

'My lord. I salute your return, in such triumph.'

He takes my hands and raises me to my feet. Then his hands are on my face and he kisses me welcome. We both gasp as our mouths touch and for a second press together. But we're not children any more. We draw apart (Duw, it feels like tearing my own skin) and Madoc turns to the three men behind him.

'This is your lady, the mistress of Dreugyllt,' he says. 'Ceinwen Maelgwyn of Cynfael.'

The bearded man bows, so does the second man, and I realise that it's Madoc's man at arms and adviser, red-haired Owain. The third man is standing a bit apart from them and now I look at him my throat tightens, making it hard to breathe. He's dark-skinned, as dark as men who've spent all their lives at sea but his skin isn't weathered, it's smooth and has a sheen on it. His face is bony and his eyes are long and flat. He's wearing a normal cloak, but under it his tunic is made from a hide I don't recognise and is threaded with feathers and tiny animal pelts. His hair hangs down his back to his knees, as black and straight as a horse's tail.

When he bows, he looks in my eyes.

'This is Arun, Rhiryd's man at arms, come to help us,' says Madoc. 'And my man Owain, you remember him.' I hold out my hand to Arun and he kisses it; Rhiryd's man at arms, probably a lord in his own right, kisses my hand. Owain does the same. Now there's only the other one left. Madoc draws me over to him and when he speaks next his voice is deep with pride. 'And this is my prisoner and my friend – I brought him back from the Island of the Great Sea. We call him Glesig Dog.'

I hesitate but Madoc lifts my hand and carries it to the dark man's lips: quickly he touches my hand with his mouth. I turn to Madoc: he's looking intently from the stranger to me and his eyes are bright with some secret satisfaction. Well Mararcd, you saw true. But who is this man?

The stranger raises his head and looks straight at me again. His eyes are long and very dark brown, much darker than mine. I can see he's thinking but I can't tell what and for some reason I want to smile.

The presentations are over. Madoc is replacing my hand gently at my side and telling Eiluned to show me to my chamber. He will come to me when he has finished his business.

Reluctant I am, to let his hand go. And he seems to be loath to take it away: it slips from mine slowly, his fingers brushing my wrist. I look up at the stone hall towering above me and then I follow Eiluned in through the great open door.

So this is a lady's chamber. It's almost as big as our whole house in Cynfael but squarer and higher. When I came to Dreugyllt before there was nothing where this room is, just air. Now there are stone walls with a window high up to let in light and fresh rushes spread ankle deep on the floor. A cloth woven out of different coloured threads hangs on the wall: it shows a man with a too-big head, a ship and a woman who looks tall and fierce, like a warrior queen. The chief colours are dark blue and green and the cloth has holly leaves woven round its edge, studded with scarlet berries.

'It's a gorgeous arras, isn't it Madam?' Eiluned says. 'Prince Madoc had the best weaver in Gwynedd make it, while he was at sea. Mind you,' she goes on, 'Illtyd the Loom's never seen you my lady, so he had to make you from hearsay.'

The woman's face is bold and nothing like mine. Her lips are too thin and her eyes are proud and angry. Yet I keep looking at her. There's something there I seem to know, just as I know something in the face of Madoc's prisoner.

And his friend, he said. That means that he'll be my friend too. In Marared's seeing, we touched hands. And Madoc sang. Duw, I wish I could remember it more clearly.

I've sent Eiluned away. I need to be quiet and think. I'm sitting on the low stool at the foot of the wide mattress, our marriage bed. Thinking.

There's footsteps on the stairs, footsteps growing faster as they leave the hall behind. There's the sound of uneven breathing, the leather curtain is pulled aside and Prince Madoc runs into the room.

He stops in front of me, laughing, and I jump up from the stool into his arms.

'Mother of God,' he keeps saying. 'Ceinwen. I love you. I've loved you every day since I left you. I've wanted you. Mother of God. The things I did for you. I've done so many things for you, Ceinwen.'

'My love, my lord, my prince,' I say, sometimes gently, sometimes exultantly. 'My love. My lord. My great prince.'

My great prince is laughing like a boy and tugging at my hair and my breasts, trying to get them free from my clothes. Duw, I love him.

'God, my love, I've got to have you,' he says.

'Tell me about what you did on the seas,' I say.

'Later. I'll tell you later.'

'No, tell me now. Tell me and love me at the same time.'

He groans happily, releasing my breasts from my dress and nuzzling them.

'I sailed west, further west than anyone's ever been.' He kisses the base of my neck and throat. 'I boarded a Norseman's ship off the little northern isles and killed a tenth of his men before taking tribute.' He licks the swell of my breasts.

I imagine the ransacked ship and the blood of the dying men and don't let myself shudder.

'And then?'

'We were nearly becalmed in a sea full of weeds, that pulled us off course. It took us four days to navigate a path through the weeds – floating islands of terrible strong weeds that clung to the hull.'

He plunges his hands down between my breasts to my stomach.

'And then? The country you found, the great island?'

'Such a great island, Ceinwen. The coast went on and on, too far to follow. And the heat, and the strange tall birds and sea creatures in the shallows.'

I draw up his hands and loosen my dress, letting it fall limp so it bares all the top half of my body. He bites his lip.

'And the men?'

'The men wear no clothes but have silver and gold body plates and are the most skilled, fearless fighters.' Madoc is laughing and talking in gasps. He stretches out his hands to me again but I still them.

'And the women?'

'The women wear no clothes either! They're well protected by the men. In raids they're taken by the winning side and they're looked after well.'

Slowly, I am gathering my skirts in my hands.

'Are they beautiful?'

Madoc grins, teasing.

'Some of them.'

'What about your prisoner? Has he brought a woman with him?'

'Glesig Dog? Dear God, no. We picked him up several months' journey away from his home. Far from his kindred and without protection from any warband. Glesig Dog's brought nothing with him.' Madoc pauses and comes closer. 'Perhaps you'll have to find a wife for him.'

'Are there any beautiful enough to match his countrywomen, though?' I say.

I lift my skirts a few inches and reveal my feet in their strange webbing. Madoc gazes at them and gives a short, breathless laugh. He puts his hands on my skirts. He lifts them further, drawing them slowly up over my thighs and my secret hair. White and black my body gleams in the dimness of the shadowed room, visible to Madoc but kept from him. His smile is full of delight.

I feel my own smile grow strong as I stretch out my hands. 'Madoc, touch me.'

He leaps forward and seizes my thighs, tumbling me back down on to the bed and searching for me through the netting. His eyes are full of passion and happiness. I laugh out loud.

'I'm your prince,' he says seriously. 'You're not allowed to tease me. I've cast my net over you forever.'

As he touches me through the net, the first touch after so many months, I close my eyes and smile.

How I love him.

13

The morning was white when Jane opened her eyes on it. She struggled to focus, forced down three of the paracetamol tablets Eirlys had left by the bed and sank back into sleep.

Once more Jane awoke, this time with a smile on her lips and a laugh stopped somewhere in her throat. She lay still for a while, looking at the ceiling, and allowed the feelings to linger in her mind.

Jane turned on to her side and put her arm round Gwyn. She lay like that for a while, curled around his body, and watched the curtains flutter in the cold air that blew in through the window. Eventually she got up, closed the window and padded shivering through to the bathroom. In the shower she let the inadequate trickles of water play on her body and tried to think.

The paracetamol had taken the edge off her headache and left her with a sensation of pulpy weakness. She struggled to overcome it and concentrate.

Her dreams, lovely, enticing, voluptuous, eluded her. She couldn't remember more than a few snippets of them, impressions of colour and depth, but the feeling of them still hung round her. It distracted her from her task.

Be logical.

Jane knew there were connections to be made, between last night's half-remembered dreams and the business with the picture in the gallery.

She knew that somehow the painting and the talk with Goff had been triggers.

But for what? For the Bloomingdale's hallucination to return? Yes.

It wasn't the same, though. The Bloomingdale's hallucination was a visual one; last night's was harder to describe – it was non-specific, something between a voice and a touch.

But it was the same woman. I recognised her instantly.

Jane, drying herself, pulled the towel closer round her, hugging herself. She had a sick feeling low in her stomach – fear – but it was a nerved-up, exciting kind of fear, shot through with adrenaline. And she couldn't quite push down the sensation of pleasure which bubbled away somewhere deep inside her, a remnant of her dreams.

After all, she had wanted to dream again.

She jumped when she saw Eirlys in the kitchen. She was sitting at the table, a folded newspaper in front of her.

'Hallo. I thought you were at work.'

Eirlys smiled.

'I thought I'd go in late this morning. I had one or two things I wanted to do, you see.'

Jane glanced round the kitchen. As usual, it was immaculate and there was no sign that Eirlys had been working on anything. She'd heard no telephone conversations or doors opening and closing.

'I hope you're not feeling too poorly. Did you take the paracet-amol?'

'Yes thanks.'

'Have some orange juice. It's freshly squeezed this morning.'

Eirlys got up and reached for the glass jug on the clean white surface. She poured Jane a long glass of it.

'We shouldn't have given you so much to drink. It was naughty of us.'

Jane let herself gently down into a chair and sipped. Orange juice: it was what Gail had bought her after the time in Bloomingdale's. Eirlys's face didn't have its usual composure; there was a trace of unease in the hazel eyes.

'Did I do something awful?' Jane asked warily.

'Oh no, nothing like that. But you got – well, very groggy after those fellows bought us the drinks.'

'Mm. I don't recall anything much after that except giving a speech and going home.'

'A speech?'

Eirlys was very still, watching Jane with her chin propped on her hand. She wore a very good watch, fine but businesslike with a gold strap.

'I did give a speech, didn't I?'

'Not exactly. You sang a song.'

'What? Oh Jesus. I have no voice. God, that must have been so embarrassing.'

Eirlys nibbled on her little finger.

'No-o-o,' she said, giving the world a multi-syllabic Welsh intonation. 'It wasn't embarrassing. But it did give everyone quite a shock.'

'Why?'

Jane was beginning to feel cold. Eirlys was going to tell her something and she didn't know if she wanted to hear it.

'It wasn't like our kind of singing. It was more like yodelling, in a strange language. Very powerful. Quite bloodcurdling, it was.'

Jane stared at her. She didn't know what to think. Yodelling? Was this a joke?

'I've never yodelled,' she said. 'And I'm a terrible linguist. I don't know any other language except tourist Spanish.'

'I'll play it for you,' said Eirlys. 'I've got it on tape, on the walkman. I turned it on when we were toasting.'

She led the way into the living room. Jane noticed that the walkman was already lying on the glass coffee table; Eirlys must have been playing it back already this morning.

'Where's Gwyn?' Eirlys asked suddenly.

'Asleep.'

'Oh. Well, sit down and have a listen. See if you recognise it.'

Jane placed her glass of orange juice down on one of the cork coasters Eirlys kept on every surface. She sat back on the sofa and linked her arms around her knees. She had a curious instinct to put something between her and the little metal machine, to protect herself.

Eirlys pressed a button – Jane noticed she didn't need to find the right place on the tape – and as the sounds hit the air, her eyes met Jane's, full of frank curiosity.

Jane clasped her knees and stared at the flowers and vines of the sofa fabric. At some point Eirlys had gone upstairs and Jane was now alone with the high, insistent voice, hers and not hers, that thrummed with such terrible, distorted passion. As the sounds died away into an unnatural silence, she leaned forward and pressed the rewind button yet again.

Eirlys was busy upstairs getting herself ready for work. Jane hunched into herself on the sofa, pressing the edges of her teeth together to stop them chattering. She knew that Eirlys hadn't been fooled by her smile and her shrug; they'd both heard the uncontrolled note in her voice when she'd said 'How weird. Interesting, isn't it?' but at least Eirlys had left her alone.

'If you're sure you're all right. I thought I'd better wait and make sure.'

She wasn't all right: how could she be all right, hearing this savage noise that was her own voice? It tore into her, plucking at her viscera like guitar strings. The incomprehensible syllables spilled out, catching one another up into a rhythm that was almost a melody. The song, the chant – it was really almost a keening – was shockingly, abandonedly passionate.

That was what set it apart from the others she'd heard. But otherwise it was a sound she knew: it took her back to the nights of her fifteenth year and the broken signs over the bars on Toller Street, the smell of the abandoned cars in the lot and the lighted trailer windows dotting the dark lake-shore.

Jane had never spoken a word of the Mandan language. She could swear, though, she knew as surely as she knew her own name, that she was hearing it again now.

Jane had left a message on the kitchen table, telling Gwyn she'd gone out. She couldn't bear to sit in the house with that tape any longer; she didn't want to be tempted to play it again. The tape was in her pocket now. She couldn't risk leaving it for Gwyn to find and, idly curious, switch on.

She paused in the curve of the lane and looked down over the valley. The winter hedges and trees were a tangle of green and brown, leading the eye down to the river which flowed quietly beneath the bridge. She had to try and unscramble her mind. There were too many things in it, signals relentlessly registering, jamming the receptors. There was too much going on, too much to try to understand.

This morning, she had been half-way to accepting the presence of the unknown woman. She had walked downstairs with the pleasures of the night before still tickling her mind and she had known, softened as she was by hangover and intimacy, that she would no longer deny it. It might be a manifestation of her love for Gwyn, it might be a delusion, it might be something elemental and female in her responding to the idea of marriage, but she had decided that she wasn't going to fight it.

And then, waiting for her in the living room before she could work out any of the connections between this woman and the things Goff had told her yesterday, was that song. The violence of it still clanged in her inner ear. She had sung a song she didn't know she knew, in a language she had only ever heard in passing. She had sung it in the presence of a roomful of people, astonishing and embarrassing them all with her abandon.

And she had sung it under the influence of the woman. She had thought her so friendly, loving almost, but now in the baldness of the morning she heard what the woman had made her do. She had dragged out of the depths of Jane's past the unhappiest, most disturbing associations. If this woman were a part of Jane's pysche, she was not, after all, a benevolent part.

Jane ran back up the short path and fitted the key into the front door. Gwyn wasn't in the living room, nor in the kitchen. Surely he wasn't still in bed?

The bedroom was untidy and empty. Gwyn's towel hung over the radiator and his shoes were gone. Jane realised that the house felt deserted.

Back downstairs she found an addition to her note on the kitchen table: 'Near death. Gone for life support.' He had obviously been trying to work: his blue folder was beside the note, with his usual collections of pens and pencils. Gwyn always carried a bunch of writing implements, just in case the first two or three should fail him at the same moment.

Jane opened the folder. Gwyn had never made an issue of his privacy; he had never needed to. Jane had always assumed, with the exaggerated respect of the non-writer for the writer, that she should keep her distance unless invited. Now she felt that she needed to know what he was writing.

She slid out the sheaf of loose papers, covered with Gwyn's writing and doodles. She saw at once that many of the papers were heavily scored with crossings out: whole blocks of text had been scribbled over and then obsessively filled in with squares of solid ink. These were the evidence of Gwyn's 'wall' during their last weeks in America.

Flicking through, she found what she was looking for: a sheet with clean handwritten lines neatly centred. It was the poem Gwyn had read in the Russell Room. Her eyes scanned it swiftly, scarcely resting on it but words leapt out at her, bringing the scene back, and the rhythm seemed to feed itself into her heart-beat.

Written above the poem, in different-coloured ink, was the number: '1'.

Her eye fell on another sheet near the top of the pile. It was less clean but still legible. The lines written on it stopped in mid-sentence, obviously unfinished, and above it, in the same dark blue ink as the first number, was written '2'.

The waters are bright blue, said the voice. Blue as a speedwell. And full of ships.

The men are swarming up the rigging, checking the masts. Sacks of grain are being carried across the planks on to the decks. There is blood on the quaystones where the hunters are carving up the stag-meat, and people keep crossing from the shore to the ships and back again, touching their possessions, saying goodbye.

From here in the prow of the first ship I can see them all. I can see the crowds on the headland, their cloaks and hair blowing in the breeze as they wait to see us off.

The masts sway as the waves take the ships. And through the masts, on the other side of the harbour, on the green spit of land . . .

* * *

Jane put the sheet down on the table, very carefully. Her stomach felt hollow like a drum.

'Hallo my darling. Christ, I feel bloody awful. How was last night?'

Gwyn leaned against the door jamb, pale and smiling sheepishly.

'It was – weird.'

'Oh? They didn't book you a male stripper or anything terrible, did they?'

'No, nothing like that. Gwyn, come and sit with me.'

'Just a second, I've got to get some of this into me.'

'What is it?'

'Shandy. The best pick-me-up when you're like this. Beer and lemonade, honestly, it works wonders.'

'No thanks. I've had Eirlys's fresh orange juice.'

'So have I. It didn't work, though. I'm just not used to drinking like that any more – not dedicated, all night, blast-your-brain drinking. I must be turning American.'

Gwyn shouted the last sentences from the kitchen, where Jane could hear him pouring himself the shandy. He brought it back into the sitting room, walking unsteadily.

'Can I make it across the room? Yes, yes, look at him go.'

He flopped down beside her and groaned at the sudden movement.

'You'll never guess what I did when I got up. I actually tried to work.'

'Yes, I know. I saw your folder.'

'I must have been mad.'

'Gwyn, I hope you won't mind, but I read your new poem.'

Gwyn paused, his glass raised to his lips, and his face went very still.

'Oh. Well. Why did you do that?'

Jane searched his face. It was guarded, with the beginnings of a frown in his eyes.

'Some strange things have been going round in my mind. I've had some very odd experiences since we've been here. I was – I was anxious, and I wanted to know what you'd been working on.'

'Hmmm. I don't see the connection, sweetheart, really. Why should your experiences have anything to do with my writing? Anyway, what do you mean by "odd experiences"?'

There was a distinct edge to Gwyn's voice. Jane heard it and felt herself flush.

'I've had my hallucination again,' she said, looking straight into his eyes. 'The one I had in Bloomingdale's.'

'Cruella de Ville?'

'Don't call her that. She's not a cartoon character, she's a – an overwhelmingly powerful presence. She's real.'

'Real in your mind,' muttered Gwyn.

'She's in your poems too.'

'What the fuck do you mean?' Gwyn's head jerked up from the shandy glass.

'The narrator in both your new poems, she's the woman I see. I feel. I dreamed her last night. I recognise her voice, Gwyn.'

'Bollocks.'

Gwyn got up and walked heavily to the other end of the room. He stood with his back to her, leaning his forehead against the window.

Jane watched the silhouette of his shoulders. She hadn't meant to say it so abruptly and challengingly. She realised how idiotic it had sounded.

'Please listen,' she said quietly. She gathered her strength and concentrated on pouring it into her voice; she must keep things level and calm

'The woman isn't the only thing I recognise. The harbour you describe in your second poem, I know what it looks like. There's a green headland on the right-hand side and a flat green spit of land on the left. There are ten ships at anchor, with their sails being unfurled. They're full of people and animals – you mention cows and stags in the poem, but I know that there are chickens on the ships too. Chickens tethered together in a line. And – '

'Jesus Christ Jane!' Gwyn turned round to stare at her. His face was ghastly white. 'What are you doing?'

'There's a rational explanation for this,' she said hurriedly. She couldn't bear the way Gwyn was looking at her: with horror and fear, and with an unwilling recognition, as if he were a little boy and she some implacable adult about to inflict pain. 'This part's explicable. There's a painting in a shop in Cardiff which shows the scene. Or almost. It was painted by a man named Haydn Phillips, who Goff knew. The painting's called *Madoc's Dream*. But the thing is . . .'

Gwyn gave a strange sigh, half of relief, half of anguish.

'You've seen a painting,' he said. 'Jesus, is that what this is about? You've seen a painting.'

'That's not all. It wasn't quite the same as your poem. There was – '

'Don't,' he said, his eyes closed and his hands clutching his head, pressing the shandy glass against his temple, 'don't ever, ever try to mind-fuck me.'

There was a silence while the unfamiliar vehemence sank in to her ears.

'It's like Goff all over again. Fucking leeches fastening on me. I won't have it. I won't take it.'

Gwyn had turned slowly round to face her again. His forehead was gleaming faintly with sweat. The words Jane was going to say died in her mouth.

'I didn't mean it that way,' she said eventually. She tried but failed to think of a way to go on. 'I truly didn't mean that.'

Gwyn took a swig of his shandy.

'Didn't you?'

Jane sat very straight on the sofa. There was no way now that she could tell Gwyn about the wreckage in the painting, nor the Mandan whose face was so familiar. The tape in her hip pocket was digging in to her. She could play him that and tell him that she was frightened, ask for his comfort and his help. But his last words still sounded in her ear, light and cynical and bitterly hurtful.

'How dare you,' she said quietly and left the room.

They made up at tea time. Gwyn came into the bedroom and sat down on the bed, not quite touching her.

'I'm sorry,' he said. 'Please forgive me.'

He looked pale and vulnerable, his face uncertain what expression to take.

'You meant it about the leeches,' said Jane.

'Only at the time. Only for a second. I'm sorry.'

Jane looked at him bleakly. She didn't have the energy to talk about it. She'd been sitting here for hours, thinking, and she knew that the accusation was fair. She did feel herself drawn to meddle with his writing. She couldn't help it, it was like being hot in the summer and seeing a cool green lake where you weren't supposed to swim.

She felt ashamed and indecisive. Gwyn was so afraid of people interfering with his writing, it was the one thing she couldn't admit to him. So how should she make a start in confiding the rest? Everything began, she realised, with his poems.

'Please say something,' said Gwyn. 'Look, I'm sorry. It's being back here, I suppose. It brings back old feelings. And you said you'd spoken to Goff.'

The apprehension in his voice made her ache for him. Could she tell him?

'I went to see him yesterday evening, to ask about the painting.'

'Why?' Gwyn's face was strained. 'What was so special about it?'

Jane touched his cheek. No, she couldn't. She couldn't start talking about an ex-lover, not now.

'Oh, just because it was called *Madoc's Dream*, and he'd told me about Madoc.'

'You're not getting interested in that stuff, are you?'

Jane shook her head.

'Uhn uhn. One of us is enough.'

'One of us? What do you mean?'

She stared, opened her mouth to say well, your poem . . . then stopped. Gwyn had said he didn't know where the first poem had come from; and so far there had been no mention of Madoc in either poem. He didn't know yet — or else it really was a coincidence.

'Well, you've had a belly-full of it all, haven't you?' she said vaguely. 'Enough for both of us.'

Gwyn touched her leg gently.

'I'm sorry,' he said. 'I'm sorry I'm so touchy about my writing. I'll try not to be.' He took a paper bag out of his jacket pocket. 'Look, I've brought you a present.'

Jane pulled out the flat package: it was a pair of fishnet stockings, the mesh displayed in a little cellophane window in the packet.

'They're really going it down the Old Post these days,' said Gwyn. 'I thought, nothing's too exotic for my wife.'

Jane began to laugh. It was such a bizarre, unlikely choice. The sight of the criss-cross pattern did something funny to her.

'Don't cry, cariad,' said Gwyn. 'You don't have to wear them, honest. Dunno why I bought them, really. God alive, I think I must be losing my marbles.'

14

The hall is filled with people, all looking at me. From the foot of the steps to high table seems a long way and I walk quickly, swishing the rushes. The company is a blur in front of my eyes. No, not a blur — a sea: a shifting, lilting mass of people, their faces turned towards me. And here and there I recognise someone with a little burst like a wave breaking.

Eiluned takes me to a place on the bench one away from Madoc and now, as I greet Madoc and the stranger beside him, and sit down, I see that she and Marged have moved to sit a few places from me, near enough to come to my side quickly but too far away for me to be able to whisper to, if I needed to ask something. But then, I wouldn't ask Eiluned anyway. Her eyes are too sharp and curious on me; I didn't need Cadell to tell me that she's higher up in her kindred than I am in mine. And little Marged's a child, like Buddug.

The man between me and Madoc is our guest of honour, Llywelyn ap Senych. I received him when he arrived, late this afternoon — in the doorway of the hall, I welcomed him, my first duty as lady of Dreugyllt. Madoc has told me all about him: a powerful man is Llywelyn, the overlord of eight trefi and man at arms to the Lord Rhys. He is a kindred to Rhys — but then almost all the great men of the southern cantrefi are — and to Cuhelyn, as well. Cuhelyn, that young boy who married Rhiryd's sister. Llywelyn wasn't at Caer Llion with us, but he has heard of me.

He's quite a bit older than Madoc and has a hard face with bloodshot eyes. He is very courteous to me, and I'm trying to talk to him like a great lady. But there's nervous he makes me. I have to keep telling myself he isn't as high-ranking as Madoc and there's no need to feel afraid, but I do. I keep thinking of Cynfael and how men like Llywelyn gallop scornfully past us on their missions for the Lord Rhys, and don't even come into the tref to collect their tribute but send an underlord in for it.

And then I hear Madoc's voice and see his face turning towards me, leaning forward so he can peer past Llywelyn to look at me. That warms me up. And after a while I begin to enjoy it. Duw, who wouldn't? Here is a man who could send Hywel and Teilo and Bran and Elydyr Tewdr himself to shoe his horse for him, and he's paying respects to me.

Llywelyn is now making me a toast, in fact, to my beauty. Madoc says he'll have to drink it in a silver cup, and claps his shoulders, but his eyes are sharp on my face while this lord of Rhys's makes his toast. I look straight back at Madoc, letting him know he has no need to be jealous.

While they drink the wine, I drink in the feeling of it. The funny thing is, I want Mam to see me.

The talk is all about Ynys Llyr. The lords at the heart of the table were all on the voyage: Arun, Rhiryd's man, and Wenlyn and Owain and a young member of Madoc's kindred called Beuno. I realise now that I glance around that Bredmor and Cadell, who I'd have expected to be close to Madoc, are seated further away, leaving the central places to the voyagers. And I see too that Madoc is encouraging everyone to talk about Ynys Llyr for me and for Llywelyn. And talk they do.

They have named it Ynys Llyr, the Island of the Great Sea and the sun shines yellow and white on it the whole day long, every day. At noon, they say, it's too bright to see in the open and you have to hurry into the shade of the trees or to the edge of the swamp, where the bushes grow six feet tall and have thick long leaves.

They love to talk about it and they can go on for hours. From here I can watch Wenlyn's pretty face grow quite enthusiastic and even grumpy old Owain has got a shine in his watchful eyes. The people who stayed behind, like Bredmor and my lovely

Cadell, lean towards us and join in too – they've heard it so often that by now they can tell it as vividly as the others.

The terrain is of three kinds – white sand shores, thick, swampy forests with big curving rivers flowing through them, and – so the people of Ynys Llyr told them – mountains further inland. The people are dark-skinned and wear no clothes because it's so hot, but lots of ornaments and jewellery. They grow a type of corn taller than a man, whose grains are each as large as peas, and beans, and fruits. They have no swine or cattle but eat fish, great fanged lizards that live in the swamps and forest beasts. On the inland mountains there are stags.

The people have kindreds like us and they live in trefi which are very like ours, except that they make their houses from tree-branches and grasses rather than earth. The men have lots of wives and the great elders and lords have more wives than anyone else. But they each have one special wife.

'Rather like our own princes,' says Llywelyn to Madoc and everyone laughs except me. I see Cadell look at me; Madoc sees it too.

'But the special wife is very powerful,' he says, and I know that's for my ears. And I lift up my head and look at Madoc with my dark eyes and smile at him with my red lips.

I am beautiful. The dark blue silk robe shows the tops of my breasts and my white neck; my hair is under a dark blue head-dress, embroidered with holly leaves in green and red threads. Duw I stared, when Eiluned brought this dress out of the trunk in our room. Five dresses there are in there: each one chosen by Madoc for me to wear. Each one rich and beautiful and bought from the trade posts of the Mediterranean, as Madoc sailed his ship on the last stretch of the voyage home.

The nets the old woman gave me are tucked safely away now, under the grand dresses in the trunk. Her eyes would open wide if she could see me here.

I am learning fast. If you listen and watch, you learn. People tell you so much. From Llywelyn I've learned (without him knowing I learned it) that the sea called the Mediterranean is very blue and has no tides, and that the countries east of it are hot, with palaces built of pink and white stone with circular roofs, and the people there eat sticky sweetmeats. And across the seas to the north, the people of the northern islands drink cloudberry wine. The foreignness and the excitement of it all crowds my mind like the smoke from the fires and the flaring rushlights. I blink my eyes at the faces jostling the high table and try to get used to being a great lady.

There is one person here, mind, who is even more an outsider than me. And trying even harder to hide it.

The dark man with the arched cheekbones and the proud nose is sitting just below the voyaging lords, on Madoc's left. And as they go on describing Ynys Llyr and remembering, he joins in. It's strange to watch him, because he uses exactly the same movements as the others — he slaps his palms on the table, he leans across, he throws back his head to laugh, and yet the actions don't go with his face. Nor with his body. It's like watching one of the players who go round the monasteries at Easter representing the saints and the miracles.

He is popular, this dark man. At least, he's popular enough for a foreigner. There are many jokes and jibes being thrown at him about his country and he takes them well, and though some of the men around him are putting a lot of strength into their elbowings and clappings, no one is actually hurting him. There's one young man across the table from him who doesn't like him; his eyes go back again and again to the dark man's face and whenever he speaks to him it's with an angry sneer. The dark man sometimes pretends not to hear him, and sometimes answers briefly. I can't usually hear what's being said but just now I heard the dark man reply: 'Pink like yours.' I don't know what it means but everyone around them is shouting with laughter and the young man has gone red with rage but pretends to smile too.

Madoc has turned at the sound of that laughter and, now he sees that the dark man is in the middle of it, he smiles. It is an easy, happy smile, and it reminds me of when we rode from Cynfael to Caer Llion.

'Come here Glesig Dog,' he shouts. He waves to him and turns back to Llywelyn. 'You'll like this,' he says. 'This is my Islander. A clever one, keep your eye on him!'

As the dark man walks up to us, Madoc calls for a stool to be brought for him. The man is still wearing his odd tunic with animal pelts sewn on to it, and no cloak. But his hair is different from this afternoon: he's loosened it from its long tail and divided it into four plaits which fall in front of and behind his shoulder, down to his waist. His eyes are on me as he stops and bows and I can see that Madoc is right: he is clever.

'My lady wants to hear stories of your country, Glesig Dog,' says Madoc. Glesig Dog gives one deep nod, glancing at me from under his eyebrows. They are very black like Madoc's but long and curved. 'Ask him what you like, my lady,' says Madoc. 'He can speak quite well now. I taught him,' he adds to Llywelyn.

The dark man is waiting. He's young – about my age and Madoc's, I can see that, now I'm close to him and have time to look. The bones of his face are so pronounced that you think he's older at first, but his skin is young and his eyes are sharp and lively. And I think that now they're a little humorous too. It's as if he knows I'm not at ease playing the lady with him.

'You'll tell my lady anything she wants to know, won't you my friend?' says Madoc commandingly.

'By God, yes!' says the stranger, in the same voice.

I stare and then, when I realise Madoc is laughing, I laugh too. Llywelyn and everyone else do the same. The dark man sits on his stool looking innocent, which makes Madoc laugh even more gleefully. He shoots a look down the table at Owain, who's frowning into his cup of wine.

'Gently Glesig,' he says to him. He shakes his head, still chuckling. 'You've got to speak gently to your mistress.' He gives another wicked look at Owain. His eyes are shining: he's teasing, but whether it's Glesig or Owain or me, I don't know.

Glesig looks at me. He gives a quick smile. It was so fast it's gone by the time he looks back at Madoc.

'Yes, my lord,' he says, in a perfect imitation. There's gentle his voice is now, just like Madoc showed him. It's peculiar: he doesn't say the words quite right, they have a funny hollow sound.

'Ceinwen?' says Madoc. 'Go on my lady.'

Down the table, I can see everyone looking at me. They are waiting for me to say the right thing for the lady of the house, for Madoc's wife.

Glesig is looking at me too. For a second he seems the friendliest person in the great hall. An outsider, far from home, like me.

'Do you miss your country?' I ask.

There. That surprised him. He looks startled and interested, and – momentarily, as he gazes into my face – very very sad.

'Yes Ceinwen,' he says, in that gentle way.

There's a rumble of gasps and smothered guffaws and Madoc punches him on the arm and shouts happily, 'My lady, man. You've got to call her my lady. I'm the only one who can call her Ceinwen.'

In the leaping flame-light of the torch, Glesig Dog smiles. It is a bright, subtle smile and it makes him look splendid, like a king or a warrior, not a slave.

'My lady,' he says, smiling.

Oh, he isn't stupid, this Glesig. And I don't think he's very safe either.

'Ask him something else,' says Madoc.

'Who is king of your country?' I ask.

Glesig pauses. He seems to be thinking how to reply.

'Madoc ap Owain ap Gruffydd!' shouts someone from the far end of the table and everyone cheers. A flicker of relief shows in Glesig's black eyes. He didn't want to answer that one. Now Wenlyn is making a toast to Madoc's future fame, and the glory of Gwynedd, and Madoc is turning to Llywelyn and toasting the Lord Rhys, and Llywelyn toasts the joint glory of Gwynedd and Rhys's line and their future triumphs, and the talk turns back to politics. Glesig moves his stool back down the table: I watch him go, stool in hand, looking down on the honoured heads of Madoc's warband.

Marvellous it is, to walk out on the hall battlements in this early morning, with Madoc at my side. Marvellous and queer. Directly beneath us lies the outer bailey: it's crowded with traders and men at arms and people of the castle, many of them working at the benches and huts that lean against the palisade. On the other side of these protecting walls is the green of the clifftop, spread with fighting men and craftsmen and their families like harvest fruits on a platter.

Madoc was holding my hand as we climbed the stairs but he let go of it at the top. I know he wants to see me standing alone up there, and he wants the people to look up and see us both, together but independent. My Madoc wants me strong.

The wind blows my skirts and buffets my face. A fat gust takes my head-dress and tears it off, whirling it down and out across the half-dug moat, and my hair is whipped into dancing dark streams around my head. Madoc exclaims and steps towards me to steady me but I laugh. I look out at the clifftop, where some children have caught my head-dress and are waving it up at me, and at the outer bailey, where faces are turned up, and behind me at the inner bailey where the best horses are being exercised on one side and Eiluned and Marged are talking with a crowd of women on the other. I look to the other side of the castle and the grey-green sea. And I look back at Madoc and laugh again.

There's happy I am. Nearly a month has passed and I am settled now, here where I should be. Dreugyllt is my place; I belong here, with Madoc. Oh there's beauty in a feeling like this; more beauty than I've ever thought of.

'Great lady' is what Glesig Dog calls me. He pretends not to know it's funny, but he does. I can see it in his eyes. Dark, dark brown his eyes are; even darker than mine, and they glint and shine as he works things out. Always thinking, is Glesig.

Madoc's shoulder is where he's usually to be found. Madoc takes Glesig with him in almost everything – when he goes down to the shore to inspect the shipbuilding; when he rides out to meet the lords who come, at least one or two a week, to visit him and sit in conference with him and Arun in the great hall. Glesig is usually at these meetings as well.

But Glesig doesn't accompany Madoc when he rides out to the cantrefi to the north-east, visiting neighbouring lords, nor when Madoc goes to do his duty as settler of disputes in the people's courts in his own cantrefi, which edge the sea in a strip to the north of here.

At such times – like today – Glesig Dog stays in Dreugyllt and learns to handle the horses and to ride them better, taking lessons from Idris Stableman. And he talks to me. I can see him coming now – he has just come out of the stables, which are built against the walls of the inner bailey, furthest from the hall. He looks around and spots Marged and me here in the shelter of the tower;

I smile at him and watch as he comes quickly across, his animal pelt cloak swinging.

'Busy, great lady?' he says as he reaches me.

'Yes Glesig,' I say, ignoring Marged's giggle. She's sweet, Marged, and doesn't mean anything nasty by it. 'We're going to make a herb garden,' I say. 'Do you know what that is?'

'Herb? Yes, I know. It was one of the first words I learned. Herbs are plants with powers for change. Is it?'

'Yes, that's it. Do you have them on Ynys Llyr?'

Glesig nods his head graciously.

'Of course.'

Marged giggles again.

'Well, we're going to make a garden here so that the people of Dreugyllt don't have to go gathering them from the woods any more, or walking across the river to the friary to buy them from the brothers.'

'Poor brothers,' says Glesig. 'You'll take away their trade and make them angry. Is that wise?'

I laugh. Glesig is making fun of Owain: 'Is it wise?' Owain's always asking Madoc in that low, solemn voice of his.

'You'll have to ask Madoc when he gets back.' I say. 'He's expected soon.'

'With another of your great men.'

'Yes.'

From her group of kindred women, Eiluned bows to me and waves to Marged. Marged turns questioningly and I nod to her to go. Glesig and I watch her half-walk, half-scamper away, not wanting to be rude to me by hurrying off but not wanting to make Eiluned cross by dawdling either. Duw, I know Marged's privileged by good birth but I'm sure it's easier to grow up in one of the unimportant kindred, in some hidden little tref, like I did.

'She's yours, even if the other one isn't,' says Glesig.

I look at him nonplussed. He nods to where Marged is now being talked at by Eiluned. 'You're winning,' he says.

'There's no game, Glesig,' I say, trying to sound cold. But it's hard: he's sharp, this Glesig, and besides it pleases me to think he sees me as winning. 'I'm Madoc's lady,' I add, just in case he hasn't understood.

Of course he's understood. He nods, and his eyes meet mine without deference but with the clearness of a man seeing and respecting an equal.

'Madoc's winning too,' he says. 'But it's different for him. It's his game. He owns it.'

'What do you mean?' I ask.

He has this strange way, Glesig, of keeping his face very still, but you can see his thoughts moving in the little twitches of his eyebrows and at the corners of his wide mouth. Now there's a tiny tuck in the skin at the right-hand corner of his mouth, a half dimple coming and going.

'He's a prince,' says Glesig, looking at me full in the face. 'A prince in his country. I'm a prince but I'm a long way from my country. And you're a princess but you haven't got a country.'

I stare at him. He does look prince-like, standing with his head thrown back and the pelts fluttering on his tunic.

'You're a prince, Glesig?'

'Oh yes great lady. I'm a prince like you're a princess.'

He smiles wickedly, then laughs. I feel a wash of fear – this man knows I'm not a princess and can never be one. But there, that's stupid: everyone knows where I come from. There's nothing to hide.

And in a way, it's a relief to have someone look at me like this again: not with servility or fascination or dazzlement but a straight, bare look, like a friend.

'You wouldn't dare say that in front of Madoc,' I say, with just a hint of a threat in my tone.

Glesig shakes his head easily.

'I'm not going to say it in front of him. Why should I? We're the same, a lot the same, great lady. We know we have to make our own lives.'

'Ssh,' I say, as Cadell comes towards us. But Glesig is already turning to him and the expression on his face is the hearty, deferential one he always wears among Madoc's men at arms.

'My lord Madoc is just two valleys away,' Cadell calls. 'My lady, he's got his brother Dafydd and two of his father's men at arms with him. We'll have to prepare a royal welcome, quickly.'

'Go and see to the men in the hall,' I say to Cadell. 'I'll organise the women. Glesig, go to the gates and tell the men to raise the standards.'

As I turn from Glesig, he bows and I hear him whisper:

'Yes, the prince is winning them all.'

'Let's hope so, for our sake,' I reply.

It's a gentler season than when I arrived. The trees are in leaf further inland and along these cliffs the hedges are green and frothy with tiny pink flowers. There's new kinds of bird-song to be heard now – thrush and greenfinch and wagtail appear on the battlements, beside the gulls and cormorants.

My herb garden is dug and walled now and I'm starting to plant it. I've already been two hours this morning, sorting through the young plants the brothers have sent us. The sun is shining thin but almost warm on my shoulders; my bleeding hasn't come this month . . .

Did the nets work? Have I got Madoc's son in me, already? I want to give him a son for Dreugyllt, a son for me and Madoc. But just like Madoc isn't telling me of his plans until he's sure of them, I'm not telling him of my secret hope.

There are two nuthatches here in the herb garden, and a chough, looking comical with its fat black body and startling red feet. Marged and I have been planting all morning: thyme and rue, fennel, sorrel, marjoram, rosemary. Here in the inner bailey, when I look at the newly turned earth and at the kitchen building in front of us, I can imagine this garden in high summer, busy with growth and fragrant. But I only have to glance up to see the men on the battlements, and one look behind me and I see the horses tethered to the walls and kept three in one stall and of course the men, here as they are everywhere, talking and arguing.

No one expects the peace to hold. It's not peace anyway: out in the unprotected trefi there are raids going on. Two days ago one of Madoc's townships was raided by kindred from his brother Gruffydd's territory. The news was brought by a party of men from Rhodri, the brother closest to Madoc. Madoc and I were in the hall with Arun and Llywelyn ap Senych, who is back on another visit.

When Rhodri's men panted out their message, there was a dead silence for a few seconds. Then the men at arms in the hall began swearing and shouting.

'We'll ride down on them!' one of the men said. 'Prince, let's ride down on the kindred and smash them.'

'On Gruffydd,' someone else said.

'Yes, on Gruffydd!'

'On Gruffydd. Let's attack Dolgellau!'

Madoc banged the table furiously. He'd gone white.

'No,' he said loudly. He said it again, quieter and more commanding this time. 'No. I'm not being provoked into attacking Gruffydd. Not yet. We're not ready.'

'But lord,' said Owain. He had appeared at the opposite side of the table from Madoc – he does this, Owain, when the moment matters. 'Gruffydd has raided your people. How are you going to answer him?'

Owain's voice was carefully controlled and his expression was grim. He was reminding Madoc of his duties. Madoc looked across the table at him and his face didn't show any response.

'We'll send a deputation at once, to demand galanas.'

'A deputation? But surely . . .' this was Llywelyn, who looked startled.

'With fifty men at arms,' said Madoc. 'And a priest. We'll do this by the law.'

An uncertain murmur started. People didn't know whether to be outraged or impressed. I was watching Madoc, trying to work him out. I was frightened: frightened of the wars that were coming down on us and frightened of the murmuring in the hall and what it meant for Madoc. I didn't understand what he was doing.

'We'll settle this by law,' he added. 'This time. And we'll finish our preparations.' He smiled suddenly, a quick, wicked smile as he looked around the crowd of men. The murmuring dropped as he stood behind the table, his eyes moving slowly and almost casually round the hall. He looked relaxed but he wasn't; I could feel his willpower working on them all. He was holding them, trying to turn them.

'And then,' he said lightly, as if he was telling a joke. 'And then, my people . . .'

He grinned as they began to laugh.

'You see,' he said to Rhodri's men. 'You can tell my brother that he can count on me.'

They cheered then – everyone except Owain, who had stepped back into the shadows, and Glesig, who was listening hard, trying to follow what was going on. Madoc had turned them round to believing in him. Though he was some inches away from me, I swear I could feel the energy pumping in him. And I still didn't understand.

That night in bed I asked him about it.

'What are these preparations for, Madoc?' I asked. 'What are we getting ready for?'

I was already in bed; he was still undressing. He shrugged his cloak off his shoulders.

'To defend ourselves, my lady.'

'Surely we've got enough men here now? We've got more men this week than we'll have next week, when Llywelyn goes.'

'Yes, but when Llywelyn goes, he should be leaving something more important than men behind.'

'What?'

'Ships.'

The word made my heart beat fast, I don't know why.

'What do you mean? Llywelyn hasn't brought any ships.'

'But Rhys ap Gruffydd wants to build some with me. If Llywelyn takes favourable news back to Rhys, then we can expect Rhys here to settle terms in a week or so. I can't have Dreugyllt being attacked before that. I can't jeopardise Rhys's visit. I need his partnership.'

Madoc was dropping the rest of his clothes on to the chest in the corner. His belt, tunic, undershirt fluttered down in a heap. He watched them fall intently, almost dreamily.

'How many ships are you building?'

He turned, naked, and looked at me.

'I don't know yet. Four, definitely. Three more, I hope, if I can agree terms. And if Rhys comes in – ' he looked at me and smiled – the same wicked smile he'd given in the hall – 'who knows?'

'What are you going to do with them?'

I was sitting straight up in bed. My hair tickled my naked back and by contrast my breasts felt cold.

'Don't you know, Ceinwen? You should. You said it. "Cast my net over the seas".'

'Duw Madoc, stop teasing me!'

He chuckled and leaped on to the bed. His body is stronger now, muscled like a man's, but still slim.

'No,' he said. 'You told me. I'm doing it. You'll just have to wait a little longer. Wait and see.'

He was that pleased with himself. Half of me loved him, half of me wanted to hit him. But a little later, when we were making love hard and urgent (no, neither of us was feeling gentle that night) he swore:

'It's going to be glorious, Ceinwen. It's going to be great, no one can imagine how great.'

But he still didn't tell me.

The earth is damp on my hands and it's rubbed in under my nails. It reminds me of planting the crops in Cynfael. I like thinking about my life in Cynfael and comparing it to now. Mam told me I'd miss it but I don't. I'm more at home here with Madoc than I ever was there.

In the future I'll bring our children here to this herb garden and teach them the properties of the plants.

Here he comes, my prince and husband, with Glesig Dog. Madoc looks excited, he's walking fast with his arm round Glesig's shoulder.

I go to meet him and we sit on the low wall that the men have built around the soon-to-be herb garden. Honey, the little yellow dog, is prancing round Glesig's feet as usual. She belongs to one of the stable men but she loves Glesig and already walks at his heels without a leash and lies, springs and fetches for him. Glesig thinks she's funny and slow; in his country, he says, the dogs have longer legs and run like deer.

'I can smell the herbs,' says Madoc in surprise. He picks up my hand and looks at the dirty streaks on it. 'My queen,' he says. 'Queen Dirty Hands.'

'Dreugyllt needs a herb garden, my king,' I say. 'Especially if we're to have lords and princes staying with us all through the summer.'

'Well, I don't know about *all* through the summer.'

'No? Why not?'

'What do you think, Glesig Dog?'

Glesig looks across the inner bailey, at the men leading horses out of the stables.

'I think, not quite all summer.'

They are both looking pleased with themselves – Madoc's got his excited air and Glesig looks different – brighter and bigger, somehow more fleshy.

What is it that Glesig thinks when he's silent? I am more and more interested in knowing. Madoc pretends he knows; 'Dear God, Ceinwen, don't ask him,' he says to me, 'He's only remembering how his people won the love of the man in the sun's house. Either that, or he's trying to find a new way of telling us how much better they train their dogs in Ynys Llyr.'

It's true. Glesig does like to talk about their dogs. And he keeps explaining the story of the man in the sun's house, which is what they call God. And then there are the other stories, like the tale of the wolftrack and the tale of the house of the moon. But I like those tales. Weird they are, and so different from ours. When Glesig tells them to us, in his top-of-the-throat Welsh with its funny traces of Madoc, I seem to see a different country, which can't really be described by words like hills and meadows, and which is bathed in a light unlike any light I've ever looked on. It's a light which only shines in Glesig's voice.

Now as he glances away from the horses I see that he's smiling to himself. But it's not one of his dreamy smiles, not at all.

'Why?' I ask. 'What's happening later this summer?'

Madoc is still holding my hand. He strokes it with one finger, tapping its way across my skin. I can feel his pent-up energy and suddenly I'm afraid.

'Is it the galanas against Gruffydd?' I ask. 'Have you heard news from the deputation?'

Madoc makes an obscene gesture with his fist.

'The galanas, huh! The galanas isn't important.'

'My lord, for God's sake tell me!' My laughing tone isn't natural, and it doesn't quite fool Madoc. He shoots me a sideways look and places my hand down in my lap.

'Can't you guess?' He's staring at me, wanting me to guess, but my mind's empty. I shake my head.

'I've heard from Rhys ap Gruffydd. Llywelyn sent a man to him yesterday and he returned this morning. Rhys is going to build three ships with me.'

'I'm very pleased my lord.'

I am pleased, but I still don't understand.

'Now that Rhys is in, my father will come in. He'll have to. Then we'll have ten ships.'

Ten ships. Cast your net over the seas. What's Madoc planning? It can't be a raid on Gruffydd or Maredudd – his father wouldn't join him in that.

I think of all the lords who have been here in the last months. There must have been half a dozen of them, coming with their warbands to Dreugyllt. When we've received them and made them welcome Madoc takes them down with him and Arun and Glesig to the shore. Sometimes I go with them. It's like an ants' nest down there: on the broad sloping grassy sands, sheltered by the arm of the bay, over a hundred men are working on the huge wooden frames, treating and bending and joining the wood, measuring angles and thicknesses, carrying weights, whittling and sawing and cutting.

The number of working men is growing all the time, as these lords go home and send back special parties of their serfs, with the skills Madoc needs. It has been puzzling me, why they should do all this. But there are so many things I'm ignorant of, and I haven't liked to ask.

'What are these ships for, my lord?'

Madoc looks at Glesig. It's a mild day and Glesig has shrugged his cloak back from his shoulders, so that the animal pelts stick out, tails and paws in the air, behind his bare arms. Madoc reaches out and gives one tiny red-brown tail a tug.

'I think your lady's about to guess after all, Glesig Dog.'

'Are you going to raid the northern isles?' I look into the blue-green eyes. They say the sea's that colour in the north when the sun shines on it. I'm frightened and excited at the idea of Madoc sailing down on those distant islands.

'No. We're going to islands but not to the northern islands. And we're not going to raid. We're going to settle.'

Settle. Duw, what does he mean?

His hand comes down on mine again and closes on it.

'We're going to be great, Ceinwen,' he says. He's speaking slowly but furiously, as if he's striking some unseen person with every word. 'We're going to do something that hasn't been done for years, not since the oldest of the old kings came to our country.'

His face is radiant, like it was at Caer Llion, in that dawn. But it's stronger now and instead of just hunger, there's a gleam of satisfaction in it too. I've got an idea – I saw Glesig staring away into the soft March air, as if he could see something I couldn't – but it's such a big idea it fills my head so I feel that I'm falling, falling off this little low wall.

'Listen,' says Madoc urgently, hurting my hand. 'My father's dying, Gwynedd's finished. Powys has already gone to the Normans. Deheubarth and Morgannwg and Gwent are slipping to the Marchers, for all Rhys's politics. If we stay here, in this little corner, we'll grow old fighting my brothers and watching the Normans eat into the cantrefi.

'So we're going to go to the Island of the Great Sea. Ten ships, Ceinwen, each filled with people of the kindreds and the ancient houses. And you and me at the head. We're going to go back to Ynys Llyr and rule over it.'

He's mad. He can't mean it. I'm making my herb garden. Next year, when our son's here, it will be thick and scented with herbs. Butterflies will land on it in spring. Bees will drone in it in summer. Do they have butterflies and bees in Glesig's country?

I asked Glesig, and he didn't know what I meant. I looked round for a butterfly or a bee to show him, but there, it's too early.

Madoc. I wanted to say no, but how could I? This is a prince of Gwynedd and I've got to be worthy of him. He's not to know what a distance I've already travelled from Cynfael to here. Cynfael: for the first time since I left there, the thought of it wrenches my heart. But not as much as leaving this, not as much.

How can I be loving something so much, so soon, as I love our stronghold here? Will you build me a new Dreugyllt, Madoc?

I've been walking back and forth out here for over an hour. I couldn't stay in the herb garden any longer and I couldn't go into the hall for the midday meal. I brought Marged out with me and she stays several yards back; I think she's frightened of the cliff edge. Down there on the shore the tiny figures are clustered black on the frames and trestles. Behind me, around the outer wall of the castle the moat is finished, and the camp of men at arms, axemen, farriers and their families has grown.

Now I understand why. Madoc's planned this well. A real prince of Gwynedd, he is.

The lovely strong walls of Dreugyllt are at my back. Before me is the sea, grey-green and churned into white-topped waves. Ships often sail across it to Ireland. So will we, but we'll be going further west still. How far west, and for how many months?

Well, so I'm to be a warrior princess after all. I'll be casting my net over the seas too, all the way to Ynys Llyr, a strange country where the people are dark like Glesig and live in round houses, telling stories about the sun and the moon. I keep my back to Dreugyllt and desperately, with the sea wind in my face, I urge my courage to rise.

15

Outside, the town hall clock struck eleven thirty. In the small wood-panelled room, Jane and Gwyn stood facing each other. The three lines of plastic chairs were empty save for Roy, Eirlys and Goff. The flower arrangement on the desk wafted the scent of carnations into the air.

Jane was unprepared for the emotion that had risen in her. It was the sight of the rings: she had seen them before, of course – they had bought them together earlier in the week. But now as they each held an identical gold circle in their hands, she began to shake.

'Jane, will you now give your vows?' said the registrar. She was in her forties, wearing a soft woollen dress and a necklace. Her voice was up and down and melodious, like Eirlys's, but firm like a schoolteacher's. 'Repeat these words after me . . .'

They were finally here, in the register office in Cardiff town hall, with all the bustle of a Saturday morning outside the tall sash windows. Gwyn had a white winter rose pinned to his tweed jacket and Jane had a white ribbon tied round her wrist, which Eirlys had insisted on giving her for luck.

For the first time since Wednesday and the terrible row with Gwyn, Jane's vision was unclouded. There had been days in between when waking and sleeping, indoors and out, whether she was with others or alone, Jane had had a secret companion.

But no longer. There was nothing distracting Jane now. It was as if an invisible membrane had just wrapped itself round her and Gwyn, sealing them off.

Running backwards like the frames of a film, she saw the short months they had known each other. It was such a brief time; they knew so little about one another, but he was necessary to her. They had to be joined.

The love they were confessing in this neat, carnation-smelling room, was overpowering. It was an assault on her identity. She knew who she was – Jane Alice Pridden of Renoxia – but she wasn't herself without this man, Gwyn Thomas of Graig, so what did that make her?

Urged by the registrar, Jane held out her left hand and stared at Gwyn's hands as he slid on the gold ring. It encircled her finger, and she felt the metal band warm and unfamiliar on her skin as she took Gwyn's hand and gently fed the ring's mate on to his finger. Their heads bent together, they both stared down at their hands.

The registrar declared that Jane Alice Pridden and Gwyn Dafydd Thomas were now legally husband and wife.

Jane looked up into Gwyn's face. He was staring at her with a mixture of love, surprise and puzzlement. She thought she was probably looking at him in exactly the same way. They leaned together and kissed, out of politeness to the registrar and the three guests, who obviously expected something like it, and as their lips touched they both began to laugh.

Gwyn was elated. Jane was impressed. The village hall looked stunning, transformed from a concrete oblong into a scene of almost pagan revelry. Huge branches of holly were fixed to the walls and roof joists, their berries clusters of bright colour against the dark leaves. Bunches of white-berried mistletoe hung from scarlet ribbons and more holly stood in big glass vases on the tables and bushed from the windows, shutting out the night.

Among the greenery the sixty-seven people Gwyn had invited were well into the merry-making, surging in and out of groups, drinking a strange assortment of wines, beers, ciders and soft drinks, and talking, talking, talking.

The wedding party had been going on for two hours, since eight o'clock, and Jane had been kissed by almost everyone here. She had been fussed over by half the older people present ('Oh, let me look at you. Well, isn't she lovely? And so tall and slim. Love her.') and had been greeted with a shy formality by the other half ('Very pleased to meet you dear. Thank you ever so much for inviting us.'). She had re-met the women from the hen night ('Hiya Jane, do you remember me, I'm Janice?') and their men ('Congratoolations Jane. I've heard a lot about you.'). And she had met other women and men, old friends of Gwyn's, some old enemies of Gwyn's — 'Oh well,' he'd murmured to her at one point, 'It all adds up to the same thing in the end, doesn't it?' — a confusing array of faces and voices, and interested, speculating eyes running over her.

It was easy being the bride at a wedding party. Everyone talked to you; no one demanded anything of you. Everyone assumed you must be very happy and indeed, you were; if a little disoriented.

She was now standing in a group of men, Gwyn's old school and local television friends. They were all rather handsome (or did she just mean rather Welsh?) and paying her a lot of attention.

'Deck the halls with boughs of holly,' sang Roy, winking at her as he walked past with a plate of sausage rolls.

'I bet that's the twentieth time he's sung that this evening,' said John, a stocky, freckled school-friend of Gwyn's, who was standing on her right. 'Where'd they come from? Up the Pengroed Way?'

'I think so,' said Jane. 'Roy and Eirlys went out one night last week and did some deforesting. They brought the cuttings down in Eirlys's car and hid them under a tarpaulin in the shed, so I wouldn't see.'

'That'll be Roy,' said John. 'He loves surprises, the big baby. Hallo Roy,' as Roy came back again with the sausage rolls. 'I was admiring your holly,'

'Spectacular, isn't it?' agreed Roy. 'We're still picking bits out of Eirlys's car. We gave poor old Goff a lift to the register office this morning and he had prickles working their way through to him all through the ceremony.'

'He never said,' said Jane, laughing. She looked round for Goff. Where was he? Oh yes, there, over by one of the small tables with chairs around it. He was easing himself down on to one of the chairs, probably about to join the group of older women and one man who were already at the table. They were his generation, the women with wool frocks and tightly curled grey-black hair, the man with an ancient suit and roguish smile. Jane waited for them to welcome him. But as Goff lowered himself into the chair a little hush fell on the other three. Then the woman nearest Goff turned away from him, a small but definite movement which shut him out of the circle.

Goff leaned his walking stick against the side of the table and showed no reaction.

Bewildered, Jane looked up at Roy, but he was nodding in the opposite direction, off on another tack.

'Alun Edwards looked surprised when he came in too,' he said.

'Did he?' John grinned, and looked in the direction of Roy's nod, towards a grey-haired man in a suit and waistcoat. He was in a group of two other similar men, all talking at once.

'Who's he?' asked Jane.

'Woodlands and meadows officer for the regional Countryside Council,' said Roy gleefully. 'The man who's supposed to stop us cutting down the holly. Hallo there Alun, fancy a sausage roll?'

Jane watched him amble off to the three men, plate in one hand, glass in the other. She smiled.

'Yes, he's a good friend, Roy,' said John. 'I bet he and Eirlys were organising you high and low all week.'

'Yes, they were. I've only just realised how much they've done. Would you excuse me, I want to say something to Goff.'

She threaded her way through the people to Goff's table. An open-faced woman in her late thirties had got there ahead of her and was pulling up a chair, chattering.

Jane saw her cast an impatient glance at the three stiff backs still turned to Goff. Perhaps it was one of those village feuds that the older generation seemed to love so much. It was odd, though; Goff didn't seem the type. She turned her head, smiling – that was Gwyn's voice. He was standing with a group of contemporaries and from here it looked like he was doing an impersonation of Professor Jewell. It touched her to see him so happy. And it touched her the way his face lit up now that he saw her. She went across and slipped her arm round his waist.

At eleven o'clock Steve, a friend of Gwyn's from his Welsh television days, began to set up his deck and speakers and as the first intermittent bursts of music sounded, the older generation began to leave. Jane went over to Goff.

'I haven't had a chance to speak to you this evening. Thank you for coming this morning.'

'I wouldn't have missed it,' said Goff. He nodded at Gwyn. 'The lad looks well.'

'Yes, I think he is.'

'It's good to see him happy. He's always had to fight for what he wants.'

'He's all right, Goff.'

'Yes. I know. His writing going well, is it?'

'Ye – how did you know he was writing?'

'I can always tell when Gwyn's writing, it shows in his face, mon. Good, is it? Different?'

'Yes to both.' Jane met Goff's level gaze. She shouldn't tell him anything about Gwyn's work, she knew that. 'The picture – *Madoc's Dream*. Gwyn seems to be writing about it.'

'Is that so? Have you talked to him about it?'

'I tried, but he didn't – he didn't want to know. He doesn't like people reading work in progress.'

'No.'

'He doesn't seem to recall the painting. But then, he could easily have seen it and forgotten it.'

'He's almost certainly seen it, Jane.'

It wasn't said to reassure her; on the contrary.

Jane looked into Goff's face. Clean-shaven this morning, his reddish stubble was already beginning to shadow his skin. Under his double-breasted suit he wore a moleskin waistcoat with green glass buttons. Every line of his face and every fold of his clothes spoke of past secrets.

This was a stubborn old man. If he understood something of what was happening to her, if he held some key, why didn't he offer it? But then, maybe he was wondering why she didn't ask him outright. Maybe he was beginning to ask himself what she had to hide.

Everyone has something to hide, thought Jane, something to regret. She knew from her own experience – that extraordinary teenage affair – that when she got frightened, she ran. She didn't want to do the same to Gwyn. She wouldn't do the same to Gwyn. Something strange was happening to them, something growing out of the conjunction of their personal histories and the race memories which each of them carried – race memories Jane had never believed in before. Her ideas were changing swiftly these days as she struggled to make sense of events. All the certainties were changing. Well, she wouldn't be hurried. She wouldn't be panicked. She would see this through with Gwyn. She would stay as close to him as she was now, dig her heels in to the ground, twine her arms round his body and hold on.

Goff's hand was on her shoulder, surprisingly heavy.

'Your tickets are at my house. The reservations for the ferry. Come and pick them up tomorrow.'

'We will. Thank you, it's a very kind gift.'

'Oh no. It's not kind, I assure you. Necessary, perhaps, even helpful, but not particularly kind. Ach, listen to me. It's time I went and left you young people to enjoy yourselves. You'll be all right Jane, the two of you. God bless you both.'

Jane caught his hand as he lifted it from her shoulder.

'Goff – at my hen night – you know, the party Eirlys arranged for me with her women friends – I sang a song when I got drunk. Eirlys has it on tape. It's a Mandan song, and I never knew I knew it.'

Goff's hand tensed in hers, and his eyes were suddenly fixed on her face. She heard him breathe out a reluctant sigh, as if he'd just had something confirmed. Then his fingers closed on hers, giving them a comforting squeeze, and he said in a very matter-of-fact voice: 'Well, it's surprising what your brain stores away, isn't it? All sorts of bits and pieces. Look, Roy's trying to get your attention. I'll be off now, I'll just go and say goodbye to the lad. Welcome to Graig, Jane. May I kiss you?'

Roy was standing by the newly set up sound equipment, shuffling through a pile of records, trying to remember which song was Jane and Gwyn's special one.

'I didn't know we had one,' said Jane.

'Bloody hell, woman, you females are so unromantic. Of course you've got one. You and Gwyn were talking about it the other night.'

Jane laughed. 'I know, only kidding. It's "Never Before".'

'That's the one. OK Steve, got that? "Never Before". Hold on, don't put it on for a second, Gwyn's saying goodbye to Goff.'

They leaned against the speaker, watching the two men. They stood a foot apart, mirroring each other's movements and their completely different faces suddenly looked alike. It was impossible to hear what they were saying, but the body language was clear. They both laughed, Goff slapped Gwyn on the shoulder and Gwyn gently punched the old man on the arm, then, after an infinitesimal pause, Gwyn put his arm round Goff in a quick, awkward embrace.

Jane didn't look at Roy; she was embarrassed that she had tears in her eyes. She watched as Gwyn walked with Goff to the door. There were half a dozen older people waiting to say goodbye to him – two of them were the women who had ignored Goff before. As Gwyn and Goff drew level with them, they turned towards each other and began to talk. And a man and a woman, standing in Gwyn's path and obviously meaning to talk to him, stepped aside as he approached with Goff and then turned to stare as the two went through the doorway.

'What's that about?' Jane said.

Roy didn't say anything. She glanced up at him; he was looking uneasy.

'Come on Roy. I noticed it before. Those two women there, by the mistletoe, they turned their backs on Goff earlier this evening. What's going on here?'

'Bloody swine,' Roy said. 'Hypocritical bastards. If they accept the invitation, they should damn well be civil to Goff.'

'Roy.'

'Oh shit, Jane, you don't want to hear rancid old village gossip. It should have died the death a long time ago. Bloody wicked, it is, to go carrying it on. And libellous. If I was Goff I'd sue the lot of them.'

Jane had been thinking it was some silly dispute, over property maybe, but the anger and contempt in Roy's face told her otherwise. Her lungs tightened. Roy was right: perhaps she didn't want to hear.

'It's something to do with Gwyn, isn't it?'

Roy nodded.

'Yes. Jesus, Jane, they're just a bunch of sanctimonious, filthy-minded old swine. Look, you know about Gwyn's parents splitting up, don't you?'

Jane looked at her hands, gazing at her gold wedding ring. She did know. Gwyn had told her and she had filled in the gaps in his words. She interlaced her fingers and nodded.

'Well, he was glad to get out, I think. He moved in with Goff and at first everyone thought it was all right. He was nearly sixteen, see. Anyway, Richard Burton had done it first, hadn't he?

'But, after about a year, it was obvious he and Goff weren't getting on too well. You know about that as well, don't you? And then these rumours started, really nasty rumours.'

Roy turned to a man who was waving at him.

'Just a minute Howard, I'll be with you mon. Eirlys? She's over there.' He turned back to Jane, picked up a record and began fiddling with it. 'There was talk that Goff was, you know, interfering with Gwyn. Abusing him. We never knew who started it, but those things don't go away, not in a village.

'Gwyn got to hear the rumours pretty fast. He didn't know what to do, like. He wanted to move out of Goff's anyway, but he didn't want it to look as though the story was true. Then the headmaster had him into his office and asked him about "trouble in his lodgings". Gwyn was beside himself with rage. He told the head it was all a load of cobblers, of course. But it was getting too much to handle, the whole thing. He came and lived with my family after that.

'He always stuck by Goff. He went to see him regularly, he visited him in the university holidays. He dedicated his book of poems to him, for Christ's sake. But it didn't stop a few people believing the gossip and it doesn't take much to ruin a man, especially down here.

'Goff took early retirement two years after Gwyn left school. He was forced into it by the headmaster and the governors, poor old bastard. His life was teaching.'

Across the crowded hall, Gwyn reappeared, alone, in the doorway. The people who had refused to speak to Goff converged on him to say goodbye. He shook hands with them politely, but his smile was cool.

'Vultures,' said Roy. There was disgust in his voice. 'They've been living off the corpse of that old libel for years.'

'Why the hell did he invite them?' Jane was finding it hard to speak; her throat was thick.

'Well, Gwyn's like that, isn't he? He doesn't like accepting unpleasant things. He thinks that if he goes ahead and acts as though everything's fine, it'll *be* fine. Don't you find that?'

'Yes,' said Jane slowly. 'I suppose that is what he does.'

'Survival techniques. Oh look, lovely, I didn't mean to spoil your evening. I shouldn't have told you, I'm sorry.'

'You haven't spoilt it.'

'It's all in the past, isn't it? And you know, the way they've been today, Gwyn and Goff, I haven't seen them like that for years. Jane . . .' Gwyn was coming towards them; Roy put his hand urgently on Jane's arm. 'Be happy with him, won't you?'

Jane kissed Roy's cheek.

'Hands off my woman,' said Gwyn. 'Or we'll have to take our shirts off and have a bare-knuckle fight.'

'Can't,' said Roy. 'I promised Eirlys I wouldn't do that any more. Anyhow, there's no coal dust to rub on our faces.'

'Ladies and gentlemen.' Steve's amplified voice boomed out of the speakers, making them jump. 'Dance time. Turn some lights down, will you?'

At the far end of the hall, Eirlys began flicking switches and the pale yellow spotlights went off and red and orange ones came on.

'Sophisticated, isn't it?' said Gwyn. 'I had to go to Cardiff for the coloured bulbs.'

'We usually put a pair of socks over ours,' said Roy. 'Or Eirlys's knickers.'

But in truth they were all blinking at the difference made by the new lighting. Deep shadows had sprung up in the corners of the hall; the boughs of holly had grown thicker, and the broad red ribbons hung down the wall like heraldic banners. The bunches of mistletoe swayed gently in the air currents and their silhouettes, oddly magnified, moved on the walls.

In the indeterminate light, faces were turning towards Jane and Gwyn and the guests were shifting around them, clearing a horseshoe-shaped space on the floor. The music sprang out of the speakers – the insistent bass line and the high melody in minor key.

Jane saw Gwyn's face, strong in the shadows before her. Taken off balance by the sudden change in mood, she felt she was watching him like a figure in a pageant. She was watching them both; she saw herself clearly, standing very straight, her head lifting to look into his eyes. She smiled to herself, knowing what would happen next. Almost as if it were a dance step they had practised, she waited for his sign. And there it was: his hands stretching out towards her in a controlled movement, a gesture both of recognition and invitation. She took the single necessary step towards him, placed her hands in his and let him draw her closer until their lips met. As they moved into the dance the sound of clapping broke all round them.

Then other figures moved on to the floor and Jane recognised Eirlys dancing with a television man, a handful of the women from the hen night and Roy moving surprisingly well with a very small, striking blonde called Clarys.

'How do you feel?' said Gwyn.

'Bloody weird.' She heard her own excited laugh.

'Yes, funny isn't it?'

She linked her hands behind his neck and moved her hips on the off-beat.

'Did Goff have a good time tonight?'

'I think so. I'm glad we had him to the ceremony. Meant a lot to him.'

'And to you,' said Jane. Gwyn smiled.

'All right, and to me.'

The first song turned into another, easier to dance to, and they began to dance more loosely, weaving in and out of other people.

'Happy?' said Gwyn as they came together again.

'Yes,' said Jane. 'It's been a good marriage so far.'

She watched Gwyn move to the music: he had his own chunky grace. She remembered how that had surprised her the first time they'd danced together in Brockham. She half wanted to ask him about Goff, but only half.

The party had thinned but there were still about fifteen people to help carry their cases and coats, shake their hands, kiss their cheeks and gather under the branches of holly in the porch.

Looking past them, Jane had a last glimpse of the hall, quiet now that the music had stopped.

'Thank you again,' she said to Roy, tightening her arms round him. 'I never expected this.'

'Well, you couldn't have your wedding night in our spare room, could you mon? We don't want to have to sleep with cotton wool in our ears.'

A few feet away, Eirlys and Gwyn were also embracing. Jane thought that she saw a fleeting sadness on both their faces. Then she and Gwyn found each other's hands and walked to the taxi, and their escort came with them, and suddenly the dark blue air around them was filled with arms and hands and there was whiteness floating all over them, like snowflakes but not cold and not wet, warm and soft, brushing their skin, staying on it, tickling and irritating it. It filled Jane's vision and made her eyes water. She put her arm up to protect her face and felt something warm and feathery on her tongue. She spat it out, half panicking.

Gwyn groaned beside her and pulled her into the car. Through the open door the group of people was blurred behind the shower of whiteness.

'Not in the car, thank you,' she heard a deep voice say and the driver slammed the door shut.

Frantically Jane brushed at her face.

'What is it?' she whispered. 'Christ Gwyn, what is it?'

'Local version of confetti,' said Gwyn. 'White feathers. They've probably opened an old pillow and picked out all the white down. In the old days they used to kill a dove.'

'God, how horrible. Why?'

'I don't know. Do you know?' Gwyn asked the driver as he got into the front seat. 'Where the white feather tradition comes from?'

'No idea,' said the driver, revving the engine. 'I only know it makes a hell of a mess in my car.'

'Here, cariad,' said Gwyn, 'We'd better have a kiss as we drive off, to please them.'

They kissed, the tiny feathers still clinging to their skin, hearing discreet cheering from the guests left behind at the hall. Then the car had turned the corner and was driving them under the streetlights, past the houses and out on to the main road. They passed the church, the Old Post and the rugby ground and were in the open valley. They sped towards Cardiff, picking white feathers out of one another's hair.

The island had been a shadow in the sea-dusk, then an emerging, hardening silhouette, and now it was coming out of the half-light as a shoreline, with the two arms of the bay sloping gently from the water, pitted with rock pools and scattered with boulders, and the headland a bulk of grass and dank earth and granite.

Gwyn stood on the deck, watching the harbour move around them as they came into berth. He looked up at the headland, sweeping back from the harbour. He hadn't wanted to come here but now, to his surprise, he felt excited. Perhaps after all, Gwyn thought, as the salty air stung his face, the comforts of the Cardiff Royal Arms were a bit oppressive.

They'd had two nights in the high-ceilinged, four-postered bed-room, a breakfast in bed and a breakfast in the red and cream dining room, and they'd sipped gin and tonics in the bar. It had been a perfect way to recover from the wedding and to enjoy being married. Yesterday morning they had sat at either end of the huge enamel bath in their old-fashioned bathroom, drinking coffee and comparing rings. Yesterday afternoon they had wandered round the castle and then gone to see an early showing of the Christmas family blockbuster film.

The train journey from Cardiff to Bristol, then from Bristol to Bideford, had been a real bore. But the sight of the coast, and the Bristol Channel blue-grey and choppy with waves, had blown his lurking ill humour away. He didn't think Jane had noticed the change; he'd been trying hard to seem enthusiastic about Lundy all along, for her sake. But now he didn't have to pretend any more. He had enjoyed every minute of the two-and-a-half-hour crossing, watching the coast of North Devon recede behind them, tracing the distant shoreline of South Devon and Cornwall to the east, turning north to see the coast of South Wales, the low green hills surprisingly touched with winter sun.

The best parts of the crossing had been when he had been alone, on deck. Jane and he had stood on the deck at first, then gone downstairs into the warm. Jane, feeling queasy, had got them brandies from the bar and they had sat in the passengers' lounge reading and sipping their drinks for a while. They had gone back on deck after half an hour, at Gwyn's suggestion, but Jane had felt cold and drowsy – 'Symptom of sea-sickness,' Gwyn had told her knowledgeably, surprising himself – and had gone back into the lounge in search of a seat. From then on, Gwyn had alternated between the deck and brief trips to the lounge to check on Jane. She looked vulnerable curled up on the red plastic banquette and he had massaged her back and felt guilty at being preoccupied. Not that she'd minded. 'Go on deck, sweetheart,' she'd muttered. 'I'm fine.'

So, especially for the later stages of the journey, he had been alone on deck. Not literally alone – several other people were leaning on the rails, or huddled on the fixed seats, but they didn't impinge on him. Gwyn had sat on a stack of lifebelts in the bows and looked across the widening sea to the changing shape of the horizon, directly in their path. His head was full of the smells of the salty air and the ferry engine and the rank wet wood of the deckboards and every now and then, as the next line came to him, he had written in a cramped hand on the back of his ticket.

He was just thinking that he must go and get Jane when she appeared beside him. She looked pale but steadier and she smiled at him and looked eagerly round the harbour. Gwyn watched her dark eyes move across the scene, taking in the quay, the harbour master's house, the road leading off to the right, the people waiting, and the land rising up behind them, shutting off the rest of the island from view.

What had Goff told Jane about this place? She knew something she wasn't saying. Goff was pulling his old tricks again, of course; he never stopped. Now that Gwyn was proving such a hard nut to crack directly, he would try to get to him through the woman he loved. Well, bringing home a wife from the mid-west had been asking for it, he supposed. The mid-west; Madoc's country. Goff had always had a soft spot for Madoc, even though he wasn't really in the old stories canon. He was a semi-historical figure who dated – if he'd ever lived – from the twelfth century, several hundred years after most of the old stories had been written down, let alone devised. He bet Goff hadn't pointed out that time lapse to Jane.

But he'd told her enough to get her interested. She had gone to see him on her own, after all. Gwyn thought that had probably been to do with the Mandan connection. He knew that Jane felt tangled up about her past and her love affair with the Mandan boy. She'd told him so during their early weeks together at Brockham when they'd been learning about each other. She hadn't gone into many details but Gwyn had learnt enough – he'd been able to join the dots and get the pictures of one of those intense, disastrous teenage love affairs. He had even thought of basing a poem on it, but then he'd begun writing his new stuff.

Had it been the Mandan element in the story that had sent Jane back to Goff alone? Whatever it had been, Goff had obviously seized his chance. He'd spun her some story, good enough to convince her that she wanted to spend her honeymoon on this god-forsaken birdwatcher's isle. So here she was, arriving on Ynys Wair, the island that featured in more than one of the old stories, looking around her with avid eyes.

Gwyn thought about asking her outright but decided against it. It wasn't Jane's fault that Goff was a relentless mixer, and if he asked her now, after that blow up they'd had on Wednesday, she'd think he was blaming her again. Gwyn was ashamed of what had happened that afternoon. He could still hear the fury in his own voice and see her stricken face, white against Eirlys's sofa cushions. He'd been bloody hung over, mind, but all the same, the violence of his reaction had shocked him.

Put it down to pre-marriage tension and to being back in Graig. It wasn't easy going home, especially with his and Goff's history. And Goff was provoking him.

Anyway, he was making amends now. He hadn't complained any more about going to Lundy. He hadn't even let on that he'd remembered the part Lundy played in the Madoc legend, much less that he minded. He did mind, but not really as much as all that. Goff wasn't doing anything he hadn't tried to do before. It was a nuisance but it wasn't that important. It certainly wasn't Jane's fault. He put his hand over hers on the rail and breathed in the cold, darkening air.

Walking inland, along the rutted path, they were climbing all the time. It was mid-afternoon now and in town it would be dark. On this island though, with the wide sky swooping above them and arcing down in every direction to meet the sea, there were still gradations of colour and light. The sky was rich blue, the hedges and trees purple, the sea a glistening silver-black.

Gulls were crying on a high lost note above their heads and from the hedges came the whirring, clicking call of some unseen birds.

Gwyn held the National Trust torch they had been given at the harbour; it had a sticking plaster wrapped round it with 'Property of the Hotel' written on it in ink. He and Jane struggled up the path with their bags, knocking into one another and giggling hilariously.

'Jesus, is this for real?'

'Perhaps we should be dropping pieces of bread to mark our trail. Hell, the school said I'd regret refusing to join the scouts. Ouf, sorry.'

'Ow, that's me not the hedge. Hey look.'

'Lights! Lights!'

'My God, what a place. Why do you think the lights are flickering like that?'

'They're signalling SOS. They want to be air-lifted out.'

'I don't think so. My guess is they're aliens signalling home. Captain, this a job for the marines.'

'Ssh, there's someone there. Hallo?'

'Well, it sure makes a change from the Royal Arms.'

Jane lay on the bed, feeling the curves of the mattress under her spine. The overhead light flickered again. She rolled on to her stomach and struck a match from the box on the bed-side table, holding the flame to the candle. 'Turn out the light, would you?'

Gwyn nodded dreamily. He was sitting in the armchair, unlacing his shoes.

'Gwyn.'

'What? Yes. Sorry.' He got up and hit the wall switch. The room immediately changed shape, became smaller and more substantial in the candlelit gloom.

Jane watched Gwyn wander back to his armchair. She knew what he was doing. He was writing. He had been at it all evening, while they read the hotel literature and studied the maps on the walls, throughout the surprisingly good dinner they'd eaten with the other four guests at the long refectory table, while they drank whiskies by the fire.

She rolled over again on to her back. She didn't feel like playing second fiddle to Gwyn's writing tonight. After the long journey to get here, and the clamber up the hill in the dark, she felt tired but invigorated, like someone who'd been trying out new muscles all day. She sat up, shook out her hair and began undressing. Shoes, socks and jumper first. Then shirt; she unbuttoned it carefully and shrugged her way out of it, baring her breasts and shoulders to the cold air. It was a shock at first, but not unpleasant. She stretched, lay back voluptuously on the bed and began unbuttoning her jeans. She was easing them down over her hips when Gwyn's eyes focused properly on her. She went on undressing, pulling down first her jeans, then her panties and she saw the struggle in Gwyn's eyes as he held on for another few seconds to his composition.

She kicked her panties gently on to the floor and raised her hands and her knees in welcome as he bent down over the bed.

She woke knowing the bed was empty. The candlelight, coming from the window-ledge, seemed very bright. It lapped at the pillows and ringed the armchair with a yellow radiance.

In the middle of it sat Gwyn, naked except for a large blue sweater. He was hunched over a notepad on his knees, writing. His face was exhausted but vibrant with concentration, his downcast eyes two dark scoops of lashes, his lower lip pushed out, his cheeks hollowed. The tiny movements of his writing hand made the bunched muscles of his shoulders quiver.

'It's finished.'

Gwyn laid his pen on his notepad. He lifted his face to hers; his eyelids were drooping but his eyes shone triumphantly. His face was rosy in the candlelight. 'Shall I read it to you?'

'Go on.'

Jane's voice was painful but he didn't stop to wonder about it. He bowed his head to the notepad and began to read.

Jane saw the harbour and the ten ships gathered in the water, heard the shouting and banging and music, and the cry of the gulls and the swish of the waves, looked into the eyes of the man beside her and lifted her face to the open sea.

In the shadowed bedroom the unknown woman was back.

16

'Where's Meurig?' Madoc is walking up the side of the deck, searching. 'Who's seen him last? Is he on his ship?' His voice is sharp. There's tense he is. Ever since we got to this island he's been bound up tight with energy. Energy so fierce it's like rage.

'He's on the quay, my lord,' says Wenlyn. Wenlyn doesn't look at me, he's concentrating on keeping Madoc sweet, but behind his smooth pretty face I think there's a smile. Wenlyn sailed with Madoc to Ynys Llyr the first time; perhaps he knows how to handle this.

'Christ's bollocks, what's he doing there? He should be on his ship, ready.'

'He's talking to Arun, prince. Probably quite a good idea in the circumstances.'

'Huh!' Madoc screws his face up as if to spit. 'He's late for that, isn't he? Keep an eye on him. Go over, take men with you.'

'We've already got men on the headland, prince. They'll see if anything happens.'

'Don't argue with me man, do it. Why are they taking so long with the stags?'

'They're nearly ready, my lord,' says Cadell as Wenlyn strides off furiously. 'And they're checking the nails again.'

Madoc's superstitious about the nails, since he had his dream. And he's suspicious too, suspicious of everyone, especially Meurig ap Rhys. He thinks that even now at this last minute Rhys might give a signal to his people and they'll turn on us. He's got men posted at all the high places of the island to watch for ambush parties who might have got here first, and for strange ships on the skyline.

I don't know why he's this way about Rhys's son. But since the attacks on Dreugyllt when two of his brothers joined with the lords of Powys, he can't be sure of any of his allies. Except Rhiryd, he says. He trusts Rhiryd because he is his foster brother and because he's sending some of his own warband with us. So is Rhys, I point out: Rhys has sent two of his warband, his son and his cousin Cuhelyn to join our voyage. But Madoc is angry that Rhys insisted on Meurig commanding all three of the ships Rhys built; he can't forgive him that, because Meurig is hardly a seaman at all.

So Wenlyn is on the quay now, with half a dozen men, pushing through the crowds to Meurig. Even his cloak swings in temper.

'We've only got an hour and a half of the tide left, prince,' says Cadell. He looks nervous; he keeps glancing over his shoulder at the people on the quay and the headland.

'I know, I know,' says Madoc. 'God give me strength. Ceinwen, it should be our ship that has Pryste on board. How can I answer to Rhiryd when Meurig drowns her?'

'You won't have to,' I say. 'Rhiryd's man Gringal will take care of her. And of Meurig, if necessary. You know that, my lord, you planned it that way. And it'll work.'

'Mmm. Yes. Gringal's one of the best seamen, after all. Glesig Dog — where is he? Where's the Dog?'

'On the spit, Madoc. You let him go to make a prayer, remember?' I say it low, trying to get him to take hold of himself.

'Oh yes. Well, I didn't know he was going to take so long, though.'

Madoc turns and looks, across the decks of the other ships, through the forest of masts, to the green spit of land. Glesig Dog is there, on his own. He's squatting on the ground, and it looks like he's nursing a fire. Madoc's face is eager for a moment as he watches him, and he narrows his eyes to see better in the bright sunlight. Then he looks back at me.

'My lady, you look pale.'

There's news. I've been pale for weeks, Madoc.

'I'm all right, my lord. Look, the stags' horns are cut.'

'Good. Bring them aboard!' Madoc shouts, striding down to

the stern of the ship, standing on the plank that joins it to the quay. He beckons Cadell to go after him and steps on to the quay, crossing quickly to the pile of stag carcasses now being roughly quartered on the stones.

What a time to be cutting up stag meat. But there, Madoc has decided that we might find the lodestone on this voyage, so we'll need stag's horn for nails. If we have iron nails, you see, the lodestone's magnetic pull will wrench them from their sockets. All ten ships have been made with nails carved out of stag's horn. Hundreds of stags have been hunted down for us, many of them in Rhys's forests.

And these last-minute stags – well, they're just in case. Madoc hasn't stopped ordering things to be done since wc left Dreugyllt.

That was two days ago. I thought my heart would crack as the little boats rowed us out from the shore, with the people from the trefi lining the clifftop, watching us go. Many people on board were weeping and I cried too, but I kept my head up, so it looked as if I were crying with joy and pride.

I'd wanted to ride back to Cynfael to say goodbye but it was too dangerous. Since the raid on Dreugyllt I haven't been able to leave the castle, unless it's to go down to the shore. Gruffydd and Maredudd, in one night, raided Rhodri and us. They took the north-eastern corner of the encampment and killed the sentries, the axemen, the people in the huts. Sixty in all. They rode off with some horses and when our men went out the next day they found them in the woods, their faces bleeding. They'd cut off their eyelids and the horses were blinded with blood and dust.

Madoc rode with Arun and Rhodri and their warbands and raided Maredudd's stronghold in Machynllyth. They almost broke through, but not quite. They came back the next day, only two thirds of them. I didn't live while they were away; I didn't know how to breathe. But I had to behave well, you see, and act strong, as Madoc's lady. My lord came home shaking and when I heard what they'd done, I was sick.

There were no more raids on Dreugyllt after that but there have been attacks on the trefi. And Madoc had to ride out to answer them. The trefi are well defended now – we have all learnt fast. Some of them sent their own warbands out to make revenge raids.

This is how Madoc said it would be. Fortified at Dreugyllt, fighting this brother and that while the trefi splinter and break up. And the Norman lords are waiting comfortably in their castles in the Marches, ready to reach out and take a bit more, and a bit more.

I don't want to live like that. But it's still been hard to leave. I keep turning to look across the sea to the north, and the coast of Morgannwg and Gwent. I lived there once, inland up a few of those green valleys. Mam and Buddug and little Dafy are there still. I hope Buddug is happy with Meilyr as her husband. I hope Rhys protects them and keeps the troubles of the north from touching them.

Madoc is talking to Rhiryd and Arun now. He's gesturing at the people who are gathered in the harbour and up the hill, the envoys of all the lords and princes who are sending people out, the men at arms and bards, the kindred who are staying behind. Madoc nods out to sea. He's saying that it's time to go.

It is. We've been on Ynys Wair nearly two days now and everyone is gathered and we're all waiting to go. It was Madoc's idea that the ships should sail here to meet and he sent seamen here ahead of us, to make sure the waters were safe. He didn't send all his own men either: just like with the ship-building, he arranged for parties to be brought together from Deheubarth and Ireland and Gwyndd, Dyfed and Morgannwg and Gwent, so that everyone in the expedition is involved. It makes a combination of powers too strong for a single enemy to attack and it stops any of Madoc's partners having second thoughts.

The last two days, all through the feasting and the songs and the harps and trumpets, Madoc's been walking from ship to ship, checking and testing things. Sometimes his face is alight with vigour, like a boy's, and he laughs; and then I see him think of something and his hand falls from Glesig's shoulder or from Arun's and he's turning to shout an order or call for someone, or to send Cadell or Wenlyn off on an urgent job.

I remember how he handed Wenlyn his mare's reins, the day we met on the track above Cynfael. Arrogant and teasing he was, the way he flicked them over and said he was tired of riding. The only people he teases now are me and Glesig and then only in private. Now when he tells Wenlyn and Cadell and the others to do things, the orders are serious.

There's a lot you've done Madoc, and so fast. All these men at arms and bards and traders and kindred are here to celebrate you.

They're separating. Madoc and Arun and Meurig are standing back from one another and now they're taking formal leave. They're wishing each other Godspeed. Arun and Madoc embrace and then they embrace Meurig too. The other lords are coming forward too: Iestyn and Beuno from Gwynedd, Brynden and Gran from Ireland; Gwynwynwyn, Rhos and Tewdr from the kindred of Deheubarth and Morgannwg. These seven men each command just one ship; Madoc and Arun and Meurig have their own ship each and share the high command of the others — Madoc has four under him, the others three each.

They are laying hands on each other now. Back and forth the arms go and the pledges. The trumpets, carried over in the little ships from Gwent, begin their fanfare.

Around the men the standard bearers step forward with their standards: bulls, dragons, stags, oaks, holly.

Roaring the crowd is, yelling and cheering. The sound is like harps and voices and the wind: from the bushes on the headland birds fly up, startled, and wheel against the sky.

The people on the shore are waving their cloaks; there's drinking round some ale tubs. Young women have woven garlands of flowers and herbs and are running forward to give them to the lords. Oh God, look at their white head-dresses pointing up in folds, and at the short over-shirts and bright belts of the boys, and at the pipes and knives they carry. There's a pipe cut from white ash, like we make in Morgannwg. And that girl's playing a crwth, like I had, but the music is lost in this great noise. She's about fourteen, the age I was when I met Madoc on the track by the ladyrock.

I can't see for tears. I feel as if I'm never going to see any people like these again but that's stupid, because the ship is full of them. All ten ships are full of them.

Madoc and the others are decked in flowers now, but Madoc most of all. There's laughter and some young men come forward carrying — very carefully — a huge green shield. It's woven of holly and on it is a crimson insignia – the shape of a single prickly leaf.

Duw. Make the tears stop.

Look away, look away. Out to sea, where it's clear and there are no people. No one but Glesig.

I'd forgotten Glesig. He's been quiet all morning and almost as tense as Madoc. Of course, today isn't the same for Glesig as for us. We're setting out on an adventure, but he knows the place we're going to – that's why he's praying now. We have Owain Gwynedd's bishop here to bless us, of course, and brothers from monasteries in dozens of cantrefi, but I'm glad Madoc asked Glesig to make this prayer. After all, Glesig knows the special powers for helping us in to his shores. He's sending them a sign, letting them know we're coming.

Windy it is, so it's been hard for him to get the fire going. But now it's alight: tiny orange sparks show in the smoke. The smoke is white-grey and is blowing this way and that. Glesig kneels by the fire with his arms stretched high over it. There's funny: it must be hot but instead of wearing his cloak back over his shoulders he's wound it round his arms so it falls like a curtain round the fire. And though the smoke must be in his eyes, he's not moving his head away.

But wait. The smoke isn't in his eyes, is it? It's blowing from side to side but it's not random. Glesig's pulling it. His arms are moving slightly, like someone rocking a cradle, and now I look I can see his hands are working, making fast, busy movements. Is it just his hands?

Changing shape, the smoke is, as I watch. Glesig's hands and something else – something he's passing from hand to hand, some small object I can't see – are pulling at the smoke, funnelling it so it's rising into a column. Now drifting up into the air are blobs of smoke, first circles, then bigger, rougher drifts, then a whole series of uneven clumps. And there's a shape trying to get out of them.

Glesig is so far away I can't see his face, only that his head is tilted back and up. He's watching the form that's struggling to come out of the smoke, that's becoming clearer with each cloudy surge.

The shape darkens and its outlines resolve; the sides become long and curved, the top curls to a point and I know, oh Duw I know what I'm going to see.

The bird rises slowly from the fire, grey-black and coiling. Sweet God, our ladyrock, what is this?

Madoc, look at it. Turn to him; call to him. My mouth is open but no sound comes, and how could I make him hear me with all this din? The people are turning though – look at the heads, they're turning like a field of wheat rippling in the breeze, all looking up at the ragged shape that hangs in the blue sky. Ohhhh. The sound is surprised but pleased. Why aren't they afraid? Duw Madoc, aren't you afraid?

The smoke bird writhes, holds its shape a moment, then its wings begin to lengthen, its head twists and becomes smaller and it's breaking up and spinning off, its wings, its fantail, its beak visible for one more second against the blue and then gone into puffs of dirty cloud, drifting fast out to sea.

Madoc is standing gazing up at the sky. When everyone else starts to shout and question, he goes on gazing.

Glesig is still kneeling by the fire, pouring earth on it and singing. I can see his mouth moving and I even think that through the noise the wind carries the song to me.

'What did you say Ceinwen?'

Madoc has moved in front of me and placed his arms on either side of my shoulders, pinning me to the gunwale. His face is inches from mine, and it's very still.

'I've seen that dark bird before.'

'In a dream.'

'No, not a dream, it was a sign. I went to a seer, my lord. It was just before you came back from your voyage. She showed me a vision of you, and of Glesig.'

Madoc stares.

'You imagined it.'

'No. I saw it true. When I saw Glesig in Dreugyllt, I recognised him from the vision.'

'My lord.' Cadell's voice breaks in on us. He's standing discreetly turned away, helping to shield us. What does he think we're doing? Making love? 'Glesig Dog is here.'

Madoc puts his hands up to my face and cups it swiftly, and

not very gently. Expression has suddenly flooded his face, and it's an expression I remember. It's how I saw him looking at Meilyr on that first night in Cynfael, during the skill sticks.

His eyes are burning with it as he turns away from me and strides to the stern. He stops on the very edge of the deck and looks at Glesig, who is half-way along the plank between the shore and the ship.

'Did you speak to your spirit, then?' he asks. It sounds like a challenge.

Glesig looks strange. He looks as if he's seen something terrible or something wonderful – I can't tell which. His mouth looks even bigger than usual and when he tries to speak, it moves slowly.

'Yes. You saw.'

'That bird. Was it a sign?'

'Yes, prince.'

'Was it a good sign?'

'There isn't good or bad. There's only the spirit. I asked it for help to get us home.'

Madoc is still standing there. For a second, I wonder if he's going to refuse to let Glesig on, to order the plank taken away and sail without him. I half hope he will. But he holds out his hands and pulls Glesig aboard.

'Well done, man.'

He walks towards me, his arm on Glesig's shoulder. Madoc is wearing an expression too complicated for me to understand. His eyes are on mine and now he pushes Glesig away and moves to my side.

'Pull up the stones,' he says to the waiting men. 'Throw down the plank.'

Madoc takes my hand. It makes me tremble. For days his attention has been given to other things; suddenly he's back. I can feel every inch of him concentrating on me, flowing into me through the touch of his palm on mine.

We walk together through the kindred who are cramming our deck. I see their faces turned towards us; they clear a ragged path for us and they're all talking.

'God be with us, prince.'

'God bless us, my lady.'

I'm wearing a new silk cloak Madoc gave me: it's dark blue, edged in dark green, and embroidered with holly leaves and berries. Ceinwen of Dreugyllt no longer; I'm Ceinwen of Gwynedd now.

Madoc's hand is on mine as the ship lurches and moves slowly forward, leading the way out of the rocky bay.

'You saw Glesig Dog, Ceinwen.' His voice is low and his eyes move to mine and away. Beneath the sea warrior's sun-browned skin there's a flush and his eyes are wide, the pupils huge and dark.

'You saw him before, with the seer. Why didn't you tell me?'

His fingers are closed around mine; as I try to move my hand I realise that I can't.

'I didn't know what it meant, Madoc.'

'What did you see?'

'You and he and I, my lord, we all touched hands. And – there was something being passed between us.'

'Something being passed? What?'

'I don't know.' I frown, trying to catch the memory. There wasn't time to see, Madoc – I just felt it. Something hard and small.'

Madoc is silent. We're out of the mouth of the bay now and with a huge noise our sister ships are following us. In between us and the other ships coracles are adrift, the men resting on their oars. All around us sails are being unfurled, opening into white squares and rectangles against the speedwell-blue sea.

'It's an omen,' says Madoc. 'A sign.'

Then he's quiet. But his face is exultant. The wind blows his hair and my head-dress.

'Look, Ceinwen,' he says in a different voice. 'There's your old country, the hills of Morgannwg, over there on the northern horizon.'

'I know.'

I know. My eyes are full of them.

'Don't cry, my lady,' says Madoc. 'This voyage is going to make us great. Like the old kings. I swear.' He turns and takes my face in his hands again, but gently this time. 'Cast your net on the seas,' he says. 'You're mine, Ceinwen and I'm yours. Forever. Do you remember?'

'Yes, my lord. I remember. Always.'
He laughs and it's a laugh of pure happiness.
'Then why are you crying?'
'For love, my lord.'
Yes, for love. And for pride. And, a little bit, for fear.

17

'There's Barry Island. Or is it Porthcawl? Barry Island's where we used to go – the real old 1950s article, fairground rides and hot dogs and pickpockets. We only went to Porthcawl once or twice, to investigate. It was smarter than Barry Island, it had a watersplash on the big dipper. I think that's Porthcawl, I can see the caravan park.'

'Caravan park? A trailer park? I didn't know you had them.'

'Oh yes. People go and stay in them for their holidays.'

'God, how bizarre.'

'Why? We stayed in one once, when I was twelve. It was in Saundersfoot, next door to Tenby, on a clifftop. Lovely it was.'

'It was? Oh well, perhaps that makes a difference. They're not generally very scenic where I come from.'

'That's because in the States they're for poor people to live in. Here they're for holidays, a treat. You can make anything a treat by calling it one. Look, if you look all the way along the coast to the end, that's probably Tenby there.'

'Oh yes.'

'You're not listening, are you? God, what is it that happens to you on hillsides? I didn't know I was getting tied up with the demon rambler.'

'Just one more rise.'

'Why? What is it with you and these bays?'

'They're beautiful, that's all.' Gwyn had fallen a few steps behind and Jane had to shout to him over the wind. 'Look, why don't you wait here and I'll go on alone?'

'Not bloody likely. I know your one more rises. I'll be sitting here for hours, watching the ferry leave without us.'

Jane laughed, a little out of breath from her fast stride and the relentless winds.

'We have plenty of time.'

'It'll be nice to have time for some lunch in the pub first.'

'We will. We're nearly there.'

'Oh aye? Good. Where's there, by the way?'

Where? Here. At last. This was their third day on the island and just in time, the secret hunt for the bay was about to be complete.

Gwyn showed no sign of knowing what she was doing. She hadn't confided in him. Jane had told him that she could visualise his harbour poem and he had seemed pleased rather than touchy: she'd taken care not to suggest that she knew more than his poem described.

She didn't know very much. Impressions ran beneath the normal flow of consciousness and occasionally popped up into her mind – colours, birds, a cacophony of noise. Nothing that wasn't there in Gwyn's poem, but so immediate, so physical. The honeymoon was real, of course, and she and Gwyn, feeling slightly hilarious among the healthy families and the wind-cheatered naturalists who liked their beer, were real. More than that, they were acutely, sensually aware of each other, just as they should be. But then, whenever the sights and sounds of the harbour slipped into her mind, they were real too.

She wanted to find the bay. Surely, even allowing for erosion and development, it would still be there in some form? This was a bleak, hard place where little could have changed beyond recognition.

Yesterday and the day before she had looked in vain. But now:

This was it. The curve of this was familiar to her. She took three strides, pulling away from Gwyn up the final few yards and she was there, on the summit. Before her the rocky bay opened up: the body of the headland to the right, the land falling steeply away to the left in a jagged swoop down to the shore. Rocks stuck out from beneath the turf and darker shapes of stone broke the grey waters. The wind tore at her, making her stagger, and swept two seagulls squawking and wheeling over the flat spit of land on the far side of the bay.

Here: it had been here. She saw the water bright blue and scudded with white foam; a forest of masts shimmered in her eyes and the wind sounded like the roaring of a great crowd.

Jane smiled. She didn't try to hide it from Gwyn. The unknown woman, her inconstant companion, smiled too.

'Christ, it's beautiful.' Gwyn had come to stand next to her. He was looking over the bay in wonder and surprise. 'God. It feels – holy, somehow. So secret and still.' There was a softness in his voice but no recognition.

Jane was silent. Strength was seeping into her as she stood above the bay; she seemed to draw vigour from the land itself. Oh God, what was it that she remembered, too deep in her mind for words? What was it the woman was trying to tell her? She felt an impossible mix of emotions: there was longing, happiness, grief, and something else that pierced her and made her shut her eyes.

'Do you think this was where Madoc set off from?'

Gwyn's voice was matter of fact in her ear. She opened her eyes. His speaking had broken the spell and she was bewildered by what he had said.

The woman was gone.

'Madoc?' she said. It sounded odd saying the name aloud. 'Gwyn?'

Gwyn chuckled.

'Well, Goff did tell me quite a time before he told you, Jane. About fifteen years before.'

'You didn't mention it.'

Gwyn shrugged. 'I didn't remember at first. Then when I did, I'd just sounded off at you about Goff. So – well, you know. I didn't want to bring it up again.'

'You bastard.'

'Why?' said Gwyn reasonably. 'What's it to you? Did you think there was any big secret about it? You weren't getting interested in all that Goff stuff, were you?'

Jane turned to face him; he was laughing.

'Goff stuff?'

'Yes, about Madoc and legends and old heroes. Oh Jane, you

were, weren't you? Is that what all this hill climbing's been about? Have we been looking for something? Trying to trace your ancestors from Renoxia back to the Bristol Channel?'

'No.'

'Oh shit, cariad, don't look so offended. I didn't mean to take the piss. It's just that I know what Goff's like. He can sell the Celtic twilight to a born-again Aryan when he's going.'

Hidden in Gwyn's eyes, Jane thought, was a sliver of steel, a warning. Instinctively, like an animal covering her tracks, she feigned indifference.

'You're right,' she said good humouredly. 'He could.' She looked back out over the bay and the angry sea. On the northern horizon lay the green hills of South Wales; to the south-west the sea spread out without break or encroachment, vanishing under the sky. From this inhospitable bay ten ships had sailed together, their square white sails carrying them down that south-western stretch of water, towards the ocean and the great lands of America.

Fuck Gwyn.

The silence deepened between them and Jane felt again the marvellous vigour rising from the ground and filling every inch of her. She let it run through her arms and legs, deep into the marrow of her spine, out to the floating ends of her hair. At last, she threw her head back and gave a long exultant cry.

'For fuck's sake, what's that?'

Gwyn had backed several yards away from her and his face was shocked. 'What the hell are you doing?'

Jane smiled and stretched.

'Celebrating this place. What's the matter? Didn't you like that?'

'Don't! Don't do it again!' Gwyn turned and looked over his shoulder. 'What was it?'

He was frightened. He was seriously frightened. Jane watched him with interest.

'Native American call,' she said, after a pause. 'I'm not sure which one. We all learned them in junior high, every kid in Renoxia can do that.'

'Well, it's unearthly,' said Gwyn, sounding more normal. 'Spare us a repeat.' Jane shrugged. 'I thought you'd be interested. You do have a Mandan ritual in your poem.'

'What?'

'The smoke from the fire, on the spit of land? That's a Mandan ritual, making prayer fire before a journey.'

Jane was surprised to hear her own voice saying this, so smoothly and so spitefully. She had made up her mind not to mention it.

'Don't start that crap again,' said Gwyn uncertainly.

Jane smiled. Yes, this was her all right, and she couldn't stop herself: suddenly she really wanted to hurt Gwyn.

'Come on sweetheart,' she said. 'Surely the prayer-fire isn't a Welsh thing to do?'

Just like the last time, Gwyn's face seemed to have gone black. It must be the effect of blood vessels constricting around his eyes, Jane thought.

'If you buy Goff's theory of Madoc,' said Gwyn, the words coming out in hard spasms, 'the whole bloody lot of contemporary Mandans are descended from the Welsh, so their rituals would have to be based on our rituals anyway. Wouldn't they?'

'There aren't any contemporary Mandans,' said Jane. 'They've all died out.'

'Oh shut up!' Gwyn shouted. 'For Christ's sake. Madoc, the Mandans, give me a fucking break!'

As the echo of his voice bounced off the cliff and was whipped away by the wind, Jane felt the poison drain out of her. She stood gazing out over the bay for several long minutes. What had that been – that vindictive rage, that longing to hurt at any cost? She didn't look over her shoulder to see what Gwyn was doing; she could hear the rustling of the grasses as he paced around. Jesus, what was happening to them? Even now she didn't feel remorse: the fury was gone but somewhere in her a hard little nub of resentment still lodged.

When she judged it was time, Jane turned round and went over to Gwyn. It was her turn to apologise, she reckoned, even if she wasn't yet, quite sorry. Besides, she wanted to look again at what she thought she had seen: the unwilling light of recognition in his eyes.

18

'What are you doing, Glesig?'

'Making something, Ceinwen.'

'Yes but what?'

I bend over him, hands on my knees. There's a swell in the water today and I'm still not steady on my feet, even after all these weeks at sea. Glesig is sitting here in the stern, among the chickens and the goats, carving something.

At first I thought it was a pipe like our pipes are, for playing tunes on. But now I see he hasn't carved any holes in it, and he's making an end piece for it – a little round bowl-shaped lump.

'It's a –' Glesig glances up at me. There's a teasing look in his eyes. There often is, these days. He says I ask him too many questions but I keep on asking. It stops me going mad with boredom on this stinking ship and it teaches me a bit (a very little bit, as Glesig likes to say) about Ynys Llyr, which will be our new home. Glesig shakes his head. 'As usual, great lady, there's no word in your language for it. It's an ik-ho-map-kee. You put the – the sweet grasses in here and you burn them.'

'There's clever,' I say. 'It's to make your houses smell nice, is it?'

'Yes.'

'Do you put it on the walls?'

Glesig grins at me, shaking his head. He often does this when the two of us are talking alone. Never in public, though.

'No, Ceinwen. You put it in your mouth.'

'Your mouth?' I imagine all these people in Glesig's country

223

sitting round with the grass burners in their mouths, scenting their houses, and I start to giggle. 'How do they talk, then?'

'They don't talk.' Glesig bends his head over the bowl-shaped nob and goes on hollowing it. He's chuckling too.

'What do they do?'

'They breathe the smoke. Then they pass on the ik-ho-map-kee to the next person.'

'Ah.' Now I think I understand. Marared breathes the smoke of her herb fires sometimes when she wants to go into a trance. 'If you go on whittling that hole,' I say, 'you'll go right through the bottom of the lump.'

'Of course,' Glesig says. 'How else can you breathe the smoke out?'

'You mean, you suck it out, straight into your mouth?'

'Yes, great lady.' Glesig gives me a comic, patient look. 'How would your people do it?'

'Well – they'd just lean over the fire and breathe in,' I say, but I say it reluctantly and grinning because even as I imagine it the scene is a ridiculous one. Glesig thinks so too; he laughs outright.

'Like this?' He leans forward, his nose lifted and his eyes screwed up, and opens and shuts his mouth like a fish. It does look very silly too, and I laugh with him and put my hand on my abdomen to protect the baby before I remember.

Glesig's eyes go to my hands and then up to my face.

'Do you still get pains?' he asks quietly, and he's not laughing any longer.

'No. Nothing any more. Don't talk about it Glesig, it's bad luck.'

We both look up to the foredeck where Madoc is arguing with Cadell and one of the crew. He argues a lot since we left Ynys Wair; I wish we had Owain here to calm things down, but Owain asked to stay in Gwynedd. He wanted to die there, he said, and be buried near Madoc's father, his prince and friend, the man he'd been named for. I never thought I'd miss old grim-face Owain, but I do.

I haven't told Madoc about losing the baby. It's never safe to tell a man early, Mam told me. Wait till you show. So I did. I thought it would be safe, mind; after what the woman said in the rock pool, about the nets. A man on you a son begets. But then the first week in this western sea was so bad, we were all so sick, and then the horses broke free and stampeded.

We knew it was a risk, bringing the horses: we've brought the smallest mares and their foals and there's no more than one pair to each ship, but they can still be dangerous. When ours broke loose, the foal was caught at once but the mare rushed across the deck and back. She trampled some of the chickens and Angharad ap Rhys was crushed by the mare against the gunwale. No one knows if she'll walk again, and her only twelve. It was Glesig who saved me: he ran in front of me and hurled his weight against the mare's neck, making her skid and then Gwilym the horseman managed to get a harness on her.

I wasn't touched. But that evening when I was sitting on the sacks, dozing, I felt the cramps come. I crawled further into the sacks and pulled my knees up under my skirts, trying to squeeze the pain to sleep. But I could feel it coming.

'I'm sick, Madoc,' I told him when he came past me and asked what was wrong. 'Leave me, my lord. It'll pass.'

He got up and went to look for Marged, who's come with us. I saw him stop and say something to Glesig, who was standing by the ship's side looking up at the stars. Beneath the sacks I had hiked up my robes above my waist. I could feel my womb squeezing, squeezing and the blood flowing.

Glesig came and sat with me. He put his hand on mine, where it twisted the sacking, and said quietly, 'You're bleeding.'

'No one must know,' I said.

'I'm sorry,' he said. He looked sorry, too; I'd never seen Glesig look as if another person had touched him before. But there was no teasing or wariness in his face. He looked angry and grieving, and his mouth was turned down, looking like a gash in the moonlight. 'Forgive me, Ceinwen,' he said roughly. 'It was the mare.'

I couldn't find the strength to say it wasn't his fault. That deep the pain was, tearing at my womb and my mind.

'Get Marged here,' I whispered. 'No one else. Madoc mustn't know.'

So much blood, there was. The next day Marged and I broke a chicken's neck and put it under the sacks and said it had been trampled there, and we washed the sacks over the side.

Madoc's never known. But Glesig had known already, see. He's a watcher, Glesig. And then, since we've been at sea there's not been much he can do to help Madoc, so he and I have become companions. Almost friends, really, but in a very different way from his friendship with Madoc.

Glesig is watching Madoc, at the same time as whittling his ik-ho-map-kee. Duw, are my eyes seeing right? This ik-ho-map-kee of his, he's making it out of Madoc's precious stag's horn. I move, and very quick, to stand in front of it.

'Glesig, what are you doing? Where did you get the horn from? You know Madoc had those men flogged on Meurig's ship, for taking stag horn.' It's true, and they'd taken so little as well, just to powder and put in their drink as a love charm.

'He knows I'm doing it.' Glesig glances up, amused. He's braided his hair today: it hangs down in four plaits, one before and behind each shoulder. 'I told him I needed the stag horn.'

Told him, mind; not asked.

'And he agreed?'

'It's prayer. Madoc knows we need it. We're going to my people's country, we need my people's prayer.'

He holds up the end lump, now shaped like a round funnel. He puts down his knife and picks up the pipe part, then brings the two together. Just as they're about to meet the ship pitches down, hitting a swell, and Glesig drives the pipe into his left hand by mistake. He curses in his own language. I steady myself against the water butt and stare down at the deck. I've learned that I can look up at the sky or down at the deck, but if I see the ship pitching against the horizon, I get giddy and sick.

This voyage. Five weeks we've been at sea and it feels like forever. This ship is so small for thirty people, two horses, goats and these fowl. At night, half the people go down into the hold to sleep and Duw, the smell down there is terrible after you've been up here on deck. In the day, when it's fine, we stay up here. And even up here there's always people jostling you, like now – these women and their children will back into us in a few moments.

At first we put the goats down there but we had to bring them up after they panicked on the fourth day out of Ynys Wair and went mad in the hold, kicking the timbers and screaming. The noise was uncanny – it travelled through the timbers, making them boom and thunder all round the ship, even up on deck. And above the echoing boom, like the sea shaking, came their bleating.

On all our sister ships, people were rushing to the sides; they crowded the decks like stampeding animals themselves, gazing at the *Gwenllyr*.

We spend quite a lot of time looking at the other ships. It's something I never expected about sea travel: I knew it was dangerous and uncomfortable and crowded and that people got sick and food went bad and water was rationed to half a cup a day each – but Duw, I didn't know it would be so boring.

We sail and sail across hundreds of miles of sea. There's no land in sight anywhere. I try not to think about how deep the waters are beneath us or how far they stretch all around us; the men sail the ship and plot the course and make repairs and see to the horses. We make bread from last year's grain and cook and mend clothes and mix herbs. We tell stories and play games like chucker stones and ffensi – the Gwynedd form of still sticks – and quarrel. There's a lot of fighting: it breaks out in a choked, furtive sort of way and is over quite quickly. But then it's simmering, ready to come back.

I spend a lot of time with Glesig. He doesn't know about being a seaman, so he's not at Madoc's shoulder as often as he used to be. He helps with the mare and the foals – he so badly wants to take the first horses into Ynys Llyr – and he occupies himself with private things like this ik-ho-map-kee. Glesig seems more confident now we're at sea, but then he would be. We're going back to his country. With every day at sea, we're further from Gwynedd and less far from his country. Last night Madoc came over to join us, briefly, where we were talking.

'Well Glesig,' he said. 'By my calculations we'll be half-way across this sea in three days. We'll be landing on Ynys Llyr in September. What do you think of that?'

'Uk-tonk-ahi-ito-pai,' said Glesig, or something that sounded like it. Madoc frowned and asked him to repeat it, then he laughed and cuffed Glesig on the head.

I'm trying to learn some of Glesig's language, too; many of us are. We have times when he sits in the middle of us all and tells us stories about his country and teaches us words. Being Glesig, of course, he has fun with us. You never know what to believe. Many of his stories are about animals of strange shapes and with special qualities. Animals in his country, he says, often have magic properties, the way that places do in our country. I've told him about our ladyrock you see, and Madoc's told him about the floating island in the Gwynedd mountains, and about the stone seat near Conwy that makes you confess your crimes and then there's the lake in the cwm that dried up one night in the middle of the spring rains.

Glesig says they do have places like that in his country. There's the sun's house in the west, where no one's been for many generations. There's the dust hills, where the dead people go. There's a special place near his tref, for his people, but it's not so much the place itself that's powerful, it's a presence that lives there. He won't tell us what it is.

They call God the sun man.

Sometimes when Glesig talks to us the strange light shines in his words and I almost see the land that waits for us, such miles and miles, weeks and weeks, of sea away. And sometimes, when it's over there in the west, the sun seems to be growing unfamiliar. As we sail and sail on, it seems to be turning into Glesig's sun.

The other afternoon, a few days ago – I can't remember how many, Duw how they run together – Glesig and I were standing together at the side, just back from the main mast. The sun was strong (we've been sailing south-west for weeks) and reflected off the dark blue water to make us frown. We were looking at the company of ships alongside us. Surprising it is, how close together the ships stay.

'Tell me about your kindred, Glesig.'

Glesig looked fast at me, then away.

'I've told you, Ceinwen,' he said.

He has, too: he's told me about how the kindreds live and rule themselves, and who's honoured for being fierce in war and good at catching the huge horned bulls. I know all that. But it's Glesig's story I want to know. It's been itching at me for some time now, especially since he's been talking more to me, alone. Since I miscarried Madoc's child.

'You haven't told me about your kindred,' I said that afternoon.

'Not about your Mam and your Da and your wife and your babies.'

It was only a guess. But I was fairly sure; I could sometimes almost see her shadow behind Glesig.

He didn't turn his head but from sideways I could see his face stiffen. There were no lines on the smooth brown surface but underneath his flesh and muscles were tightening into sharp edges.

He didn't say anything and I didn't know how to break the silence. Frightened I was, at what I'd done. The silence went on and on until in the end I said something completely different.

'Do you know about Glesig's family?' I asked Madoc last night, when he came in under the thick brychan with me – it's made of double linen to wrap right around us because we've got no rush-stuffed mattress here, only loose rushes.

'They live at the northern end of a great river,' Madoc said. 'They're called the Bird people. They take their name from the swallows, I think: Glesig Dog got very excited one day in Dreu-gyllt when the first swallows came.' He finished pulling off his cloak and shirt and wrapped the brychan round us. Under the brychan his hands took hold of me; his palms are rough from the ropes now. He dropped his head to kiss my mouth. 'Do you want me to speak the name of his kindred, Ceinwen? I can do it in his language.' But I didn't ask him for it and I didn't ask any more about Glesig. Madoc was driving all the questions from my lips, if not from my mind . . .

Dear God, this swell. I slide down the side of the ship, next to Glesig, and close my eyes. Close my eyes: the motion is heavy and horrible and regular and my eyelids are too weighed down to move.

It's like falling straight into a dream. I am in a dim place with a dark roof overhead. It's like an enormous cave but it has no walls – it goes on as far as I can see in every direction, and it's got hills and forests and streams and there are birds flying in the gloomy air.

I look up at the roof. It's very far away and brown and thick, and made of earth.

I open my eyes. Up down goes the ship. Up down, sickening. I blink at Glesig. He's put the two pieces of the ik-ho-map-kee in his lap and he's holding something else now; holding it very secret, hidden in his fist. He sees me glance at it. And he's wondering if I've noticed.

I don't say anything. There's something about the way his fist is closed round it and his arm hanging down by his side, trying to deceive, that stops me speaking. Suddenly, I'm thinking about our ladyrock, the cold grey woman standing deep in the woods.

Glesig is looking into my face. His eyes are in my mind, seeing the woods and the track and the ladyrock. I can't keep him out – he slipped in so fast. No. Close, leaves and branches, close round her. No one's supposed to see her –

It's gone. There's stupid I am. Glesig can't see. He's not magic – is he?

He's speaking, anyhow.

'Do you want to hear a story, Ceinwen?'

'Yes.'

He smiles and I start to smile with him but stop. This smile of his is foreign and sad.

'If we were in my country we'd be breathing from the ik-ho-map-kee. You hold it while I talk.'

'What about you? Don't you want to hold it?'

'Ssshh. Don't speak now.' He picks the two pieces out of his lap, one-handed, and gives them to me. Light and skilled his fingers are, scooping up the pieces of carved horn and closing my hand around them. Now he smiles again.

He sits back against the side. Up down, the ship goes, up down, and I have to close my eyes again. The sun is on my eyelids, making them orange with a thin black line where the mast casts its shadow. Swoop, swoop.

'Long ago,' says Glesig, 'before any of us were born, my people lived under the earth. Our name was See-pohs-kanuma-kakee, you would call us the Bird people. We lived a long way down, thousands of feet below a sky of earth and rock and we couldn't get to the sun.'

Swoop, swoop.

'We knew the sun lived above the earth and rock sky, but we had never seen him. We wanted to go to his house and sing to him but we didn't know where his house was. We were very unhappy and grieved for the sun and the above-land.

'One morning, a young man gathered his wives together and

told them he was going to look for the way to the above-land, where the sun's home was. The wives loved him so much, they said they would go with him, although it was dangerous. Perhaps we'll be eaten by the worms in the earth-sky, they said. Perhaps the beetles with poisoned claws, who live in the between-world, will reach down and sting us. But we will go with you.

'Well, when the rest of the people saw that the wives were going, they said, we'll follow the young man too. So they packed their bull meat and oats, put their belongings on the dog-sledges, and followed him.

'They walked two days along a river until they came to some low hills. There were many paths they could follow into the hills and the young man didn't know what to do. Then he noticed a bird sitting on a small boulder.'

Rock, swoop, rock, goes the ship. There's gentle the motion is, it makes me smile.

'The bird was black with white wing tips and a white beak. It looked at the young man and felt pity for him. "Come with me," said the bird, "and I will show you the way to the above-land." The bird flew off into the heart of the low hills and stopped at a bean plant which grew very high. It grew higher than the people, higher than the low hills, higher than the earth and rock and rock sky.

' "Climb up this bean plant," said the bird, "and you will find the above-land." And it flew up the bean plant and vanished.

'The young man and his wives and all the people climbed up the bean plant and their dogs, carrying their belongings, climbed after them. When they came out on to the earth, it was night. The sun had gone beyond the rim of the earth to walk the long walk back to his house, and there was no light.

'Then one of the young man's wives saw something shining ahead. It was the white beak and white wing tips of the bird. All through the night the bird led the people through the country they couldn't see, showing the way with its white markings. And then, just before dawn, it vanished.

'The people lay down to sleep, waiting for the bird to come back. When they woke up, they found they were at the foot of a hill, with trees growing on it, but there was no sign of the bird. Then the first wife of the young man told them she had had a dream. In the dream, the bird had been singing to her from the trees on top of the hill, and it was the loveliest, sweetest song she had ever heard. "Husband," she said to the young man. "I know the bird is on the hill, up in the tallest tree. Climb up its branches and see."

'The young man went up to the tallest tree and from its branches he heard singing that made his heart fly with happiness. He climbed up and found a nest and instead of eggs, in it there was a little black stone shaped like a bird. It had a white beak and a white tip on each wing and it was singing.

' "You will always hear me in your dreams," it sang, and then it was silent. When the young man went back to his people they had all heard the song. So they went down the hill and made their houses at the bottom, where they could hear the stone singing in their dreams. That's how the Bird people came to live in the above-land, around the Hill of the Dark Bird, where the dreamstone stays.'

There's hard it is, to open my eyes. They're weighed down. No, I'm wrong – they are open, but everything dazzles and I can't see. There's too much glare from the sun – it's too strong, see, it's in my eyes.

I can see Glesig now. He's watching me; his head tips slightly with the boat, going over slowly, coming back again, I don't notice it so much any more, the motion's still there but it's fallen away.

'Are they still there?' I ask. 'Your people?'

'Yes.'

'What happened to the bird?'

'Ssh.'

'Why?'

Glesig doesn't answer. His eyes are on me, unmoving.

His right hand is still clenched. An odd shape it is; he's had to hook his thumb round his knuckles to stop it showing. And suddenly I know.

Of course. My mind is working now, fast to make up for how slow it's been before. That's what was in the vision Marared showed me; the unseen object that passed through my hands. A sign, you see. A sign. And I'm not the only one who's seen it:

remember what Madoc said as we set sail. Does he know what Glesig carries hidden in his shirt?

'Why did you bring it away?' I ask. I'm breathing hard. I'm excited and frightened both together.

He moves his head against the side of the ship, like a cat with an itch.

'I had to,' he says. 'It was in danger. I had to take the stone and keep it safe.'

A long time seems to go by without us speaking. I'm caught by his gaze, I can't look away.

'What kind of danger?' I whisper back, but Glesig only smiles.

And suddenly there's shouting all round us. The crew are rushing to the masts and other people are stumbling to the far side of the ship, yelling and shrieking. The ship dips and sways horribly; I scramble to my feet. Above the women's flapping head-dresses I can see a bigger, whiter flapping: the sails of one of our sister ships. Duw she's close! Men are swarming up her masts, tunics tearing this way and that in the sudden wind, struggling to trim the sails. I can hear Madoc's voice, furious and boyish suddenly, yelling at our own crew. 'Hold her. Don't turn her yet, you stupid bastards, in God's name hold her!' For a few seconds we ride dangerously alongside the other ship, then she's turning away. Her stern swings round into ours; the people clustered along the side of our ship panic and fall back, stepping on chickens and stumbling over the water butts. The stern is that close I'm not breathing any more, but no shock comes.

Glesig has both his hands together over the dreamstone, and his eyes are staring at the other ship's mast. It swings as the ship keels and then it moves away.

Our people are shouting with relief and a row has broken out among the crew, but I'm not listening. I'm watching Glesig.

For several seconds more he just sits there, then he lifts his clasped hands furtively to just under his chin, mutters something and hides them in the folds of his shirt. He brings them out empty.

'Sssh,' says Glesig quietly. 'It's nothing, great lady.'

I nod, but I'm staring at his tunic, trying to see where the dreamstone must be hidden. He's got a secret pocket sewn in there, then. This stone – I wish I could see it.

I clasp my hands together quickly under my chin, like Glesig did. Perhaps the stone is working for us and keeping us safe. It doesn't do to be disrespectful.

'What are you going to do with it, Glesig?' I say, speaking low.

'I'm going to take it back, Ceinwen.'

'Back where?'

'Back to my people's country, where it belongs.'

'What about the danger?'

'Perhaps it will be gone.' Glesig doesn't look at me. He flicks a pellet of chicken droppings across the planks. Uneasy, he is. He reaches out and takes the two pieces of his ik-ho-map-kee from me, holding them up and squinting at them. 'The dreamstone must go back,' he says briskly, as if we're discussing sending a lame horse back to the seller. 'It shouldn't have left the shores. I didn't mean it to come across the sea. Some things belong in their place – you understand that, don't you Ceinwen?'

'But Glesig – ' the row among the crew is so noisy now, I have to lean towards him till our heads touch: my white head-dress, with the dark brown wisps of hair escaping, and his black plaits – 'what would you have done if Madoc hadn't decided to return to Ynys Llyr?'

Glesig turns and looks at Madoc.

'I don't know,' he says. 'But he did decide to return.' And then, sounding quite passionate, he says, 'He's a great man, Ceinwen.'

'I know,' I say.

Of course I know: Madoc, who so much wanted to be great, has become great. He dares to do things that other people don't; he takes risks, he has three times the heart of anyone else. Sometimes he frightens me, just as much as he makes me proud. But I didn't know that Glesig saw it.

'Well, Glesig,' I say, teasing him slightly, 'this is good to hear. You haven't always been so ready to praise him – to me, at least.'

Glesig gave me a quick, smiling look.

'Well, great lady,' he says at once. 'He has faults. He needs a lot of good luck to get him by, but somehow he gets it. That's part of his skill. Mind you,' he goes on, 'you and I will have to look after him when he gets to Ynys Llyr. The great need their critics, especially in times of success.'

I smile at him and touch his hand. I pretend it's a scolding slap but it isn't. Glesig is clever; he has clear eyes, even though he loves Madoc. And I think we might need him, in the times ahead. Perhaps it's the near escape we've just had; perhaps it's the story Glesig told me, but despite the noon-day heat, I shiver.

19

'Oh, stop thanking me,' said Eirlys. 'It's been lovely having you. Next time you'll have to stay longer.'

'We'd like the two of you to come to New York.'

Jane fingered the extra sweater she had tied round her shoulders, thinking that she would be wearing it in twelve hours' time. Packed and with the airline tickets in her bag, she felt she was already half-way across the ocean. The kitchen, which she had grown used to over the last ten days, suddenly looked foreign and quaint again.

'We'd love to, at some point,' said Eirlys, pouring herself a second glass of orange juice. 'I've been there with work, but Roy never has. Gwyn's very happy there isn't he?'

'Yes,' said Jane. 'He gets homesick once in a while but yes, it suits him.'

Eirlys looked past Jane into a far corner of the kitchen. She was wearing a chestnut-brown woollen dress with a wide turtle neck; it clung to her gentle curves and made her look sophisticated, like one of the well-dressed blondes in a Hitchcock movie. Her face was guarded, further echoing the likeness.

'It's funny, isn't it?' she said. 'I always knew Gwyn would leave, even when we were still at school. I was surprised when he came back here to work in television.'

Her eyes strayed to the two suitcases, packed and strapped up by the kitchen door.

'I'd like to see him in New York, settled.'

'I don't know if I'd say we were settled,' said Jane, thinking about Gwyn's bare apartment and her tiny cramped one.

'No,' said Eirlys, looking up at her. 'Gwyn was saying about only having a one-year contract. But you're together, aren't you?'

Jane looked politely back at Eirlys; now this was a loaded question. She supposed Eirlys had picked up on the nervous tension that was buzzing between her and Gwyn. Eirlys was a watcher and a listener and she was very fond of Gwyn; in a way, Jane had come to realise, she looked out for him. It was understandable: Eirlys had been around during Gwyn's years with Goff. But Eirlys wasn't the one with Gwyn now, was she? Whatever went on between Jane and Gwyn was their own business.

'Yes, we're together,' said Jane flatly.

'He loves you very much, you know.'

'And I love him.'

Eirlys looked away first.

'Well, I'm glad,' she said, putting her glass down on the draining board. 'You're not at all alike and that's good. I'd better be off, are you sure you've got everything you need?'

'Positive,' said Jane. She felt rather contrite now that she had frozen Eirlys out. She smiled apologetically and crossed the quarry tiles to Eirlys. 'Hey, I know you don't want me to keep saying thank you but I have to. You and Roy have been terrific to me, you've made such a difference.'

Eirlys smiled back, relieved.

'It's been a real pleasure. We like organising, Roy and I.' They kissed, shyly but with real affection. 'Damn, I must dash. Goodbye Jane. We'll look forward to seeing you soon, either here or there.'

The clock on the dresser said ten to eleven. Their taxi wasn't due till half one. Their coffee was finished and Gwyn was talking to Goff about an Irish poet he had met on the readings circuit, who had a residency at Princeton.

'Hates it there, mon. Mind you, I'm not surprised, it's like a doll's house, that place. But he's doing some bloody good work. They publish him in the *New York Review*, I'll find you a copy when I get back and send it on.'

'That would be kind, lad. I've been following O'Farrell for years, since he was runner-up in the Schools Four Nations.'

There was a pause. Gwyn looked flustered and Goff winked at Jane. 'This lad came first.'

Something was going on. Gwyn was leaning down to the old briefcase he'd left by his chair, and rummaging inside. He straightened up self-consciously and Jane saw that he had his blue folder in his hand. Goff, sitting back in his armchair, looked at it and behind his spectacles his eyes sharpened.

'There's something I'd like you to read before we go. If you want to.'

'Oh aye, lad.'

'I've been doing some new stuff the last few months.' Gwyn was stammering slightly. 'The verse form should please you anyway, you difficult old sod, even if you don't like what I've done with it. You'll make a bard of me yet.'

Gwyn was nervous. He covered up with a shrug.

'Give it here then, lad.' Goff's throat had reddened with pleasure and his hand trembled slightly as he took the folder and opened it.

'The top three sheets are the finished versions,' Gwyn said. 'The rest is notes. There are two complete poems so far. I've just started a third.'

Jane looked at him, leaning forward, his elbows on his knees. When had he started the third?

'I tell you what,' said Goff, his voice suddenly deep. 'Why don't you take Jane through to the front room and show her my library? I wanted her to see it before she left. And give me a bit of peace and quiet to read these here. Is that all right with you, Jane?' he added, without raising his head.

Jane could feel the tension in Gwyn as he led her into the narrow hall and closed the door behind them.

'This is nice of you,' she said quietly.

'I wanted to show him. I don't know if he'll like them. But bloody hell, did you see his face when I gave him that hint about the verse form? He wasn't expecting that.'

Jane ducked her head and pushed open the door to the front room. She felt treacherous, knowing that Goff already knew perfectly well what to expect; she had told him as much. She was anxious to get out of the claustrophobic hall where the brass mirror reflected her and Gwyn back to herself. She went ahead of Gwyn into the front room.

At first sight it seemed to be all books. There were four tall, dark wooden bookcases: two side by side on the longest wall, one on the door wall and the fourth placed at an angle across one of the chimney niches. Behind the glass panels the spines were dark blue, faded green, dull red. Some had barely visible lettering on them. There was a number of fat volumes, three or four times the width of the others, and some modern dust jackets stood here and there, screaming out at the eye and emphasising the quiet uniformity of the rest. From the tops of many books, slips of paper sprouted.

Jane gazed round her and obediently listened to Gwyn's commentary. Here were the books Goff himself had worked on as a student, and which had started his collection. Here were the oldest editions of the texts; there were the commentaries. These were latter-day reworkings of the stories in the original texts – what Goff liked to call the old legends.

As she stood among the bookcases, listening to Gwyn's recital, Jane heard the rapture in his voice. He might deny it, but he had caught the bug again. How could he ever have hoped to lose it, with this in his background, waiting for him to return?

Gwyn was speaking to her.

'Look,' he said awkwardly, 'I want to go and talk to Goff. All right? Can I leave you here? Give us five minutes will you, to talk over the poems.'

'Sure,' Jane said. She nodded absently. 'I'm fine.'

Gwyn pulled the door to behind him. Jane lifted the glass front on one of the shelves and ran her fingers along the book spines. She couldn't read what they said and she lifted one out at random, a faded red volume. She opened it carefully, supporting the front cover with one hand and smelt the woody, powdery smell of old paper. The title page was in Welsh. She replaced the book and took out a green one; that was in Welsh too.

Maybe I'll try another shelf, she thought, but before she had reached the bookcase in the corner, she had turned away. She knew it would be no good. This wasn't for her.

It was disorienting to be cut off from books. Her life was all about them, for Christ's sake; what had she been doing for the last six years if not educating herself to understand books?

And now Gwyn was in the middle room with Goff, sharing with him the harbour poems and the mythic history behind them and she was shut in here, not understanding anything. Jane looked out of the window: it was prosaic, just the tarmac strip of the road and the red-brick backyards of the houses lower down the hill.

One, she thought: there is a strange woman in my mind who brings me visions.

Two: these visions connect with Gwyn's poems.

Three: the visions and the poems are about Madoc.

It should be one of the most exciting and uplifting times of her life, to be experiencing these phenomena with the man she loved. They should be sharing it, talking it through and trying to explore it. But Gwyn wouldn't talk about it; he just took refuge in his poems. And that left Jane with the half-remembered visions and the occasional presence of the woman. Jane shut her eyes; she had never felt lonelier than now. No, never, not even back when she was a sixteen-year-old and leaving everything she knew behind. It was a bleak thought: to be just married, intensely in love and so lonely.

The door opened behind her and she turned, trying to ease the tension from her face. Goff stood in the doorway, bent and radiant. He looked transfigured, Jane saw, and just behind him was Gwyn, flushed with relief and triumph. The poems had been a success; of course they had.

'Gwyn hasn't been looking after you properly, has he? He left you to it.' Goff peered at Jane, smiling slyly. 'Are you getting on all right in here?'

'Oh yes thank you,' said Jane. She enunciated rather too clearly but Goff didn't notice.

'All the same, all the same, he shouldn't be walking out on you.' He leaned heavily on the door knob and thumped Gwyn on the shoulder. 'That's no way to treat the woman who's helped you write the best poetry of your life, is it boy?'

Gwyn stopped mid-smile and shot a startled look at Goff.

'Well mon, you don't think it's a coincidence that you started writing like this when you met her? Oh no. No, you can't be that dull.'

Jane saw Gwyn's eyes rest uncertainly on her. He laughed.

'I can make my own love to Jane, thank you Goff,' he said.

'It's not making love, boy, it's – oh well. Oh well, there's none so blind as those that won't see, eh Jane?'

Jane smoothed her palms against her thighs.

'They're good, aren't they?' she said.

'They're excellent,' said Goff quietly. Excellent; the word teachers use. But there was no hiding Goff's emotion. Jane smiled suddenly at Gwyn, happy for him.

'Let's have a drink,' said Goff, 'a valedictory drink. Go and see what I've got in the dresser, Gwyn.'

Left alone with Jane for a moment, Goff observed her.

'Did the books upset you?'

'No. They're beautiful. I wish I understood Welsh.'

'Hmm. Do you? Why don't you get Gwyn to teach you.'

'I don't think,' said Jane softly, 'that he's too keen.'

'No. No well, he's possessive about his work. But you know that. And this work he's doing now – well, you know that too. Come on, let's go into the other room.'

They sat sipping their drinks – Gwyn a whisky, Jane a vermouth, Goff a sherry – while Gwyn and Goff talked eagerly about other poets. They were both displacing their excitement over Gwyn's poems. Jane was touched to see them in this complicity, but she found it hard to concentrate on what they said. It was nothing to do with her, after all. Her attention roved round the room, alighting on pieces of furniture and ornaments, never settling for long. She felt frustrated and lonely, God, so lonely.

After five minutes, Gwyn and Goff fell silent. Jane smiled vaguely at them both; she was aware of Goff watching her. Goff was the first to speak again.

'You've got plenty of time still haven't you?' he said. 'Why don't you take Jane up to the ladyrock? She should see our standing stone before she goes.'

'She doesn't want to see that old thing.'

'Oh I don't know.'

Was it something in his voice that alerted Jane? Or was it the mention of the standing stone itself? Suddenly her wandering thoughts gathered themselves and focused on Goff.

'You have a standing stone here? Like Stonehenge?'

'Good God, not quite. It's just one stone, slate, and very beautiful.'

'In a wood?'

Goff turned his head and the light from the windows reflected off his glasses, hiding his eyes. Now, why did I say that? thought Jane. How did I know?

'Yes,' said Goff. 'Ye-es, that's her. Up on the Pengroed Way, she is. She guards the valley.'

'She?' said Jane. 'Why is it a she?'

'Why not?' said Gwyn. He sounded testy, suddenly. 'It's given generations of people an excuse to make up stories. You can take your pick. She's an oracle – there's a cave close to her, our very own Delphi you see. Or she sprang up out of the ground in the thirteenth century, the spirit of a woman who died trying to save the local monastery from burning.'

'Oh rubbish,' interrupted Goff. 'You know damn well she's older than that, boy. Bronze Age at least.'

'Since when did legends have anything to do with historical fact? Or she's a marker on the way to Stonehenge, when they supposedly rolled the stones down from the Welsh mountains. A druid signpost, though that doesn't account for the gender, of course.'

'You don't know your history. She catches the moon at certain times of year, and that would make her a moon symbol and therefore female to the druids. At least be accurate if you're going to scoff.'

Goff's good-humoured voice and Gwyn's exasperated one rushed back and forth at each other like rival waves on a beach. Jane lifted her own voice above them.

'I'd like to see her,' she said.

Gwyn sighed. Goff stared calmly into his sherry.

'Oh Jane cariad,' said Gwyn. 'You dragged me all over Lundy looking for natural splendour. This is the last time I'll see Goff for months. Can't we just sit here and relax for once?'

Below the belt, thought Jane. Now, why don't you want me

to go up there? Instantly she was quite determined to go. She smiled affectionately at him.

'You're right, sweetheart. Why don't I leave you and Goff together for a while? I'll go up to the ladyrock on my own. I'd really like to see it and you can give me directions, can't you Goff?'

'Of course,' said Goff. His lower lip had crept out; she thought he was trying to restrain a smile. 'It's a nice walk, you can do it in fifteen or twenty minutes. You go over the bridge just past Roy's, where you were staying, and up the hill on the other side. Go past the row of white cottages at the top, take the path into the woods and follow it to the right for about a quarter of a mile.'

'OK.' Jane was already on her feet, draining her glass. 'What then?'

'Then you get lost and I have to come and look for you,' said Gwyn.

'Shut up Gwyn Thomas,' said Goff and there was no mistaking the teacher in his voice this time. Gwyn looked up slowly, in disbelief, but Goff ignored him, as if he were a tiresome ten-year-old misbehaving, and nodded encouragingly at Jane. 'What then? Then you'll be there. You'll know her when you see her.'

The sound of Jane's footsteps had faded from the drive and she had had time to reach the corner of the road before Gwyn spoke. He'd put his glass down but he didn't stand up; he didn't want to use any cheap means of facing down Goff. They were sitting opposite one another and Gwyn, the blue folder lying within his reach, his new poems inside, felt stronger than he had ever done in Goff's presence. He put the new strength and authority into his voice.

'What in God's name are you doing?'

The old man wasn't abashed.

'She wanted to see the ladyrock, lad.'

'You're making trouble between us, Goff.'

The dark flush travelled up Goff's neck and stained his ears.

'You've got no right to say that.'

'No, you've got no right to *do* this. I know all about your obsessions but you just keep them to yourself. You've been feeding Jane up on your precious Madoc and the bloody Mandans and it's not fair, she's not able to deal with it. She had an affair with a Mandan boy when she was still a kid. It got out of hand and turned so nasty she had to leave home. I bet she didn't tell you that, did she? She was more or less run out of town at sixteen. Sixteen. She's never been back. You can imagine what that's done to her. And then you start in on her with how the Mandans are descended from the Welsh – Jesus.'

Goff was sitting upright in his chair, his hands motionless on the wooden arms, but his eyes twitched and he looked away.

'I didn't know,' he said. 'No, she didn't tell me. I didn't mean to cause her pain.'

'No, well, you never do, do you? Do you know, the night after she'd come round to see you she had some sort of black-out and spoke in tongues? Eirlys told me. They had to bring her out of the pub talking rubbish. What the hell did you tell her?'

'She came to me asking about Haydn Phillips' painting in Caradoc's shop. So I told her about Haydn and America. She asked me, Gwyn. She came to me.'

'Oh God, Haydn bloody Phillips. What's he got to do with anything except that it gave you a chance to drag the Mandans in again? You're ruthless, aren't you? You just pick out whatever you think will hook people in. Well congratulations. It's worked. She's seeing Mandans and Madoc everywhere now.

'Look, do you know what she told me the first day we came round here? She told me the Mandans weren't even bloody well there in the twelfth century. They weren't there for hundreds of years, so Madoc would have had a job inter-marrying with them, wouldn't he?'

'I know,' said Goff calmly.

'You – what?'

'The Mandans didn't arrive in the mid-west until the fourteenth century, when a drought changed the population patterns. But there was someone there before them and they wouldn't all be gone, would they? Think, boy; people are never all gone – there's always some who stay. So the Mandans migrated into Madoc's country, found the remnants of these people and inter-married with them. And those people they found were the descendants of Madoc and the people *he* found at the head of the great river.

Remnants meeting other remnants, generating their own remnants. Good God, boy, what do you think the Welsh are if not remnants of the Celts?'

Gwyn shook his head wearily. He was troubled by the image of things connecting, sending out ripples, reverberations, waves of movement that ran endlessly into one another. It was horrible.

He slapped the arm of his chair to get rid of the image.

'All right, all right, I submit! I'm a remnant, you're a remnant, everyone's a bloody remnant. But Goff, leave Jane out of your remnant hunt. You're hurting her.'

Goff didn't answer immediately. Then slowly he took off his glasses, pulled a cloth out of his cardigan pocket and began to clean the lenses. His hands trembled; Gwyn watched him, torn between compassion and rage.

'I didn't mean to hurt her,' Goff said. His voice was very deep and dragged at the vowel sounds as if he was having trouble pronouncing them. 'Or you, Gwyn. But Jane came to me, you see, asking things, and I had to tell her. She saw the picture for herself and recognised it. She sees things in your poems. Don't set your face against it, lad, please.'

Gwyn looked at the blue folder. He couldn't stop himself: he reached out and picked it up, bringing it possessively into his lap. He spoke very clearly:

'This is my work, Goff. This is the best work I've ever done. I couldn't have written these poems without you. I know there are all sorts of things from the old stories in them. I'm not denying that. But these poems are mine. Stay away.'

Gwyn heard his words hang in the air of the quiet room. He hugged the folder and watched as Goff lifted the glasses back on to his nose.

'They are not your poems, lad. Oh aye, your words, perhaps, your syntax and phrasing. You've got a gift, all right. But that gift is being used for something. Don't fight it; be glad.'

The rage blossomed in Gwyn's head, turning everything orange and black. For a moment he revelled in it. Then he opened his eyes and as the angry mist dispersed he took Goff's measure: an elderly man, his flesh shrivelled away beneath the skin, his face bony and obdurate.

Oh Christ, what was there to get in such a rage about? He'd

end up as unbalanced as Goff at this rate. He exhaled a few times to calm himself down — Jane had taught him that technique — and leaned over to touch Goff's hand.

'Let's just forget it, shall we? And hope Jane doesn't get lost up there.'

The ladyrock stood on the left of the path, grey and secret. Behind her the ground rose in an earth bank and rivulets of water trickled over the moss. The path, a beaten earth track, ran straight from Jane past the ladyrock and then curved between the trees, out of sight.

Jane stood watching. It was so still, like a memory or a dream. But it was neither. She wasn't aware of her feet carrying her along the track, nor of her lips beginning to murmur, almost croon, words which made no sense.

She was smiling as she reached her hands out to touch the stone, and so was the unknown woman.

Gwyn's arm was tightly round Jane's shoulders. He'd hardly had his hands off her since she'd come in. He wanted to protect her; or did he want her to protect him? She had that inturned look again; he was getting used to that secretive radiance in her eyes. What emotions and imaginings, what hallucinations, for God's sake, had Goff set off in her now?

Thank God the taxi was here. Gwyn just wanted to go; to leave behind this over-familiar house and the landscape that tugged uncomfortably at his heart and, above all, Goff. Goff was coming slowly along the hall now, looking from Jane to Gwyn.

'You've taken the bags out then? You're all ready? Well, I won't keep you, the driver will be waiting to go.' He paused in front of Jane and held his hands out to her. 'Goodbye, my dear. I'm so very glad to have met you.'

Jane disentangled herself from Gwyn's grip. He watched her take Goff's hands, then put her arms round the old man's neck and kiss him. It was a demonstrative gesture for her and Gwyn saw that she was trembling. Goff patted her shoulder, his own hand quite steady now.

'God bless, Jane,' he said. He hugged her to him for a few seconds, then he glanced up, over her shoulder, at Gwyn. 'And

God bless you too, lad. You will look after each other now, won't you?'

He held Gwyn's gaze, and there was an uncharacteristic anxiety in his eyes. Reluctantly, and against his better judgement, Gwyn smiled.

Part Three

20

Glesig is pressed into the side of the boat, standing very straight and still. I don't think he's moved for an hour. He's watching the shore as it comes gradually closer. I don't know how anyone could stand still for so long, especially with all this fuss and chatter going on.

There's still his face is. I don't think even his eyes are moving. But he's not calm.

He's been standing here for two days now, since we sighted the first piece of shore to the north-east. It was only a tiny pale gleam on the horizon and we soon lost it, because the wind and the current drew us away. But Glesig's been here ever since – he leaves the side to go and see to the foals and to answer Madoc's calls to examine the charts, but then he comes back. Today, Madoc's been taking the charts to him.

When day broke this morning, we could see the shore clearly. Now the sun's high in the sky and beating down on our faces, and the coast is pale yellow and dark green: there are long broad swoops of sand and places where the green comes right down to the water. No rocks, no cliffs; white birds with long necks and blue-tipped wings are flying low over the water between us and the shore.

Ynys Llyr: we're here. All the men who were on Madoc's first voyage say they know it, just by the look of the place. And someone has just shouted out that he can smell it. He's going mad with excitement and the other people are now leaning towards the shore, tipping their faces up and sniffing. There's silly they look

– most of them don't know what they're sniffing for anyway. Oh, but what was that? A smell like spices – no, like flowers – no, I don't know what to call it. It came on the wind and it was beautiful. I've never smelt anything like it before.

We're too far away to see if there are any people or animals. There are no boats. Madoc says there weren't any last time, either: the people of Ynys Llyr don't go to sea.

Madoc is at the prow, gripping the gunwale. Crushed in his fist is one of his charts. I've seen him happy, many times, but not like this. This happiness is so fierce. He looks across the green waters to the shore as if he wants to swallow them both, and now his eyes are ranging over the company of ships. I can see him looking at Arun's ship at the far end of the company, with the flag of the boar flying from its mast. His eyes move over the other ships, and even when he looks at Meurig's ship his look of fierce content doesn't change. Now he's come back to the *Gwenllyr* and he's turning, looking for me.

He's brown-skinned and thinner than he used to be. We're all thinner. Under my skirts I've got patches of red on the skin of my legs. We brought herbs with us but I can't find the right ones to make the patches go. My head-dress is torn; I lost my spares when we were washing them over the side one day. Some of the women are leaving theirs off altogether now, but I keep mine: I like it when Madoc takes it off in the night and my hair tumbles down just for him.

This voyage is nearly over, thank God. It's been harder than I expected: we lost Beuno's ship last month, in a storm, and only five people were saved from it. On our *Gwenllyr* three have died of fever; sixteen people have died on the other ships. So many of us are sick and we're all weakened. And less than half the animals are left. But we've made it.

Madoc, we've made it.

Madoc's found me now, and he's calling me to him. There's imperious he is, with his sharp gestures of summons. It makes me excited to answer him; to move slowly through the crowded deck to him, my head high.

We are sailing in closer and closer to the shore. I can make out different kinds of green now: there are trees and bushes and there are also long low plants that spread on to the sand.

I reach Madoc and he puts both his hands, crumpled chart and all, on top of mine.

'Ynys Llyr my lady,' he says, and his voice is very guttural. 'What do you think of it?'

The scent of flowers and spiced wood is blowing in our faces again. Beautiful; it's beautiful.

The coracle is too full: we're low down in the water and swaying. All around us people are swimming – they can't wait for the coracles to return, and the water's so clear you can look straight down and see the stones and shells and strange coloured fish. A few yards ahead, the sea-bed shelves upwards and men are wading. Some of the women and children are jumping out of the coracles now and wading with them.

Now Bleddyn, our oarsman, puts up his paddle and swings himself over the side, holding the coracle steady and pulling it a few more feet until it bangs against the bed. At last! I can't wait any longer, I scramble out first and stand in the thigh-deep water: my sodden skirts feel glorious against my hot skin. I help out little Angharad, whose legs are mending, and hold her until her mother, Sianed, is in the water too and able to take her. Angharad is sobbing with excitement and fear.

I join the rush through the shallows as we all move as fast as we can, laughing and shouting and warning one another – 'Don't step on the pink things! They've got spines!' 'Mind out for the jellyfish!' – towards the strand. The men are carrying their bows high above their heads, to keep the strings dry.

Glesig is out of the water already. He's left his cloak behind; it's weeks since he wore anything but a thin shirt and now that's dripping wet and clinging to him and his body looks different from the bodies of the men around him, his limbs looser. Madoc is not far from him; Madoc's out of the water too and wet only below the waist – he came in a coracle, as leader of the voyage, and waded only the last few yards – and he's standing on a piece of sand shaded by the low green stuff, and he's watching Glesig.

I think Madoc's waiting for Glesig to look across at him, or speak to him. But Glesig doesn't realise: he's walking up the yellow sand with long strides and his body tilted forward. It's nothing like the way he moved in Gwynedd yet it looks right here. He's looking up in between the bushes and trees, making little movements of his head as though he's tracking a deer or wild pig. He seems completely absorbed.

I see Madoc watching him as he moves around the rim of the trees, peering in between the trunks. Glesig vanishes into the dimness for a few seconds – from where I am I can see his shirt moving among the bushes, but Madoc can't and he strides quickly across the sand, making funny little jumping steps, and follows him. Before he reaches the edge of the trees, Glesig comes out again, a little further down. I see Madoc relax. He slows his pace and walks towards Glesig, calling him to get his attention.

Glesig turns and looks at him blankly. Then he reaches out and grabs Madoc's arm and they both turn away and look at something in the wood.

It was Madoc who calmed everyone when they appeared. Duw, that was a panic. We heard them before we saw them, coming through the wood, but the men hadn't had time to get their hands to their bows when they were spilling out on to the sand. Brown-skinned people with black hair and bony faces and with necklaces of shells and fish-bones – and naked.

We knew the people of the island didn't wear many clothes, but naked! The women's breasts showed and the men's pricks, and even the women's cunts you could almost see, because they only wore little low-slung girdles of grasses and shells, which didn't even cover their hair.

The men all wore their hair up on their heads, fixed into little knots, and some wore arrows stuck through the knots. Others had very long bows, as long as themselves, and short light spears, but the men in front weren't armed. They were carrying shiny discs and animal skins and the women carried provisions: bowls filled with berries, rush baskets piled with grain, animals like little dragons, drinking casks.

And they were all talking, or singing, or praying – we couldn't tell, the noise was like the screeching of birds. We were screeching too – screaming and shouting to each other and running back to the sea, grabbing the children. I ran to the water's edge myself but then I saw Madoc standing his ground at the top of the strand and I came back. His men were clustering round him, but he waved them clear. They shuffled back a step, their hands on their weapons. I crept forward, through the outer lines of the men, and then I was grabbed suddenly in a very strong grip. It was Cadell: his baby face was fierce, for once.

'Stay here, my lady,' he said. 'It's dangerous.'

'Let me go, Cadell,' I said. 'I've got to hear what Madoc's saying.'

'No,' said Cadell. 'He wouldn't forgive me if you were hurt. I wouldn't forgive myself.'

I looked in his face and saw what I'd never realised before — that Cadell is half in love with me himself. But I didn't have time to think anything about it, because Glesig and Madoc were moving forward side by side and I was straining to hear what they said.

What a sight it was. All our men behind Madoc, and the people of the island covering the other half of the shore, facing him. All their nakedness and brownness, their strange sharp bones and the decorations they wear round their necks and ankles. And Glesig standing next to Madoc, looking half like us and half like them. Peculiar it was, to see him there. He was the same red-brown colour as the strangers, the colour of rich loam, and under his wet shirt you could see that his body was like theirs. And Glesig had their black hair and the same bones showing through the skin and the eyes, those dark, far apart eyes.

Yes, he looked like them. But he looked like us too. Perhaps it was the shirt, or the hair in braids. Perhaps it was seeing him shoulder to shoulder with Madoc. I could see the people of the island looking from him to Madoc and they didn't know what to think.

One man had stepped in front of all the other strangers. He had dark red stains on his chest, in a petal pattern. He said something to Glesig.

They didn't understand each other at once. The leader of the strangers and Glesig and Madoc were all taking it in turns to say things and to gesture with their hands. I could hear them quite clearly because apart from those three, no one made any sound. There was just the cry of birds and the shushh-shhuuu-ushhh of the sea. I recognised some of the words Glesig and Madoc said, from my own learning of them: 'the sun' Glesig said several times, and Madoc said 'the sea' and 'friendship' and 'house'. But there were many words I didn't understand – Glesig and Madoc were trying different languages, I think.

In the end it was Madoc, not Glesig, who found some words they could all understand. The leader of the strangers was triumphant: he made a great speech and I could see that Madoc and Glesig hardly understood a word. But soon they were all three placing tributes on the ground between them. We'd brought a store of objects off the ships for that purpose and the men were passing them up to Madoc one by one: copper cups, a silk cloak, a knife with a carved handle, tin buckles, a bronze ring. I couldn't see all the things the strangers passed up for us but among them were animals' skins, the round shiny discs which were shields, and many things to eat and drink.

Then Glesig and Madoc went into the heart of the crowd, side by side with the leader, and all the other strangers began to walk forward towards us, staring curiously and reaching out hands to touch.

At last, Cadell's hand slackened on my arm. I think he'd forgotten it was there. He looked embarrassed and said he was sorry if he'd hurt me. Even with everything else that was happening, the realisation that Cadell felt like that touched me; it made me feel I really belong to the kindred of Gwynedd.

There's strange it was, that welcome party. Because that's what it was. Madoc and Glesig had told the leader we'd come to be their friends and allies, you see. I'd been worried in advance that we wouldn't get the chance to tell them, that they'd just attack us. But Madoc and Glesig said not. In his country, Glesig says, you announce going to war. You don't raid another kindred without warning, as they do in our country. And it's true, these strangers came to us with gifts and waited to see what we intended. And they've made us welcome.

But Duw, surely we can't really be going to settle here, with these people? They wear no clothes. You should have seen all the good women of the kindred, not knowing where to look. Well, I didn't know where to look either . . . it is hot, though, in our dresses. The sun beats down on our faces and backs and on the sand, so it's too hot to walk on. All afternoon, the sweat has been running down my body; I've waded back into the water several times, to get cool.

These people are called the people of the clear-water river islands; that's what Glesig and Madoc have told us. Wenlyn understands a tiny bit of what the strangers say, and he's been passing it on, too. They're called that because they live on the banks of a river on the other side of this wood, and the river has many clear-water streams with islands in it. They store their winter provisions in granaries on the islands, and swim or row their boats to them. They have coracles like ours: at least, I think that's what the two women who've been talking to me and giving me fruits meant by their pointings and their foreign words.

They've touched me and I've touched them. Their skin is smoother than mine but harder. Their hair is like Glesig's – slippery and stiff. They keep touching my head-dress and murmuring about it.

We've been here hours now, and not a word has passed between me and Madoc. He's busy with the leader and – and look at that! There are women there, with him, and women with heavy necklaces. Is one of them the leader's wife? Or wives – remember what Glesig says. There's something about the way that these women look – prouder than the two who are feeding me. Important. And Madoc is being very gracious to them.

I look around for Cadell or Wenlyn, to ask them to take me to him. I must get there. I must be presented too. I am Madoc's lady. But I can't see either of them: but here's Glesig, walking with three young men of his own age, all of them with arrows in their hair – warriors, I think they must be.

'Glesig,' I say it clear and commanding, and the three men around him stare at me. 'Who's Madoc talking to?'

Glesig follows my gaze.

'The leader, Salin-pay-o, and his first three women.'

'I should meet them, shouldn't I?'

Glesig glances at me. His face is stern, like the faces of these three young male warriors, but inside the fierceness his eyes flicker a smile. Glesig Dog knows just what's in my mind.

'You will meet them, great lady,' he says. 'After these three men have paid tribute to you.'

He turns to the three men and says something. I don't know

what it is, but from his gestures and their faces I think he's telling them that I am Madoc's lady, and a great woman.

The women around me – who have fallen back now the men are here – are beginning to exclaim. The three warriors touch their foreheads and chests to me, and then they each take an arrow out of their hair and lay it on the ground in front of me.

And now they are looking over here – Madoc and the leader and the women. I can see them out of the corner of my eye.

'Tell the men I accept their tribute,' I say to Glesig. 'Tell them that I will bring them something from my ship as a gift.'

Glesig tells them and now I can hear Madoc's voice.

'Bring my lady here,' he's saying to someone. It's Wenlyn, coming across the sand to me.

I walk with him, my head up, wearing my head-dress like a crown, and I can hear Madoc saying something halting, in their language, to the leader. He turns to greet me and holds out his hand to draw me in. For a second his eyes slide past me and I know he's looking at Glesig. My lord, you shouldn't need Glesig to remind you of me. His fingers close so tightly on mine they hurt.

Beautiful, this country is. The things we've seen this afternoon. Now we are back on the *Gwenllyr*, for the night, but we can still feel the hardness of the ground under our feet and we're all eager to have it there again. It's dark, but it's still possible to see the shore, because some of Salin-pay-o's people are there, sitting in huts of tree branches and grasses, with fires burning in between them.

Here on the *Gwenllyr*, just like on all the other ships, everyone is listening to descriptions of the clear-water river islands and the settlement there. Even I'm listening, though I've seen it myself. About fifty of us went, a handful from each ship, with Madoc and Glesig and Meurig at the head, with Salin-pay-o. And me with Salin-pay-o's wives, just behind. We walked two hours, through forest thick with undergrowth. What a forest – we've all had a go at describing it to the people who stayed on the shore. The trees are tall and some of them have black, sweet-smelling bark. There are still waters which hide creatures like giant lizards with teeth; from above they look like tree branches floating, and before you bathe or fish or even lean over the water you've got to stir its surface with stones. If the branches move, you get away from the water. There are ways of hunting these creatures, but they take lots of men and are dangerous. There are silkworms clustered on the leaves of trees and everywhere their filmy, sticky residue.

Just listen to Iolo the Songman, telling them about it. Madoc is sitting on one of the trading goods chests with Arun, talking hard. Meurig isn't here – they didn't tell him they were going to meet and talk and so he's busy on his own ship, celebrating our safe arrival. Madoc and Arun are taking advantage of it. It makes me laugh, how they despise him.

I don't know what Madoc and Arun are talking about, though; now and then Madoc stops and seems to be telling Arun to listen to Iolo – of course, Arun didn't come with us to the clear-water island so he didn't see the hide and branch houses, the mud and branch granaries which are beginning to fill up with provisions, the tall crop, three heads taller than a man, with ears of grain a foot long. Iolo is doing very well, telling these people how to imagine what they've never seen.

For a while, Madoc called Glesig over to him and Arun and he stood beside them, his back turned to me and his head bent. I couldn't tell what they were saying to him. Since then, he's been at the side of the ship again, like he was when we arrived. But he's standing at the wrong side: instead of looking east, towards the place where the settlement is, he's looking through the darkness to the west, and I can see that he's reading the stars.

Madoc is behaving oddly towards Glesig. I don't think anyone's noticed it but me. I keep seeing the way Madoc chased across the sand to keep Glesig in his sight when we'd just landed. And all the time we were being taken through the forest, Madoc had Glesig close by him. He's watching him. It's as if he thinks Glesig is going to run away.

'Glesig?'

I've come up quietly behind him. I didn't want him to hear me coming; I didn't want Madoc to notice me go. Glesig turns only very slightly, just enough for me to know he's heard. I join him at the ship's side, so close our arms nearly touch.

'What are you looking for?'

He doesn't answer.

'Your home,' I say. 'Isn't it?'

He still doesn't answer, but he goes back to looking up at the sky, at the stars that are over the land to the west and north of here.

'Is that where it is?' I don't know why, but as I say it, the idea thrills me. I don't even know what I'm looking for, but among the powdering of stars up there in the blackness is a conjunction that Glesig knows how to recognise. Below it, somewhere much further in to this strange country, is his home.

'Yes, it's there. A long way away,' he adds.

'Do you want to leave us?' Of course he does. Why should he be our prisoner any longer, now we're in his country? But the thought hurts me. 'Does Madoc know?'

'I don't want to leave you,' says Glesig. He's looking at me in surprise. 'Madoc is my brother.'

Now it's my turn to stare. Glesig, Madoc's foster brother. This can't be true; why would Madoc make his captive into his foster brother? Glesig has no warband. Glesig has nothing that can help Madoc in his ventures. He couldn't even help Madoc find the right course on the voyage; he's no seaman.

Rhiryd is Madoc's foster brother. But Rhiryd isn't here.

'You're Madoc's foster brother?' I ask.

The hand closes on my arm, I feel his shoulder behind mine and Madoc has swung me round and is holding me in a hard embrace and smiling into my eyes.

'Asking questions, my lady? You'll have to learn to keep your voice down.'

I gaze at him: Madoc hasn't spoken to me like that since the day we met, when he challenged me about having a lover.

'Why, my lord?' I say at once. 'A new foster brother of yours is something to be welcomed.'

He won't talk to me like that; I can't let him talk to me like that. Madoc steps in front of me, blocking out Glesig.

'Speak quietly, Ceinwen,' he says. 'You're not herding pigs in Cynfael now.' I gasp in astonishment and then, looking at Madoc's warning smile, I'm full of anger. I try to move away but he grabs my other hand and holds me tight.

'You're hurting me, my *lord*,' I say. Beyond Madoc I can hear Glesig move uncertainly.

'Leave us, Glesig Dog,' says Madoc over his shoulder. I hear Glesig move away, back across the deck to the crowd around Iolo.

Madoc and I look at each other. I thought he was angry when he grabbed me but now I see that it's not displeasure in his face. It's energy: the look of someone who knows what he wants and knows what he must do to get it. His eyes are moving over my face, concentrating on me. He's dragging my thoughts towards him.

'I don't want Arun to know,' he says urgently. 'I don't want any of the captains to know about Glesig. They'll suspect me of going behind their backs.'

Madoc is still holding me – one hand grips my shoulder, the other holds my wrist.

'I don't understand,' I say, trying not to flinch. 'What are you doing? Why have you made him your foster brother?'

'We're not in Gwynedd now. We're in Glesig's country. He has things to teach us. Oh, the others don't see it, but they weren't with me the first time. I saved Glesig then, saved him from starvation and bandits and he saved me and my men in return. We're bonded now.'

I look into his face and I remember him earlier, on the shore.

'Why were you following him today, then?' I whisper. 'Did you think he'd run away?'

Madoc's eyes, violet as they always are in the dark, half close.

'Don't you trust him?' I ask.

'You can never be sure,' says Madoc abruptly. He frowns and shakes his head. 'Who could be? You've got to guard what's yours.'

'He told me he didn't want to leave us. And you won't be able to watch him once we're settled. There are too many places to hide in these forests.'

Madoc's hands are easing off me. He turns me gently to face the ship's side and the great sky.

'We're not settling here,' he says in my ear. 'We're sailing on tomorrow.'

'But – ' the word comes out loud, like a cat's cry. No one

hears: it's lost in the noise of the people talking around Iolo. 'But you said to Salin-pay-o we'd stay. You said we'd settle further up the clear-water river and be his allies.'

Madoc shakes his head. He's smiling.

'That was just words. I couldn't risk offending him, could I? No Ceinwen, we're going on. In that direction.' He nods towards the north-west, at the same stretch of sky and the same shadow of land that drew Glesig's gaze.

'Glesig's country?' I speak quietly this time. It's not just because Madoc told me to be careful, but because the idea pleases me. Yes, it pleases me very much. It's too strange here in this hot country with these naked people; Glesig's country – well, I feel I almost know it.

But I understand why Madoc is anxious.

'Will the people agree?' I ask in a whisper. 'They're sick of voyaging, Madoc, and it's so far away. Up that great river. We'll never all survive.'

'Probably not all of us, no.'

'Then how are you going to persuade them?'

'With the help of my foster brother Glesig. He wants to take us there, you see. He wants to go back to his people in triumph, bringing a powerful ally to help protect them from the wars with the other kindreds. And bringing something else, too.'

I jump slightly. This is the first time he's ever mentioned it to me.

'The dreamstone,' I say.

'What?' Madoc looks at me questioningly. 'Oh yes, that. Has Glesig shown you that?'

His voice is sharp with interest.

'No my lord. I've never seen it. He's just told me the story of it and I know he keeps it on him.'

'Yes,' says Madoc. 'I didn't know he'd told you. But I didn't mean that, Ceinwen, I meant horses.'

'Ah.'

'Yes. You see, don't you? What horses would mean for the first kindred who bred them in Ynys Llyr?'

'Yes, I do. I do.'

'Power in battle. Speed of travel – some of the kindreds around Madoc's country are travelling peoples; they're always moving on, you know, building a new tref every season. Trade. But mainly battle. Think of it, Ceinwen. Glesig has travelled months across this island and seen only one coast, this one. And on all that land, there are no horses. Think of the power, for the kindred who have horses over those who haven't.'

I am thinking. And I'm seeing. I'm seeing a new Gwynedd, but much bigger, stretching from this shore to wherever the northern coast lies, embracing mountains and rivers and valleys, and our kindreds settling in trefi in the best, most fertile of all the valleys and plains.

'The foal has died on the *Gwenllyr*. And the mare is sick. What about the other ships?'

'We've got seven foals and six mares, two of them probably won't live. Four of the foals are male. We'll put them to the mares as soon as they're old enough. If only we could have brought some stallions, but they'd have wrecked the ships.'

'Well, Glesig's good with them and getting better. And we've got Idris Stableman, and the Hellynt kindred know horses well. And there's me.'

Madoc nods.

'There's you, my lady. I remember the Cynfael way with horses.'

Madoc's face is gleaming in the moonlight, and I can see he's remembering that day in our tref, when he asked me to go with him. I like him remembering that, but I want him to recognise something else too: I am his royal lady, here as I was in Dreugyllt.

'Call Glesig,' I say to him, my voice quiet but very clear. I want him to know that I won't be ignored and treated roughly.

'My lady?' says Madoc softly, half surprised, half warning.

'Call Glesig,' I say, 'and tell me, in front of him, that he is your foster brother. Commend us to each other. Like you did with Rhiryd.'

Madoc moves his head sideways as if he can't see me clearly. He watches me for a second, considering, then he turns and calls Glesig. As Glesig walks across the crowded deck towards us, Madoc looks back at me and I can't tell if he's smiling or not.

21

It was a sense of movement rather than a noise which brought her into the living room. As she came out of the kitchen she heard a scurry or a flap, like papers falling. She crossed the narrow hall into the living room and a darkness flitted at the edge of her vision. She had the impression that she's just missed something. She looked attentively at the room: the blinds were half-raised, the sofa had two books and a copy of the *New York Review* on it, her papers were still in their pile on the desk. Gwyn's sweater was hanging on the back of the armchair.

Then she saw them: on the table in the corner, on top of Gwyn's second-hand music centre. The two birds perched motionless on the shiny casing, their bright eyes staring at her.

Her coffee swayed violently in the mug and she clasped the china with both hands to steady it. There was something horrible about seeing the birds here: one was a light brown speckled bird, perhaps a thrush, the other a darker green-black colour. She could see the oily sheen on their feathers; the pale brown one blinked, showing scaly eyelids.

Jane crept across the floor. As she came within arm's reach of them, they hopped slightly closer together. She stepped backwards. She didn't want them to fly up suddenly. She waved her coffee cup at them, cautiously. They twitched their beaks. She stamped her foot. The larger bird made two hops away from its partner, then came back.

'Gwyn!' called Jane. At the sound of her voice, the birds rose into the air and began flying zig-zag around the room, cannoning into the furniture.

'Yes?' said Gwyn, wandering in. He had only just got up and was shrugging on a bathrobe. 'What the – ? Where did they come from?'

'Through the windows I guess. Look out.'

The green-black bird had flown straight at him, wings beating wildly.

'Ugh! Get out! Out. Shoo!'

Gwyn ran to the door and shut it, then he went to the window and pulled up the blinds. The window was open a few inches at the top. 'How the hell did they get in through that little gap?' He pulled the bottom sash up and the cold air billowed in. The birds had settled again, one on the desk and the other on the floor in the centre of the room. Gwyn rushed at them waving his arms and Jane flattened herself against the wall as they lifted into the air again. For a few seconds the two birds whirled round in the middle of the room, above Gwyn's shooing arms, then they flew directly for the open window and were gone.

Gwyn and Jane looked at one another.

'That was bizarre,' Jane said shakily. 'Do you know, before I called you they were just perched on your music centre, looking at me. I got right up close, they didn't care.'

'Urban birds. Squatters. Oh God, there's bird shit on the table.' Jane stared at the yellow spatters.

'I didn't see them do that, did you? I'll clean it up.'

'No, I will. You've had your shower already. Ugh. Have we got any disinfectant?'

Jane watched Gwyn scrubbing at the bird droppings, his bathrobe sleeves rolled up and his jaw set. He was very thorough, prowling round the room to check that he hadn't missed anything, rescrubbing the cleaned surfaces with new lengths of kitchen paper and disinfectant.

'Revolting things,' he said, carrying the soiled paper and the disinfectant bottle through to the kitchen. When Jane followed him, he'd wrapped the paper in a plastic bag and placed it by the door. 'Can you take it down on your way out, lovely? I've got to dive into a hot shower and get clean.'

'Sure,' said Jane. She had to raise her voice as he was already half-way to the bathroom. She watched him go, rather surprised. She'd never seen him spring into domestic action like that before; those birds had really disturbed him. She wandered to the bathroom door, reluctant to leave the apartment without kissing him goodbye. Since their return from Wales she often felt a hunger for his touch. She wasn't sure if it was passion or tenderness she craved, but either way, when the touch had come and gone she was usually left unsatisfied.

She stopped herself from opening the shower curtain and reaching for Gwyn. Instead she called out 'See you this evening sweetheart' from the doorway.

'See you,' called Gwyn.

Jane checked her mail tray in the *Review* office. There were several envelopes addressed to her, all magazine business, and one personal letter: from Miss Archer. Jane had been half expecting it ever since her return – there had been plenty of time for Miss Archer to receive the card Jane had sent her from Lundy, bearing a bulletin about her marriage and her honeymoon and a passing reference to Haydn Phillips.

Jane opened Miss Archer's letter first and read it quickly. There wasn't much of it: less than one side of a page, with none of Miss Archer's usual conversational ramblings.

Dear Jane

Thank you kindly for your news, which certainly did surprise me. Congratulations dear, and every happiness for the future. As you know, I still have access to the High School library and have asked there for your young man's book, but they don't have it. I have ordered it from Shelby's.

Your description of Wales was very interesting to me. I have never been there but Haydn Phillips talked to me about it. Yes, I knew him. He was a very talented young man and it was a tragedy, what happened. They told me he'd destroyed all his paintings, yet you say you've seen one. I've often wondered if that one would turn up, sooner or later. And where.

We have two feet of snow here; you know what Renoxia

winters are like. White Dove Pond has been frozen for weeks.

Best regards, Jennifer Archer.

Jane frowned: the reference to Haydn Phillips was curious. 'That one.' Had she described the painting to Miss Archer? She couldn't remember doing so.

Jane put some coffee on to steep and began opening the rest of her mail. She was soon interrupted by the sound of footsteps outside and she looked up expectantly. Harry usually came in on a Tuesday morning. She hadn't seen much of him in the ten days she'd been back at Brockham; she'd enjoy a few hours with him now, to chat over events and catch up with the gossip.

'Hi,' she smiled as he came in. 'You look on top of things.'

'No more than I ever am. And no less.'

Harry kissed her hallo, then went over to his desk to tidy the already tidy mail trays. He looked handsome and relaxed, like a big blond cat basking. Now that Jane came to think of it, he had been like this ever since her return from Wales.

'Harry?' she said tentatively.

'Ye-es.' He sounded gently mocking.

'Has something happened?'

He nodded, head bent, and continued aligning papers.

'Yes, oh perspicacious one.'

'Who is he?'

Harry stopped tidying and looked her in the face. He looked uncharacteristically shy.

'His name is Edward Catzberger. He's one of the theatre critics on the *Times*. And I met him – don't laugh – through Duane. He and Molly had a dinner just after Christmas and I was invited.'

'Yes, I remember.' It had been just a few days before her and Gwyn's departure for Wales.

'Edward was there. I don't think Duane exactly intended to bring us together. I think I was invited as part of his literary empire. But he doesn't seem to mind. As a matter of fact, he's been much more kindly disposed towards me since; Edward's seal of approval must count for something.'

'You didn't get together at Duane's dinner?'

'Of course not. That's your style, not mine.' Harry stretched lazily and smiled. 'Don't look so cross. I can't help being a preppy prude. No, it was all very decorous. Edward called me the next day and asked me if I'd like to take his second ticket to the play he was reviewing that night.'

'Having gotten the number from Duane?'

'Having gotten the number from Duane. And there we are.'

'Harry, I'm really pleased. Is it top secret?'

'No. Why should it be?'

'So do I get to meet him?'

'Whenever you like.'

Jane watched Harry get off the desk and sit down behind it.

'Why didn't you tell me sooner?'

Harry began counting out the manuscripts on his desk.

'One – two – three – oh no, four, and all read by Jane Pridden already. Why do you have to be so efficient? I haven't been keeping it from you Jane. The moment just didn't arise till now.'

You mean, thought Jane, that I didn't notice the change in you till now. She felt guilty and hurt in equal measure. Harry's relationship had begun even before she and Gwyn left for Wales, yet he'd said nothing about it. And these last ten days he must have been seeing Edward over and over. No wonder he hadn't been free any of the evenings she'd tried to arrange to see him.

'I suppose it didn't,' she said. 'Well, I'm really pleased, Harry. What's he like?'

'Urbane and reticent. I don't know how he combines the two but he does. He's thirty-two, slim, dark, middle height, comes of good parentage in Washington DC. More coffee?'

Jane didn't answer him at once: she was listening, not to him but to the familiar half-dreaded, half-welcome sound inside her head. It was a gentle soughing, like hearing wind in the meadow grasses or suddenly being aware of the blood rushing through your heart. 'Ah – no thanks,' she said.

She could feel Harry looking at her. He put the coffee jug down and came over to her desk.

'Jane, are you OK? You really don't seem yourself.'

'I'm fine, a little tired.'

'I don't mean this morning. I mean in general. Ever since you came back from Wales you've seemed preoccupied and – well, you don't look very happy.'

Jane moved the mess of her papers around.

'I'm happy,' she said absent-mindedly. 'Why shouldn't I be happy?'

'Truly?'

'Oh for God's sake, Harry!'

He stepped back abruptly.

'I don't want to make your business mine, of course.' He sounded very polite; she'd hurt his feelings now. 'I'll make fresh coffee.'

Too late, Jane realised that she'd been rude. Jesus, did he have to be so touchy though? She watched Harry's broad back. Clad in the expensive dark green wool jacket, it looked vulnerable and hurt.

'Look I'm sorry,' Jane said. 'I'm preoccupied. Too much work to do. Will we have lunch today?'

Harry glanced over his tailored shoulder.

'We usually do on Tuesdays, don't we?'

'Just confirming,' said Jane. 'Good.'

By lunch time she would have cleared her mind of Miss Archer's letter and she would be able to give Harry her attention. They had quite a bit to tell each other, by the sound of it.

But as they took their places in the refectory, a hand waved at them. Harry lifted his hand in response and the next moment Gail was at his shoulder, carrying pot roast on a tray.

'Hallo Harry, hallo Jane. May I join you?'

'Of course,' said Harry courteously. He gave Jane a quick look over Gail's head. Trust Gail to butt in, she thought, turning to her with a smile.

'Did you see the *Times* this morning?' Gail said to Harry as they sat down. 'Edward roasted *Pontoon by Numbers*.'

'Well it was shit,' said Harry. 'He was embarrassed to have subjected you to it.'

'Oh you know how I enjoy hating a production.'

Jane looked from one to the other as they tore delicately into the play they had both seen with Edward last night. Gail had met Edward; Gail seemed to know him quite well.

Jane ate most of her lunch in silence, while the others talked. By the time she'd finished, it was clear to her that she was no longer Harry's main friend and confidant; she was not even his second. Since when had Harry become great friends with Gail? Since I've been in Wales with Gwyn and Goff, she thought. How quickly things change.

It made her feel very much on the outside. She began playing with her fork, drawing patterns in the leftover sauce on her plate. Lots of wide-winged Vs, like birds in flight.

Gwyn pressed his pen nib over and over again into the paper, with precise, controlled movements. Stab, stab, stab. The black dots multiplied in the loop of the 'b', thickened the stem of the 'i', spread across the 'r'. When he had obscured the 'd', Gwyn moved on to the eighth line of the poem and began on the letters of the third word: 'w', 'i', 'n', 'g'. He worked across them, diligently blocking them out. They didn't belong in the poem. It was hard enough dealing with the characters who were beginning to emerge, and all the glorious things they were seeing, without accommodating these ominous bird images as well. And they were ominous: they kept sneaking in just when he was enjoying himself, casting a shadow over the mood.

Gwyn shoved the pen away from him with such force that it rolled off the desk and spattered ink on the floor. He got up and went to the window, staring down at the lighted campus square. It was nearly six o'clock and dark. It looked very cold out there: people were hurrying across the square in heavy coats and woolly hats. Gwyn still couldn't get used to those: now that the fierce cold had set in he could understand the quilted coats and the mufflers, but those woolly hats that people pulled down over their ears? He couldn't imagine being cold enough to wear one of those. He kept trying to persuade Jane to throw hers away, or at least wear it differently. 'You look like Benny Hill!' he'd said in exasperation yesterday, and she had shot him a look of utter contempt and slammed out of the flat.

They kept having stupid little clashes. Gwyn knew they were often his fault; he was so preoccupied with his writing that he found himself make careless comments or misunderstanding what Jane was saying and taking things the wrong way.

Yet he couldn't tear himself away from his work. Three poems were now complete and he was on his way to finishing the fourth.

He knew he was writing a series, and suspected that there were at least another four instalments to go. He hadn't told Jane this; he hadn't told her anything much about the poems recently. After that run-in on Lundy, and her private rapture courtesy of Goff on their last afternoon, he'd decided to keep his work to himself.

It was partly embarrassment. After all his angry denials, he didn't quite know how to admit to her that she had been right and he was indeed writing a series of poems about Madoc. The knowledge made him chuckle guiltily. He'd given her such a hard time over that; she would have every right to be fed up.

He grinned and whistled through his teeth. What a subject for a Welsh poet. And what scope, with all the characters and action and the juggling with history. Add to that the fact that it was written from a woman's point of view – it had been sharp of Jane to see that – and he had the makings of a new high water mark in Gwyn Thomas's career.

High water mark; it was funny how these maritime images kept slipping into his mind. Well, that was getting inside the subject for you. Gwyn was mildly surprised to discover how much he knew about navigation and the bits and bobs of Medieval life.

There were a number of things that baffled him, though. He could see that the Indian – because Jane was right again, there was an Indian in it – would probably be a prisoner, brought back from Madoc's first voyage as a trophy. But he didn't know why he should have thought of it – he was certain he'd never read a version of the legend with an Indian in it. And what the hell was the significance of these birds?

They gave him a strangely menaced feeling. He leaned his head against the cold window pane and wondered if he should tell Jane about them, but no – it would mean too much explanation. Too much talking about his poems and he definitely didn't want to get into that.

Gwyn searched for Jane's figure among the others criss-crossing the campus square. This was about the time she usually left her office. He hadn't been down to see her today; they had stopped dropping in on one another so regularly. They both recognised that they could do with more space.

It wasn't that he didn't want to see her. It wasn't that he did love her. In fact, Gwyn was perturbed at the growing feeling jealousy that assailed him about Jane. It was something he hadn't known for a long time, not since he was an insecure adolescent, these surges of sexual jealousy. Now, for instance, if he was honest, he had to admit that he didn't like the idea of her spending the evening with that ghastly PhD student, Robert Wendell. He had seen the way Robert looked at her. He was fairly sure it wasn't mutual; Robert resembled a monkfish, after all, but that was no comfort. In fact, that made it worse. He felt a tide of pure possessive rage rise in him as he contemplated it.

Time for a drink. Gwyn packed up his papers into his blue folder and locked up the office. The cold bit into him as he left the faculty. He hurried down the steps towards the bar but halfway there, an idea that had been hovering between the lines of his writing all day suddenly coalesced. That was it; that was how he should integrate all the diverse elements of poem number four. He veered sharply to the right and headed down the path which led off campus. The paving stones were webbed with frost; they sparkled orange-white beneath the street lamps. Forget the bar; he had whisky and wine at the flat: he walked faster and faster until in the end he broke into a run, overwhelmed with eagerness to be back in the poem again.

Gwyn had just finished. It had taken him two hours; he'd been astonished when he looked at his watch. But he had finished it: Madoc and his voyagers were sailing along the exotic southern coast, travelling west.

The telephone rang. He picked up his glass of whisky and nursed it across the room, enjoying the taste of it and the beatific haze of achievement. It was a sexy feeling, languorous but strong. He smiled as he picked up the handset.

'Yes?'

'Hallo. Is this Gwyn?' It was a male voice, with an accent that was somehow more American than those Gwyn was used to – a throaty twang. He didn't recognise it, but at the sound of it something clicked warningly in his mind.

'Yes,' he said. 'It is. Who's speaking?'

'You don't know me,' said the voice. 'I'm an old friend of ─'s.' Gwyn looked at his whisky. He had an extraordinary ─ g that he knew what was coming next. 'My name's Sam.'

'Hallo Sam. Yes, Jane's mentioned you.'

Gwyn wondered what his voice sounded like to Sam. To his own ears it was controlled and formal, quite unlike itself.

'I hear that you guys got married. Mazeltov.'

'Thanks.'

'Uh – is Jane there, Gwyn? Could I speak with her?'

It sounded so easy and so young, as if Sam lived round the corner and called up every day.

'No, she's not in. She's out. Can I give her a message?'

'Yes. I'm coming to New York on Thursday, for a few weeks, with a work project. I was thinking maybe we could all meet.'

'Sure,' said Gwyn. 'Yes, that would be great. Give us a ring.'

'OK, I will. Give her my regards, will you?'

'Yes. Goodbye.'

Gwyn put the handset down. His beatific feeling was gone. And the room looked different: shrunken and two dimensional. It was like a stage set. He drank some whisky but his mind was too busy to get the taste of it.

Who had told Jane's ex-lover about their marriage?

The timbre of Sam's voice vibrated in his ear. He had a curious feeling that if he picked up the telephone Sam would still be on the other end, listening. He moved away from the phone and sat down on the sofa. Suddenly he remembered the birds this morning and how they'd fouled the table; he could smell the disinfectant. He leaned forward quickly.

That feeling was on him again – the sense of menace prickling on his skin. It was as if that oddly familiar voice on the phone had brought with it the sound of wings, beating up a fear inside him, choking him with an intimation of danger that he couldn't understand.

22

Terrible, this country is; terrible. The heat weighs down on my shoulders like a stone and the air is thick and wet. It's hard to breathe. The trees go up and up to the sky, great cedars, and grey moss hangs from their branches like filthy cuckoo spit. Around the clearings the swamp plants rise: their leathery leaves make a wall the height of a man, shutting out the light, and their roots clutch at the earth like strong black claws. We have found two paths that lead through the swamp away from the river, but even the men who have been all the way through them have found no true open land. There are clearings, large clearings, but around the edges always the swamp plants again.

We could even be on another island, just a bigger one this time. If only we could sail our ships on, but we can't. They've come as far as they can. Up river from here the water swirls in vicious black eddies, and boils up in waterspouts. The *Pwll Annan* lies on the shore, her masts broken and her hull stove in. We are starting to make the smaller boats from her timbers, but we might as well be using the whole ships. We can't take them any further on.

No, but we could take them back. That's what our people are saying. Now we've mourned the dead and nursed the sick, and watched three of the children die of fever these last two days, we could load the animals back on to the remaining ships and sail downstream and back on to the firm, sweet shore. Far away from the swamp and black water and the thick mist which stands on the water in pillars and takes the shape of men.

There are 254 of us left from the 310 who left Ynys Wair. Nineteen died in the wreck of the *Pwll Annan*, and seven have died since, of sickness they brought out of the water. And now some of the children who weren't in the water are dying.

Duw, is it only twenty-two nights since we left the shore of the clear-water island people? So much has changed.

Madoc has a stubborn, closed in look on his face now. He won't talk to the kindred. He won't listen to what his fellow captains are telling him. Even Arun he only half hears. He cuts short their pleadings on behalf of the tired, heartsick people, and just insists that we go on north.

For all these twenty-two days and nights, I have been watching him. When we were still hopeful, sailing west along the coast, when we began to navigate the offshore islands and the inland waters, as the wet heat descended on us, I watched him. As we struggled further upstream, meeting no people, finding no land good enough to make even a temporary settlement, I grew worried.

He's changed since we left the shore of the clear-water island people. With every mile of water we covered, I've seen him become more restless, and more driven. He spends almost all his time with Glesig now, he can scarcely bear to let him out of his sight. But there's less friendship there. It's not like it used to be in Dreugyllt. Nor even on the voyage over the empty seas, when Madoc left Glesig to me and the horses. Now it does seem that Glesig is Madoc's prisoner.

Madoc is colder with me, too. He still holds me at night, and when he fucks me he sometimes weeps with passion, but when he wakes he leaves me at once and goes to find Glesig. Glesig sleeps next to us, the other side of a goat's hide Madoc had hung between us and the prow. Madoc's put him there so he can't leave the ship without us knowing. He refused to let Glesig sleep in one of the stick and branch shelters on the river bank, where some of the people choose to lie. I know why he's done it, but it means Glesig hears every sound of our love-making. It shouldn' matter. It doesn't matter when Madoc is groaning with pleasu But when he weeps I feel afraid, and I pull his head down o my breasts and cradle it to smother the noise.

Uncertain, I am − not sure what I think or believe. I

sure that night off the clear-water island coast, when Madoc said we should sail on west. No doubts then – I was filled with courage from my prince. But now I don't know.

It's all gone so wrong. In these three weeks since we first touched land we've started to run out of food, and sickness has spread on to the ships. It's as if it's reaching out from the swampy land and the rank waters. Every day there's a huddle of sick people on the aft deck, groaning and sweating with fever, and half the rest of us feel weakened with the heavy air and the heat. Our water supplies are low – it's only rained once since we turned inland from the coast and that put just a few inches in the water butts. We've started boiling the river water with herbs to clear it but it tastes foul and we're afraid to drink it.

No wonder the people are getting angry with Madoc. It's Madoc who brought us to this swampy river coast; who takes Glesig's advice and insists that everyone else takes it too. It's Madoc's fault the *Pwll Annan* was wrecked and nineteen people died. We could all see the waterspouts up ahead and there wasn't a person who wanted to navigate them but Madoc. Even Arun was against him – especially Arun. I thought then that Madoc must give way and let the ships turn back, but he didn't. He went from ship to ship in his coracle, commanding and challenging the captains, threatening punishments to the men. He managed to subdue all the protests and to get everyone sullen but following him. Then he steered the *Gwenllyr* through the spouts and the eddies, running from side to side yelling instructions to the men, and we swung and slithered between the currents until we were all white-faced and dizzy and I had to press my lips together to stop myself screaming in terror. But we got through. And the second ship, Gran's, came through after us. But the *Pwll Annan* came third and was tossed between two spouts and driven into the bank by an eddy and in trying to get free it was driven again and again into the spreading roots of a tree until suddenly with a huge heave it tipped right over.

Oh God, I can't bear to remember it. The screams and the ple and animals falling, and the crunching of the masts.

thing has been the same since then. How could it be? With ips this side of the water spouts and the other six below d none of us able to go on up river, and Madoc refusing to let anyone go back. And the wreckage of the *Pwll Annan* still here, being picked apart for land shelters and for timbers for small boats.

Madoc is determined that we'll go north on foot now, once Glesig's found us a way. The small boats will transport the supplies, when the river allows it.

But will Glesig find us a way? The kindred don't think so.

Glesig talks to no one any more but the horses: the three mares and five foals who have survived. They at least are glad to be on land. He murmurs to them a lot while he feeds them and walks them in the shade of the tall cedars and the dark swamp plants. But when the kindred try to get him to answer their questions about the paths he's looking for, and why he's bringing us up this river, he won't answer. He won't answer my questions, either; he'll speak to me sometimes, but he'll only say what he wants to say - warn me about some animal that creeps in the swamp and stings, or tell me some story about the people of his country. I listen of course, but I don't know what to make of half of it.

I get a strange feeling when I'm with Glesig these days. Sometimes I want to put my arms round him and hold him.

I can see that Glesig is worried about leading us wrong. He doesn't know this region: when Madoc found him, he was further east, on the better lands like those of the clear-water islands. But on the way from his country he had passed many trefi inhabited by war-like kindreds and had had to hide and escape many times. He's trying to bring us to his country by a different route, so we don't have to do battle.

Madoc has explained this to the people, but they don't like having to trust Glesig, the foreigner. If Madoc didn't have such close control over them, they'd have attacked Glesig by now. There's even been one or two rushes made at him, but only furtively, when Madoc isn't looking, and he's never been badly hurt. Yesterday, though, the kindred and the serfs and the captains were all so angry and so worried I thought they woul snatch him away from Madoc and that everything would turned upside down. But at the last minute, it didn't hap Duw, Madoc, you're a strong man to be able to change round like that.

It happened yesterday, in the late afternoon. Glesig

gone since early morning, taking his sticks and his sharp stones and his new-made bow into the glades of the huge, high trees to look for trails and paths – and Madoc, of course, had gone with him. The muttering on the ships and on the river bank had been seething for hours, bubbling like the scummy waterspouts themselves. When Arun came to find me, I wasn't surprised.

I was in one of the land shelters, trying to cool the foreheads of the sick people – another two children were down with fever. Outside, I saw Arun leave a group of the other captains. He was looking over at me and squaring his shoulders. I saw him shaking off Meurig, who wanted to come too. Instead, he brought with him Pryste, the sister of his lord and Madoc's foster brother Rhiryd. She looked yellow-white and sick with heat.

I knew what they wanted. They wanted me to talk to Madoc.

'I tell you, my lady Ceinwen,' said Arun, his hand working on the shabby folds of his tunic. 'There's such a feeling against Glesig Dog, there's talk of seizing him and killing him. Everyone's saying it's some kind of spell he's worked on Madoc ap Owain. Do you remember that smoke bird he made on Ynys Wair? It's bad; it's ungodly.'

'They want to kill Glesig?' I asked. I wasn't surprised but saying it like that, the words stuck in my throat like fish bones.

'They do. And I wouldn't be stopping them if I didn't know it meant danger to Madoc as well.'

'What do you mean?' My voice seemed to be shrinking; I looked at the kindred, sitting exhausted in the patches of shade, gathered round the wreckage of the *Pwll Annan*, and saw how thin they were and how shrunken their faces. And how desperate.

'The kindred are angry, my lady, and afraid.'

'But – dear God Arun, surely they wouldn't turn on Madoc? He's their prince.'

'Not everyone's prince, my lady,' said Arun. 'Not the prince of Rhys's kindred, nor of Rhiryd's.' He saw me staring at him in horror and his face went a deep red. 'I'm not saying any of us wants his overthrow, my lady. He's our leader here and we're — But – it's –'

'— now,' I said. I had looked from him to Pryste. I was staring — thin face and we hung on to each other's eyes. She had — somewhere in Ireland; she had come to the far edge of the world with a boy husband who was at Madoc's command. My love was here with me, and leading 254 people into despair.

'I'll talk to him,' I promised, 'I'll try.'

And so when Glesig reappeared on the edge of our clear stretch of riverbank, and Madoc – with one eye on him – walked into our half-built camp, I tried to draw him apart.

'Ceinwen.' He started to talk before I'd even reached him. 'We've found some tree-bark maps. We think there's a way through past the edge of the swamp plants once we cross the small streams. They're not deep.'

'Good, my lord. That's good,' I said. 'Madoc, I must talk to you.'

I could see the people around us were listening. They were crowding in on us, making my task much more difficult. I looked across at Arun and glanced from him to them, trying to make him see that I wanted him to call them away. Madoc saw.

'What's this?' he said sharply. 'If you and Arun have got something to say, say it.'

'Can we go into the shade of the trees, my lord?' I said. 'I'm so hot.'

Madoc let me walk a few paces away and then he said impatiently, 'In God's name, what is it? More complaints from the kindred I suppose?'

I had thought and thought, and decided that the way to make him listen was to be bold.

'They want to go back Madoc,' I said. 'Back to the shore of the clear-water island people.'

Madoc's face was twisted with anger and contempt. 'Back?' he said. 'Who says so?'

'Everyone,' I said. 'The kindred, the serfs, the seamen, the captains. Everyone, Madoc.'

'Oh yes? And you –' he paused and then added with an unpleasant emphasis, ' – my lady?'

'I agree.'

Like a wolf springing, his hand leapt out and struck my fa The blow lifted me off my feet and I staggered, lost my bala and fell. There was a sudden absolute quiet in the clearing.

I was struggling to sit up, my head feeling as if it ha

knocked off my neck. All the left side of my face was numb. Then Madoc was leaning over me, roughly grabbing my wrists. He pulled me to my feet and dragged me, stumbling, to the trees where Glesig was crouched. Glesig alone hadn't turned to stare at the sound of Madoc hitting me. He was squatting with his back to the clearing, cutting some knife marks in the bark.

Madoc jerked both my wrists together in one hand and with his free hand he pointed to the tree trunk.

'Look,' he said, and his voice was so unexpected I felt a shudder travel over my skin. I'd been expecting scorn or fury; perhaps another blow. But instead his voice was quiet, even gentle. It didn't sound like him; it was pushed out of shape with a strange yearning note. 'Look Ceinwen,' he said again. No, he wasn't commanding me; he wasn't even asking me. He was pleading with me like a lover.

I looked. All I could see were score marks in the bark, and Glesig's brown fingers moving over them. On my wrists, Madoc's fingers were moving too: a light, loving stroking from the same hand that had just knocked me to the ground.

'This is a map,' he said wonderingly. 'Glesig is making it, to show where the land leads from here. He's found three like it, on the far side of the swamp, showing how to go north. He's finding a way for us, a way through to his country. Don't lose faith in me now, Ceinwen.'

Then he raised both my hands to his mouth and kissed them, smoothed his hand down my left cheek where the skin was swelling from his blow, and walked with me back to the settlement huts, his eyes shining as if he had just seen God himself.

Well, that was a performance Madoc gave for our people. They greeted him with murmurings, like a swarm of bees, rising, falling away, rising again. I could feel their eyes on my cheek which was ripening into a warm, bruised swelling. Madoc was holding my hand tightly and I stood by him, looking back at the kindred. They had such different expressions – curiosity, anger, outrage – and all of them, a trace of expectancy.

And Madoc didn't let them down. It was like that time in Gwyllt, when they had wanted him to ride down on Gruffydd and he'd refused; I could feel the same energy vibrating in him.

This time it was a bigger job to carry them with him, but Madoc was glowing with certainty; he was like an iron that has been pulled out of the forge fire.

He told them about the tree maps they'd found; he told them about the plains that waited beyond the swamps. He told them about the secret rivers and valleys Glesig could lead us by, safe from the eyes of the war-like kindred. He told them about the hills with gold and silver in them, which wasn't prized by the people of Ynys Llyr, which we could mine and send back to the European trade routes. He told them of the temperate summers and the winters with snow and rain, like at home. When he asked them to choose, they were resentful but I knew, they all knew, what the choice would be.

A clever man Madoc is. He didn't pause once they had settled it; he set us all to work, on preparations. We worked until the light failed, the men on the boats, the women on packing food and supplies and trying out ways of carrying the children and the sick. Glesig has been showing us how his people make wide sledges out of sticks and hides, which they harness to their dogs and which carry their babies and their belongings over miles of plain. We're going to make some out of the ships' sails and tree branches, and harness them to the stronger mares.

The sun is high in the sky now and our morning's work is over; we're resting now, while the hottest hours last. We'll be ready to move on in a few days, going north, along Glesig's path.

I've been working as hard as the rest of them and I'll be walking with them tomorrow, at the head of them. With the bruise dark on my cheek where Madoc hit me. He's said nothing about it and neither have I. But I can't get the memory of it out of my mind, or the look on the faces of the kindred.

All day today Madoc's eyes have been clouded with a strange wildness. And I haven't been able to find any words to say to him.

23

In the last week New York had frozen hard. The sidewalks were brushed with sand but every night they froze to a slippery brown slush and it was a relief when new snow fell on them, turning them briefly clean and white again.

Jane stamped the slush off her boots on to the doormat. The heavy door swung back into its frame, shutting out the upper West Side evening, and she pressed the elevator button, flexing her gloved fingers to ease the blood back into them.

Six thirty. She wished she and Gwyn hadn't accepted Edward's invitation to go down-town to the theatre. She wouldn't even have time for a shower to warm her up.

She heard voices as she put her key in the lock. At first she thought it was Harry, come round early. Then the cadence of one of the voices stopped her hand on the key.

She stood still, listening to the loose-linked voice with its easy resonances. She couldn't follow what was being said but she could hear the rise and fall of his tone, the restless pauses, and she heard the buried tension, just the same as she used to hear it in the school corridors when teachers spoke to him, and in her family's home when her mother or father answered the door.

Sam. Sam. Jane wrenched the key in the lock and burst in.

Sam was sitting on the sofa; Gwyn on the arm of the chair. y were both leaning forward and their heads were turned ⸱ds her.

⸱t struck her first was the difference between Sam and ⸱t wasn't just the features: Sam's hawkish bone structure, straight black hair and tilting eyes. It was the way the two men held themselves. Sam was drawn up in a restless stillness; Gwyn sprawled, with a hint of aggression in his pose.

Sam was looking at Jane sideways in the familiar, anxious way. He was older, of course; broader and heavier. Jane was astonished at how excited she was to see him. She had an insane urge to throw herself on his lap and yell.

She stood where she had stopped, just inside the door, and put her hands in her coat pockets.

'Jesus, this is a shock,' she said. She glanced at Gwyn: he was turning a beer bottle round in his hands; she couldn't read his face. Her eyes slid back to Sam. 'Sam.'

She began to smile, for want of anything else to do. Then the smile widened and deepened out of her control. 'Shit, Sam, it's really good to see you.'

Sam was getting to his feet. Jane watched him, gauging his height. He was taller than before: when he'd put his beer bottle down and finished unfolding his limbs he was over six feet. His blue jeans were still loose on his hips but tighter round the legs where he'd put on muscle. The sleeves of his plaid shirt fitted snugly at the shoulder too. As he straightened, Jane's eyes fell on the hollow at the base of his throat, just above the neck of his vest.

It was a very male presence – it was odd that she had forgotten that. He stood awkwardly, his body suddenly occupying a lot of space in the little room, and made an uncertain gesture with his hands. Jane stared at the gold ring. He still wore it.

'I was going to call,' he said, 'but then I was in the neighbourhood. You didn't know I was in town?'

Sam ducked his head and looked from her to Gwyn: it was a laconic glance. She followed his eyes.

'No, I didn't know,' Jane said. 'Should I have?'

'Well, sure,' said Sam. 'Miss Archer gave me your number and I told Gwyn I'd be coming. We fixed for me to call.'

Jane looked quickly from one to the other. Gwyn had spoken to Sam? She heard the sharpness in her voice as she said, 'You didn't tell me.'

Gwyn was looking up at both of them from his chair arm expression one of mild surprise. He waved the beer bottle

'No, sorry,' he said. 'Terribly sorry, both of you. I thought I'd mentioned it, see.'

He smiled engagingly. Sam glanced down at him in an oddly dismissive way, then looked over his head to Jane.

'Oh well,' said Sam. 'Another message gone astray.'

Jane grinned in recognition: this was what they used to say to one another in the old days when the adults – parents, teachers, his Uncle Willie – had tried to keep them apart. It was bad of Sam to be speaking their old code in front of Gwyn, but then what had Gwyn been doing to keep Sam's message from her?

She nodded slowly, in the old pretend-cynical way.

'Yeah,' she said, the words coming back to her without her thinking. 'Fuck it.'

They stood mirroring each other for a second. Gwyn's eyes were on them both, watchful but uncomprehending. And I'm not sure I understand it either, thought Jane. After all this time, out of nowhere, Sam was here. And everything felt so much the same. Thousands of memories from the old days were beginning to pour through her, making her feel like a fifteen year old again.

Shit, it was so disorienting. Fucking A. She didn't know where she was. Who was this person who kept swearing like an adolescent? It's you, dick-head. Dick-head yourself, you mother. Jesus, stop it. Get a grip. Sam and her. Any minute now she'd throw on a sweatshirt and they'd slip out of the yard door together, off to the Monday game. Except that had been in the summer. In winter it had been the rink or the Yellow Store.

Jane took hold of herself. I should really be feeling anguished, she thought. Or at least embarrassed. Why aren't I?

'How've you been?' she asked, crossing the small piece of floor between them and reaching up to kiss him. She hoped Gwyn didn't see the tremor that went through her as Sam's hands closed on her arms.

'Pretty well,' Sam said. He bent his head to kiss her, lightly, like an acquaintance. The familiarity she had expected wasn't there and the disappointment hit her like a blow. She was reluctant to let him go; feeling the weight of his hands through her coat, she rested against him for an instant.

great to see you, Sam,' she said in a good ol' boy tone

284

Duane would have envied. Then she did feel embarrassed and jerked her head up to look at him.

He was looking down at her quite impersonally.

'Me too, Jane,' he said after a pause.

The atmosphere in the room was like static. Jane was almost afraid to speak in case her words sent shocks crackling between the three of them.

She had taken her coat off and brought more beers from the kitchen. She had a longing for a vodka or whisky to help her over the shock of seeing Sam, but she felt that diving for the spirits would be rude. It would be tantamount to saying, shit, how are we going to handle this? And she also remembered that Miss Archer had written about a period of heavy drinking in Sam's life, a while back. Maybe it wouldn't be politic to offer him hard liquor.

So now they were sitting in a triangle, drinking beer too fast. The bottles were so small. Sam was on the sofa; Gwyn was still in his place on the arm of the easy chair. Jane hadn't wanted to sit on the easy chair seat — it was too couply for anything and she wasn't feeling very friendly towards Gwyn just now, but then she'd hesitated to take the other end of the sofa. It was only a two seater and she didn't feel like committing herself to Sam's personal space either. So she had dragged the hard chair away from the desk and was now perched on it. She felt like a student teacher struggling to take a particularly bad seminar.

Sam was talking, but not exactly freely. He was answering her questions about his job — as a teacher — and the project which had brought him to New York — a month's exchange in a school for special needs kids on Amsterdam — but his replies were just that: replies, and they made her feel like an interrogator. Gwyn was leaning back, half sprawled on the seat of the easy chair with his legs over the arm, giving no encouragement. It was incredible that anyone who looked so dreamy and relaxed could be producing such a sense of strain.

'So how long have you been doing this teaching?' Jane s
She wasn't sure if she should curse the way the words sou
(so self-consciously gracious and interested) or be thankf
at least her tone hid her real feelings. Neither Sam no

would know from listening to her that she was as excited as a child at seeing Sam again and hungering for every morsel of information he would give.

'Three years the actual teaching. And two years before that, training.'

'Do you like it?'

'Sure I like it. The pay's shit but the conditions are quite good.'

'And the work itself?'

'Yeah. What about the work?' Sam turned his amused look on her. 'Oh,' he said, 'that stuff I have to do when I'm in the classroom? Conversing with kids? Well, that's a real pain in the ass, naturally.'

'I just never would have thought of you as a teacher,' Jane said defensively.

She wished she could stop gazing at him.

'No,' Sam said. 'I didn't think of it for myself. It was Jennifer put me on to it.'

'Jennifer?'

'Miss Archer. Your Miss Archer.'

'Oh. She never told me.' Jane was astonished to hear Sam refer to Miss Archer so easily as Jennifer, astonished and slightly jealous. She had always thought of Miss Archer as her own personal good angel. 'Miss Archer and I – Jennifer – we write to each other sometimes, you know,' she added.

'I know. She – ' A hoarse scream cut across his words.

'The intercom,' said Jane mechanically. 'Oh shit, Harry, the play. I'd forgotten.'

She went to the door and buzzed to let Harry in. Gwyn was still leaning back in the easy chair, making no move, either to get up or to say anything to Sam. Jane wondered what they'd been talking about before she arrived.

'Do you think we can cancel?' she said to Gwyn. 'Look, why don't you go on without me?'

'Don't alter your plans for me,' said Sam. 'I only dropped by say hallo. I'm expected back anyway.' He began to reach for   at, draped over the back of the sofa.

'   ' said Jane, too vehemently. 'Don't go yet. You haven't   where you're staying.'

'Tonight on 112th. I'm not sure after that. But you can get me at the school in the day, and I know where you are.'

'You don't have anywhere to stay, Sam?'

He smiled, a wouldn't-you-know-it smile.

'It's a long story. The place I was supposed to stay – my exchange's place – is some kind of sub-sub-sub-let and someone further along the line hasn't paid his rent. I turned up to find all the locks changed. The other guys there are crashing on friends' floors, and they're fitting me in with them. They're taking care of me all right.'

'You're sleeping on floors?'

'It's no big deal.'

'But – ', There was a knocking on the door. Jane glanced at Gwyn but he didn't move so she went to answer it. 'Just a minute,' she said to Sam over her shoulder. 'Hi Harry, come in.'

She had already turned away from Harry and was heading back into the living room when she remembered her manners. She paused and saw Harry's curious expression as he followed her in and looked past her to Gwyn and the man on the sofa.

'Oh Harry, this is a friend of mine. An old friend.' Harry's blue eyes were suddenly alight with interest and she knew he was ahead of her. 'Sam, this is Harry. Harry, Sam.'

Sam was on his feet and he and Harry shook hands. They were almost exactly the same height and bulk, and rather weirdly they looked like the dark and fair variation of some basic frame. The six feet plus male model, facial features Caucasian/AmerIndian, hair to match. The two men looked into each other's eyes with undisguised curiosity.

'How are you?' said Harry.

'Good to meet you,' said Sam.

'You're staying in New York for a while?'

'Yeah. I often do.'

'Do you?' said Jane. 'I didn't know that.'

'I spend some part of each year in New York,' Sam said. 'Not far from here, mostly. In fact two years ago I worked three months in the Barolo Bar. You know, the jazz-blues place on 115th?'

'Yes, we know it,' said Harry, filling in the pause on Jane's behalf. Jane was staring dumbly at Sam, trying to take in th last bit of information. Sam seemed amused; he smiled wickedly at her.

Gwyn swung himself up on to the chair arm, a compact figure suddenly asserting itself. They all looked at him doubtfully.

'Let's have another drink,' he said.

'We don't have too much time,' said Harry. 'I said we'd meet Edward at the theatre at seven thirty.'

'I'm on my way,' said Sam. He picked his coat up for the second time. Next to Harry's midnight blue wool coat, the sheep-skin looked battered and poor.

'We'll all come down with you,' Jane said. 'Listen, about where you're staying. Why don't I give you the keys to my place? I spend most of my time here now, but I've still got the apartment to do what I want with. It's crazy you sleeping on floors when there's an empty place a couple of blocks away.'

She pulled on her coat and ran her hands through her hair as she spoke, to avoid meeting Harry's or Gwyn's eyes. She knew Harry would be fascinated and Gwyn would be furious; she was surprised herself. She reiterated the offer.

'What do you say?' she said, shaking her head free and looking up at Sam. 'It's just dumb not to use it. Please.'

She saw that she had taken Sam off guard – at last. For a second he looked uncertainly from her to Gwyn.

'It's not necessary,' he said, swinging a heavy leather hold-all over his shoulder. He looked down at her and the easy smile came back. 'I've lived rough quite a bit these last twelve years.'

Jane breathed deeply to still her heart. She felt reckless and out of breath and utterly determined to have her way.

'OK,' she said, 'it's not necessary. But it's there so you might as well use it.'

All four of them were in the tiny hallway now. Gwyn was rooting in the closet for his coat; Sam looked ironically from Jane to Gwyn's back and twitched his eyebrows. Jane gave a nervous grin, aware of Harry's eyes on them both.

'Well, I don't know,' said Sam.

Gwyn shut the closet door and turned back to them, shrugging on his coat.

'Oh for God's sake take it mon,' he said. 'Or Nan Pridden here ill never shut up.'

Harry laughed; Jane had the feeling it was out of embarrassment. Sam smiled as well. Jane was suddenly self-conscious: she gave what she hoped would pass for a good-humoured shrug. She didn't think anyone but she could hear the antagonism buried deep in Gwyn's voice.

'I'll take it,' Sam said. 'Thanks.'

Jane walked out into the corridor with Sam, and Harry came behind with Gwyn. As Jane and Sam walked ahead to the elevator, they made arrangements to meet tomorrow lunch-time, and for Jane to take Sam to the apartment. Jane could hear herself fussing; she was acutely aware of Sam standing quietly next to her. Now that she'd got her way, she felt anxious about Gwyn's reaction and too shy to look at Sam – she was sure he'd be laughing at her.

She trailed off as Gwyn and Harry caught up with them and all four entered the small elevator. There was just room for them to stand without quite touching one another.

'What're you going to see?' Sam asked.

'Off-Broadway production of *A Doll's House*,' said Harry. 'It's based on a Japanese Noh interpretation.'

'Uh huh,' said Sam. He didn't give any other reaction and Jane wondered what he was thinking. She wished they had been going to see something less rarefied, but then she shouldn't make assumptions: she'd already had her picture of Sam's Renoxia-bound life shattered. Sam would probably turn out to be an authority on Japanese Nôh theatre, if she asked him. Sam's eyes rested briefly on hers and she decided not to ask.

They all shivered instinctively as they stepped out into the frozen night. At the end of the street they turned to say goodbye to Sam. He shook hands again with Gwyn and Harry, and Jane put her hand on his sheepskin covered arm and lifted her face – cautiously this time, almost flinchingly – for his kiss. It was a light touch, like their kiss of greeting, but she thought that now there was a shiver of complicity in it. Or was that just her?

'See you tomorrow.'

'Uh huh. Oh by the way,' Sam plunged his hand into his hold-all and pulled out a blue envelope. 'This is for you, from Miss Archer. She asked me to give it to you. You'd have gotten it faster in the mail, of course, but what do you know?'

He jerked out his hand in the abrupt North Dakotan farewell gesture and turned away, walking up-town with long strides.

Jane slipped the envelope into her pocket.

'Funny how people do that, isn't it?' she said. 'Give letters to people to carry. When the mail's so much faster, like he said. Can you see a cab anywhere?'

It wasn't an easy evening. In the aftermath of seeing Sam, Jane was nervous and over-excited and kept talking too much. Harry was watchful and Edward, sensing the cross currents, was obviously perplexed, but too polite to ask questions. Gwyn was the most unsettling element in the mix: he smiled lazily and stood drinks and exuded a bogus bonhomie which made everyone uncomfortable.

It was only the second time she had met Edward and Jane knew that she should be making friends with him. In the interval, as they sipped their glasses of wine in the bar, she chatted away to him about his job and hers, and Brockham, and North Dakota, and what a good man Duane Jewell was. Edward Catzberger was a well mannered, thoughtful person and Jane liked him. Unfortunately he also made her feel loud and crass. As the group separated to replace their glasses on the bar, Gwyn caught her eye.

'Steady on there,' he said mockingly.

Jane put out her hands to him, about to murmur something loving and anxious, but he turned and led the way back into the auditorium.

The scenes of the play impressed themselves on her eyes and ears but didn't travel through to her brain. She sat in the dark, Edward on her right and Harry on her left, and wondered what Gwyn was thinking.

In the end, it was gone midnight when they left Edward and Harry in the restaurant and flagged down a taxi. As they drove up Third Avenue Jane slipped her hand into Gwyn's. He didn't pull away but neither did he respond. He let his hand lie around hers and looked out of the window.

'I'll have to go and clear up the apartment tomorrow morning,' said Jane.

'Mm,' said Gwyn.

'Do you mind me asking him to stay?'

'Yes,' said Gwyn.

Jane watched his profile. He was looking calmly at the passing store-fronts.

'Oh,' she said. 'I'm sorry. I can't take it back. I can't tell him he has to sleep on someone's floor.'

'No,' said Gwyn easily.

'Well – Jesus, Gwyn! Look at me. If you're angry look me in the face and tell me so.'

Gwyn snapped his head round and grabbed her shoulders. His face, tense with fury, was only half an inch from hers.

'I'm angry,' he said. 'I'm fucking angry.' He seemed to be forcing the words out through some great obstacle. Jane gazed into his eyes, surprised at how weak she'd gone.

'For Christ's sake Gwyn.'

Gwyn held her much too tight for several long seconds. She could tell from his face that he was hurting her on purpose. Then he said, very quietly and distinctly, 'Just don't you sleep with him. Don't you bloody dare.'

Jane didn't know if her gasp was of pain, shock or guilt.

They didn't talk after that, not even when they arrived back in their apartment building and went up in the elevator together. They let themselves into the apartment in silence and went into different rooms: Gwyn into the living room, Jane into the box-like kitchen.

She sat at the table and slowly took off her gloves. As she put them back into her pockets she felt a crumple of paper and remembered Miss Archer's letter. She drew out the blue envelope; it took her several goes to tear it open and extract the folded blue paper. She smoothed it on the table top and began to read.

She read the letter to half way down the page, then stopped and went back to the beginning. It was Miss Archer's voice, just as it was Miss Archer's handwriting, but distorted by an emotion she didn't recognise. Panic was snatching at her lungs as she read the bizarre sentences. She got up and poured herself a drink of water; then she lowered herself back on to the chair and began to read again.

Dear Jane

I am giving this letter to Sam to give to you. I've asked him not to post it; I want you to receive it only if he brings it.

There is more for you to know about Haydn Phillips. It wasn't the drugs that destroyed him, although they didn't help. I was what they used to call 'the woman in the case'; I don't know if your Welsh friend mentioned there was a woman. There always has been, and she always gets left out of the telling. This is a pity, because it stops the next woman being warned until it is too late. Maybe I have left it too late. Maybe in my heart I haven't wanted to warn you.

I have always been very fond of you and Sam, I think you know that. I thought perhaps if I helped you get away, it might be resolved or at least diverted. But of course, it can't be.

I hear that Gwyn Thomas is a very talented poet. You will know that, better than anyone, just as I knew Haydn's painting. But perhaps you don't understand your own gift so well, nor Sam's. Sam knows the most of the three of you, remember that.

There's no point my trying to be more specific. If this seems to you the ramblings of an eccentric old spinster, then God bless. But if you are reading this, Sam has brought it to you, and if Sam has come to you, then it is beginning again.

I have a confession to make: twelve years ago, when you and Sam were disgraced, I envied you. I saw that you children loved each other with a passion, and I saw that it was strong. If you have found that again with your husband, then we might hope to survive the violence. I might dare to hope that this latest and last beginning will lead to a good end.

Come and see me when you return.

Your Jennifer Archer.

She's crazy, thought Jane. She's crazy, crazy. But she didn't believe it. She sat looking at the letter, trying to divide it into things she understood and things she didn't. Miss Archer had had an affair with Haydn Phillips and it had gone wrong. Miss Archer saw some connection between Gwyn and Haydn Phillips. But Miss Archer also seemed to find some connection between herself and Haydn and Jane and Sam. Sam was some kind of messenger.

Oh God, it was idiotic.

Then why did it freeze her to her seat and make her arms and legs too heavy to move?

Did Sam know what was in the letter? She thought not. It didn't sound as if Miss Archer had told him. She imagined the old librarian sitting at the cheap teak desk in her living room, at some late hour of the night just like this, the electric light shining down evenly on the furniture and the framed reproduction paintings and the collection of china shoes. Miss Archer saw none of them, though she looked around her: she was writing to Jane.

Jane sat in the kitchen feeling as if she were joined to Miss Archer by a taut wire which stretched across fifteen hundred miles and two time zones. Then, bit by bit, the vision of Miss Archer's lighted living room gave way to other images: Sam's earlier, younger face below her bedroom window, bright in the October daybreak; Sam's teenage clothes crumpled on the floor of his trailer; Sam's arms closing round her, his hand beneath her head in the summer undergrowth by White Dove Pond.

She pushed the balls of her hands into her eyes, pressing the images away. You children loved each other with a passion. Yes, but that was a long time ago and her husband was a few yards away, in another room. And they loved each other too: she remembered the pain of Gwyn's hands on her shoulders, hurting her deliberately. A different kind of passion; a different kind of love.

Hating Gwyn and longing for him to come in and touch her again, to kiss her, hit her, do anything if only he'd break the distance, Jane sat on in the kitchen. Gwyn didn't come to find her.

24

We are walking north, on pleasant rolling land, between hills which are covered with woods of pine and fir. Glesig is leading us very well, from the stars and tree-bark maps. Madoc is full of vigour and hope and he keeps taking my hand and kissing my lips. If only I could forget the way he hit me, I'd be very cheerful, because it seems that our luck has returned for the better.

Once Madoc had won the people round, the captains agreed to try again and bring the rest of the ships through the water spouts. So we cleared them of people and supplies and slowly, and with great care, they brought them through: all six of them and only one, Arun's, was holed. And it was a small hole and we had pitch to mend it.

So we loaded all the supplies and animals and people back on again and we were able to go another three weeks by river. We were only going half as fast as we had done on the open sea, mind, what with the side winds and the currents, but it seemed faster to me. We could see the land going by, and watch as the swamps changed to firmer land, wooded with fine tall cedar trees.

The weather was cooler as we went further north and we had some heavy rains which filled up the water butts. Now and then great flocks of birds flew overhead: going south they were, for winter. It made me think of home.

Two weeks ago we came to the waterfall.

'Even you can't take ships up a waterfall, prince!' said Arun and everyone laughed, even though it meant taking to the land. We were all in a cheerful mood because of the good land opening up around us and the cooler, fresher air. It reminded us of home a bit and as we unloaded the ships and built the carts to carry our supplies, we talked about what it would be like in our trefi now.

The harvests are long since over and the winter oats sown. In Cynfael the sheep will have been brought back from the summer pasture near Abercwm. It will be cold in the mornings and the men will go hunting. Meilyr will be off with the others, a man at the head of the hunt now, bringing the quarry home for his Buddug. And if I know Buddug, she'll still be spending many of her days with Mam, married or not, and so Meilyr will be bringing meat for Mam and Dafy too. Good: I like to think of them being looked after.

I didn't say too much of this, though. Instead I listened to Pryste telling me about her home in Ireland. She talked about the castle where she lived with her father and his warband, the same castle Madoc went to for his years of fosterage. She and Madoc were children together, see, and recently she's started telling me stories of what they did.

'We used to go by the river on fine days and Madoc would try and shoot fish out of the water with his bow.' She laughed. 'He'd try for hours,' she said. 'Whole afternoons at a time, getting so furious that he couldn't do it!'

'Did he ever get one?'

'Once. At least, he said so. But I wasn't there to see it with my own eyes.'

'Pryste! Can you be suggesting that Madoc would make it up?'

'Oh no,' said Pryste, her face mischievous. 'Not Madoc ap Owain ap Gruffydd. He was always as gracious in failure as in triumph.'

We began to laugh then, a really good giggling laugh like the kind I used to have with Nest and Buddug, on and on until our stomachs hurt.

She's very sharp in a quiet way, this Pryste. Ever since that terrible day in the swamp when Madoc hit me, she's made herself my friend. She used to call to me from her ship when it came alongside ours on the river and now we're on land, we work together, looking after sick people and organising the other women. I suspect that if it wasn't for Pryste, I'd have trouble getting the women of the kindreds to do what I say; I know that some of them resent me for a jumped up village girl.

Madoc would be furious if he knew. So I don't tell him. He's unstoppable now, my prince; at the moment it seems he can do anything with the people. Even when he decided that unloading the ships was not enough and we had to dismantle the timbers and take them with us, he got his way.

'Glesig says the river in his country is as big as the Tywi,' Madoc said. 'And it runs three times the length of Gwynedd. When we reach it, I want us to be able to build small ships to sail up it.'

'But prince,' said Morddyn, who's the leader of the high kindred among us. 'Is it really possible to build even small ships just like that?'

'Of course it is,' said Madoc. 'You came to Dreugyllt, didn't you?'

'There were very many craftsmen at Dreugyllt and warbands protecting them.'

'You've got craftsmen here,' said Madoc. 'You've got our warband. And,' he added, grinning, 'you've got me.'

He said it so confidently that even Morddyn had to laugh and agree. But I happened to be looking at the captains and I saw that none of them joined in the cheering.

Arun, who was near me, frowned and turned away.

'Of course, prince,' he muttered under his breath.

You see, although everything's going well now, Madoc is still not consulting with the captains. He treats them as his own men at arms, like he treats Wenlyn and Cadell, and he doesn't see that they don't like it. They don't like being ignored and overruled when they're supposed to be joint leaders and advisers. But the only person Madoc consults these days is Glesig and he does that very definitely as Glesig's master.

What happened yesterday hasn't helped things. For the first time since we left the coast, we met Ynys Llyr people and by his handling of it Madoc managed to offend not only the captains but Morddyn too. It was an exciting, frightening moment: our scouts to the east saw men marching in a long line around the foot of a hill and coming towards us. The scout who had the horse came galloping over, telling us the news.

He'd barely finished telling us when Madoc was turning to Glesig.

'Glesig, take his mount,' Madoc said. 'Get me a horse, Wenlyn, whatever's nearest. Yes, the brown mare — bring her here. My bow — quick. Arun, you and the others bring armed men after me. How many did you say were coming this way? Fifty? The same number then Arun, with others in reserve. Don't bring them too close up behind us, just so the strangers can see. Glesig, are you ready? Come on.'

He and Glesig galloped off, leaving no time for Arun or anyone to speak. Morddyn looked furious — as head of the high kindred he should be leading the muster, and Arun realised that because he walked over to him and said quietly:

'Will you raise the men in Madoc's name, Morddyn Hellynt?'

The men were gone out of sight several hours and we had no word of anything until two of them returned on Madoc's and Glesig's horses, saying that Madoc was bringing the sixty Ynys Llyr people, all warriors, to have hospitality and we should get up a temporary shelter and prepare food and gifts at once.

There's peculiar the occasion was. These Ynys Llyr people were different from the ones on the coast — shorter and not so good looking — but they wore clothes quite like ours, heavy cloaks of decorated hide and shoes of the same stuff. When they saw that many of us had bare feet, they gave us the shoes and in return we gave them the same kinds of things we'd given the clear-water people: copper and pewter cups, knives and a couple of spears.

We couldn't understand anything they said, though. Glesig said that he had never heard their kind of language before, so we all had to communicate with gestures.

They were very interested in the horses, too interested, I heard Cadell mutter. We tried to talk to them about the kinds of animals they have here — we've seen some very strange ones. There are deer with curly horns, fat furry beasts with heads like pigs and bodies like squirrels, that live in trees. And half-wolves that call with a high sad bark in the night. So far though we haven't seen any of the great wild oxen that Glesig told us about, with shaggy heads and forequarters, whose meat and hides and horns the

Ynys Llyr people use. We asked the visitors about the oxen but they didn't seem to understand.

At nightfall, the Ynys Llyr people left. Madoc had made some kind of treaty of friendship with them, but we weren't too sure of their goodwill. We posted many look-outs overnight and this morning we set off early, walking north, towards the hills that are covered in fir and pine.

Madoc is walking among the captains now, talking to them. They are listening to him stiffly and Rhos and Gran are frowning, but Madoc seems not to notice. I tried to tell him last night, when we lay under the brychan together, that he should be more careful, but he just shrugged.

'Only one man can lead, Ceinwen,' he said. 'And I've done very well till now. The people are happy, the kindred are happy – '

'Morddyn isn't,' I said. 'He feels you should have asked him to lead the muster, not Arun.'

'What? You know Ceinwen, there are always people who grumble and complain. As long as I'm this nation's prince there'll be men wanting to take over from me. I'm used to that.'

'But these aren't your enemies, Madoc,' I say, as gently as I can.

'No? You make me wonder.'

'Hallo great lady.'

I have come up to Glesig as he's exercising the foals. He used to do this under the instruction of Idris the horseman but now he does it alone. This morning he's trotting two foals at the same time, on very long pieces of rope. They have to run to strengthen their legs but we can't set them free in this open countryside, with no coppices or walled meadows in which to corner them, so we use the ropes.

'You've got very skilful at that Glesig.'

'Thank you Ceinwen. I'm learning.'

'Careful. They get tangled if you look away like that. Shall I hold one for you while we talk?'

Glesig gave me Mynda's rope and we walk companionably side by side, guiding the foals in their trots and sudden, head-shaking gambols.

298

'This is nice country,' I say, looking out over the rolling ground. 'Will we be in it much longer?'

'I hope not. I don't like it. These woods and ridges — you can't see who's on the other side of them. And I don't trust those people who came to the camp. The sooner we're out of their country, the better.'

'How do we know there aren't more of them ahead?'

'I don't know for sure. I want to take us to the north-east, where the land's more open. Then at least we can see what's coming.'

'I suppose you and Madoc have agreed that.'

'Yes. Why not? It's the right thing to do.'

'But Madoc hasn't said anything about it to the captains.'

'Yes he has. He's told them this morning.'

'Ah. How did they take it?'

'What do you mean?' Glesig looks at me, amused. 'It's the right thing to do. They must see that. It's worth taking the longer way if it's safer. Why are you frowning?'

'Because I'm anxious. It's the way Madoc's acting, see.' I drop my voice. 'He doesn't take any notice of anyone now. He doesn't bother to consult with the captains or the high kindred. And he doesn't even seem to know that they're annoyed. You must have noticed.'

'I'm very busy,' says Glesig drily. 'Prince Madoc makes me work for my keep these days.'

'I know he does. You're always advising him or teaching the people how to do something.'

'It is my country. I'm the only one of you who knows anything about it.'

'But it's not just that, though, Glesig, is it?'

Glesig turns on the spot, tightening the rope to make his foal, Betyl, wheel away to the left.

'That's enough to keep one man very busy.'

As he speaks, Glesig takes one hand from the rope and passes it unthinkingly over his left side. It's a gesture I've seen him make before: passing his hand over the place where he keeps the dreamstone. It's something he does when he's uneasy or very moved.

'It's still there,' I say. 'Don't worry.'

Glesig gives me an odd guilty look, like someone who's been caught in the act of stealing.

'There is something else between you and Madoc isn't there?' I say slowly. 'What is it? Is it something to do with that stone?'

Glesig looks fiercely at me.

'Madoc is my friend,' he says. 'He's my brother. I told you that. If he wants me near him it's because I'm his brother.'

'Foster brother.'

'What?'

'That's what we call it, when you make someone outside your kin your partner. Not brother but foster brother.'

'In my country we call it brother,' says Glesig even more fiercely. 'And Madoc calls it brother. So I am his brother.'

It's surprising, this vehemence of Glesig's. He's glaring at me like Dafy used to when I made fun of his secret game.

'Duw, Glesig,' I say, 'there's no need to be so angry. I know you love Madoc. But you said yourself that great men need their critics. And he is acting strangely with you.'

Glesig gives me a sharp look.

'No more strangely than with you. In my country, if a man hits his wife – ah, never mind, Ceinwen,' he says, as I look away. 'He's got passions in his heart, driving him. When we reach my country it will be better.'

'When we reach your country. How long will that be now?'

'Another month, maybe two.'

'Your people will be glad to see you back,' I say.

'Maybe. I don't know – I've been gone a long time.'

'Your wife will be glad to see you.' I say it shyly, wondering if perhaps, this time, he'll talk to me about her.

Glesig's face goes very still.

'I haven't got a wife.'

But I'm sure he has. I remember how he looked on the ship when I asked him.

'Madoc says you have,' I say, crossing my fingers in my skirts.

That's shaken him all right: Glesig jerks his head round to stare at me and his eyes search my face.

'You're lying,' he says slowly. 'Don't do that, great lady. Not to me.'

'Why not? You're lying to me. I know you've got a wife, Glesig, why won't you tell me about her?'

'I have no wife. Ceinwen, Madoc and I have sworn to help one another, a secret oath between brothers. I can't break my honour by telling you. It would break faith with Madoc.'

He says the last words passionately and I can't get any more out of him.

'Madoc,' I say, as we are watching the hide and stick shelter go up for tonight's stop. 'Why won't Glesig talk about his wife?'

Madoc takes my arm as if we were in the Hall at Dreugyllt.

'Probably because she's not really his wife yet,' he says. 'And never will be. He's no fool; in his heart he knows he's dreaming.'

'Why won't she be his wife? Doesn't she love him?'

Madoc grins; there's aggravating he is and enjoying it too.

'If you don't know, Ceinwen, it must be because he doesn't want you to know. And I can't tell you. Foster brothers' secrets.'

My Madoc has had a dream. He won't tell me what it was. He woke gasping and now he pushes me angrily aside when I try to hold him.

'What is it?' I ask. Listening, he is, his head turned to the edge of the camp where the watch stands, and fear makes my voice sharp. 'What can you hear? What?' I catch his arm and he turns and looks at me. His face is bewildered but twisted with passion.

He blinks heavily.

'What is it, Ceinwen?' he says, and begins to struggle to his feet. 'What's wrong?'

I was mistaken. He wasn't awake before, when he listened. He was still asleep then — it's only now that he's awake.

'Ssh,' I say. 'Ssh my love. You were dreaming. Dreaming, Madoc. Dreaming.'

I put my arms round his waist and hold him beside me. I kiss his face and stroke the hair back from his temples. I rest my lips on his straight brows and smooth the two lines that have furrowed the skin between them. He's frowning and yet there's a little smile on his mouth.

'Dreaming, that's all,' I say. 'What is it, Madoc? Can you remember?'

He shakes his head and rests it against mine. His hands start to stroke my back, pressing the linen shirt against my skin.

I don't believe him. He can remember all right, my prince. I can feel his heart beating and he gives a low, longing sigh.

'It's quiet out,' I say. 'No disturbances.'

Madoc lifts his head and his lips press on mine with a groan. I let him kiss me, and at first it's gentle but then the control of the kiss changes and I can feel him pressing into my mouth with the strength he sometimes has now. It's not the open, healthy force of the young prince of Gwynedd, Owain ap Gruffydd's son. It's a shut in strength, drawn up from a place I can't get to.

Madoc's hands are under my linen shirt and he's pushing my legs apart and pulling them round himself.

'My love,' he mutters again and again. 'My lady. My love of Cynfael.'

When he loves me like this, it's as if he's drowning me. I can't think beyond him; I can't feel anything else. I don't know where I stop and he begins – it's that confusing. I can only hold on and hope not to be swept away by this furious passion, this storm which he's carrying inside him.

Madoc's asleep again now. His lips are curled in a little smile, though whether it's for our love-making or his dreams I don't know. Such violent, passionate dreams they seem to be.

He's quiet now. He's curled up like a boy, his hands pressed against his ribs as if he's guarding some special possession.

It's how Glesig sleeps. This is the same gesture that Glesig makes when he puts his hands to his side, protecting the dream-stone. Exactly the same.

25

It is beginning again. Jane stared at Sam as he walked round her little apartment and tried to find a clue. What was Miss Archer trying to tell her in that extraordinary letter?

Sam was looking from one piece of furniture to another, his face shadowed. It was a look she knew well: it screened his feelings when they were too strong for him to handle. He'd looked like that in Willie's trailer, and the first time the principal had called them to his office, and when they'd walked through the Reservation together, ignoring his mother's shouts, and the morning the principal had come to the school gates and turned her away.

The memories made her close her eyes. It was bewildering to have Sam in front of her, big and solid and with the marks of experience on him, reminding her of another Sam.

No, not another Sam: it was the same one. Every abrupt movement told her that, every word. It was just that she didn't know what he'd been doing for twelve years. Who he'd been with; what had been happening.

Sam's ring binder lay on the desk. His name was written on it in ink: Sam Late Martin. So Sam was now using a Mandan name.

Sam had reached the bedroom doorway. He glanced in and nodded.

'It's nice,' he said, turning to her. He looked uncomfortable. 'It's great. Are you sure about this?'

'Positive.'

'I'm not homeless, you know.'

'For God's sake, Sam, I know you're not.'

'Ok. I'll take it. Have your lawyer call my lawyer.'

Jane smiled. 'Catch.'

She threw the keys and Sam swiped them out of the air.

There was a pause. Passing the keys to him had suddenly made the apartment feel different. Jane was very aware of its stillness and of the door shutting them off from the world outside. She dropped her gaze from his face to his hands, but the sight of them was somehow even more intimate.

Jane couldn't find the right tone in which to speak. But Sam broke the silence easily.

'I'd offer you lunch,' he said, 'but there's nothing in the ice box.'

'No, sorry,' she said. 'That was an oversight. There's a place I often eat just round the corner on Broadway.'

'Let's go.'

Jane breathed deeply as she led the way to the door. Sam was keeping a safe three feet behind her, outside her body space. The realisation hurt her and as he turned to lock the door, she stared at his bent back and head.

This moment reminded her irresistibly of the things they had done back in Renoxia, the doors they had opened, legally and illegally, the refuges they had found and to which they had led each other. Sam glanced at her as he withdrew the key from the lock and she saw the same knowledge in his eyes.

He put the key in the pocket of his sheepskin, half-smiled and put his hand on Jane's shoulder as they walked down the corridor. She could feel the weight of it, more weight than there had used to be, and the tension in his fingers.

'Thanks,' he said.

'You're welcome.'

It seemed to Jane that days had gone by since she'd heard Sam's voice yesterday evening. This morning alone seemed to have lasted for ever.

At least she and Gwyn had made up. They hadn't spoken about it, but when she had finally gone to bed last night his arms had closed around her. They had slept like that all night long. This morning Jane had left him sitting at his desk in his towelling robe, frowning at a sheet of paper.

Dora's was already full with lunch-time people. Jane and Sam had to squeeze on to a table where two business colleagues – a young woman and a thirty-fiveish man – were talking more than eating, planning a pitch they were about to make that afternoon. Under cover of their energetic discussion of strategies and inter-facing, Jane watched the way that Sam's thick blue jumper hugged his throat, and groped for some clues to his life.

'What school do you teach at back home?' she asked.

'It's called Hillborough Junior High. It's a new one. They shut down White Bluff and Cherrylawn and put the two together in a new building on the east side of town.'

'The east side?'

'Just south and east of the Commercial District. Convenient for the kids of White Dove and their Moms.'

'Sure. But not so good for the kids of Toller and the Reservation?'

Sam poured his soda, his elbow joggling against her arm.

'Not so good. But we've got our own school on the Reservation now. Just a kindergarten so far, funded by a welfare programme. But there are plans to get our own junior high.'

'Would you want to teach in it?'

'I'd rather run it.'

'Is that a possibility?'

'Sure it's a possibility. If for some reason I begin to fly up the promotion ladder. But you know I just can't come up with a convincing reason why that should happen.' Sam gave her his polite deadpan look. 'However, it is a help that no one in their right mind actually wants to work on the Reservation. It makes the competition easier to handle.'

'Are things any better now?'

'Where, the Reservation? Yeah, some. The programme built us a craft centre. We make traditional artefacts now, you know. We get the beads shipped from Hong Kong. They're cheaper than American-made stuff and if we buy enough, we get discount. Did you know Hong Kong has a whole new industry sector to keep us in beads and lacquered discs and blow pipes?'

Jane wasn't sure if she should laugh but she couldn't help it.

'Can people make money from crafts?'

'Not so far.'

'How are Jimmy and Suzanne?' she asked after Sam's half brother and sister.

'Jimmy's in the pen. Suzanne's in Chicago, working as a nurse.'

'Little Suzanne? In Chicago?'

'It was the furthest away she could get from us. She and Mom can't stand to see each other.'

'How is your mother?'

'The same as she ever was. Anxious, angry. Afraid. She's been picking Jimmy up off the ground for so long, she's forgotten how to stand up straight. She could be proud of Suzi if she wanted to be, but she won't.'

'Where are you living now? With room-mates from school?'

Sam looked at her with an odd mixture of dignity and offence. It was the kind of look you never received at Brockham but she had seen it in someone's eyes recently – whose?

'I'm living on the Reservation,' he said. 'And hey, guess what. I have a trailer of my own.'

Eirlys. It had been in Eirlys's eyes that Jane had seen that look, when she'd snubbed her questions about Gwyn. It was the look of someone who was being asked to deny something very important to them.

But was the Reservation so important to Sam? It never used to be. It used to be just the place he lived, with the people he loved and hated.

'I see you're using a Mandan name now,' Jane said, nodding at his folder.

'That's right. They say it's my name.'

'Who's they? Willie?'

'Willie. And eventually my Mom confirmed it.'

'So. You and Willie have gotten pretty close after all?'

Jane couldn't keep the flat note out of her voice.

Sam looked carefully at her. His face was full of complicated emotions, sharpening the strong lines of his nose and cheekbones and jaw.

'We get along,' he said.

Across the table, Jane realised, the suited colleagues had

stopped talking and were listening in curiously. She stared at them and they turned to each other again, flustered.

'He always hated me,' she said quietly. 'Always.'

She waited for a denial but the only thing that came was their food.

Sam had a girlfriend. Her name was Dee Ann and she had come to Renoxia with the national reservation funding programme. She was a Sioux from South Dakota, and she sounded passionate and witty and clever. A match for Sam, in fact.

They lived together some of the time, when Dee Ann wasn't travelling. Dee Ann travelled a lot, helping to set up programmes in the other Plains reservations, or lobbying Congress. Dee Ann's Sioux name was White Roe. Jane asked Sam if he had a picture of her and to her surprise, he took one out of his wallet. Dee Ann wasn't beautiful but she had a clever, interesting face. And a formidable one, Jane thought, looking at the energy shining out of the dark eyes.

With Dee Ann's photograph fell out a small card on which was a list of names and numbers in Sam's writing. Sam left it on the table while Jane looked at the picture, and she surreptitiously read it. It was a list of contact numbers for his New York trip. Dee Ann's name was down twice, with two numbers, each with a different area code, and dates written beside them. Evidently this was one of her travelling periods. Beneath her name were others with New York numbers: Paul, Miriam, Jed Bierhorst, AFB.

Jane felt overwhelmed with curiosity about Sam's life and irrationally agitated that she no longer knew anything about it. Who were these people? Who was Miriam? Would she be coming to visit Sam in Jane's apartment?

'She's very attractive,' Jane said, handing the picture back. 'She looks interesting.'

'She is,' said Sam. 'I can't keep pace.'

'What about you?' he asked, sliding the card and picture back into his wallet. 'You got married fast. Are you happy?'

'Yes,' said Jane. 'I am. Very.'

'Gwyn seems like a guy with a lot to him.'

'He is. But he's not always like he was last night.'

'He wasn't very keen on me, you mean? Coming to see his two-moons bride?'

'One moon.'

'Huh?'

'We've only been married one moon.'

'Congratulations. You got a celebration coming up?'

'Oh fuck off, Sam,' said Jane amiably.

Sam grinned and pushed his plate away. Then he picked up his fork and stole a piece of Jane's ravioli. She laughed but the action brought back too many memories, too vividly. Sam had always filched her food, was always hungry and the traumas which had made her unable to eat just sharpened his appetite. The gesture of pushing her plate towards him was so familiar it confused her.

'Still always hungry?'

'Uh huh. Can't seem to get enough. Can't seem to gain weight.'

Jane watched him scrape the last envelopes of pasta off the china.

'Sam, did Miss Archer tell you what was in her letter to me?'

He soaked up the last sauce with bread. 'No.'

'Has she ever mentioned a man named Haydn Phillips to you?'

'Uhn uhn, but Willie has.'

'Willie?'

'Willie was his friend too. Didn't you know?'

Jane shook her head slowly. 'No. I didn't know. I hardly know anything about Haydn Phillips. It's just, he keeps appearing.'

'In what way?'

'Well, first of all – hey Sam, we never heard of him before, did we? When we were kids?'

Sam shrugged.

'I don't remember it,' he said. 'It's not exactly the sort of thing kids'd know about, is it?'

'I know but . . . I've heard so much about him just recently, and the story did seem kind of familiar when I first heard it.'

Sam had stopped eating. His eyes were on her face with a quizzical attention: he seemed to be trying to gauge her seriousness.

'So, when was that?' he said.

'In Wales. Earlier this month. First of all, I saw a painting by

308

Haydn Phillips, and I thought I'd seen it before.' Jane paused but Sam didn't speak. 'It was bizarre,' she said. 'I was so shaken by it. I went to Goff, an old teacher of Gwyn's, and asked him about it. He told me the Renoxia connection.'

She blinked at Sam, observing him through her lashes. She didn't know how much to tell him; if she could put into words the dark woman's presence and the feeling of terror the bird in the painting had aroused in her. She didn't know if she wanted to.

She wavered and drew back. Stick to the scientific facts.

'Well, later on I mentioned Haydn Phillips in a letter to Miss Archer and she wrote back that she'd known him.'

There was a pause.

'That was it huh?' said Sam. 'That was what was in the letter I had to bring to you personally?'

'No. That wasn't all. Sam, is Miss Archer OK? She hasn't said anything strange to you?'

'No,' he said cheerfully.

'Because her letter was really off the wall. She had some kind of affair with Haydn Phillips, did you know that?'

'Let's say I put two and two together.'

'And – the rest of the letter was about, well, us.'

Jane raised her eyes to Sam's face. The quizzical humour had faded from it at her last words and suddenly he was looking at her with an odd, naked softness. She breathed in sharply. So after all, it was still there; somewhere in him too, a remnant of their love was still alive.

But almost as soon as she thought it, Sam spoke and his voice seemed to contradict the look in his eyes.

'What about us?' he said easily.

Jane searched for the words to go on, striving to sound brisk and matter of fact.

'Oh, well, it didn't make much sense. She seemed to think something bad was going to happen to us. She implied that you and I were somehow linked to her and Haydn Phillips. She wrote that,' Jane heard her breathing falter, despite herself, 'she wrote that if you came to see me, it would mean it was beginning again.'

She was watching Sam's face closely. She was so confused now, she didn't know what she expected him to do: maybe laugh at her or shrug or even roll his eyes and say 'Yes, It has Begun.' But he did none of these. He just frowned at her for long seconds and then shook his head.

'Shit, Jane, I've missed you,' he said.

'Did Sam move in OK?' Gwyn stood in front of her desk almost shyly. The snow sky outside was filling the office with a yellow-grey light. He looked tired and rumpled and endearingly boyish.

Jane thought of the way she had just left Sam, their quick, tentative embrace on the sidewalk and the swirl of emotions that was still in her head.

'Yes, no problem.' she said. 'He wants to buy us a drink tonight to say thank you. I said we'd meet him in the bar at six.'

'I've got a class,' said Gwyn. 'This post-war poetry course I've been roped into.'

'Oh shit,' lied Jane. 'I didn't know it was a six o'clock class. All the same, you can come afterwards.'

'Yeah,' said Gwyn vaguely. 'I'll need a few drinks after I've faced all those smart-arse graduate students. I could do with a few in advance. I haven't prepared.'

'Been writing all day?'

Gwyn nodded. His eyes had the slight squint Jane had come to associate with a sustained writing binge.

'Pleased with it?' She knew she needn't ask. His mouth curved in a secretive smile. While she had been talking to Sam, he had been lost in that world where she could only half follow him.

'Look,' Gwyn said. He glanced at her uncertainly. 'I'm sorry I was a bastard last night.'

'It's all right.'

'No it's not. Understandable maybe, but not all right. I was jealous, see.'

'I know.'

'It was your mysterious hulking ex just turning up like that.'

'Not quite just turning up. There was a phone call.'

Gwyn pulled his mouth down.

'Yes. All right. Well, the thing I'd like to ask *you* is – ' he smiled at her to soften it, and then glanced to the door. 'Oh Christ, do I hear who I think I hear?'

Jewell's big voice travelled fast down the corridor, ahead of the footsteps. They had time for a brief exchange of glances before he came in.

Professor Jewell was overpowering in a thick, mustard yellow wool cardigan and sewage brown trousers. He took in Gwyn and Jane with one aggressive sweep of his head and broke off his conversation with Harry.

'Gwyn Thomas, what a surprise. The poet serenading the fair lady? Very touching. But in working hours, dear boy, she happens to be my assistant, try and remember that and restrain your uxorial passion. Now Jane, shall I rid you of this turbulent love priest?'

Jane gave her best rootin'-tootin' grin and leaned her elbows on the page proofs before her, to draw attention to the fact that she was working.

'Ah excellent,' said Jewell, glancing at them. 'So far on, so soon? What a paragon you are. As it happens Gwyn, I have something to discuss with you, so you can stay awhile.'

'Oh yes?' said Gwyn mildly.

'Assuredly. A reading. A special reading of heroic verse, with selections from the Greeks, the Norsemen, the Persians and Arthur's fair race. Including, brave fellow, your own latest compositions.'

'Mine.'

'Yes. Oh, not the well observed stuff, carved on an inch of stiletto blade. Your recent creations. The fruits of your latest and ongoing labours. The Gwyn Thomas bardic/heroic vein to which you treated us at the last reading, and which was really, I venture to say, not altogether contemptible.'

'No.'

'What did you say?' Professor Jewell paused in mid-circuit of the room. He looked at Gwyn with a tolerant leer then, as he registered Gwyn's tension, his facial muscles drooped and his eyebrows began to twitch together disbelievingly.

'What, Master Thomas?'

'No,' said Gwyn quietly. 'No reading of my new poems. No.'

'You jest, you son of a gun,' said Jewell.

'No I don't.'

'May I ask *why* you don't wish to favour us with any of your poems? Ah, wait a moment. Is it that you have omitted to write any more? Well, that is reprehensible of course, but in view of your nuptials forgivable. This time. But the reading will be scheduled for the end of semester; it will in fact be a reading under the auspices of the *West Side Review* and we'll want to flag it in our next issue, of course, so you'll have time to buckle down. Dear boy.'

Jewell was smiling again, but not for long.

'No,' Gwyn repeated. His voice was still low but now it was shaking with reined in violence. 'No reading of my new poems. No reading of them.'

Professor Jewell was staring at his protégé in fascination. His grey head was thrust forward on his neck and waved slightly from side to side, like a huge snake.

'Now let me see. You have written the works, but you don't wish to share them with us. Far be it from me to invoke anything so vulgar as the legal contract you signed with us, as our resident – I believe – *poet*. Shall I just remind you of your duties under common courtesy to those who have taken an interest in you and helped further your career?'

Gwyn stood in the middle of the room, his fists clenched at his side. His face looked oddly blind as he shook his head.

'No,' he said with desperate finality. 'No. No.'

Jewell turned to Jane. His eyes were shining with the excitement of the scene. Behind him, Jane could see Harry trying to blend into the wall.

'Jane. Would you like to intercede and make things – shall we say – less embarrassing for our mutual relationships?'

Jane looked at the menacing figure of Jewell, now leaning over her desk. He was her boss. He had employed her. He could sack her. He could and probably would finish her chances of working on a similar magazine. The fear of it rose in her throat. She thought quickly and tried for a conversational tone.

'I think perhaps Gwyn's not ready to show anyone his poems yet, Professor Jewell,' she extemporised.

'That much is evident, Jane. The question is, why?'

'I don't know,' said Jane. She glanced at Gwyn and forced herself to give a rueful smile. 'I haven't seen them either.'

Jewell looked from her to Gwyn. Gwyn was gazing at him with an expression of agonised defiance. The taller man stared back, his chest swelling ominously, and then, unexpectedly, he chuckled. It was a self-conscious, rumbling chuckle that grew into a guffaw.

'God help us,' he said. 'God save us from these goddamned anal-retentive poets! Get out of here Thomas, you Welsh word-monger, and leave us to get on with some work.'

'Jee-sus,' said Harry, when they were finally alone. 'What in hell was all that about?'

Jane folded up the page proofs with shaking hands. While Jewell had been going over them, she'd kept her emotions in check but now a reaction was sweeping over her.

'I don't know,' she said. 'Christ Harry, I don't know.'

'You were lying about the poems weren't you? You have read them.'

'No. Just one of them. Not the others.'

'Do you know what Gwyn's so wound up about?'

Jane folded her trembling hands under her chin and looked at Harry. His face was full of real concern and she longed to confide in him, as an uninvolved friend. As someone outside the pattern; the pattern she was beginning to see.

'Yes,' she said. 'I do.'

Harry waited.

'Well,' he prompted. 'Do you want to tell me about it?'

Yes, thought Jane. Yes. But all at once there was someone else in her mind, the familiar presence that was never far away since their return from Wales. This time, the presence was not just intimate and caressing. It was warning.

Jane shrugged and smiled tightly.

'I can't,' she said. 'I'm sorry but I can't tell anyone.'

Sam looked good in Brockham bar. Several people turned to look at him as he walked in and Jane went forward to meet him thinking, 'Yes, and he's mine, from way back.' She resisted an urge to take his hand as she led the way to their table.

'No Gwyn,' said Sam.

'He has a class but he'll be along later. I'll have a Beck's,' she said to the graduate student who was taking their order.

'Two.'

They waited till the student was out of earshot.

'Did you have a good afternoon?' Jane asked.

'OK.'

'Do you really enjoy it, Sam?'

He shook his head irritably. 'Yes. Why?'

'I just never imagined you being a teacher.'

'There's not much else I can be. Wall Street's not big on unqualified Indians with a history of alcohol abuse.'

'You could train for something else. You *were* the brightest kid in school.'

Sam leaned back while the graduate student placed their beers on the table. He sighed.

'Yes I was,' he said, looking straight at her. 'And do you know what? I am still.' He picked up his bottle and drank. 'Ah, leave it, Janey.'

Jane felt heat rise into her face at the endearment. She leaned forward to grab her beer, hoping to hide her confusion. It was dangerous to let Sam affect her so much, and pointless: Sam had a lover of his own and a new life, just as she had. But forgotten feelings were welling up inside her – no, not forgotten, just lost, for too long.

She cooled her palms on the chill glass and waited for Sam to speak. He was leaning his elbows on the table, his shoulders hunched, and there was a faintly despairing look on his face.

Sam knew she was watching him. He linked his hands round the base of his bottle and spoke without looking at her:

'The Haydn Phillips painting you saw – it definitely had a bird in it?'

The words were so unexpected, it took Jane a moment to hear them properly. But the image was vivid in her mind at once: Haydn Phillips' bird, with wings outspread and head bowed. And with it came a secondary image of another, less substantial bird: the smoke bird Gwyn had written into his harbour poem. But she didn't see it in the context of the poem itself: instead she saw again the wind-battered cliff, and herself taunting Gwyn: 'That's a Mandan ritual, making prayer-fire.' She swallowed, her throat suddenly dry.

'Definitely. Why do you ask?'

'Was it a gull?' Sam sounded tense, almost aggressive.

'No. It was a dark coloured bird.'

Sam was silent for a moment. Then he said, angrily, 'Shit!'

'Why?' said Jane apprehensively. 'What's important about the colour?'

Sam shook his head.

'I can't tell you,' he said shortly. 'I'm sorry, I shouldn't have said anything. It's a Mandan thing.'

Jane stared at him. 'You're not serious?'

'I'm sorry.'

'You're really not going to tell me the significance of something *I've* seen, because it's a Mandan thing?'

Sam shrugged.

'As you say,' he said apologetically.

'You're not serious.'

'Jane, I can't help it. Don't push me.'

She looked at him. Sam was sitting back in his chair with his long, powerful legs stretched out before him. His hands made half-fists and he was kneading his knuckles together unconsciously.

'I don't understand,' she said angrily.

'You wouldn't, you're not Mandan.'

Jane blinked at the dismissiveness of his tone. She'd heard him speak like that to other people often enough – to teachers and her parents and to Willie in the past, once or twice to Gwyn last night – but never before to her.

'Shee-it,' she said quietly.

Sam jerked his head back uneasily, shaking his black hair over his shoulders.

'Come on Jane, it's not as bad as that. We're nearly all gone, near as makes no goddamn difference to anyone except us. Surely you don't need to know our secrets too, before we go?'

'No. "I" don't. "I" don't know why the fuck you're in such a lousy mood this evening. "I" don't know what you're talking about.'

'No, you don't!' snapped Sam. There was another silence, then he exhaled slowly. 'Jane, I'm sorry – I shouldn't be beating you up about it.

'Janey, I know Willie wasn't fair to you in the past, but I've gotten very fond of him. He's been good to me. Now Willie truly

315

believes there are some things in Mandan culture – what's left of it – that shouldn't be told outside. But it looks like someone told Haydn Phillips.'

He looked bleakly at Jane.

'Willie was his friend,' she said. 'You said so yourself.'

'I know. That's what I've been thinking. But shit, Jane, if Willie knew that Phillips had used it in his paintings – I think it would kill him.'

'Well you can relax. There's only one painting left. Phillips burned all the others.'

'One's still one too many. I just hope to God Willie never gets to hear of it. Oh, I know it sounds stupid, I know it's nothing to do with me, but when you told me about the painting, I felt like I'd let him down. Absurd, huh?'

Jane stared at Sam. He was telling the truth: he was serious about this Mandan secrecy business. He had picked up his beer bottle and was examining it as though he were trying to trace the genesis of Haydn Phillips' bird in the glass. But what he didn't know of course, was that it was not only Haydn Phillips' bird; now it was Gwyn's bird too.

What had Goff called Renoxia? Madoc's country. No, no, no; it couldn't be.

'Maybe it was just an intuition of Phillips',' she said, and heard her voice too loud. 'Maybe he just picked it up accidentally, out of the ether.'

Sam turned quickly. 'Why do you say that?'

'Well, you said yourself that no one would tell him. And funny things happen in the subconscious.'

Their eyes met and held. Once more Jane was seeing Haydn Phillips' painting, as plainly as if it had been hanging in front of her. But this time she wasn't looking at the terrible oversized bird but at a detail in the bottom left hand corner of the scene: a detail which at the time had seemed impossible, so impossible that she had ascribed it to her own overwrought state. But it was funny how clearly it came back now, how she could see every detail of the brushwork: the dark horizontals that were the eyes, the red-brown strokes of the skin, the white gleams which highlighted the bones of the face, the outstretched arms and the bended knees. And seeing the figure in her mind's eye, she looked once more at this painterly, stylised representation of a human form and knew she recognised it.

'Maybe you're right,' said Sam. 'Maybe you're right twice over. Ah, forget it. I've been sleeping badly recently and things get all out of proportion. Do you know the feeling?'

'Very well.'

Too well; much, much too well. For a while back there she had thought Sam's presence was going to afford her a relief, but now it seemed that even he was part of it. The pattern was growing, closing around her.

Jane swallowed the last of her beer, forcing the liquid down her throat.

'Another beer?' said Sam. 'No, let's wait. I can see Gwyn coming in.'

Jane's eyes flew to Sam's face and before she knew what she was doing, she had reached out both hands and clutched his arm.

'Hey,' he said quietly, 'what's this?'

'Oh nothing,' said Jane. 'Just something I thought of – nothing important.'

She took her hands off him and folded them in her lap. Gwyn was walking towards them, smiling at her over Sam's head. Her nails dug painfully into her palms as she tried to control herself. Why did the sight of the two men, Gwyn coming ever nearer behind Sam, suddenly infect her with such fear?

26

The country is changing. In the hours we've been walking since dawn, we've seen the land begin to rise to the west. And now the mist has cleared to show a river gleaming black-brown in the clear morning light.

For a while now, Pryste has been looking anxious at my side. Her fair head turns this way and that, assessing the land. Glesig has noticed it too: a few minutes ago I caught his eye and we smiled.

'Are you worried, my lady?' he asks her now.

'A little,' says Pryste. 'I can't help wondering what Madoc and Arun think about this country – and my husband, of course.' Poor Pryste; she always tries to be so respectful to Cuhelyn. 'The high land's closing in ahead,' she goes on. 'Look, it's coming round in a curve. What happens if we're attacked from the hills? We'll be driven into the river.'

A few months ago I'd have been surprised to hear Pryste speak like that. Duw, I'd have thought; there's a warlord's sister speaking. But now we're all used to thinking of these things, every day.

So Glesig needn't look at Pryste in that admiring way, as though she's said something extraordinary.

'You're right to be cautious, Madam,' he says. 'But I've already spoken to Madoc and Arun about the ground – I know it, you see. You can't see it from here but where the high land comes in, the river turns off to the east so the plain is still as wide. Besides, there are no clans living here. The river floods in spring and would wash their livestock away.'

He smiles at Pryste and she smiles gratefully back.

It irritates me: these days Glesig has smiles for everyone. I cut across their exchange.

'Where are we going to stop, then?' I ask.

'This side of the river bend,' says Glesig. 'It's not far – we'll be there by early afternoon. It's a good place to camp – I've camped here before, when I was a boy, with my people.'

Pryste puts her hand on Glesig's arm. Very splendid she looks too, in her deerhide cloak. Many of us are wearing them now, since we had the great deer kill two weeks ago and Glesig taught us all how to smoke the hides over fires. We didn't have time to smoke them properly, and they're stiff and they still smell of the animal. But they're warm and God knows we need that now that the winter has come. It hasn't snowed yet, but there's frost on the ground every night and every morning. We've made deerhide shoes for ourselves to protect our feet from the iron cold. I feel stupid in my clumsy cloak and large shoes, but Pryste looks noble in hers: like one of the Irish ladies from the old battle stories.

'It must be good for you, to be back in your own country,' she says gently.

'We're not there yet, my lady,' Glesig answers. 'Ynys Llyr is a huge island. We have many more weeks to travel.'

'Further into winter,' I say sharply, pulling my cloak around me. Little Buddug stirs in the sling which holds her next to me. I put my arm round her to soothe her. Little Buddug, named after my own Buddug, is the daughter of Elen of Tydraeth. She was born two weeks ago and Elen is too sick to care for her. There are other nursing mothers here who feed her, but I often carry her. I don't know why I do it: it always makes me unhappy, what with thinking about my own child that I lost. I should be heavy with him in my belly now.

Glesig is looking at me; he's heard my cross tone.

'Poor Ceinwen,' he says. 'You didn't like the heat, now you don't like the cold.'

'I just hope you're not leading our people wrong, Glesig,' I say. 'There's funny, isn't it, how often we've walked through friendly country and only stopped when we're in some miserable place, with foul water and bad weather and hostile neighbours.'

'But at least we've never been attacked,' says Pryste. 'And if we tried to stop in the better country, we might have been.'

'Hmm,' I say. I don't know why but I can't stop myself teasing and provoking Glesig.

He smiles broadly.

'Ceinwen knows better than to trust anyone who has power or knowledge, don't you Ceinwen?'

'Are you speaking against Madoc?' I say, although I know he's not. 'Are you saying Madoc isn't trustworthy?'

Pryste gives me a quick, shocked glance. I ignore her; over little Buddug's head I watch for Glesig's reaction. I expect laughter or an angry denial but instead I can see a look of uncertainty on his face. Glesig's head twitches; he half turns in Madoc's direction then checks himself. I've taken him off guard, but what exactly is it that I'm seeing?

'Well, well,' I murmur, not quite sure what to think. Glesig recovers now.

'Of course I trust Madoc,' he says. 'But if you mistrust me, my lady, I'm afraid you mistrust the prince as well. You see, *he* trusts me so you'll have to decide if you trust both of us or neither.'

'He's got you there, Ceinwen,' says Pryste. She's seen nothing in this except word play. Well, that's probably a good thing, but I know what I saw. And I know what I'm seeing now – Glesig's right hand moving to his left side, to touch his chest beneath his cloak. He sees me watching him but he can't stop himself from doing it.

It's the dreamstone again. Something is wrong between Glesig and Madoc and I know, I know it's to do with the stone.

'No Ceinwen, why should I worry about a scrap of stone?' Madoc raises his eyebrows at me. 'Don't you think I've got enough to keep me busy with all our other concerns?'

'Glesig says the stone is very powerful,' I argue. 'And a lot of the people are beginning to wonder what it is he uses in his prayers. They know he's got something there.'

'So?'

'I don't like it, Madoc,' I say slowly. 'The stone's a talisman. You think so too, don't you?'

'I promised my father's bishop not to believe in anything but Christ and the Virgin,' says Madoc piously.

I shake my head at him, smiling.

'My lord, you had the eye carved on every one of our ships in recognition of the old powers. Christ and the Virgin won't mind company, is what you said then.'

'Quite right,' grins Madoc. 'Seafarer's hospitality, that is.'

'You're still a seafarer and we're still travelling. Look at the people building the shelters, have you noticed something about them?'

Madoc stares at the people who, for the last few hours, have been labouring to put up a brushwood and hides shelter for the night. They are gathered in groups round different tasks: finishing the trench, forcing the upright branches into the ground, binding together the hides. Yet they are all positioned with their heads turned north, towards the glow of Glesig's solitary fire.

'You see, my lord? They won't turn their back on him while he's making prayer-fire with the dreamstone. They're reverencing it.'

Madoc shrugs.

'Ceinwen, they don't know anything about his precious dreamstone.'

'No, but they know he's got something. They all saw the smoke bird at Dreugyllt.'

'There are many ways of doing tricks like that.'

'You didn't think so at the time,' I say, and then I flinch instinctively as Madoc scowls at me. Since he hit me, I've been wary of his temper.

He notices my movement away and after a pause, which seems to cost him a big effort, he chuckles.

'I confess,' he says. 'I'm superstitious before a voyage, all seafarers are. What's the matter, Ceinwen? Why do you want me to bother about Glesig and his stone?'

I look into his face: he's impatient and annoyed. But he's uneasy too, his head is tossing from side to side as if he's trying to get away from this conversation.

'Do you remember Marared's vision?' I say. 'The seer in Cynfael. She saw – '

'That's enough, Ceinwen.' Madoc is agitated now, his voice

321

has dropped low and rough. 'It's bad luck to go dwelling on these things. We've done well so far, we've got a long way to go. If the people want to put their faith in Glesig's stone, let them. I'm not worried by it, God's bollocks, I've got enough on my hands leading them through this country. Because it is me leading them, Ceinwen, not Glesig. I'm the prince of this nation. And if they bow their heads to anyone in this island, damn them, it'll be me.'

The last words he says under his breath, peering angrily at Glesig's distant figure where he kneels before his fire.

So. Something is not right, but Madoc won't tell me. Well, that's no surprise: he tells me less and less these days. The shelter is almost all erected now: the last tasks are being done by the light of the fires, and women are cooking amongst the sawing and knocking and strapping, the digging and packing. Madoc has been going around the great, flimsy shelter, checking it, and now he and the captains have gone to inspect the watches. The men have taken up their positions on the rugged little cliffs that fringe the river: from there they command a view in every direction.

Madoc is beside himself tonight. In the wooded lower slopes of the hills to the west, a scouting party of our people have found many fallen trees. They've been down several years, so the wood is good for ships. And Glesig has told Madoc that soon, not far to the north, the river will become navigable.

Now that they're talking about ships again, the captains are flocking round Madoc, their grudges apparently forgotten. They're together on the river cliffs. I can see them, tiny in the moonlight, just little dark marks against the silver water. When I took Madoc some wine just now, he brushed me away almost angrily; there's far away he seems. There's lonely it makes me feel.

'Did you get a sign, Glesig?'

'What do you mean?'

'From your prayer-fire. Is the smoke bird going to guide us safe to your country?'

Glesig pauses, staring into the fire. He does this nowadays, turns away from me as much as he can.

'If you don't want people to ask questions, you shouldn't make your prayer-fire in front of us all.'

'I don't know,' he says.

'What?'

He looks at me now and I can see something I didn't expect – he's troubled.

'I don't know if we'll all be safe. I just don't know.'

'What are you afraid of?'

His face has grown stronger since we've been on Ynys Llyr land; it's sombre, brooding with thoughts I can't see, but which make my heart feel strangely tight. It shouldn't be a pleasant feeling but somehow it is.

'I'm afraid of us, Ceinwen.'

'Us? You mean your own people?'

'No. You and me and Madoc. We want things. We want so many things – so much.'

I look down at the ground. I'm not sure what Glesig is telling me but the tight feeling grows around my heart.

'Glesig Dog! Meurig wants you to draw that map for him. Come and explain to him.' It's Madoc's voice of course, prince-like and abrupt. 'Come on!' he shouts and Glesig has to get to his feet and go in answer to his command, leaving me alone again.

This morning we stood up on the cliff the other side of the river. The sky was white-blue and the land went on for ever. A bitter wind was blowing in my face. Madoc stood beside me gesturing up the course of the river, telling me how we'd sail up it to Glesig's country. And I looked on the endless, undulating land and remembered another time when Madoc and I had stood high up in the teeth of the wind. That morning, that second morning of our reunion, when he'd taken me on to the battlements of Dreugyllt.

I'd laughed that morning in Dreugyllt. And I laughed now, but an uncertain laugh. Did Madoc hear the difference?

Glesig leads me along the river bank, his head bent. We are going herb picking; I asked him to show me where the herbs grew, and he agreed. We have been out an hour and all our talk has been scratchy and difficult. Neither of us wants to mention what we said last night but I could swear we are both thinking about it.

Duw, it makes me angry and hot inside when Glesig won't talk to me. Look at him now, avoiding me: he's staring down at the coarse grasses and rushes; the light of this early afternoon is pale yellow-green, coming down in vertical sheets from the sky. It's a funny, metallic light and it shows planes and hollows in Glesig's tense face.

'There's the warrior's plant.' He points to a tall, straggly plant with ugly pale flowers on its thin stems. 'The leaves increase courage.'

'I'd better get some for Madoc, then,' I say, kneeling down and starting to pull off the leaves.

Glesig doesn't help me. 'Madoc's brave enough,' he says. I go on picking leaves and cramming them into my leather bag.

'You used to criticise Madoc,' I say. 'You used to talk to me about the way he was planning things and giving orders.'

When he doesn't reply, I glance up. Last night's brooding look is back – he seems heavy and tired. And he seems sad too – which I've never seen in him before. He's got the look of a man who's been struggling a long time against a weight that's on him, and who's just begun to realise that he can't throw it off. His eyes half close and he shakes his head.

'Glesig,' I say gently and I reach out my hands to him.

He bends down slightly to give me his hands, but although he's standing over me, it's me who's comforting him. And not just comforting him; I kneel there quite a while before he pulls me to my feet and says,

'There's a little jut of land on the bank there . . . can you see it? Covered with tall grasses. You can usually find herbs for curing stiff joints in those grasses.'

'There's useful. Let's go there.'

So we're walking there, and my hand is almost brushing his. My feet rustle on the frosty grasses and as we come to the jut of land, he stretches his arm out behind me, holding the snaggly branches of the river bushes away. I can feel the strength of his arm.

I feel very easy with Glesig, see. He knows how I think. And

I know what it's like to be poor and despised like him. What is it he once said: 'We have to make our own way, you and I?'

'I'm worried,' I say. 'I'm tired and worried and there's so much to watch out for.'

'I know,' Glesig says.

He looks down at me, where we've paused on the edge of the jut. His eyes are black, like flood-water, and they've drowned all his expression. The bushes and grasses growing around us are already closing over our heads, hiding us. Glesig steps ahead of me, his hide tunic swishing against my cloak and clears a path into the tangled undergrowth. He leads into it with his shoulder, then he turns and holds out his hand and I take it.

Glesig's hand is warm and sinewy: its clasp sends shocks through me. The rushes are in my eyes and I can't see but touching his hand is like being joined to something very powerful and alive, burning and beating in the darkness. His muscles flex and he draws me gently into the dim greenness with him.

I don't think he hears my sigh. For a moment we stand very still and then Glesig's arms come round me, burning where they touch. They burn, but not to hurt: where he presses against me my flesh ripens and heals.

I put my arms round him. Big, he is; so much bigger than Madoc. To hold him is like a gap being filled, when I didn't even know it was there. His head comes down for my mouth.

There's gentle his kiss is for such a big man, and deep. My hands are holding his head. I'm stroking him and pulling him down closer to me; I'm lifting my mouth into his and bending my back so he can hold me, hold me. Glesig's arms are round me, lifting me up and he kneels down, carrying me with him. I'm clinging to him; I can feel the muscles in his arms and the adam's apple in his throat and the pulse on his neck.

He puts his hand inside my dress and strokes my legs apart and I lift my knees and call for him, but without words.

He's sliding on top of me and my hands are pushing at him, trying to open his tunic. His weight comes down on me and I struggle, fight, to get his tunic open. There's a tearing noise and my hands are against his skin. Against his ribs I feel a hard bump, where the stone is strapped in its leather pouch. I place my right hand gently over it and smile up at Glesig, venturer to venturer.

I seize him, he enters me, and I pull his strong body against me and up into me, and my womb is open to him and I smile on his smiling mouth.

Glesig lies inside me, spent and quiet. He looks down into my eyes.

'My friend,' he says softly.

Neither of us speaks again. His face is against mine; our cheeks touch gently. There's no stubble on his chin.

It seemed right then. Few minutes ago, it seemed right. But now that we've drawn away from each other, the other feelings are creeping in: a realisation of what we've done. A guilt. It began to come as we lay there, not speaking. And when Glesig finally lifted himself off me, I began to shake with loneliness and a frightened shame.

We're on our knees, fumbling to straighten our clothes. Glesig fastens his tunic again, tying the thongs over his ribs, and I turn my eyes from the hard bump in the leather where the dreamstone lies. It makes me think of Madoc; it's like having Madoc here, watching us.

We're standing up. My head-dress is destroyed, but who has a whole head-dress any more? My breasts I put back into the dress and I have to tug tremblingly at the fabric to stop the tear showing.

In the yellow-green gloom I see Glesig clearly. His face and my face looking at each other across the imprint of our bodies on the ground.

He leads the way out and I pass very close to him but we don't touch. We don't speak, all the way up the bank, on to the plain and across the flat, hard grassland towards the camp. We walk and walk the stretching distance, until it seems that the camp is as far away as the distant hills to the west and the impossible horizon that rings everything round. We don't touch and we don't speak and I carry my half-full bag of herbs.

27

The wind was blowing from the west. It came rushing in from New Jersey, raced across Broadway, was funnelled between the Brockham faculty buildings and exploded on to campus square. It drove Gwyn onwards like a huge hand in the small of his back and nearly swept his feet from under him.

Like Mary Poppins, he thought, blown into Cherry Tree Lane with her carpet bag, and felt a pang of pure nostalgia for home. It would be good to be back in small streets where children splashed through puddles in wellington boots and students got cold in damp libraries and bought themselves crumpets for tea. Instead the imposing grey facades of Brockham's faculties loomed at him. The unnervingly well-dressed students of this private university were muffled in lambswool and cashmere. And Sam Mandan was walking towards him, with Gail at his side.

Sam was a familiar figure in Brockham now. It had happened quickly and apparently without effort: a few introductions from Jane and the man was known in the bar, the campus shop, Dora's... he seemed to have no self-consciousness about his invidious position here, and certainly no one reminded him of it. They all seemed to accept him as one of the gang, no questions asked.

Look at Gail, talking away to him, her clear face turned up to his. It stung Gwyn to see that. It wasn't as if Sam made any special effort with these people: he just took their friendliness for granted. He used Brockham as a base for his job and his social life, and the bar as a starting point for his evenings with his own friends – Jed and Nathalie, Miriam, and the pretentious man called Anstrom who played acoustic guitar in the Barolo up on Columbus.

Sam had been here a week, getting his hands on Gwyn's life and Gwyn's wife, and still Gwyn didn't know who this man was. Watching Sam bend his body, instinctively adjusting to the force of the wind, Gwyn thought that he really was like a sinister Mary Poppins – a stranger who had blown in from nowhere and who was making himself at home, for motives Gwyn could not fathom.

Or could he? Day by day, since Sam had arrived, Gwyn found himself less sure of Jane, less able to talk to her.

'Hallo Gwyn. Some wind.'

'Morning Sam. Gail.'

Gail smiled civilly at him.

'I was just telling Gail about the band last night. Did you guys stay long after I quit?'

'Half an hour or so,' said Gwyn. 'We left before the next set. I can only take so much amateur blues.'

'It's a good thing I didn't stay on or I'd have been even later out of bed this morning. I've got to run. Are you coming to Jed's tonight?'

'I don't know. What's happening?'

'A bunch of us are meeting there. Jane will tell you about it, I'll be in the bar first anyway.'

Sam sketched a farewell gesture that took in both of them and loped off, his back looking muscular and preoccupied.

'Sam says the band was quite good last night,' said Gail, as they hurried up the faculty steps. Gwyn thought he heard a hint of tutorly correction in her tone.

'Oh yes it was,' he said. 'Great.'

He didn't know if it had been or not; he was no judge of music. But having agreed to go with Sam and Jane and the ghastly Anstrom to an R & B club, he'd been determined to outstay Sam. He'd hoped to get some time alone with Jane, but of course Anstrom had stayed on too. Not that Jane had seemed to mind.

He wondered how Jane came to know about tonight's arrangements.

'Sorry?' he said to Gail, who seemed to have asked him some sort of question.

'I just asked how your work was going,' said Gail hesitantly.

Work; that was one thing, *the* one thing, that was going well. He could have talked to Jane about that if she'd asked him but recently a heavy silence had fallen between them on the subject.

'Bloody marvellous,' said Gwyn defiantly.

He hadn't meant to get drunk. It was the sight of Jane there, fitting so neatly into Sam's body space like that. Relaxing beside him, leaning towards him; looking so right with him. So bloody at ease. And all their colleagues here in Brockham bar were seeing it too.

Sam and Jane looked so much at home together that this woman Robert Wendell had brought in from outside thought they were a couple. She had just asked Gwyn if he was going out with them later or if he'd like to go to the movie with her and Robert.

Gwyn wished that he could flirt with this woman, Kate. She was giving him enough opportunity, looking up into his face and asking him arch questions about rugby players. But all he could think about was Jane. His eyes kept sliding over Kate's shoulders towards her. Jane looked lovely tonight: rosy and happy like a little girl. He wanted to hold her and kiss her.

Just then Jane looked up and saw him watching her. She cocked a do-you-need-help eyebrow and smiled. He glared at her.

'Is anything wrong?' Kate asked, beginning to look put out.

'I'm sorry,' said Gwyn. 'My – friend was just showing me her watch.'

'Oh,' said Kate, dumbfounded.

'Excuse me,' said Gwyn. 'It was really nice meeting you. Bye now.'

He walked purposefully to Jane's side and then had to loiter while she listened to what Gail was saying to her. Oh Jesus, the Kate woman was looking across at him and saying something to Robert. Was he making a complete fool of himself?

'You'll have to ask Gwyn about that,' he heard Sam say.

'What?' said Gwyn, striving to sound interested and pleasant.

Sam sketched one of his quick gestures at Gail.

'Gail was asking me about the Madoc myth. I was telling her you'd know more about it than me.'

'What the hell do you mean?'

Gail's eyes were large and troubled; Jane put her hand soothingly on Gwyn's arm.

'He's only asking you because you're Welsh.'

Gwyn scowled at her – he couldn't stop himself – and spoke across her at Sam.

'What do you know about the Madoc myth?'

Sam looked askance.

'Nothing more than anyone else,' he said. 'That's just what I was telling Gail.'

'And you think I do?'

'We'd better go,' said Jane, looking at her watch. Her hand tightened on Gwyn's arm and she leaned against him, rubbing her head against his for a second. 'You ready, sweetheart?'

Gwyn longed to return her caress but he couldn't: he was too preoccupied with staring at Sam, turning over in his mind a sudden paranoid idea.

Gwyn waited until Gail and Harry were gone, then moved out of the shelter of the stacks. That had been close. Thank God he'd seen them in time; if he hadn't dodged round the corner between the chemical engineering shelves, they'd have met at the borrowing counter. He could imagine their eyes roving curiously over his books:

American Indian Songs and Poems. The Trickster: A Study in American Indian Mythology. Myths of the Plains Indians.

They'd have put two and two together fast enough. They'd only have arrived at two and three quarters by doing it, but it wasn't any of their bloody business anyway. He didn't need to be humiliated any more.

Gwyn glanced to right and left under his brows; no one he knew was around. He walked purposefully to the borrowing counter and kept his head bent while the librarian checked his books. Then he heaved them into his canvas bag and made for the doors.

The cold bit at his face as he crossed the campus square. It made his stubble hurt, but the thought of shaving made it hurt even more. He thrust his head down and strode on, then ran up the faculty steps two at a time. Shit, he'd forgotten about his poetry class: they'd have been waiting for ten minutes already. This made the second time this week he'd lost track of his schedule. It was getting harder and harder to focus his mind on Brockham and the daily round.

He hugged the canvas bag to him, feeling the hard edges of the books dig into his side. He wouldn't be able to look at them for two hours now; two hours in which Jane and Sam would draw even further away from him.

But he'd catch up, Gwyn thought, as he listened with half an ear to Nadia Hagan and James Thankhorn reading their dialogue poem. He'd catch up and overtake. He looked at the eleven students gathered in the seminar room and wondered if their minds were really on the class. He smiled a quick, appreciative smile as James made a poetic witticism. Don't you imagine you can shut me out, wife and former lover. There are more ways in than one.

It was four o'clock, the dead time of the afternoon. Outside it was dark; in his office Gwyn's reading lamp cast a pool of yellow light over his desk and the open books. Three storeys above the campus square he was floating, half-way between afternoon and night, unmoored to anything.

So, there was no doubt about the appearance of a white man myth in the Mandan legends. In some versions a white man; in some versions a man from the other side of a huge water; in all versions arriving in a canoe and saving the Mandans from a flood. The Noah story. Goff's theory, he remembered, had been that the flood was a bit of Christian mythology interposed into the Mandan – an addition of the surviving Welsh. Originally, Goff had surmised, the canoe would have been the ship, boat or boats, in which Madoc had arrived.

According to the books, there was a white dove who popped in and out of Mandan mythology – well, that figured: if the Welsh had brought them Noah they'd have thrown in the dove too. What, no olives?

Nothing about other birds though; nothing about dark ones. Which was odd, because they were cropping up in the poems more and more. And not only in the poems: Sam's Mandan name, Late Martin, was a bird's name.

Martin: look it up, each book had an index. M – Ma – nothing. Nothing here either. Ah yes, here in *Songs and Poems* appears in a footnote on page 143. Yes, blah, blah, nice song about the Old Man giving all the animals their characteristics . . . here. The fruit bird that couldn't fly from the ground: 'Thought to be a reference to the purple martin, which the agrarian Indians welcomed for its ability to fight off other birds who came in search of young grain crops. Indians would tie hollowed out gourds high on poles to make nests for the martins.'

Well, that was clear enough.

All the same, there was something here Gwyn couldn't see. It was like a blankness in his vision, as if someone had drawn a picture and then scribbled over a patch of it. He felt that if he stared long enough at the scribble, the lines would begin to separate into layers and resolve, and he would glimpse through the furious scratchings to the forms beneath.

But he couldn't. He knew he couldn't, because it was getting like that in the poems too. In the one he'd finished yesterday, for instance, there was a camp, a river and an island jutting into the river. He'd wanted to write about the island, but he couldn't. For some reason, he couldn't see on to it or past it. He'd felt his Madoc character tugging him towards it, urging him on, but he just couldn't get it. His narrative voice veered off course every time he tried to describe it. So he'd replaced the island with a lovely, plangent line about the herbs of home, but it had left him unsatisfied. And tense and brooding and increasingly, dangerously angry.

But then he felt angry almost all the time since Sam had arrived, and jealous. That's why writing the poems was such a relief.

No, there was nothing here that made things any clearer. He wasn't sure what he was looking for anyway. It was the same with the letter of Goff's that had arrived this morning: a perfectly nice letter it was, affectionate and unsentimental, with a considered but on the whole very enthusiastic appraisal of the poems Gwyn had left with him. Yet Gwyn couldn't shake the feeling that there was something Goff wasn't saying.

He wondered, if he asked, whether Goff would be able to help him understand what was going on in Jane's mind about his poems and this Madoc thing. She still regularly had that look of inturned dazzlement – he didn't think they'd had a day without it since their return, certainly not since Sam's arrival – but now it often had an attentive quality, as if she were trying to puzzle something out.

Whatever it was, Gwyn wanted to get at it too. So that when he bought drinks for Jane and Sam in the Barolo, or sat with them in the darkness before the flickering movie screen, or followed them in through his door to his apartment, he would understand the messages that passed between their eyes. He would know what it was that threatened him.

The sound of the electric bell made him look at his watch. Six o'clock; how had it got to six o'clock? Jane would be closing up the office soon. Gwyn reached out and switched off the reading lamp. Then he rose and felt his way around the desk to the window, where he stood a little way back from the pane, doubly sheltered by the darkness and the curtain. Anyone looking up from the square would think his study was empty.

He watched students and faculty members come out of their buildings and cross the square. He stood there watching for fifteen minutes before he saw Jane's figure appear below him. She seemed to be waiting, looking around for someone. A voice called her name and she turned and there, coming in from the Amsterdam side of the campus, was Sam. He ran up to the faculty steps, put his arm round Jane and gave her a hug. She kissed his face. Then she glanced up at Gwyn's dark window and the two of them wandered off in the direction of her old apartment, arm in arm.

Gwyn stared after them till his eyes stung. A few yards in their wake, hopping and fluttering in the evening breeze, a small bird was following them.

28

Madoc knows something happened. I don't know how he knows; I don't believe anyone has told him. No one knew, to be able to tell him. But somehow, he suspects.

He looks at me as if I'm some strange, foreign creature and at night he wraps himself in his hide cloak and leaves me in the brychan alone. With Glesig, he's sometimes friendly, sometimes cold and harsh.

He often tells me to go and walk with Glesig, or puts us together to talk with one another by the fire at night. We have to try and find some way of talking, under his watchful, accusing eyes.

Meanwhile Madoc calls other women to his side to play and sing to him, where he used to have always only me. Rhian, and round-faced blonde Heledd are the ones he most favours and Heledd has taken to smiling slyly at me when I pass. Everyone's noticed, of course; they're all chattering and wondering.

Whenever I am alone with Madoc I wonder if he's going to accuse me but he never does. He ignores me. Or in a soft voice he goads me, asking me if Glesig's taught me any secrets of Ynys Llyr lately. Or he even makes princely conversation with me.

'You sent for me, my lord?' I reach Madoc, where he stands talking to a group of kindred. Blonde Heledd is among them, her fair head turned up attentively to Madoc.

Madoc turns politely towards me.

'Glesig needs you, my lady,' he says. 'Would you give him your help?'

'Of course. Where is he, prince?'

'Behind the shelters, with the horses. One of them has an infected leg and we need your Cynfael skills.'

I return his smile and walk away with my head up, trying to look graceful and not to stumble on the black, frozen earth. I know that some of the kindred Madoc has gathered round him will be watching me under their lashes. I walk as if I don't dread this encounter, as if my skin isn't already shrinking from the prospect of Glesig's closeness.

I can hardly bear to look at Glesig now. I'm haunted by the memory of what happened; it comes back, as vivid as if his body were still on top of mine. It makes me shake; it makes me want to vomit.

Yet I must go and stand next to him again and look into his dishonourable eyes with my own.

How could I have betrayed Madoc with this man? With Glesig, Madoc's captive and his foster brother. Duw Madoc, if you knew how unworthy of your bond this Glesig Dog is. A dishonest man and a dangerous one.

I've been thinking back to all the things he's told me and done with me. He's like an enchanter – he knew about my miscarriage before I told him; on the ship he put me in a trance with that story about the stone. Yes, the dreamstone; it's all to do with that. Because I've been thinking about how he used it to conjure the smoke bird on Ynys Wair. And the way he prays to it every time we enter new land.

Oh, Glesig is a dangerous man all right. And that is a dangerous talisman. It gives him power over people. It gave him power over me.

I walk the long way round the big shack shelter, to put off the moment of seeing Glesig. He'll be waiting for me; by now he'll know, he'll have followed the murmuring voices and the turning heads. Madoc is punishing both of us well.

Sometimes, in these last dark weeks, I've wondered why he doesn't just kill us.

Or cast us out, to take our chance. That's what really frightens me.

The darkness spreads out beyond the shack and the stars are brighter. Glesig is watering the horses and feeling the legs of one of the foals. It must be the bay: I can see from here the white blaze on its face. The blaze is widening as the foal grows.

I begin to speak as soon as I'm in earshot, to keep as far away as I can. And I speak loud, so people who are passing can hear what I'm saying and no one can imagine otherwise.

'Madoc has sent me to help you. Does Mynda have a swelling?'

Glesig's shoulders seem to twitch inwards, but he half turns his head and says,

'Yes. And it's hot. I'm afraid of an infection.'

'Let me see.' I move the long way round the foal's body past his head; his eyes are dull. Glesig stands back so that no part of my cloak or skirt touches him as I lean down. The swelling is bad, it raises the hair and the flesh beneath is shiny. I don't know what to do with this; in Cynfael the women helped feed and break the horses and heal small wounds, but I've never seen this kind of swelling before.

'Is there a cut?' I say. 'Or a bite?'

'I can't see one.'

I stand up and put my hand on Mynda's trembling flank.

'I'll make a poultice. There's some mouse-ear left, and some comfrey.'

'We use a special herb for poisoned swellings in my kindred,' says Glesig. 'The leaves of spiky berries that grow on the sandy hills. There should be some here.'

'We'll send some people to look tomorrow. I'll make a poultice for tonight.' And I walk away, too fast, wanting to put the shelter and the people between me and Glesig and those words of his, which make me think of herbs growing in tangled secret places.

Elen, one of the young women of Rhys's kindred, and the mother of the baby Buddug, is sitting by my store of herbs. She's nursing Buddug and talking to Marged. Marged jumps up when she sees me but Elen stays put. They do that, these days, the women of the kindreds, when Madoc's not around.

'Pass me the second bag behind you, Elen,' I say sharply. 'The one with the stalks.'

Elen glances over her shoulder and lazily stretches out an arm, pushing the bag towards Marged, to pass to me.

'Making potions, Lady Ceinwen?' she asks, faint scorn sounding in the 'lady'. 'Love potions?'

'A poultice,' I say. 'For the bay foal, Mynda. To take the poison out of his leg.'

Elen cradles Buddug's little head against her breast and looks at me above the child's head.

'Poison,' she says. 'There seems of be a lot of that around now, Lady Ceinwen.' 'Lady' again. 'Poison, getting into animals and into men.'

'And I do my best to cure it,' I say coldly. My hands are shaking as I take the bag of herbs from Marged. What is this woman saying; what are all the kindred and the people saying against me?

'The brothers in our friary used to say that the cure and the cause of poison were one and the same. Do you agree with the holy brothers?'

I've set the bag carefully on the ground and now my hands are inside its neck, picking through the herbs. The leaves rustle against my skin and the brittle stalks stick into me.

I look this Elen full in the face; her eyes are sneering.

'Be careful, Elen,' I say quietly. 'I know why you couldn't nurse your child properly. There's things a mother does stops her milk flowing and I know what you did.'

And I stare hard at her, to convince her. There's appalled she looks. Her face has gone yellow in the firelight. Did she really think no one had noticed the flirtation she was having with her husband's nephew? Does she really think I care if she wants to cheat on Wyngyn Dawr, the pompous old bully? But she should understand: if she speaks against me I'll use what I know against her.

'Pass me the little bag by your elbow,' I say to her, pleasantly.

Another hard night, all pressed together for warmth in the shelter that's no more than a screen, flung together in a few hours. The fires around the edges keep the wild animals away, but not the frost. All night we doze and wake shivering, to see the men on watch walking and stamping, and we huddle down again, seeking warmth from each other. Madoc is dreaming again: a tormenting dream which makes him shudder and sigh and makes his hands creep across the brychan, like the hands of a beggar, pleading.

I hold him. I hold him and he doesn't move away, even though he wakes up. He buries his head in my shoulder and I feel wetness on my skin: he's crying.

'Oh my lord,' I whisper, thinking that he's weeping about me, but before I can say more he's speaking, very, very low, and in a voice of utter desire:

'The stone. Please, please give me the stone.'

We are packed and walking by the time dawn has spread its half-light. Every day for weeks we've been following the course of the river north. Madoc won't let us stop and build a settlement for a few days, as we used to; he insists we go on, to try and reach Glesig's country before the worst of winter. Every day there are more people sick; we pull them on the land sledges, people and mares taking the weight together, and when they die we bury them where we stop for the night.

We eat the meat of the shaggy bulls, which parties of our men go and kill as the rest of us walk. They've given up trying to kill them with bows; now, they do as Glesig taught them and round up companies of the cattle and chase them, driving them over the river cliffs so the fall kills them, or wounds them badly enough for the men to get knives to them.

We eat some of the meat fresh and smoke the rest, pounding it into paste to eat in the days ahead.

Madoc and Arun are hopeful that the river will soon be navigable.

Madoc wants to be at sail again. He longs to be steering a ship, driving it on through the waters, feeling the great craft and its passengers responding to his command. And he wants something else, too; wants it very badly. I can still hear his voice from last night, speaking so longingly: the memory turns my back-bone to water.

The afternoon light is fading, and it makes the land look indescribably, terrifyingly beautiful. The weary flatness across which we've been travelling for so long is changing: from here going northwards the land begins to ripple into long, rounded hills and there are glimmers of water between them, rivers and lakes.

On the hills, which are skeined with white frost, the small dark shapes of animals move. The little black dots are visible way into the distance: goats and horned cattle and the big shaggy bulls, supported by this grassland. Since we have been standing here we've seen three birds of prey hover in the skies. There are enough small animals here for them to live, even in winter.

We are entering Glesig's land. Not the heart of it; not his country, where his people live. But as Dreugyllt belonged to Gwynedd and not to the southern lands under Rhys, so these hills before us belong to Glesig's land.

Glesig has gone ahead, down the short slope to the tributary stream, across it and up the other side to the edge of his people's land. Many people are watching him, as they go about their tasks. He's making the usual preparations, kneeling down to nurse the fire, his back to us, facing north. What mesh is he weaving for us now with that stone's powers?

Madoc is coming back up the sloping land from the river, with Arun and the other captains. A strong, excited company they are.

As they come within talking range, everyone turns to them hopefully. Madoc stops where we can all hear and see him, and the captains move a little way back. Triumphant, he looks, and excited, so furiously excited. He raises his arms to quieten the calling and the questions and then shouts,

'We'll build a settlement here, enough to stay six or seven days. Tomorrow we'll start hunting for food. Enough to keep us for twenty or thirty days. It's time to build our new ships, as fast as we can. The river's navigable to the north!'

The women are scurrying, heads down, as I cross the ground to Glesig. We've all been on edge since the scouting party was spotted yesterday. A marauding kindred, Glesig said, who raid their neighbours like Madoc's brothers used to. We've been here five days and nights, see – too long for safety.

'Glesig!' I call hoarsely, trying to keep my voice low.

Glesig looks up from the foal. It's that familiar movement of his – so horribly familiar, that turning towards me – which has filled me with shame and made me helpless for these past weeks. But now my anxiety carries me forward. 'Glesig!'

There is a peculiar noise in my ears. No, it isn't in my ears, it's outside, coming from much farther away: a yelling, thudding noise from the high ground to the west, where the look-outs are running along the ridge towards each other. No, towards us.

They're waving their bows and spears and now the earth is thundering with hoof-beats – can all that be from one horse, just the one mare, which the boy Ifor from the Draellan kindred is riding? I saw him go out this morning, as the emergency watch, to bring us early news of any trouble.

Trouble: Ifor's mare gallops towards us, growing from a small thing I can cover with my hand to the size of a rabbit, a dog, a big sweating horse, steam snorting from her nostrils, and I can see Ifor's face, elongated with fear and excitement, shouting, 'A raid! A raid! Everyone take arms! A raid!'

The waiting seems strangely long in the middle of all the rushing and shouting and weeping. Pryste and I have been working non-stop, herding the women and girls and the very little boys into the shelter. We were going to go on to the ships, but Madoc and Arun decided no, the ships would be too defenceless if the raiders broke through to the river. So instead we're in the shelter, digging with our hands to try and raise the low earth ridge that surrounds the sunken floor, trying to make something like a wall that will hold up any raiders who get through.

We need more time, much more time, and out on the plain the men are trying to arrange themselves into a formation, but they don't know where to go. Up on all the high points, where they can rush down on the attackers? Or should they be deepest just behind the look-out points?

I keep losing sight of Madoc as the men crowd round him for instructions, and I can't bear not to be able to see him.

The first news was of hundreds and hundreds of them, coming from the west. Now another look-out has come gasping by to say there aren't so many, perhaps one hundred, perhaps we can hold them off . . .

I'm frightened. Duw, I'm frightened. My blood feels thin and white in my limbs, like sap.

Madoc: I want to go to him, but there's no time. He's taken Glesig by the arm, he's got him standing at his side. Glesig holds a spear, Madoc a spear and a bow and there are men with bows thick around them and beyond them, the serfs with axes. The three mares all have riders, but there's puny and small they look stretched out among the men like that, sticking up above the line.

Dear God, here they are.

The yelling and the clashing of weapons and the blood. The thrashing arms and legs, and the faces. The men staggering away from the line, towards us, and their faces twisted with pain, grey-white with hurt and bleeding, as we run out to bring them in. Some of them scream as we touch them.

There's some older women here, some from the kindreds and some of them half-free and serfs, who know what to do. The rest of us are doing what they tell us, tearing our last few linen shirts and tying them in strips around the men's wounds to staunch the blood flow; laying herbs on — there's no time for poultices — and holding them down so they can't hurt themselves worse with their thrashing.

The sights are terrible. Out there a wall of men, our men and the Ynys Llyr attackers; the wall shivers and boils and crashes apart, swells up again. I can't see Madoc.

They are coming towards us; they've broken through. Horrible, terrible men with patterns painted all over their arms and legs and faces, and some of them with animals' pelts on their heads. There's some of our men, running across to try and stop them, throwing their spears. The attackers turn and they fight fiercely and strong, with their long sharp spears of bone, and small axes like I've never seen before, and our men are going down, horribly. We've got spears in here too, from our wounded men, and Pryste and I look at each other and we each pick up one up and run to the little earth ridge and squat down, and as the head of the first Ynys Llyr man appears against the sky I drive the spear up, with all my strength, into his stomach.

Oh God. They're in here, and we're breaking out of the sides and the back, running, throwing what we can. Many of the women are picking up fallen spears. There are things falling and bleeding. everything's crashing, oh God, everything.

Here, in the middle of this field of dead people, we're stumbling, looking for our own. There's so many lying here – scores.

My eyes are filled with the sight of blood. Arun is dead. Madoc is sitting next to him, his arms round his chest. Pryste is dead too. She killed two Ynys Llyr men with her spear and then the third one drove his little axe into her head. I saw her dying but I didn't have time to go to her, I was running not to die myself.

They've gone, though; we drove them off. There are forty or fifty of them lying here. The men are going round finishing off the live ones with their knives; to have live prisoners would only mean trouble for us, strangers in their country. And our only hope, Wenlyn said to me just now, is to be seen as cruel and pitiless. Then, perhaps they won't be so ready to attack us again. Cadell is dead.

But Madoc is alive, and Glesig. Wenlyn's just told me Glesig is one of the men out here on the field, wounded, needing to be brought in to the shack. Not that we've got anything we can do for him there.

I've just trodden on a dead man's arm: springy it felt, under my foot. I crouch and touch it in apology: it's no man, it's a boy, thirteen or fourteen. One of the Hellynt kindred.

Picking my way more carefully, I reach Glesig. He's lying on his side, his hair spread out over the ground. It's matted with blood. He's bleeding from the leg, too, a deep gash that runs from his left knee to his thigh. He's trying to get up, but he can't.

'Glesig.'

He turns his head slightly and groans with the pain. His eyes struggle to see me.

'It's Ceinwen,' I say. I kneel down beside him, carefully.

He says something but it's in his own language and his voice is too thick for me to understand. I know what he's asking though. His right arm keeps trying to move to his side.

'It's gone, Glesig,' I say. 'Gone. The dreamstone. You've lost it.'

He gives a terrible little cry in his throat and moves his hands slowly to his ribs. I glance over my shoulder: two women are coming towards me, ready to help me carry Glesig back in. There's hardly any time. I reach out for his injured leg and pull it hard. Glesig's cry turns into a gasp and his head drops to the earth in a faint. Leaning over him, my body shields the knife as I cut my way through his hide cloak and slice out the pocket containing the stone. Through the leather I can feel a small, very hard shape. It seems to draw my fingers tight round it, like the lodestone draws a needle. I thrust my hand, leather pouch, stone and all, into my skirt pocket, and straighten up.

'He's alive,' I say to the women. One of them is Elen, another is a serf; battle makes strange comrades. 'Be careful of his head.'

The light is beginning to go. Up on the high ground, the men who have returned to the watch are black smudges against the yellow-grey sky. The ships are mysterious shapes on the still river.

'We've got no horses now,' Madoc says. 'None.'

'I know, my lord. You said.'

'They were all killed,' says Madoc. 'Even the foals.'

'We'll bring out more horses.'

Madoc shakes his head.

'Yes, my lord, we will.'

He shakes his head again. He hasn't asked about Glesig; he hasn't asked about Pryste.

'There's nothing to save us,' Madoc says. 'I've led us here and we're finished.'

'You can lead us on.'

'No.'

I've never seen Madoc like this. He won't get up from the ground; he won't go to see Meurig, who's badly wounded, or talk to Wenlyn, who's trying to get the dead buried, or meet with the captains who are left – Gran and Rhos and Gwynwynwyn and Iestyn – to give the order to move on. He just sits by this piece of ground where Arun lay, and won't move.

I look down at him. I love that dark head, bent now and filled with despair. I've had those hands on me, strong and loving and brave, but I don't know if they'll ever be like that again.

In my own hands is the most beautiful thing I've ever seen: a small black stone shaped like a bird taking flight. No one has carved this – it's been worn smooth by the winds and the tides. Its head is slightly turned from its body and its tail is two-pointed. Lovely it is; lovely.

It's time to show it to Madoc but I can't speak for happiness. In the middle of all this wreckage, and this death, and these people groaning with pain, I'm glad. This little thing I hold fills me with love and longing. It floods my heart.

Meanwhile Madoc sits here, broken on the ground. I've been standing next to him some time, holding the stone, and the longer I stand, the harder it is to tell him about it. Should I really give it to him? Can he make any use of it? It hurts me to stand here looking down on him, not touching him; it makes my arms ache.

Madoc places his hands on his knees and stares at them. It's a lost, restless movement and it pierces me like a needle pierces linen; it slides through me, between my ribs and into my heart.

'You can lead us on,' I say. Rich, my voice is, and sure. 'Now, tonight. We haven't got horses, but we've got something else. I've got it for you: look. Look.'

I hold out my cupped hands to him and he lifts his head to look. I watch the top of his head as he stares at it, unmoving.

The dark stone lies graceful on my blistered palm, a tiny swooping thing, caught into stillness.

'Isn't it beautiful?' I say softly. 'No wonder it's so precious to Glesig's people.'

Eventually Madoc raises his head from the stone and looks at me. His face is a dozen different feelings, all locked together. He holds out his hand like a child.

'Help me up,' he says.

I reach out my right hand to him, the stone still cradled in it, and he grasps it. As he pulls himself to his feet, the weight of his hand bears down on mine and I feel the dreamstone pressing itself into my palm. There's a strange thing – I can feel the shape of it sinking into my flesh as if I was being branded.

I have a sudden wild yearning to keep it, and a premonition of the loss that will come.

Madoc's hand is still clasped on mine. I can see by his face that he, too, feels it beneath his palm. His left arm comes tightly round my waist and grips me to him.

'How did you get it?'

'I took it from Glesig when we carried him in.'

Madoc's face is level with mine and hard, but it's the hardness of eagerness and hope.

'Why?'

'You know why. The stone has virtues – I know it is powerful;

344

you too, you fear and want it, you've talked about it in your sleep.'

Madoc is silent, watching me.

'Does he know you've got it?'

'No. I told him one of the raiders must have taken it.'

Madoc's expression is changing, becoming subtler and more complicated than it's been for a long time. The hand that's clasped over mine begins to close on the dreamstone.

'Well,' he says, half to himself. 'I'll have to have Glesig guarded from now on. Or he might go running off to look for it.'

His fingers lift the stone away from me, grazing my palm. It hurts so much that I wince and look down at my hand, expecting to see blood.

Madoc's face is pale; his right hand is clutched against his chest.

'So,' he says, his left hand pressing me to him so I can't move, 'you do love me after all, my lady.'

29

In Riverside Park, at lunch-time, they strolled like lovers and friends. It was a beautiful day, with a pale blue, crystalline sky. Winter sunlight reflected off the iced puddles and the old snow and cast a stillness over the Hudson. Across the water, the industrial buildings of New Jersey looked splendid and strange, like the great buildings of some long forgotten empire.

'Neat, isn't it?' said Sam.

Jane, who was biting into her hero sandwich, nodded.

'Mmmm.'

'Eloquent,' said Sam. 'Poetic.'

'I have enough goddamn poetry in my life,' said Jane. 'I like to look at things and feel them, not shit on about them.'

'You're in the wrong job, then.'

'I'm beginning to think so.'

'You'd do well in Romona Amsterdam, though. We could use you as liaison personnel. "Hey, Mr Martin, Sir, old buddy. Why you giving us this shit to do?" "Go ask Ms Pridden, asshole." '

'Having some problems with attitude are you?' said Jane.

'Nothing I haven't come across before,' said Sam. He pulled a strand of her hair clear from her face. 'Do you remember the mouth you had on you at school?'

'Only when I was mad.'

'You were frequently mad.'

'So were you, but you were too clever to do it my way.'

'Yeah, I handled it really well, didn't I? I got to stay.'

Jane's hand felt tense around the remains of her hero sandwich.

She looked out at the waters of the Hudson, black-gold and rippled by a string of barges going upstream.

'You could always leave.'

'I could.'

Suddenly the unspoken question of what they still felt for one another was all around them. Jane couldn't look at Sam; she was too afraid of what she might see. Or of what she might find herself doing. She stood where they had stopped on the path, staring out at the river, wishing that she could think. Sam was at her shoulder, blocking out the wind, his body heat crossing the tiny space between them to warm her.

Gwyn seemed very far away, dwindled to a speck in a Brockham office.

Jane felt Sam's hand on her shoulder, turning her round. He was watching her intently, and what he saw in her face made his eyes open wide and brought hunger into them. He put out his other hand and yanked her towards him. Jane wound her hands into the folds of his jacket and clung to him as he cradled her head and lifted her face up to his.

They stood kissing in Riverside Park like teenagers; clutching one another, resting their faces against each other for a second to draw breath then kissing again, unable to leave the tangle of skin and mouth. Jane's hero sandwich was crushed somewhere in between them; she kept her face turned up greedily to Sam's, feeling the bread crust digging into her breast and not caring.

Sam dropped his head to her neck and kissed her quickly, passionately down the length of her throat, nuzzling her under the jawbone. Jane closed her hands around his muscled plaid shoulders and felt the remains of the hero tumble down and bounce off her hip.

What the hell are we doing? she thought to herself and decided that she didn't much care.

Sam's arm was slung around her shoulders as the two of them walked down towards the river wall. Jane had fallen easily into Sam's loping rhythm; her arm was under his jacket and her hand hooked on to his belt in the old way. They stopped where the ground began to fall away and leaned against the sheltered side of a tree.

'Shit Janey,' said Sam, and his voice was at once rueful and happy, 'we're in trouble again.'

Jane couldn't stop herself walking most of the way back to the school with him. She couldn't bear to leave him and go back to the complications and anxiety awaiting her at Brockham. It was Sam who insisted they part company on this side of Amsterdam.

And then it happened. One moment Jane was lifting her hand to Sam's cheek, the next the presence had swooped down on her and seized her, freezing her hand in mid air. Through a barrier which was like splintered glass, she stared at Sam.

'Jane?' Sam was four-square in front of her, his head tilted to one side. 'What's happening?'

Jane tried to speak and failed. Her tongue was pinned down by the force of the visitation and she stood helpless and speechless. The woman was back but this time she was neither gentle nor warning – she was angry.

'Janey. Janey, what is it?'

Sam's hands were reaching to her but falling short. Her arm was still raised towards him and painfully, she stretched it out further, but he didn't take it. She saw him hesitate, his hands half held out, his eyes scanning her, and then the presence lifted slightly and Sam stepped forward to support her.

'OK Janey, it's OK.' He hugged her protectively. 'You feeling all right?'

'Yes,' she said. The presence had receded but it was still there, like someone yelling at her from a distance, like a blanket of noise, low down in her head. Sam's arms round her were uncomfortably tight. 'I'm fine,' she said. 'I was dizzy, that's all. Listen, I have to go. See you later.'

Later was an evening at Jed's place, with Gwyn and Nathalie. Jane spent the evening measuring a scrupulous distance between herself, Gwyn and Sam, as though if she could keep equidistant from them both, things would work out all right. And all the time she wondered why she couldn't think straight, and whether Gwyn could see anything wrong.

Jane jerked awake, half sitting up, her hands clutching the quilt.

The fear seemed to be alive in her body – pulsing in her arms, her throat, her chest, like drumbeats reverberating through her.

She gasped for breath, struggling to fill her lungs. Her hands were sweaty on the quilt, she noticed. She had a sudden detached view of herself, as if from above, sitting very still in bed next to a sleeping Gwyn. It looked an oddly peaceful picture.

In her head she felt a scrabbling, like something making a desperate retreat. Something; someone: the woman.

Jane unclenched her fingers and smoothed the edge of the quilt. The woman was gone now, and so was the fear. But there was a different fear left behind in the bedroom; a horrid little sensation which Jane was used to carrying in her mind most of each day. She couldn't quite expunge it during even the busiest times and when she had nothing to do, it rolled tinnily into the centre of her consciousness. It was the fear of what was happening to her.

She looked down at Gwyn. He lay on his side, turned away from her, and his face was anguished. His eyebrows were drawn together, gouging creases into his forehead, and his jaw was set and vibrating slightly, as if he were carrying on some concealed argument in his sleep.

He'd looked like this for over a week. Jane knew, because she lay awake almost every night and watched him.

Everything was wrong between them. They still made love; Gwyn still groaned and thrust and kissed her and she moaned and responded and writhed, but it was oddly unengaging. Each time, Jane's mind would drift away, no matter how hard she tried to anchor it, and she'd find herself thinking about Sam.

They were seeing too much of Sam and Sam's crowd. And she was seeing too much of Sam alone. Gwyn suspected of course and she hated herself for putting him through this.

But she couldn't keep away. Now as she sat next to Gwyn in their bed, she longed to see Sam again.

It wasn't just that she was still attracted to him. It wasn't just the remnants of their teenage love, refusing to die. It was this fear, which grew with each new, unremembered dream, and each new sheet of paper Gwyn covered with dark blue ink.

Gwyn was writing more than ever. He was taking refuge in it from what was happening between the two of them. He wouldn't let her ask him about it; he warned her off with sly smiles as he sat writing at his desk and in his office and even on his lap in the bar.

Being with Sam gave her a relief from that. The woman still came to her in Sam's company, but somehow Jane felt less alone with Sam's arm around her, with Sam's head against hers. She was able to cling to him until the moment was past and draw comfort from him, without either of them speaking of it.

Feeling treacherous, Jane slid out of bed and took the bathrobe from the back of the chair. Gwyn stirred as she opened the door and she held her breath, looking at him. He whimpered, muttered wordlessly and went on sleeping.

Oh God, what was he dreaming? Shivering, Jane went into the bathroom. She couldn't go on keeping all this to herself. Sam had seen Miss Archer's letter; Sam knew something weird was going on. And Sam was in it too, wasn't he? Only she couldn't work out where he fitted in.

She turned on the shower and waited for it to run hot. Yearning for Sam's arms round her, she planned how she could sneak away and see him this afternoon.

'Shall we look at Wendy Turner's piece next?' asked Harry. 'We might as well try and get it down between the two of us. It's awful stuff for you to have to plod through on your own.'

Jane glanced at her watch.

'Well – I was planning to leave early today. Like in five minutes. Leave it for me to start tomorrow.'

'How can I do that, and live with myself?' Harry sighed, rifling through the pages of laser-printed copy. 'No, I'll be a martyr and make a start on it. Where are you going?'

Jane bent her head over the manuscript she was marking up. She searched for inspiration but found none.

'To Sam's school,' she said reluctantly. Damn it, why couldn't she have lied? Now she'd have to ask Harry not to tell Gwyn. No, she couldn't do that, she'd just have to risk it.

'Oh,' said Harry, very non-committal.

'Like I said, sorry.'

'How much longer is he in New York?'

'Two and a bit weeks.'

'It must be strange, resuming a relationship after so many years.'

Jane darted a startled look at him. Resuming: what was Harry getting at? Harry met her eyes levelly, and she saw the hint of a rebuke in his face. It irritated her.

'It's terrific,' she said.

'I saw Gwyn in the library,' said Harry after a pause. 'He looked tired. He said he was working hard.'

'He is.'

The silence remained unbroken for a while, then Harry stood up abruptly.

'I'll see you,' he said and left the office.

The Romona Amsterdam School was housed on the first two floors of a red-brick building, and separated from the avenue by a bush and tree-filled yard. A sign directed Jane to go in through the central door; she found herself in a wide corridor, hung with information posters and children's paintings. A wall sign with an arrow said 'Office'; inside the office a blonde girl with a ponytail was talking to a boy of about twelve.

'Excuse me,' said Jane, trying not to sound impatient. 'I'm looking for Sam Martin. Do you know if he's here?'

The blonde girl (she was older than Jane had first thought, about twenty-five) glanced around the room as if Sam might be there. The boy looked Jane up and down very deliberately.

'Sam Late Martin,' he said bossily. 'That's his name. Not Martin, Late Martin.'

'Yes I know,' Jane smiled. 'But it's a mouthful, to say the whole lot, don't you think?'

'No,' said the boy, staring at her.

Jane shrugged.

'Whatever,' she snapped. 'Look,' turning to the girl, 'do you know where he is?'

The girl seemed to think.

'Well, he hasn't left, I don't think,' she said. 'I expect he's somewhere in the building.'

'I'll go and look for him then,' said Jane. 'Shall I? Thank you.'

She walked off before they could stop her or delay her any further. She was as nervous as a cat. She had to see Sam; she had to touch him and kiss him again, feel his hands taking hold of her. It was what she needed, it was their unfinished business. First, she had to have that, then perhaps when the craving had been soothed a little she could think sensibly about what was happening and get it all in proportion.

Sam wasn't in any of the rooms on this floor. They were all empty except for one in which several boys were playing basketball. Jane climbed the staircase which wound in a broad spiral to the next floor. One room at the front had voices coming from it; Jane peered in through the glass panel and saw it was a staff room, and that half a dozen people were in it, writing, chatting, examining timetables. But no Sam. She went along the corridor from the front to the back: Sam was in the very last room, with windows that looked out on to a dark yard.

It was arranged as a conventional classroom with a teacher's desk at the front, and Sam was sitting at it. He was turned slightly away from the door, looking towards the window.

'Sam,' said Jane, and her voice was self-conscious. 'I wanted to see you before – '

'Look,' said Sam. He sounded peculiar. 'Look.'

Jane was crossing the floor to his desk.

'What?'

'There, the bird.'

The face he turned to Jane was blank with fear. Jane looked around, bewildered, but couldn't see anything. Sam pointed at the window.

'Out there. It's been there all day. Just sitting there. Shit, all day.'

His voice rose. Through the glass, Jane began to make out a small shape. It was a small dark-coloured bird, perched on the window ledge, looking in.

'It's just a bird.'

'It's been there all day,' Sam whispered, and Jane could hear the panic he was fighting to control. He had his hand up across his mouth.

She went to touch his shoulder but he shrank away from her. The gesture filled her with a fear of her own.

'What's going on?' she said sharply. 'What the fuck's happening here?'

She strode to the window and tapped on it. The bird fluttered into the air and came back down on to the ledge a few inches further along. It didn't even turn its head towards Jane: its bright little eyes were focused on Sam. Jane saw the rich, dark shades in its feathers.

'It's a purple martin,' she said.

Sam looked at her, his face haggard.

'Let's get out of here.'

They walked down the corridor, wrapped around one another, past the office and the glaring twelve-year old boy, and across the hibernating front yard to the avenue. The roar of the traffic and the dazzling lights were comforting. Sam's arms were round Jane, hugging her, but she hardly knew what she was doing. She was too agitated to speak. She stood in his embrace like an infuriated child, bumping her forehead over and over again on the fleecy lining of his sheepskin.

'What's going on?' she said, clenching her teeth. 'You haven't been honest with me, Sam. You've been stringing me along. Oh God, what's going on?'

Sam pushed his mouth against her hair.

'I haven't been stringing you along. I can't tell you. I'm not permitted to.'

'Who doesn't permit it? What don't they permit? You just cut it out. You have to tell me about the birds. You have to.'

There was a silence, then,

'OK Janey. I'll tell you about the birds if you tell me about the woman.'

Jane was aware that she had gone still in his arms. She leaned against his chest, confused. Sam knew about the woman. How? She couldn't think, couldn't get her brain to work.

'But,' she shook her head, trying to understand. She was clinging to his coat again, but differently from the way she'd done it in Riverside Park. 'But she's to do with Gwyn, not you.'

The bar was optimistically large for its location, and almost empty. Jane and Sam sat at a table away from the window, just in case Professor Jewell walked by. It felt strange to be drinking cocktails at five in the afternoon, and even stranger to be worrying about Duane Jewell at the same time as all these other things.

'You start.'

Sam nodded, glancing from her to his drink.

'I'll try. Jane – shit, Janey, do you promise me you won't laugh?'

'Why should I? What's funny?'

'Well – we were always so down on all that back-to-the-land shit. All that fake mysticism people like Carol Falls went in for. I'm still not comfortable with the things Willie tells me.'

'And what are they?'

'Folk tales mainly. And separatist lectures about preserving my Mandan identity. These last few years he's been telling me my family history, how my father had Mandan blood as well as my mother. It has made me think – made me interested.'

'Don't apologise for that,' interrupted Jane.

'I'm not apologising.'

'No. Sorry.'

'Willie's talked me through the Mandan legends and customs – the sun dance and the sacred canoe and the buffalo dance, all the stuff that you get in the local bookstores anyway. But he told me a few other things, that he said were only ever handed down verbally, and between a few people from one generation to the next.

'It's a kind of counter culture. The white settlers had gotten hold of one of our legends – the white dove. They named their own places after it, like White Dove Pond. But Willie says that was only ever a cover story, and that the real legend was about a – a dark bird.'

Sam dropped his voice to a murmur. He hunched his shoulders and toyed with his glass: he looked acutely uncomfortable, almost hunted.

'He said I should never tell anyone who wasn't a Mandan,' he muttered. 'I didn't think I took him seriously, it's funny how tough it is to tell you.' He smiled wanly. 'I feel like I can hardly breathe.

'Willie said that before the man with the canoe came, long before, there was the dark bird. Our people were supposed to have lived under the ground originally, and the bird led them up to the surface. It stayed with them then and looked after them,

354

for generations, until the First Man – that's the man with the canoe – came.'

'White people know about the First Man, of course. But what they don't know is that there was a First Woman too.'

Sam stopped talking. He seemed to be thinking hard and picking his words.

'Something bad happened. I don't know what, that part's not told. But something happened between the woman and the dark bird and we lost them both. I don't know what it is. I can't get at it. But the bird and the dark woman – that's what she's known as – have become this secret story that gets passed along. It's passed in secret, just a few people know it at one time. They're a special group within the Mandans; they're supposed to be descended from the First people. They – we – are called White Mandans.'

'We?'

Sam glanced uneasily up at her.

'I'm supposed to be one of the line. Willie says. So is he, of course. And my father, but he was never very interested – he never talked about it, he thought it was all voodoo crap.'

Jane drank her cocktail: it was a margarita, just like she'd had that time in the Blue Bar. Maybe, she thought wildly, the woman liked them.

'So. What about these birds you've been seeing?'

Sam's pupils shrank as he looked into the overhead light.

'I get these dreams. I've been having them for a month or so. Dreams of large flocks of birds, flying overhead. And they're just so frightening.'

The fear passed into Jane again, just as it had done in the classroom. She fought to keep it at bay.

'And the woman. You asked me about the woman. How come you did that?'

'Jennifer,' said Sam. 'Miss Archer. It was that letter she wrote you, that she asked me to bring. She said that there was always a woman in the case, but no one talks about her. Do you remember? When you showed me that letter, I knew she must mean the dark woman. It had to be – a woman who no one talks about and that guy Phillips who painted birds, and Phillips and Jennifer having something going.

'Don't you see? Jennifer said if I came to see you it would be beginning again. I'm seeing birds. And you're seeing something too, I've watched it happen to you over and over since I've been here, you think I don't notice but I do. It happened to you yesterday. And I reckon that if I'm seeing birds, you're seeing a woman.'

Jane was concentrating very hard: she had to, to follow Sam's story and keep her mind clear of all the other things that were clamouring to come in.

'Why didn't you ask me about her before?'

Sam laid his hands slowly on the table between them, palms turned upwards.

'I was frightened,' he said, and he sounded ashamed. 'I've been thinking I'm going out of my mind.'

Jane shook her head. The way Sam told it, the story was simple and convincing, but there was so much he'd left out. So much she hardly knew how to begin to tell him.

'No,' she said. 'You're not. There are all kinds of other things too. Listen . . .'

'Christ,' said Sam. He looked punch-drunk, gazing at Jane over their empty glasses. 'So you think that Haydn Phillips told this man Goff whatever he knew? And Goff told Gwyn?'

'No, not told. I don't think Phillips was together enough to tell anyone anything when he got back. I can't be sure, of course. But I don't think Goff positively *knows* anything about the Mandan side. It's the Welsh side of it that he seems to understand. But he never came out and told me anything, and I'm pretty sure he hasn't told Gwyn either.'

'But something happened with Phillips and Jennifer. And Miss Archer reckons it's beginning again, with you and me.'

'And with Gwyn.'

'Yeah, with your husband.'

The word was like an unexpected touch on Jane's flesh. It brought Gwyn vividly to her and made her shiver with love and bewilderment. What was Gwyn doing now? Would he be thinking of her?

She put her hands up to her eyes.

'Don't say it like that, please.'

'It's OK,' said Sam, after a pause. 'I love Dee Ann, you know.'

'Yes,' said Jane. 'I don't know if that makes me happy or sick.'
She found that she was giggling, rather unevenly. Sam joined in.

'This trouble we're in,' he said.

'It's worse than you thought,' said Jane.

'I'm frightened Janey. The birds have been coming more often
in my dreams, every night they're here now. And you saw that
thing today.'

'A purple martin. Member of the swallow family. Who gave
you your Mandan name, Sam?'

'My grandfather. But it was Willie who told me about it.'

'Willie. Always goddamn Willie.'

Sam took her hands and began kneading them gently. The ring
she had given him for his sixteenth birthday glinted on his fourth
finger.

'Maybe he really has sent me crazy,' he said. 'Maybe all this
is just hocus-pocus.'

But Jane was thinking about all the birds that had cropped up
in her life recently. The two birds in the apartment, the white
feathers the guests had showered on her and Gwyn at the wedding
party, the bird in the painting, the smoke bird in the poem. With
a small, hard jolt, she realised that when she had met Gwyn she
had been wearing her bird mask.

There were too many examples for it to be coincidence. Besides,
she didn't believe in coincidence any more.

'Sam, I have to go,' she said urgently. 'But take me outside and
hold me before I do.'

The apartment was in darkness. Jane closed the door behind her
and leaned against it, not knowing if she were disappointed or
relieved. It was nearly seven; Gwyn could be still in his office, or
in the library, or in the bar. Maybe he was banging on the door
to her old apartment, expecting to drag her out from underneath
Sam. If he had been here, she could have flung herself at him and
gabbled out her fears and asked him to show her, please just
show her, what he had been writing.

But he would very likely have refused, just as he still, ada-
mantly, refused to agree to Duane's reading. It was probably
better this way.

Jane flicked the lights on and went swiftly into the living room, and to the corner which held his desk. She pulled at all the drawer handles: one of them was locked. That would be where he kept the copies of his poems. Gwyn carried the blue folder with him everywhere, but he was too nervous to keep all his work in one place: she knew he took copies on the faculty machine, and this must be where he stored them.

The key was gone, of course. Jane went into the kitchen and got a sharp, thin vegetable knife. She had no luck with it. Then she tried fiddling inside the lock with the wire head of a coat-hanger, but she made no impression. Finally, her adrenalin starting to surge, she braced one foot against the desk, seized the drawer handle and began to wrench. The desk was a cheap one and at the fourth pull there was a splintering noise and the drawer came away.

The photocopies were folded away inside a plastic bag. She carried them to the sofa and began leafing through for the recent, post-harbour poems. She scarcely had time to read them: she could hear the footsteps coming along the landing, and then the click of Gwyn's key in the lock. Her eyes skidded down the lines.

'What the fuck – ?' she heard Gwyn say, and then she saw his furious face as he rushed into the room and lunged at her.

She rolled out of his way as he fell on the sofa and hit out, punching him on the face. Her fist made a thick, oddly dead noise on his jaw; she hit out again, striking his arm down, and scrambled to her feet.

'It's full of birds!' she cried. She heard the fury in her voice, a wild, vindictive fury beyond her control. 'You stupid lying bastard! It's full of birds!'

Gwyn was slumped against the sofa arm, holding his jaw and looking up at her in astonishment. She gasped for breath and shuddered as the fury burned white and then changed into something else, into something that made her moan and drop the sheaf of papers: into terror.

The birds seemed to come flapping into her mind, filling her ears with the noise of their approach, darkening her spirit with their wings.

30

'You see?' Wenlyn nods towards the huddle of men in the bows. Their heads are outlined against the silver-grey water of the river, looking like a crop of indignant toadstools. They stand there expostulating and nodding to each other and shooting glances across the ship to Madoc. Wenlyn smiles, turning his back to them so they won't see. 'Madoc's really outraged them this time, they're all huffing and puffing fit to burst. They say to do the jobs he's ordered would insult their dignity as higher kindred.'

'Oh we can't have that,' I say. 'Can we, Wenlyn? Dear God, what a bunch of squawkers. I suppose Madoc's not aware of it?'

'Of course not.'

'No. Well, we'd better settle it. What'll we say? That everyone who does their hand's turn now gets precedence when it comes to choosing land in Glesig's country?'

'We can say that, but they'll soon work out that if they all work, they'll all get precedence, and that'll be like having no advantage.'

'Yes, but who'll dare to be the first one to lose precedence? As long as one of them works, the rest have to follow.'

'And you're sure enough that one of them will work, are you?'

'Yes, my pretty Wenlyn,' I say. 'I'm pretty sure.'

'There's a few you can smile at, are there?'

'One or two.'

And a few I can give hard looks to as well.

'I'll escort you over to tell them the choice, shall I?'

'Oh all right. But I tell you, Wenlyn, I prefer the company of the half-free and the serfs to that gaggle of useless geese.'

'Hush, lady,' says Wenlyn, offering me his arm. 'Be gentle with the foolish things.'

'Now what's this?' I say, as we come up to the little knot of aggrieved high kindred. 'My lord Wenlyn says you don't want to take your turn at the oars and the cook pots.'

The men – fourteen of them, important men back in their own cantrefi – murmur and do some shuffling.

'My lady, it's not right,' says Morddyn Hellynt, their leader. 'We shouldn't be doing serfs' work. How will we command them when we're landed again if we've worked alongside them now?'

'If you could do skilled craft work,' I say, with an amused smile, 'then we could put you to making the bows and arrows and knife hafts, the wheels and copper jewellery and crwths and other gifts for the Ynys Llyr people. But there – you've got no craft skills. The women can cook and prepare food and sew the hides – as I do. Now you pencenedl will have to take the oars and the sails and the board mending, to release the skilled people for the urgent tasks.'

'I've got prince's blood in me,' says a gruff voice, furiously. It's Merewyd ap Bran, Elen's cousin. 'Royal blood, from Rhys's house. No great man of my line has ever done slave's work.'

'Then no great man of your line is likely to hold land in Ynys Llyr,' I say calmly. They gape at me. 'There is a system,' I say, 'agreed by Madoc with lord Rhiryd of Clochran, with the lord Rhys himself and with all the other lords who sent goods and people over. In times of hardship and danger, the kindred work. Yes, even the highest kindred. And when we settle, the best choices of land and livestock and title go to the kindred who have worked their share. Those who don't choose to work will have to be content with what's left.'

'But we've never heard of this before!' Morddyn says, his chest swelling. 'When did Madoc agree this? Why hasn't he told us about it?'

'Does the prince tell you everything?' I enquire, in polite surprise.

Morddyn stares.

'Something of this magnitude . . .' he starts, but he doesn't finish his complaint.

I look at the higher kindred until the muttering subsides. In the silence we can all hear Madoc's voice, travelling clear to us from the masts.

'Tell him if it's not ready by nightfall I'll have the skin off his back — again. And if he thinks the last time was severe, let him try me now.'

It's one of the serfs he's talking about, Tegwyn Sailpatcher, but it has its effect. The way Madoc's been handling his people recently, the kindred can almost believe he'd have them flogged too. Almost.

I let the threat die away on the frozen air, then I look around the faces before me.

'Is there anyone here who wants to refuse to work?' I ask. I make my voice light and interested, as though I really would like to know what they all think.

No one speaks a word.

'Well, then,' I say. 'I'll go back to doing my work and you can make a start on yours.'

I nod at Wenlyn, who bows courteously, and walk back to my station at the side of the ship where I'm trying to make cheese from the milk of our two remaining goats. I'm hoping to have some tablets ready to offer to Glesig's people as gifts, when we arrive. Every gift, every show of wealth and skill, will help.

'That put a stop to the protests, my lady.' Wenlyn's long-lashed eyes are watering in the wind that blows off the river, but his suave face is amused. 'You make a good pair, you and the Prince.'

'I know,' I say. In another life, I would have worried whether that was impertinence on Wenlyn's part, and if I should rebuke him. 'We do very well together now. With help from you, Wenlyn.'

'I don't like waste,' Wenlyn observes. 'And I'd like to keep my life, in the most favourable circumstances possible.'

I laugh.

'We'll see what we can do.'

'Are you getting anything useful out of Glesig yet?'

'No. He hardly speaks. I wish he would.'

'So do we all. He could help us if he wanted to; it would make all the difference for our chances.'

'Yes,' I say. But that's not the only reason I want Glesig to talk. I miss the friendship he and Madoc and I had; and I miss my own understanding with him. I even, in a funny way, miss the bickering that went on between us before – well.

Now it's as though his soul has gone away and all that's left on this ramshackle ship of ours is his body. Madoc has that guarded well. Chained, Glesig is, nothing more than a prisoner.

It's a terrible sight, this broken man. I can hardly bear to see him, though sometimes Madoc asks me to go and try to make him talk, and sometimes I go anyway. I don't know why I do. He will only give me dead-sounding, angry answers to my questions and to ask, again and again, where the stone is. Now he's lost the stone, it's hard to remember how powerful it made him. And I wonder if I was right to think what I did about him and the way he was using it on me . . .

Of course I was. The stone is powerful; we have proof of that in the way Madoc's strength has returned a hundredfold since I took it from Glesig and gave it to him.

There's no sense in my pitying Glesig. There's no sense in my still feeling this tenderness for him. I must save it all for Madoc.

My Madoc: he's glorying in his leadership now. And in my help. Madoc gives the orders and assumes that everyone will obey. And when Wenlyn and I have applied a little cleverness, they usually do.

Wenlyn is busy now organising the reluctant high kindred. Oh damn this goats' cheese – it isn't going to come right. I put the cloth down on top of the barrel to keep the mess covered, wedge the barrel steady with sacking and go to Madoc. He's turned away from the sails now; he's looking across the water at the shore: the line of flat land, backed by ripple upon ripple of brown hills, which keeps pace with our thrown together fleet.

'My love,' he says as I approach. His nostrils twitch and he looks down at my hands, which are still whitened from the milk curds. 'Cheese making?' he smiles. His eyes are soft and I know he's remembering when I sat straining cheese and he galloped the

Cynfael horses in front of me and he was secretly making up his mind to take me away with him. How near it still seems.

I smile in understanding.

'We've come far,' I say.

He nods. Then he gestures towards the bows, where the higher kindred are drifting apart. 'Trouble over the work?'

'The usual grumbles,' I say impatiently. 'I told them that if they didn't do the work you gave them, they'd forfeit their precedence on choice of land. You agreed it with Rhiryd and Rhys and the others before we left, see.'

Madoc grins.

'That was astute of me.'

'They thought so too. Wenlyn's setting them to work now.'

'Good. We have to get going on the weapons and tools as soon as we can. The shores are beginning to converge – it might just be a temporary thing but I think we could be nearing the head.'

'Glesig's not saying anything, then?' I ask.

Madoc spits on to the deck.

'I'd break his nose if I thought it would grease his tongue.' He pauses. 'I've even tried being gentle with him,' he says. 'You know, Ceinwen. As his foster brother.'

'And he doesn't respond?'

'No,' says Madoc. He leans on the gunwale, staring at the shore. He looks a bit sad, even hurt. 'Do you think he'll ever speak again?' he says.

'I don't know,' I answer. 'Perhaps, when we get to his country.'

'He's not coming ashore with us,' says Madoc quickly. 'I'm taking the men at arms ashore with us, and the kindred elders of course. But Glesig's staying guarded on board. I'm keeping him as a hostage.'

'I'm coming too,' I say.

'What?'

'I'm coming ashore with you, Madoc.' I say it smoothly, as if the choice was all mine. 'As your lady. You and I are king and queen of this nation now.'

Madoc turns and tilts his head at me. Dusk is gathering – it comes so swiftly on this river – and he looks closely, crinkling his narrow eyes.

'Very well, queen. Now we'd better go and count our tools

and weapons, because we'll need all the help we can get when we land this nation of ours.'

The shores are drawing distinctly together in the distance – we could see that as soon as light came this morning. The work on gifts and weapons is going on furiously. A sorry collection they look, the wheels and knives and longbows and musical instruments, all being crafted together and makeshift. But we hope Glesig's people will be impressed. And warned into respect.

Madoc came up to me just now and took my wrists in his grip and said, 'We are nearly there, Ceinwen, nearly there.' The bitter cold stung my face and made my throat raw but inside I felt the warm surge of excitement.

Our long thin ship is making slow progress to the north, as the wind is blowing from the north-east, but the men and the strongest serf woman are labouring at the oars and forward we go. In our wake come our two company ships. 'Ships'; these are boats and disreputable ones at that, but today they look very brave and heroic as they plough their way up the narrowing water.

'I want you to talk to Glesig,' Madoc says to me now, with his hands triumphant around my wrists. 'He won't tell me anything useful. You try once more.'

'He won't respond any better to me, my lord,' I say. 'All he does is ask about the stone and say there's no point to anything. And I – I hate seeing him.'

'I need you to try. Tell him we know we're nearly there. Tell him we're bringing him into his land. Go and show him that fierce queen's face, my love, and see if it breaks his silence.'

So I'm making my way to the stern with the barrels and water butt, where Glesig is chained to the side. One of the young boys of Rhys's kindred, Dawyl, is guarding him. He looks awkward as he stands aside – it's a wary, half-resentful look a lot of the people have for me now. They became unsure when Madoc was so cold to me, you see, and they never knew why we became close again. And they don't like me telling them what to do.

I don't care about them. I nod graciously at Dawyl and sweep past him to Glesig. I have to prepare myself for the first glance; it's always painful. Now he's a prisoner and in disgrace, he's like an animal in a hunter's trap. It's such a change, I find it hard to look at him.

He's sitting on the boards, his head tipped back, looking blankly at the sky. His face has got no expression at all. It's as if someone has sucked all the living things out of it and left a darkness. You can see it in his eyes and underneath his skin.

His eyes move to my face, where I stand a yard from him, and stay on it. I look at him but get no response. I can't bring myself to say his name; it seems too mocking.

'We're nearly there,' I say. 'The river is narrowing, we're nearly in your country.'

Silence.

'Can you hear me?' I say, with a touch of the new command in my voice. He blinks, slowly.

'Yes, my lady.'

'You used to call me "great lady" once,' I say. 'As a joke. Why don't you do that again?'

'It's not a joke now,' says Glesig, and now his voice isn't completely dead, there's some hint of expression in it: bitterness, or is it accusation?

'Don't you like that, Glesig?' I say.

The sound of his name makes him look quickly away. It makes me feel heavy too, as if I'm eating something bilious.

'Shall I help you stand up, so you can watch the shore?'

Glesig stares at the deck.

'Don't you want to see your country?'

'No!' he says violently, and thrashes his head as if I'm torturing him. 'No.'

'Why not?' I persist.

Slowly Glesig looks up. His eyes are incredulous and bitter. I try to hold his gaze but I can't.

'Well,' I say, looking above his head, out at the eastern river-bank. Why are these stupid tears in my eyes? 'We'd like you to tell us about your people and how to greet them peacefully. What gifts to give them.'

'Send Dawyl away,' says Glesig.

I look at him quickly. He's watching me, to see if I'll do it. There's something urgent in his face.

'Go, Dawyl,' I say.

'But my lady —' I turn and look at him and he steps briskly backwards out of the enclosure.

I turn back to Glesig. He's still sitting, making no attempt to move, and his strong face staring up at me from a beggar's position is disconcerting.

'Do you know what the dreamstone does?' he says.

I raise my eyebrows. I'm not going to give him any sign about the dreamstone, though my stomach has begun to churn.

'It makes stronger what's deepest in your heart.'

I say nothing. Glesig smiles, a very faint, hopeless smile that makes me feel unbearably sad.

'What you desire,' he explains, looking into my face, 'you desire more fiercely. What you fear, will come to overpower you. What you love, will no longer be denied.'

'A powerful thing, the dreamstone,' I say, smiling back.

'Yes, powerful. The stone can bless people.'

'Yes,' I say, thinking of the small, lovely thing I held in my hand. I miss it, even knowing it's so close, on Madoc's body, even being able to touch the rough leather of its pouch now and again.

'And it can burn them,' says Glesig, very low and quick. 'If you're cruel, if you're angry, if you're a coward, if you're treacherous. I've found out which of those I am, which are you?'

I gasp; I feel winded, as if Glesig's punched me in the chest. He's leaning forward, watching me with eyes that are suddenly full of energy, black and wriggling with it.

'I haven't got the dreamstone,' is all I can say. 'I haven't got it.'

I'm backing away from him, still saying, 'I haven't got it' when a cry comes swooping towards me from the masts, repeated and echoed by a clamour of high and low voices.

'A tref! A tref! Glesig's country!'

I look up to the man who's signalling from the mast. Everyone has stopped in the middle of what they were doing; people are rushing to the starboard side. Madoc is scrambling to stand on the shoulders of two of the men; as they clutch his legs he's straightening up and his arm goes out, pointing wildly.

'Glesig's country!' he seems to be yelling. Then, as he goes on shouting, I realise that's not quite it. His words travel through the cold air to me. 'Our country!' he's shouting. 'Our country!'

When I look back at Glesig, he's standing up too. But he's not gazing at the shore; his face is turned up, with a look of dread, to Madoc.

31

As he heard the lift mechanism clatter into action, Gwyn looked at his watch: half past midnight. He stretched his cramped legs into a more comfortable position. He had been sitting here on the floor outside Jane's old apartment for nearly an hour.

He had his notebook in his hand as usual, and his pen ready to work, but for once he was using neither. His head was too full of all the things he and Jane had talked about, facing each other for hours in their shared living room that evening, trying to find their way round the barriers that had gone up between them in recent weeks.

Jane had been hysterical at first, but after that her deadly calm conviction had been even more unsettling. She had told him things he didn't want to hear about his own poems, forced him to recognise connections that could not logically exist. She had shocked him out of his own defensive anger and made him feel her fear.

It couldn't go on. Jane swore there was no stopping it, but Gwyn knew damn well there was. He knew who was responsible for Jane's terror and her tears: that unscrupulous piece of shit, Sam Never-Too-Late Martin.

Gwyn had promised Jane he wouldn't fight Sam or hurl accusations at him. Jane had actually seemed to believe him, too. Not that Gwyn wanted to take on a man several inches taller and broader than he was. But whenever he thought of him, the hurly-burly in Gwyn's head died down beneath a pure, white-flowing stream of rage.

And this was Sam. It must be: the lift was coming to a stop on this floor and Gwyn had seen everyone else come in. He put his notebook away in his pocket and stood up.

The lift doors clattered open and Sam came out, walking along the corridor with his head down, his hands jammed into his jeans pockets. He caught sight of Gwyn when he was only a few yards away and his stride faltered.

'Hi. What are you doing here?'

'Waiting for you.'

'How was your emergency meeting?'

'We didn't really have one.'

'No, I didn't really think you did.'

'At least,' said Gwyn softly, as Sam stopped a few feet away from him and got out his keys, 'it was only between Jane and me.'

Sam nodded.

'Is she all right?'

'I haven't beaten her up, if that's what you mean.'

'It isn't.'

Sam said it easily, pushing open the door and leaving Gwyn to follow him in. Gwyn did so, stepping lightly. He was nerved up all over: he felt as if his veins were filled with air.

He looked carefully around as he shut the door behind him, seeing Jane's old apartment through new eyes. He'd been here several times in the last week with both Jane and Sam, but then it had seemed unreal, like a wendy house in which they were play acting. Now, with just him and Sam inside its walls, it felt quite different. It felt very definitely real and dangerous.

Sam took off his jacket and went into the kitchen alcove, re-emerging with a bottle of bourbon. He sat himself in the only comfortable chair, long legs spilling out in front of him and poured out two glasses.

You insolent fucking bastard, thought Gwyn, feeling a rising surge of fury. No, don't let that happen. Don't lose control – that's what he wants. Gwyn thought about Sam stuck in a classroom five days a week with screaming, impossible children, and smiled at the picture. He sat down in the other chair and prepared to take charge. Don't be angry; don't let him get to you. Take him off guard. He selected a cool, detached tone.

'What do you know about your past?' he asked.

Sam handed him a glass.

'The American past? Let's see . . . the pilgrim fathers. The wild west. Buffalo Bill. The Alamo.'

'Don't piss me around.'

'That's mine too, you know.'

'Of course. Like the Civil War and the Battle of Trafalgar and Queen Victoria are mine. But the other bits, Sam – what about them?'

Gwyn heard something unusual in his own voice, then he realised what it was. He'd never called Sam by his name before. And he knew why – it was too much like an acknowledgement. It put them in a partnership that he for one did not want. He shot him a cold look but the bastard wasn't even watching him.

'I never went to the reconstructed Mandan village in Bismarck until I was fourteen years old,' Sam said thoughtfully. 'But since I've been teaching I've gone there five times in three years.'

'You know all about the Madoc legend, then.'

'Like I told Gail, I knew the outline. I know more since this afternoon.'

'You knew enough anyway,' Gwyn challenged him, 'didn't you?'

Sam leaned back in his chair and sighed. But he grinned at the same time.

'Ah shit,' he said. 'I'm just a hick from the sticks. Never was much on book learning, know what I mean?'

Gwyn stared in disbelief. If Sam was just pretending to be relaxed, it was a bloody good pretence.

'Knock it off,' he said roughly. 'Cleverest boy in the school, Jane told me you were.'

'Yeah, that was my mistake.'

'Hmm. Mine was only being able to do one thing.'

They sat in silence for a while. Gwyn found himself watching Sam's right foot swivelling on its heel against the wooden floor: it turned in until it almost touched the instep of his left foot, then turned out again, in out, in out, like a pendulum. When he looked up he found Sam's brown-black eyes on his, anxiously. Immediately Sam looked away.

Gwyn struggled with a sudden curiosity: what was Sam thinking? Why had he looked at him like that? He hardened his heart. Don't get side-tracked. Keep going.

'So anyhow,' said Gwyn heavily, 'you know about the Madoc legend. Already *knew* about the Madoc legend. And Jane's told you about my sequence of poems on it.'

That hurt; as he said it his throat narrowed, forcing his voice into a higher octave.

'She did.'

'Well, I want to know what you told her about birds.'

'I don't know that it's any of your business, is it?' said Sam, suddenly fierce.

'It fucking well is. When I got home she was going through all my poems. She'd broken into my desk to get them. They were all over the bloody floor – everywhere.' Gwyn clenched his fists and tried to stop his voice from going staccato. 'She was out of control, she was trying to tear them up. Do you realise, if I hadn't got copies locked away somewhere else she could have destroyed them all? All of them!'

Sam shrugged.

'Maybe you should be more open with her. Show her what you're doing.'

'What the fuck would you know about it?'

'What Jane tells me.'

Gwyn flinched. Then he sat forward on the very edge of his seat. Suddenly he was so angry he had to keep gulping down air.

'Keep – your – hands – off – her, you no-hope Indian bastard.'

Sam put his glass down and stood up. The sound of his own words had glued Gwyn to his chair. He was immobilised by the shock of hearing himself say such a thing – and by a pang of sheer physical fear. Sam stepped towards him, tall and menacing. He leaned over, reached out and took the glass out of Gwyn's hand.

'Asshole,' he said bitterly and walked to where the bourbon bottle stood.

Suddenly released from his catalepsy, Gwyn jumped up and snatched his glass back, so that bourbon splashed on to the floor. The inside of his chest felt scratchy and choked with rage, as if it were full of barbed wire.

'What do you bloody well expect? You're pulling this Mandan

secret bird crap on Jane, trying to get her away from me. You're trying to come between us, you're trying to break us up. I tell you, you keep your hands off her, you *Mandan* bastard.'

Almost casually, Sam punched Gwyn in the stomach. It wasn't a vicious blow but Gwyn was no longer expecting it: it was the shock more than the pain which doubled him up.

'Grow a dick,' said Sam scornfully. Then, as Gwyn tried to straighten up, drawing his right arm to punch back, Sam's hands struck his shoulders firmly, knocking him back into his chair.

'Here.' Sam refilled his glass and handed it to him. 'Shut up now, you've said enough. This is serious shit we're dealing with. Drink it and listen.'

Stunned, Gwyn sat still. The anger still whirled in him but shrunken, like a trapped wasp in an empty room. Get up and hit him, he thought to himself, but he couldn't.

'I've been having dreams,' said Sam. 'Did Jane tell you?'

Gwyn gazed stonily at him.

'For Christ's sake, man.'

'Yes. She did.'

'I didn't know what the dreams were about, but they kept coming. Flocks of these dark birds, always flying in an arrow shape. The flocks grew too, as the dreams went on. It's been happening for over three months now.'

The same time Jane and I have known each other, Gwyn thought involuntarily.

'A month ago it got so I was afraid to sleep. I mentioned it to my uncle, Willie. I didn't tell Jane that – she and Willie didn't see eye to eye in the past and – '

'Yes, I know. He threw her off the reservation. For being a bad influence on poor little Sam.'

'He did it, not me.' Sam paused, suddenly less confident. 'So she talks about what happened then, does she?'

Gwyn raised his eyebrows. 'Privileged information, is it? Well, so is what my wife tells me.' Did he imagine it, or did Sam wince? 'Wife,' he said distinctly. 'She's my wife, Sam, remember?'

'How could I forget?' said Sam bitterly. Then, eyeing Gwyn's face, 'That's a nice wifely bruise she gave you.'

Gwyn touched it and smiled softly.

'Seems to be my night for it. But this one's a badge of love.'

Sam looked away first.

'Willie said it was the dark bird, coming back. Did Jane tell you about that too?'

'Yes.'

'She shouldn't have done that.' Sam's body had tensed up; he flashed an angry glance at Gwyn. 'That wasn't hers to tell.'

'Grow a dick,' said Gwyn mockingly.

They stared at each other in silence. Gwyn felt something dangerous buzzing in between them: not the earlier anger but a different, restrained violence that couldn't get loose.

Suddenly and illogically he felt exasperated with Jane for forcing him into an enmity with this man. In other circumstances, he was sure they could have been friends.

Friends? Come on, you must be joking. Never.

'Oh for Christ's sake, mon,' he said impatiently. 'Get on with it.'

'You know it already,' said Sam, grinding his knuckles against his knees. 'I don't understand it and I didn't use to believe in it, but I'm getting these dreams every night now, and today there was the bird at the window.' His head dropped an inch and he closed his eyes, as if he were trying to drive out the memory. The gesture chilled Gwyn. He blinked hard.

'Well, it looks like we're all in it together,' he said flippantly. 'Cheer up, mon. I bet Jane and I have seen at least as many birds as you – probably more if you count everything in.'

'You don't take it seriously.'

Don't I? thought Gwyn. Do I?

'You think it's *funny*?' said Sam, his eyes contemptuous, 'that Jane's frightened almost out of her mind and that she recognises something in my experiences?'

'I don't think it's funny that it's connected to you,' said Gwyn quietly.

'Ah fuck you,' said Sam. 'Look, what are you doing here? It's past midnight. Why aren't you at home in bed with Jane? Your wife.'

Gwyn stared into his empty glass then reached for the bottle. It was funny, but his anger had almost completely drained away now and in its place was a perverse desire to talk.

'I'm not buying this crap about hauntings,' he said. 'I'm not,' he repeated more loudly. 'I deal in the subconscious every day, mon, it's my trade. The birds in my poems don't bother me, they don't even baffle me. You want to know where they come from? The subconscious – my personal subconscious. And that's where Jane's woman comes from too – her subconscious. And your birds from your subconscious. And so on. And there are times when people's subconsciouses run together – especially people who are close or who've been close.

'Jane likes to think her woman is the narrator of my poems. Well, she's not. My work is mine, and only mine. Jane doesn't understand, see, she doesn't realise what it's like, working on a sequence like these. How preoccupied you get. The thing is, she's jealous of my writing. I can understand that. I don't like it but I can understand it.'

In the brief silence that followed, Sam shook his head.

'Holy shit, do you have any idea how conceited you are?'

'I am *not* conceited,' muttered Gwyn through his teeth. 'I'm just stating the facts. I love Jane, Jane loves me. I am a poet, Jane is not. Got it?'

'Sure. I got it.'

'I'll tell you something else. Jane and I are slightly telepathic. I don't know if it's going to last, I think it's something to do with being in the early stages of our life together – so passionately in love,' added Gwyn with a throb of brutal pleasure. 'We do seem to be plugging in to each other's subconscious – she seems to be dreaming some of the events in my poems as I write them.

'It's only since you came on the scene that the dreams have begun to frighten her. And you're right, she is frightened. Really frightened. Scared to death. So what are we going to do about it?'

'What do you suggest?' Sam hooked his right ankle up on to his left knee and balanced his glass on it. It was a provocative gesture, as if Gwyn's demands were too unimportant to command his attention.

'I suggest you get out of this apartment,' said Gwyn. 'Leave. Go and stay somewhere else. And stop crawling off behind my back to see Jane.'

Sam steadied the glass with his index fingers. Through the

distorting surface, Gwyn saw the dull gold of his ring. What was it, a signet ring? But he wore it on his wedding finger.

'I've got a better idea,' Sam said,

'Oh yes? Are you going to grace me with it?'

'Let's all three of us go back to Renoxia.'

'What?' Gwyn was so staggered he actually laughed. 'What did you say? You must be off your head.'

'No.'

'Jesus mon, why the fuck should Jane and I want to do that? Jane's life's been half ruined by that place, she still has nightmares about it. If you think your showing up here has made any difference to that, you're wrong.'

'Did I say that?'

'What, you think I should take her to Renoxia anyway, against her will? With you, of all people? You think I'm actually going to throw the two of you together in all your old love haunts?'

Sam slammed his glass down on the floor.

'Shut the fuck up, for one goddamned minute, will you? And give me that bottle.'

Gwyn seized it by its neck and rudely filled his own glass to the brim before shoving the bottle at Sam.

'God give me strength,' said Sam, looking at the ceiling. 'You're like one of my goddamned special needs kids.'

Gwyn tried to glare at him but the childish action had exhilarated him and broken the tension. He saw how ridiculous it must have looked and against his will, his face creased into a sheepish smile.

Sam looked surprised then he laughed, an unexpectedly nice low chuckle.

'Sorry,' said Gwyn.

'OK. Me too. Now look, can we talk about this a minute? I don't know what in hell is going on, but I'm frightened and Jane is frightened. And I don't think you really are stupid, so I reckon you're secretly frightened too. No, don't say anything. I've been thinking about this all evening. Look.'

Sam got up and took two strides across the tiny room to the bookcase. He picked a cheap blue atlas off the shelves, turned its pages and laid it down on the floor in front of Gwyn.

'A map of America,' said Gwyn. 'Good for me, I recognise it. So?'

'I want you to show me something,' said Sam. 'This sequence of yours, about Madoc coming to America. Can you show me the route?'

Gwyn took a long, thoughtful drink of his bourbon. He was beginning to feel incredibly drunk.

'How do you mean?'

'Well, presumably your poems are charting his journey, aren't they? Like the *Odyssey*?'

Gwyn stared at Sam, who was now squatting down by his chair, their faces level.

'That's what I thought,' he said. 'That's how I thought about it once.'

'Hell Gwyn, it's not the world's most original thought, if you don't mind my saying so.'

'No, maybe not. The poems are though,' Gwyn said aggressively. 'The poems are completely original and bloody good.'

'I didn't say they weren't. So now, in different poems, Madoc's at different stages of the journey, right?'

'Yep.'

'Show me. Show me where he comes ashore and where he goes next, poem by poem.'

Gwyn narrowed his eyes. It was funny, he'd never thought of it like that. He'd just written the poems as they came.

'I haven't imagined it geographically,' he said. 'I'm not sure if I know. Let's see. It's interesting, this. Now, they landed somewhere hot, where the coast was fragrant, that must be Florida, then they sailed on west and up a swampy river –'

His hand lifted from Florida to the Mississippi delta.

'– that'd be here. Then they sailed up river to some falls and struck off across land, a plateau –'

His hand hovered indecisively and came down on the Ozarks.

'That'd be about right. Then on north, with a different river coming into view on the east, hmm, yes, that'll be the Missouri or one of its tributaries. Then there were some hills starting to appear in the west and river cliffs in the east –'

His hand slid from the eastern edge of the Rockies across to the bluffs of the Missouri feeders, then north.

'Here they saw the rippling hills ahead of them. Then they went up the navigable river and now they've seen the settlement which makes it just about – '

His hand, shifting eagerly up the map, stopped. Instinctively, on the last move, he'd veered slightly west and now his fingertips were resting in the very heart of the North Dakotan rectangle, just below Lake Sakakawea.

'Oh,' said Gwyn softly.

'You see?' said Sam. He was chewing his lower lip and he looked so strained that, without thinking, Gwyn passed him his own glass. Sam drank from it and coughed.

'Thanks.'

Gwyn stared at him. Interesting: for the first time ever, Sam looked really rattled.

They both jumped as they heard the knock on the door.

Jane stood in front of her own door and waited to be let in. What were they doing in there? She could hear voices and the creaking of chairs. She shouldn't have come, but she couldn't stay away.

Oh God, what had happened? Where *were* they? She raised her hand to knock again and froze as the door opened. It was Sam, with Gwyn only inches behind him. She saw anxiety pass into each face – she must look as ghastly as she felt – and they both spoke at once.

'Are you OK?'

'What's up?'

'Ohh. You *are* here,' Jane said. 'You were gone so long, Gwyn, I thought I'd come and see . . . you know,' she smiled nervously, 'if you'd killed each other yet.'

She was only half joking but Gwyn and Sam seemed to find it funny. Shaking his head, Sam ushered her into the room and closed the door behind her; Gwyn took her hand and led her over to the armchair. Their different touches on her one after the other made her disoriented.

'Come here cariad,' said Gwyn. 'No need to worry, we've cleaned up the blood, see. Sit down now.'

'You'll need some bourbon,' murmured Sam.

As Gwyn settled her in the squashy chair and Sam emptied the dregs of a bourbon bottle into a glass for her, Jane's bewilderment grew. She looked from one to the other but kept having to drop her gaze: each time she met the eyes of one man, it felt like a betrayal of the other.

Then she looked at the floor and saw the map of America.

'What is this?' she said shakily. 'A geography lesson?'

'In a way,' said Gwyn.

'Hey, why are you guys looking at each other like that?'

'We have a proposition for you,' said Sam, handing her the glass. 'Take a drink.'

'Yes,' said Gwyn. 'Knock it back. Now then – ' He bent down, shut the atlas and perched on the arm of Jane's chair. 'Don't look so terrified, lovely. You're not being tried for witchcraft. On the contrary, you and Sam are going to take me on a trip. To your home town.'

'What?'

'We want to go to Renoxia. This weekend. The three of us. We can talk to Sam's uncle Willie and your Miss Archer and find out what Haydn Phillips has got to do with anything and perhaps we'll get this whole thing over and done with.'

Jane tried to laugh but it came out as a gasp. She couldn't believe what she was hearing. After all these years, to go back to Renoxia, to let herself be taken back by – of all people – these two men. It was impossible, it was insane.

She said the first thing she could think of.

'We can't afford it.'

Gwyn laughed like his old self.

'I'll pay.'

'That's not necessary,' said Sam.

'Never mind, I'll still pay. It's worth it. Jane cariad, we can't have you living in this state of hysteria. We all need to calm down. Sam and I have become buddies,' a tiny spark of amusement danced in Gwyn's eyes, 'and between the three of us we can sort this thing out. Besides, you've seen my home town, I want to see yours. Don't look so worried, darling, I swear it's the best thing for all of us.'

Jane looked up at Sam. He was leaning against the bookshelves, a slightly worried expression on his face. But he gave no sign that he disagreed.

She wanted him to hold her. It should be Gwyn she turned to,

Gwyn her lover and husband, who had come round here to sort Sam out. But there was something wrong in what Gwyn was saying. Or perhaps it was the way that he said it.

Renoxia: the home of Jane's childhood, the place she had left forever. She saw it again: the town on the lake-shore, blown by the winds that swept over the endless plain. Still and open in the heat of summer, frozen iron hard in winter, keeping its secrets as the seasons ran out one after the other. The prospect of going home blossomed slowly in her mind, dark-shadowed, tempting, terrifying.

Part Four

32

We are facing real danger now. There's no question of going back: we'll do it. With Madoc's brave prince-like gestures from the prow of the ship, and me going smiling among our people, forcing them to stay calm and do what Wenlyn and I told them, we'll do it.

But Duw, it's nerve-wracking, coming into shore. There is Madoc, standing at the prow, making the gestures of peace that Glesig showed him so long ago, in Dreugyllt. The river-shore below the tref is alive with Glesig's people, writhing with them. Young men are running up and down in warbands as we're rowed into the shallows, groups of women and children seem to melt into one another and out again, and there are wolf-like dogs hurling themselves at the wash from our ships.

We're coming closer and closer. There, in the centre of the shore is a group of older, important looking men, two of whom wear animal skin head-dresses; arguing they are, and shouting orders and the young men at the water's edge are drawing bows in preparation. I'm hard put to keep the people round me quiet; moans and babbles of panic are breaking out and I can feel my own fear rising.

Madoc is up at the prow, making their sign of peace, but they haven't seen him. We're drifting sideways towards the shore and the Ynys Llyr people are looking at the mid-ship, at the panicking mass around me.

'Wenlyn!' I hiss. He comes running to me. 'Lift me up, high as you can. Quick!' Wenlyn ducks down, grabs me round the hips and lifts me clear of the others on deck. I sway in his arms like a bundle of rags put out to scare the birds and my arms wave wildly in the same way. But the elders on the shore have seen me, and they follow my pointing arm to Madoc, and now they are standing very still, and the warriors are pausing with the bows at their shoulders, and at last one of the elders steps forward and makes the sign of peace back.

It's been too close for comfort, this one. I don't let the people see my relief though, nor my fear.

'Put your swords away,' I say sharply to Morddyn. 'And for God's sake Rhys Eliadr, unstring your bow. Wear your weapons, good, but wear them with discretion or you'll get us all killed.'

I think I hear a hiss as I sweep through them to join Madoc at the prow.

The ladder sways under me. I go down as quick as I can; I don't like to have my back turned to the shore and the Ynys Llyr people, who are all gathered in a huge semi-circle. Madoc went down before me with Morddyn and two of the crew. They are up to their necks in water and I can hear them handling the coracle that has just been let down from the side to take us to the shore.

I have reached the water. It's so cold it grips my feet and ankles like a vice, squeezing the blood out of them. I gasp in pain, turn and there is Madoc's hand, stretched out for me. The coracle is ready but he's waited shoulder-deep in this freezing water to hand me in. I step in and feel the coracle lurch; I sit quickly and it lurches again as Madoc, hauling himself a few steps back up the ladder, climbs in beside me. Then Morddyn comes in too. The crewmen, their faces blue-white with cold, pull us towards the shore.

The four important-looking men are in the centre of the semi-circle, making a reception party. From down here in the coracle, they look fearsome. Now that we have splashed out of the coracle into the last inches of water, and are wading up to them, they are standing their spears in front of them in some ceremonial salute.

I can tell by the way their eyes keep darting to me that they are surprised a woman has come ashore with the leading party.

I hold myself straight, despite the cramping cold in my legs, and don't let myself look at Madoc.

'This is the Bird People's country,' says one of the men wearing a head-dress. 'What are you doing, coming here?'

Madoc and Morddyn and I exchange excited glances. We can understand. Glesig has taught us well – we can all understand what the elder says!

'We have come from a long way away to be your allies,' Madoc says, speaking slowly in their language. 'We have one of your people with us, who is coming behind us, and he told us about you and your country and your wars with your neighbours. We have wars in our country, that's why we left. We are a strong people, with many gifts for you and skills we can teach you.'

The elders are frowning over Madoc's speech – they can't understand all of what he's saying. The first elder speaks to him again:

'What sort of gifts and skills? Why should we need them?'

'Gifts and skills to help you defend your country in war. We know where to find animals as fast as deer which men can ride in battles. We can help you make spears and arrowheads sharper than your enemy's. We can give you breastplates twice as hard as leather.'

The four elders are listening in concentrated silence but the Bird People gathered round them are all talking. They must be explaining Madoc's words to each other: after each gift he names, the noise surges upwards.

The first elder makes a sign and the other three turn away from us, into a circle where they talk. There's a long moment when I feel the wind blowing through my cloak and dress and chafing the wet fabric against my legs. Then the first elder turns back.

'Why would you give these to us?'

This is the second really dangerous moment. I hold my breath as Madoc's voice sounds: steady, my love, steady; you've got to make them believe in our strength.

'We are not a travelling people,' Madoc says simply. 'We want to settle. To do that in safety, we need allies. We ask you to be our allies – help us to find a country where we can live and we will give you the gifts and teach you our skills and lend you our support in wars against your enemies.'

'And in return we'll support you?' The elder's tone is full of expression but we know so little about these people, we can't tell what it means. 'You'll need a lot of support at first. Everyone will want to attack you.'

'We have very good weapons,' says Madoc. 'Shall I ask my men to bring them for you to see?'

The elders confer.

'Yes,' says the first elder. 'Bring your people ashore.' As Madoc goes to shout the order, he motions him to keep still. 'First we want to know one thing. You said you have one of our men with you. What is he called?'

And suddenly there's a silence – an absolute, dead silence. All the Bird People, even the children, have stopped talking.

'We call him Stray Dog,' says Madoc, a look of great interest on his face. 'That's the only name we know him by. We met him many months to the south of here. He has led us to this country. He's sick now with the river fever and will not be ready to leave our company for many days.'

Every single one of the Bird People is looking at Madoc. He seems to enjoy it – he's smiling slightly. But this stillness among so many people is uncanny – it makes me afraid. The four elders are staring at Madoc as if they are measuring him. Now they are turning away again to make their close circle: they are in conference for a long time. Not once do they look back at us or the ships.

At last, they are breaking up. One of them comes forward – it's the second elder this time, the other one wearing a head-dress. He takes something from his cloak – it's an ik-ho-map-kee, like Glesig made on the *Gwenllyr* – and he puts it into Madoc's hands. Madoc thanks him and reaches out for my waist. He takes the bronze-handled knife from my belt and gives it to the man.

'It cuts much sharper than stone,' he says.

The second elder carries it back to his companions. The first elder examines it, peering under the flap of his head-dress; he runs his finger along the blade and exclaims. Giving it to one of his fellows, he looks past the three of us to the ships.

'Bring your people ashore,' he says. 'If you're not aggressive, you have our word we won't hurt you.'

We have walked from the river to the tref. It's built quite a way back from the river: we've had to climb a sloping cliff face to reach it. Once we reached the top, we could see why they had built it here: the river flows in a bend round the land, protecting it to the south, east and north. To the west the land unfolds into a wide valley plain: we can't see all of it (the tref blocks some of the view) but what we can see is beautiful and looks fertile too – a huge valley floor, rising further away in gentle swells of land, these swells flattening out into plains again, then rising, then flattening like ripples on water as far as the eye can see. To the north-west we can see four other trefi, also built on river cliffs like this one: these, the elders say, are other, lesser Bird People trefi. Further west, and hidden from our view by the buildings of this tref, are a further six.

Never, never have we seen so much good land, all owned by one people.

'Dear Christ,' Madoc muttered as we stood gazing at it. 'Dear Christ. Ah, God, yes.'

West, beyond a long gradual ridge of land, live the Bird People's main enemy. They are a travelling people, apparently, who move their settlements from season to season, circulating over a vast area of their own land and encroaching regularly on to the Bird People's. At least, I think that's what they do. The Bird People don't explain it quite like that, and we're having trouble under-standing some of their words.

We have come inside the tref itself now – guarded, it is, by a double ring of wooden posts, with a moat dug between them. It is a huge tref. There must be nearly two hundred houses here, as many as in Caer Llion. And they are all built of packed earth, like our homes in Cynfael. But this is very, very different from anything I have seen in Morgannwg or Gwent or Gwynedd.

There is no land to speak of in here – the houses are built so close together it's hard for more than two people to walk between them at the same time. When we began the trek up here, our people were all in a big block, sticking together, but now we've all got separated into groups and are all mixed in with the Bird People.

'All the men are armed, aren't they?' I whispered urgently to Madoc just now. He nodded, a tiny, sure movement.

And it's comforting to see the tips of our people's bows and spears sticking out between the houses, in every direction. Impressive, it looks, and Madoc was right to show them the sharpness of our blades. Just in case.

The first elder is leading us a winding route through the houses. At every turn, we come across other parts of our party, being led and questioned by the Bird People: everyone seems to be heading for the same point.

These houses are like and unlike our own houses at home. They are round, like great big pots turned upside down, and they have packed earth roofs like low hills. On almost every roof, there are people standing. They are calling to one another and to us; they even have dogs up there.

Some of these Bird People — especially the men — are very fiercely and beautifully dressed. They wear leather tunics and long cloaks, decorated with pelts and animals' teeth and brooches of shaped and polished bone. They wear leather shoes, like those we now wear but much stronger and more finely made, sewn with beads and dyed. Shabby we look, next to them.

The men's hair falls long down their backs, made into cords with a red and black sticky stuff like clay. Some of them wear head-dresses, each different from anyone else's.

There's funny it feels to be here among these people who are so strangely familiar. You see, they are Glesig's people. I can see his likeness in so many of these faces, and in the way the men stand on the roofs, with one leg forward and their weight on the back foot. In the faces of the young warriors especially, Glesig is present. Oh Glesig, you should be here with us, returning to your tref. But it can't be — and you didn't look as if you wanted to come anyway, huddled down on your haunches among your chains, your eyes staring straight past me as I explained why.

You must stay hidden for a while longer so that we can be received as honoured friends.

Madoc is still with the first elder and I am still with Madoc, or at least near him. But it's hard to keep up with him with the narrowness of these paths and the way that the Bird People women gather round me. There's a woman here who is, I think, the chief elder's wife. She is about the age of my Mam and has the air of being used to respect. She wears a complicated necklace, several layers of thorns and animal teeth and shaped bone, dyed in reds and blues.

She's saying very little, she seems shy. Or perhaps I'm supposed to talk to her. I have just told her that I'm Madoc's wife and asked her if she's the wife of the chief elder.

Yes, she says. Her name is Wara Cah. At first I don't hear it properly and she has to repeat it several times. She has difficulty with my name too – eventually she says it as 'Keen wee.' I quite like the sound of it, on her tongue.

It's glorious, being able to understand people again. I can't understand everything, of course, I'm not nearly as skilled as Madoc is in this language. When several of the Bird People talk together, I struggle to hear one word in ten, and even when one person speaks to me directly they have to speak slow. But when they do that, I can get the meaning.

And not only me: Glesig did his teaching well – almost all of our people are finding they can make some kind of talk as the Bird People lead us through their tref. There's a noise of Gwynedd voices and Dyfed voices and Ynys Llyr voices all mixed up together! Just behind Wara Cah and me, my little Marged is walking (she still sticks loyally to me). 'I'm Marged, from Gwynedd,' I keep hearing her say, in her soft-voiced version of this country's language. 'Marged, from Gwynedd. I have a big journey.' And the girl walking alongside her – a beautiful girl with the strangest long, silver-grey hair – is saying, 'What's Gwynedd? Where are you going?' until Marged chokes with laughter.

'We have *finished* a long journey,' I hear Elen say, glaring at the girl (Elen's lover Gwildyn Hen has sent several eager looks in that direction). 'Finished, you understand?'

'A very long journey? From the end of the river?' says the girl curiously.

'And beyond,' sighs Elen.

Suddenly, we are out of the endless jumble of houses and in an open space. Ah, now I see! The houses, which seemed to be built anyhow, are actually in a pattern: they make circles within circles within circles, and here at the heart of the tref is a large space like a circular courtyard. And in the middle of the court one house stands alone.

People – ours and theirs – are spilling into the court. They don't press forward, though – this is obviously a special place, where precedence matters. I edge my way quickly through the people who have come between us and stand again at Madoc's side. The first elder, who is asking Madoc to accompany him to the middle house, looks at me uncertainly. Madoc hesitates, then he takes my hand with a courtly gesture and follows the elder. The other three elders have reappeared out of the crowds and the six of us converge on the house. We walk around the curved walls and find ourselves in front of a doorway.

The second elder goes to stand in the doorway, blocking our view of inside, and he motions to us to turn round. We turn, so we are facing the outer edge of the court, and we look at the people's faces, and the curving roofs behind them, thick with more people and dogs. And then we see it.

The houses directly opposite us are aligned differently from the others. A narrow opening runs all the way from the edge of this court, through the curving rows of houses to the outer palisades. It is so narrow that only one person at a time could pass through it, but it is wide enough to show us the land beyond. Like a passageway it is, like the aisle in the brothers' church above Dreugyllt. It leads from the heart of the tref across the plain to where a single, steep-sided hill is outlined against the white sky. The hill is coloured in the dark greens and browns of winter; its summit has a crown of trees.

The sight of it sends a tremor through me. I know at once what it is; I recognise it from Glesig's story, the strange one he told me on the *Gwenllyr*. It is the Hill of the Dark Bird, where the bird vanished and left the dreamstone in its place.

The first elder, standing on Madoc's right, is tapping his spear on the ground and saying something – giving us a formal welcome, I think. I don't know; I can't listen or look at him. I can only look at the Hill.

Now we are all moving forwards – towards the Hill. As we walk, I am directly in the line of it, it's as if I'm being drawn on a string, I don't think I could step aside even if I wanted to. But Madoc's hand pulls me and I swerve my feet to the right and here we are, gathering round the doorway of another house, the house nearest the lone building in the centre, and which stands at the start of the passageway.

'Welcome to my house,' says the first elder to Madoc. Madoc lets go of my hand; I catch a glimpse of his face white and set as he follows the elder inside.

'It's good,' Madoc says yet again. 'It's good. Yes, Ceinwen, it's going well.'

'I think we should go back to the ships for the night,' I say. I'm that anxious about our shelters – made of hides and sticks, barely dug into the ground at all, they leave us exposed. Some of the Bird People have come over here with us, to help us build the camp, but the shelters look so frail compared to their solid houses. And there's no moated palisade for us. 'Madoc, this camp isn't secure enough yet. Darkness is coming. We should go back now, and be sure of a safe night.'

'No!' says Madoc. 'No more of this! I've told you why not.'

'But how do we know they're not tricking us?'

'Why should they be? We've given gifts and exchanged people as hostages. They know our weapons are better than theirs. And they know damn well that we have something they want.'

'Did you tell them? Is that what you did when Mah-jo-poh took you into the holy house?'

'Mah-jo-*pah*. Their names are important, we'll all have to get them right. I – hinted. I indicated. I didn't need to do any more – you saw yourself that they half guessed we've got the stone. They won't attack us. They can't.'

'What do you mean? Of course they can. We may have better weapons but there are less of us and we're weak.'

'They can't attack us.' Madoc's right hand drops to his waist and rests on his belt. That's where, under his hide tunic, he wears the leather pouch.

'Dear God, Madoc,' I say impatiently, 'that's the very reason they will attack us. They want their dreamstone back.'

He shakes his head. There's infuriating his smile is – but lovely too. A smile of power.

'No,' he says. 'The Bird People worship this stone. They won't take it by force. They're not allowed to. It has to be freely given.'

For some reason, I shiver. I wrap my arms together beneath my cloak, trying to find some warmth from my own flesh.

'Who told you that?' I ask curiously. 'Mah-jo-pah? You believe him? It might be a lie, to put us off our guard.'

'Glesig Dog told me, a long time ago.'

'Oh.' I look across to the small square shelter made of hides and logs, in which Glesig is hidden. Carried from the ship, he was, in a wooden chest, so that his people wouldn't see him. And now he's guarded in there. 'Why didn't you tell me earlier, my lord?'

Madoc laughs. He seems to think it's really funny.

'My lady. My proud princess. Your prince doesn't have to answer to you, does he?'

And before I can answer, he turns and walks away, still laughing, as if he'd never asked my advice, never relied on me and Wenlyn to keep the kindred in order, never taken the stone from my own hands.

It's slipping. I can feel it slipping.

'Marged, are you looking after Ko-ka?'

'Yes Ceinwen. She's showing us how they cook the shaggy bull meat to make it less horrible!' Marged giggles; she looks really happy. She and Ko-ka, our number one hostage, and other women of the kindred, are gathered round the big pots which are bubbling over the sunken fires. There are quite a few men around the place as well, working on the shelters and offering help that the women don't need. This Ko-ka, she's very beautiful, and Marged's never had so much attention before. Ko-ka doesn't seem to mind either.

'There's kind,' I say, smiling at Ko-ka. I'm very friendly to Ko-ka. I saw the way the first elder handed her to Madoc. 'The Bird People are coming down from the tref soon, to feast with us. They'll be bringing more food but we must give what we can.'

'Our women, for instance,' says a bitter voice at my side. It's Olwen, Heledd's mother.

'Heledd is the Bird People's guest, like Ko-ka's ours,' I say.

'And we all know why she was given to them, don't we?'

'Because she is beautiful and from a good kindred. You heard what Madoc said to Mah-jo-pah.'

'And I saw you speak to Madoc beforehand. You made sure she went, because you're jealous. Like the village slut you are.'

A gasp – or is it a laugh – goes round the little knot of women. Olwen glares at me, her bony face flushed with misery and loathing.

I put my own face – bony too, but still beautiful for all that – close to hers.

'This village slut can have you whipped. And will, Olwen Henged, at one more word.'

I wait but no other word comes. Sick of them, I am, sick to death. I leave them muttering their resentment, and walk through the groups of people to the three small shelters that are already up.

At the door to the middle shelter stand Dawyl and two of the half-free. They are dragging sacks of supplies into the doorway. From the outside and to the Bird People this shelter looks like a store, but it's also a prison.

'I want to see Glesig,' I say to Dawyl. He lifts his boy's chin, fluffy now with the beginnings of a beard.

'Orders are to let no one in.'

'Don't be stupid Dawyl, you know that doesn't mean me.'

'The prince said no one.'

His eyes are confident, insolent almost. What is this, that's happening? In the tref Madoc was respectful to me, but here in the camp there's something going on that I don't understand.

'I've just come from the prince,' I say coldly. 'Do you want me to go back again and tell him you wouldn't let me in?'

Dawyl's eyes begin to flicker and his boy's mouth goes uncertain.

'He can't talk,' he says. 'I'm not taking the gag off.'

The gag? Duw, what are they doing to him?

'Just let me in. Now.'

Inside the hut it's very dark – there's no fire lit to see by or to give warmth. It takes me several moments before I can see, and then it's only dimly. There are sacks and crates piled around the walls of the hut and in one corner, slumped on the ground, is Glesig.

His hands are tied behind him, and his ankles are bound to one another with rope. There's another rope around his waist and that's fixed to an iron peg, driven into the ground. But the worst thing is his face: they've tied a long strip of leather round and round his mouth so he can't make any noise.

'Oh dear God, Glesig.' I kneel down in front of him. He looks at me dully and tries to shake the hair out of his eyes.

'Holy mother. Sweet stone lady of Cynfael. What have they done to you?'

He can't make a sound. He can't make a gesture. I stroke the hair back from his forehead.

'Is it Madoc?' I say. 'Is it Madoc who's done this?' But of course it's Madoc; who else could it be?

'My lord, I *must* speak to you.'

Madoc's eyes gleam at me, boyish, amused. He moves away from the fire and the men, into the shadow.

'You're very flustered, my lady. What is it?'

'Why have you gagged Glesig like that? He's in pain. He can hardly breathe.'

'So what?'

'Madoc, Glesig's been your friend.'

'He's hardly my friend any more, my lady. Or yours. He's made it clear he won't help us; well, I've got to see to it that he doesn't get a chance to harm us. What if I left him ungagged, to shout out to his people?'

'But if they see him like this they'll know something's up.'

'Why should they see him? Who's going to tell them about him? You, Ceinwen?'

Madoc looks interested.

'No. I – why should I?'

'You tell me. Why did you go to see him just now?'

'I just wanted to see him. To see if he had anything to say. To tell him we're in his country.'

'Oh, he knows that. Don't worry. I'm keeping him informed.'

'Madoc. Why don't you just let him go?'

'It's too late now,' Madoc says with satisfaction. 'As you said, we can't afford to let the Bird People know how we've been looking after him. It would destroy their trust in us. Speaking of our new neighbours, I can see them coming down in procession from the tref for the feast. Get yourself organised, Ceinwen. You should be ready to greet them.'

This woman keeps looking at me. She's several people away from me and sometimes the fire flares up and obscures her. But when the flames die down again there she is, watching me.

She's one of Mah-jo-pah's wives – she must be, to be sitting so close to me. She's my age or a little younger and she's strangely pleasing to look at. She hasn't got Ko-ka's delicate loveliness: her face is broad and so is her nose, and her mouth's so wide it looks as if it's been stretched. But she's got a brightness that burns in her slanting eyes and lights her whole face.

There's funny – I feel as if I know this woman. Wara Cah is sitting next to me, talking. I have to wait till she's finished, then I say, casually,

'Who's the woman with the feather clasp on her cloak?'

'With the long eyes? Rokai. She's the daughter of our most famous warrior, Kutaimah. He killed forty-nine Ridge People in his life.' Wara Cah looks as though she could say more but she doesn't.

I'd like to meet Rokai. I'm tired and I want someone my own age and my own mind to talk to, someone who knows what it's like to be a young woman making your own way. I want a friend.

A few yards away Madoc sits at the head of the men's fire, sharing the top place with Mah-jo-pah. The Bird People seem very stern in the firelight; among them Madoc looks ruffled and young. His hair curls against his skin, making the shadows shift over it. His eyes are turned away from me; he hasn't looked over here once since the feast began.

I look back at Rokai and find her eyes on me again. Perhaps I could talk to her.

It's taken me a good while to work these changes in our circle. I could just have called Rokai over to me but then all the other women would have listened in – the Bird People women, our kindred, Ko-ka and Marged. I don't want that. So I've managed, bit by bit, to get the people mixed up around the fire, and now I'm within touching distance of her.

Her head is bent, her long hair spread out around her shoulders like a shawl. My fingers work on the dried fruits we've been given.

'You're a wife of Mah-jo-pah?' I say.

'Yes,' Rokai answers. Her voice is clear and low, deeper than mine. 'And you're the first wife of Madoc.'

'I'm the only wife of Madoc,' I say. But I don't sound as sure as I'd like to.

Rokai glances at Madoc and then at me.

'Is it true that in your country a man has just one wife?' she says curiously.

'Not always,' I say, thinking of Owain Gwynedd and his three wives. 'Great men have more. But only one woman can be recognised by everyone as the wife. And I'm that woman for Madoc.'

'How are you chosen for that? By birth? By beauty?'

I could easily say yes to her. She's not to know about my birth and even after this long journey I'm beautiful enough. But I want to tell her.

'Usually a great man chooses a wife by birth and beauty,' I say. 'And because he wants her kindred as his allies. I don't have birth. Madoc chose me for beauty and for love. And I chose him,' I add suddenly, though I don't know if she'll understand.

Rokai's hand brushes against my skirt, the tiniest touch.

'I chose a man,' she says, very very quietly. Both our heads are bent and I strain to catch her words through the curtain of her hair. 'I chose him for love and he chose me. But I wasn't allowed to have him.'

'Why not?'

'He was no one. He hadn't proved himself in war. The expeditions he went on weren't lucky. And I am Kutaimah's daughter, and Mah-jo-pah had chosen me for his house.'

'What happened to your man?'

Rokai turns her head and through the streams of shining, oiled black hair, her eyes are avid.

'I think he's with you.'

Duw, she talking about Glesig. So this, this is Glesig's woman, the one he would never speak about. This is who he was coming back for.

'Yes,' I say, and my voice is a whisper, very far away. 'He's sick.'

'How sick?' There's desperate she sounds. 'Will he live?'

'I don't know.'

'They say he led you here? He led you back to us? He wanted to come back?'

I nod.

'He wanted it very much. To come back in triumph.'

'Then he must still have it. The dreamstone.'

I'm silent but my eyes have flown anxiously to Madoc.

'No,' says Rokai in horror. 'No. He hasn't let it go!'

'Does it matter?' I say. 'He saved it from the danger in the first place and brought it away. Now we're bringing it back. Does it matter who has it?'

Rokai puts her hands up to her eyes.

'I told him not to do it,' she says fiercely, turning her head from side to side. 'I told him not to. I said I could find another way.'

'I don't understand,' I say lamely. 'What way? He told me about the danger. He had to get the stone away, to safety.'

Rokai draws her hands down to shield her mouth. She's smiling bleakly.

'That was the story. That was what people were supposed to believe.'

'What do you mean?'

'You don't know my man, do you? He was impatient and desperate – all that bad luck in the expeditions, and everyone jeering at him whenever he asked for me. He was only going to take it and hide it for a day. He was going to lead the search to find it; he was going to restore it by night.

'He wanted to prove himself. He said the dark bird would bless us. He thought it would understand and help us. I knew it wouldn't. It isn't like that,' she says despairingly. 'It's never like that.'

There's something gritty between my fingers – I've ground the dried fruit into powder. Glesig, my friend, my rival, my enemy, my equal.

You even match me in love.

Glesig has lain with me, and I've been in his arms. *You don't know my man, do you?*

I do. I do, though.

There's funny, how long it's taken me to realise it.

I can't look at Rokai, only into the fire which burns my eyes. 'He did that for you?' I say softly. 'I didn't know.'

But Madoc knew. He's known for a long time: this is the foster brother's secret he wouldn't tell me. Why not, Madoc? What reason did you have for keeping this back?

He's looking at me now, my prince. Something about me has attracted his attention. He's leaning forward to have a clear view and his face is alight with a hungry, menacing interest. I wish I could hide my feelings from him. I wish I could draw a cloak over my face to conceal my thoughts.

But I know he sees them all. His eyes narrow and his mouth curves: he's smiling at me, deep into my eyes. It's the playful, ruthless smile that I've loved, that I still love, but now its danger is all for me.

33

It was eight twenty-three in the morning at Renoxia bus station. A man Jane did not recognise was sliding crates out from the side of the bus and loading them on to a trolley. Behind him, selling tickets in the booth, was Mr Wilcomb. Jane had never known him: the name came back to her unbidden, as a visual memory – black letters printed on white on his breast pocket.

She descended the steps on to the road and breathed in cautiously, as if the air itself might hurt her. It smelt of frost and diesel and the lake.

Gwyn had bundled out of the bus ahead of her and now stood hunched over his canvas bag, his back to her. He'd been getting increasingly edgy ever since their plane landed in Chicago. When they'd left Brockham yesterday there had been a camaraderie between the three of them but it hadn't survived the night. It had been an uncomfortable ride in every sense.

She heard Sam follow her on to the ground, then the clang of the bus's doors shutting. Sam stepped to the left of her: they were all walking round one another so carefully, taking pains not to touch. She looked up, seeking Sam's gaze. He met her eyes almost reluctantly and gave a stiff smile.

'What now?' said Gwyn abruptly, as they stood in the station car park. His voice was deep and hoarse; anyone would think, thought Jane, that she'd persuaded him to come rather than the other way round.

In the parking bays were two pick ups, a Manwell's taxi cab and a Winnebago.

'We check into an hotel,' said Jane. 'We can take a taxi or walk.'

'Let's walk. I want to get a good look at the place.'

Gwyn said it with relish. Jane looked beyond the car park to the gas station and the sports store, new since her time, and the billboards that lined the way into the Commercial District. To the right a shabbier road led to Toller and the Reservation.

'Where did you live, then?' Gwyn asked.

'The other side of the Commercial District. All the residential streets are there.' She faltered. ' – Apart from the Reservation. That's to the north, on the lake-shore.'

'Pushed into the worst bit of land,' said Gwyn neutrally. 'There's marginalisation for you, eh Sam?'

'That's right.'

'Well come on then, I'm freezing my arse off here.'

They walked towards the Commercial District, passing beneath the traffic lights and signposts, watching the shops opening up. The hardware store, the grocery, the savings bank. The liquor store and the gun store behind their grilles. Jane recognised exactly which stores had been here twelve years ago and which were new. She could even tell which were missing: she used to know this street very well. It was where she and Sam had come to buy their supplies when Toller was too near the reservation and White Dove not far enough from school. In the hide-out days.

During the last four days, Jane had imagined this walk a hundred times. She had prepared herself for pain, grief, nostalgia; she'd armoured herself against an onslaught of violent, irresistible emotions.

But it wasn't like that. She didn't feel any of those turbulent things: she was simply home.

She was home. She knew the smell of the air, the shape of the Uxor Company building at the corner, how to pause at the intersection in case a truck was coming out of the blind entrance to the left. She knew that it was Saturday, so kids would be down on White Dove pond to get the early skating. She knew Sam's footsteps on the sidewalk next to her and the way he used his body to shield her from the wind . . .

Gwyn swore and pulled his collar up.

'Christ it's like a hurricane. Not exactly a clement spot, your home town, is it?'

After the wind blasted streets, the warmth of the hotel lobby hit them like a blanket. It was as dusty as a blanket too: Jane had to blink through the floating specks to focus on the leatherette sofas, the framed photographs of the Lakes and the Rockies, and the reception desk.

There was a family checking out, the children giggling together, the mother discussing the dust with the woman behind the desk.

'It's the AC? It was working fine in our cabin this morning, at least I think it was – oh, a separate system? Yes, I suppose it would be. Well I don't know, how's a person to see in this atmosphere? It makes your eyes sting, doesn't it?'

Jane turned to Gwyn, tugging his sleeve and nodding at the children, who were beaming up at the receptionist whilst peeling the wood-look vinyl paper off the sides of the desk.

Gwyn looked but showed no reaction.

'Very Renoxian,' said Jane. 'What do you think of it all so far?'

Gwyn shrugged. 'It's a small town. It's a motel. It's much as I expected.'

He twitched his shoulders irritably and as the family finished their transaction he barged forward, almost elbowing Sam aside, and asked for a double room.

Jane watched as the receptionist, a middle-aged blonde woman with eyes hard inside blue shadow, took the measure of the three of them. She paused when she looked at Sam and her mouth puckered.

'A bedroom for two. For tonight only?'

'Probably,' said Gwyn.

Jane looked anxiously at Sam. She felt sick and over-tired. Gwyn had been all right on Wednesday when they'd decided to come here; more than that, he'd been loving, almost tender. But for the last twenty-four hours he'd done nothing but push her away.

Now he was leaning his elbows on the desk, excluding Jane and Sam. It was so different from the last time they had checked into a room: Jane remembered the snug hotel on Lundy, with the bare wood staircase and the open fires and candlelight in the bedroom. She wished that it could be like that again; that Gwyn would turn around and take her hand, and they could be going off to their room as lovers, people just married, glowing with excitement and shared jokes. Instead they were here with Sam, the three of them strung tight with tension and haunted by ghosts, on a nightmare quest to track down an old legend.

It's all Sam's fault, Jane thought for a second, but then she recalled that the woman had come to her long before Sam reappeared; even that first night on Lundy she had been there, conjured up out of the candlelight by Gwyn's poetry. Gwyn appeared to be trying to charm the receptionist, with little success. Why the hell was he bothering?

'Thank you very much,' he said as she handed him the keys.

'You're welcome,' she said in a voice that suggested they weren't. 'Number thirty-four is out of the door and to the left along the walkway. One in from the end.' Her eyes kept flickering from Gwyn and Jane to Sam. Now with a small, decided gesture she turned towards Sam and let her cool smile freeze. 'Number thirty-four is for two people only. Are you looking for a room also?'

'No, ma'am,' said Sam. 'I live here. But I'll see my friends settled.'

'Bitch,' said Gwyn just too loudly as they walked off.

'Jesus, Gwyn, shut up!' Jane whispered angrily.

'What's the matter?' demanded Gwyn, barging through the door ahead of her. 'She is a bitch. She was rude to Sam.'

'You don't make Sam's life any easier by doing things like that.'

'Don't talk about Sam as if he's not here,' Gwyn said, as Sam followed them out on to the walkway. 'You don't like it, do you Sam?'

'Just knock it off,' said Sam.

Gwyn strolled down the walkway humming to himself. He smiled at Jane and Sam as he turned in front of door number thirty-four and fitted the key.

'Speaking of knocking off,' Jane heard him say, quietly, so only she could hear, 'how do you find my wife?'

The door opened and Gwyn walked into the cabin. It was dim,

402

thanks to closed brown curtains, and smelled of rubber paint. Jane walked unsteadily over the threshold and sat down on the nearest bed. This was a side of Gwyn she had seen in disturbing flashes before but never for so long, never so relentlessly. He seemed to have thrown off all his gentleness and humour. It was as if another, darker person inside him had emerged and taken over.

'Make some coffee,' she said bleakly. 'I suggest we each take a shower and then decide what to do.'

As the hot water washed away the grime of the journey, Jane began to feel better. She was tired and light-headed, but coffee and breakfast would fix that. They could go to Delaney's – if it was still there, of course, and eat pancakes and hash browns and plot out their course of action. They could pretend it was a vacation: they might pass as old college friends, for instance.

But when she went back out into the bedroom, wrapped in a towel, Gwyn was lying on the bed reading the Renoxia civic guide and Sam sat as far away from him as possible, drinking coffee.

'Who wants the shower next?' said Jane. Gwyn didn't respond. 'Looks like you, Sam,' she said.

Sam frowned questioningly in Gwyn's direction. She shrugged.

'Well, OK. I'll take my coffee with me.'

Gwyn waited till they could hear the sound of running water through the closed door before he said,

'Don't mind me. Why don't you go back in and join him?'

'Cut it out Gwyn.' Jane pulled a creased but clean shirt and jumper out of her bag and began to get dressed. She hurried into her underwear, keeping the towel around her.

'It's all right,' said Gwyn sardonically, 'I'm not going to – '

'I said, cut it out! What's the matter with you?'

Gwyn lowered the civic guide and looked at her, his eyes deep grey and unfriendly.

'What's the matter with *you*?' he said softly.

'You wanted to come here,' said Jane. 'You're the one who ran around buying tickets and arranging flights.' She was panting; she could feel an emotion building inside her and she thought she might be about to yell or burst into tears or possibly both. 'I never wanted to come, never. So don't give me this *shit* now! And don't you dare take it out on Sam either.'

She finished dressing and went to the coffee jug, which was steaming with the brew Sam had made. Trembling, she poured herself a cup and took it to the chair Sam had sat in.

Gwyn sat up on the bed and stared at her.

'What is it?' she asked.

He didn't answer.

'Don't be childish.'

But then she realised he wasn't looking at her. He was staring without seeing, and his lips moved soundlessly.

'Oh Christ, snap out of it,' she said despairingly as he reached for his blue folder, but she knew it was already too late.

'He won't come,' she said to Sam, ten minutes later. 'Look at him. He's gone for hours now.'

'Gwyn,' said Sam. 'GWYN.' No answer. He went over to where Gwyn had drawn a hard chair up to the bedside table and put his hand square on the paper he was using.

'Oh for God's sake, mon,' muttered Gwyn, shoving his hand off. 'Go off together, why don't you? Leave me alone. Can't you see I'm working?'

'You can put it off till later. We have to go find Jennifer. We agreed.'

'You find her. Oy!' As Sam tried to put his hand back on the paper, Gwyn gave it a hard sideways chop. 'Keep off. I'm warning you.'

Sam hesitated, shooting an uncertain glance at Jane.

She shook her head, struggling with an angry ache which had lodged in her chest and was now growing, threatening to dissolve into tears. She put her hand out tentatively to touch Gwyn's shoulder but drew it back again: she couldn't bear another rebuff.

'There's no point fighting,' she said. 'Oh hell Sam, leave him. We can go alone.'

'I don't like it.' Sam was standing irresolutely behind Gwyn, and it hurt Jane to see him gazing at the back of Gwyn's curly head while Gwyn scribbled on, taking no notice. She couldn't work out which aspects of the scene hurt her, or why; she only knew she didn't want to stay there any longer.

'Come on,' she said, gathering up her bag and coat and making for the door. 'Leave him to it.'

So Gwyn was left behind in the hotel room and now there was just Jane and Sam, together as they used to be. Walking along the empty streets in the white Renoxia morning, Jane felt the coils of her identity shaking further and further loose.

Before, Jane had felt at home. Now, with Gwyn left behind in the hotel, the town felt even more familiar. Now it wasn't only a familiarity of space but of time. The membrane that separated the past from the present had dissolved and she couldn't have said, as she walked across the western edge of the Commercial District with Sam, and entered the streets of Middle Renoxia, whether she was twenty-eight or sixteen, a grown woman or a hungry, love-perturbed teenager.

As they walked, the blocks of commercial buildings flattened out and changed into houses, their yards furnished with bicycles, children's toys, car parts. The Connors' house still had bushes shaped like toadstools lining the drive, but much, much bigger now: they stood nearly six feet tall, as if someone had pumped them up overnight. A group of kids hung out alongside the basketball courts, just the same as Sam and Jane had been, exactly the same, even wearing a different version of the same clothes – jeans and sweats.

Sam walked by her side, not saying much. In New York she had found it impossible not to touch him; here the pull was so powerful she didn't dare take the risk. Her whole body ached to feel his touch, even the pressure of his arm through his coat. But she was afraid: this wasn't twelve years ago and these small town streets were not as prosaic as they seemed.

They crossed the street where she had lived, both glancing at the house, now painted green, but not slowing down. They crossed two more intersections, avoided four kids on bikes and were at Miss Archer's. There was a light on round the back, in her kitchen window.

'OK?' said Sam.

Jane nodded. She didn't trust herself to speak.

'Well, here goes.'

The door opened unexpectedly quickly, as if someone had been watching their approach. And Jane was looking at Miss Archer, her old school librarian and friend, and Haydn Phillips' lover.

Miss Archer was wearing a dark pink jumper and a brown pleated skirt. She had always had a taste for coquettish clothes. She looked more womanly than Jane remembered her, less of a librarian, but perhaps that was because of what Jane now knew. As she stood in the doorway Jane could see that this woman in her sixties was attractive and even mysterious: her fine bones had blurred and her delicate skin had wrinkled, but there was the stamp of passion on her mouth and eyes.

'Hello Miss Archer,' said Jane self-consciously.

Miss Archer had gone very pale upon seeing them, and her eyes darted from Jane to Sam and back to Jane.

'Oh my dear,' she said in her slightly harsh voice. 'Oh my dears. Only the two of you?'

'Gwyn's at the hotel,' said Jane. 'He was going to come with us – it was his idea in the first place – but as soon as we arrived he started writing.'

'Oh,' said Miss Archer. 'That's a – a pity. Come in, both of you. Hallo Sam,' she said quietly as she stood back for him to pass. 'Jane, you look well. You haven't changed at all. Let me see you.'

She shut the door and turned, taking Jane by the shoulders. 'You're taller. Girls go on growing such a long time. You're taller than me now. You look tired.'

Jane couldn't find any words for a moment; she was busy remembering the last time Miss Archer had been kind to her, when she brought her into this house and advised her on how to get out of Renoxia, away from the trouble that roared around her.

'I am tired. There's been a fair amount going on.'

'Yes, I know. I knew when Sam told me he was going to New York. I didn't say anything to you, Sam, but then I didn't need to, did I?'

'I'm sorry?'

'You understand me, Sam.'

Jane looked from Miss Archer to Sam.

'What's this? Sam? What's happening?'

'I don't know,' said Sam, but his voice was thick.

Miss Archer pulled at her jumper, a little nervous tic Jane remembered, and opened the living room door.

'It's no good,' she said. 'You'll have to be honest with each other. It was the same way with us too. There's no point holding out on her, Sam, it's gotten too dangerous for all of you. I knew it was likely to be this way, I watched you and I knew.'

'Sam?' said Jane again. He was standing against the wall, his arms folded in front of him. He looked defiant and afraid.

The hall seemed to change: the colours, the distances, the framed reproduction art on the walls suddenly all seemed very definite. Hard edged and irreducible. Inescapable. The woman was here.

Cautiously, Jane moved past Sam and into the living room. She didn't touch anything – not the door nor the walls nor the furniture. In the middle of the room she stopped and looked around her, at the square-spindly furniture, the bright cushions and the collection of china shoes on its special wall rack. The shoes were more whimsical than she had remembered them: some were sharp-toed, others had trims of gauze and ribbon, still others wicked-looking heels.

Every instinct told her that she was in the presence of danger. But the danger wasn't coming from this room; it was locked inside her.

'Help me,' she said to Miss Archer. Her voice rose like a little child's. 'Please help me.'

Miss Archer's touch was firm.

'I will,' she said. 'Sam's going to go now, and then we'll talk. You just sit here and I'll be back in a minute.'

'I can't leave her,' Jane heard Sam say from the hall. And then Miss Archer's voice:

'She won't come to any harm with me, Sam. Go home for now. I'll send her on.'

'I want to stay. I want to hear what you have to say.'

'You know enough.' Miss Archer's voice sounded regretful, but not angry. Sam said something else but Jane could no longer hear. There was the click of the front door opening, then it closed behind him again, shutting out the day.

Miss Archer made them both coffee while Jane sat, her mind

numb, in the living room. When Miss Archer brought in the cups, Jane sipped at hers and laughed shakily: there had to be a double measure of whisky in it.

'Yes, there's some in mine too,' said Miss Archer, pulling up a chair close to Jane. 'I don't know what to say to you. I feel so responsible. I had hoped that with you moved away it might not happen again. I always thought it would be you, you see – well, once you and Sam fell in love I thought so. You reminded me so very much of myself. And when you left I believed it might have been averted. So did Willie.'

'*What* might have been averted? Miss Archer, are you saying that you've had the same experiences as me? But you don't even know what mine are.'

'Yes I do. I saw it on your face as soon as you walked in the house. It's happening to you and Sam and your husband, just as it happened to us.'

'To you and Haydn Phillips?'

'To Haydn and Willie and me.'

Jane's hand trembled on the hot cup.

'Willie? Uncle Willie?'

'Why, yes. To the three of us. It's always three, every generation.'

'*What* is? Please, I don't understand. I just don't understand.'

Miss Archer sighed.

'Neither do I, Jane, not truly. I sometimes think Willie and Sam know more. They are keepers of the story, after all, and they're kin.' Miss Archer paused and dropped her voice. 'Did Sam speak to you about the dark bird?'

Jane felt a tightening in her head, as if the woman had clenched her fists in anger.

'Yes. He told me that it was the real symbol of the Mandan people, the original one. He said that it had been driven away somehow by a woman who came with the first man.' There, again: a convulsive jab in her soul.

'Jane. It's all right, dear. Drink your coffee. He's told you that much, I'm glad.'

'But what's the rest of it?'

'I only know one thing more. It comes back; to every generation, it returns. Always to three people and each time they choose.'

'Choose what?'

'Whom to sacrifice.'

'No!'

'Dear, I'm sorry.'

'No!' said Jane again. She felt as if she were in a nightmare, trying to swim her way out of treacle. It was ludicrous and horrifying at the same time. 'No, this is crazy. *Listen* to yourself, Miss Archer. Do you – do you *believe* this? It's impossible. What you're saying is insane.'

'You mean I'm insane. An old woman who's not quite all there. But I was a young woman when it happened, like you. The evidence is gone because of course, Haydn destroyed his paintings. He painted them and they did what they did to us and afterwards he destroyed them – except for one. One he saved; I think he hoped it might act as a warning. And you recognised that one yourself.'

'What did they do to you – the paintings? I don't understand.'

'I think you do, dear,' said Miss Archer gently. She took the cup away from Jane and placed it on the table. 'You're spilling it, you'll burn yourself. The paintings did to us what the poems are now doing to you – drawing you in. Making you go through it. There are many ways it can come back, you see – art is one. There have been others: business, religion, working the land . . . you see, when a man gets a glimpse – even the faintest passing shadow – of the bird, it inspires him. He takes it and uses it in his own way. And once that's begun, there's no help for it. Then the bird uses him, and the folk who permitted him to see, and makes it happen over again. To try and get restitution.'

The pain was so bad, Jane felt herself turn white. Like cymbals clashing she heard Miss Archer ask, 'What is it?'

'I have a terrible headache. Like claws in my head.'

'She's here, isn't she? I thought she was, I can see her in your face. It's odd, I thought I might be able to feel her again myself, but I can't.'

The wistfulness in Miss Archer's voice made Jane stare. It seemed more horrible and absurd than anything else she had heard, and more convincing. She staggered to her feet, flinching at the way the movement jarred her.

'I have to go, I have to.'

'Yes of course.'

'No, not of course. I feel nauseous. Oh never mind. I want Sam. Where did he go?'

'He said he'd be in Eddie's, on Toller.'

Eddie's: Eddie's was the bar they had always used to go to, where Eddie and his sister used to give them room to meet in the back kitchen.

Jane moaned at the pain and felt her way into the hall. She turned and looked back at Miss Archer.

'If you were so keen to help me get away,' she said accusingly, 'why did you bring me back?'

'I didn't,' Miss Archer said with quiet dignity. 'I did not bring you back, Jane, remember that. You came willingly. I don't know if it was you or Sam or Gwyn who first made the decision, but it wasn't me. I just knew that it was likely you would come, once Sam had reached you. And I thought I might be able to help you when you did.'

'Once Sam reached me.' Jane echoed the words flatly. 'But you told him where to find me.'

'He had begun to look for you; he would have gotten to you on his own eventually.'

'Are you saying –' she heard the reluctance in her voice; ' – that Sam wants to hurt me?'

'No. Not necessarily. But be careful, Jane. There's so much anger and pain in this place. And so much darkness.'

Jane stared at Miss Archer as she stood, fragile but erect in her hallway, twisting her hands in her dark pink jumper. She was flushed and her eyes were shining with moisture. Jane wished she hadn't come. Jennifer Archer was a hysteric; whatever her involvement had been with Haydn Phillips and Willie, it had unhinged her. She had given Jane no help and she had sent Sam away just when Jane most needed him.

'I'm going to Sam,' whispered Jane.

'Of course. And Jane – be ready for Gwyn when he comes.'

Jane opened the door – she had to drag at it; it seemed to swing inwards in slow motion – and went.

The streets of Renoxia were bald and dangerous. The light filled them: it sharpened the edges of the houses and garages, intensified the colours of the cars, added to the density of the people so that as they walked along the sidewalks she could see the air being displaced.

Twice people passed Jane and turned to look at her; they were people she knew from school, her own age, one time companions. She walked on without a second glance and they became uncertain and left her alone.

The claws were deep in her mind.

Toller Street had changed, a little. There were patches of regeneration on it. Shuttered, dirt-blackened store fronts still gaped on the sidewalk like the gaps in a mouth, but a few of them had boards up, announcing that the premises were under new lease. At the corner Jane went by a yellow and blue chalet-shaped building with Burger Brother written across its windows, and people behind those windows – mostly whites. On the south-facing side of the street a block and a half had been renovated and a number of modest stores were open for business. They looked south towards Middle Renoxia and White Dove, their window displays like hopeful smiles.

But Jane looked at the other side of the street, where she recognised the barbers' shop and the diner, despite its new name, the derelict lots and the bars which hid themselves behind plastic curtains and unwelcoming thick wood doors.

She pushed open the door of Eddie's and became entangled in the curtain. It wasn't the old pvc one but a handsome wool and leather hanging, whose smell rushed into her nose like a tide. She fought her way out, trying not to panic. The leather fold parted and she could see other new things in the interior: some new tables and chairs made of wood rather than metal, and store-bought shades on the lamps. But it was the same. The light was dim and a sediment seemed to lie on everything – the surfaces, the people, the air.

Sam wasn't at any of the wood tables near the front, nor the metal tables at the rear; he was at the bar, half-turned on his stool and watching her.

The claws eased their grip and she sighed. She crossed the bar to him quickly.

'Sam,' she said.

He met her eyes apprehensively and said nothing.

'What are you drinking?' she asked. 'That can't be soda?'

Sam nodded and drew his head further back into his hunched shoulders.

'I have to stay in control.' He spoke reluctantly, as if he didn't want to be distracted.

'I need a real drink,' said Jane. The more she talked, the looser the woman's grip became. It was such a relief. 'Have one with me. Get me a scotch,' she said to Eddie, who was behind the bar. Eddie was staring at her, his broad face shocked with recognition. Jane couldn't face a reunion now: she nodded at him as if she'd seen him yesterday and turned back to Sam. 'Let me get you a scotch.'

'I can't, I daren't.'

'Don't, Sam' said Jane. 'Don't let Miss Archer get to you. She's an hysteric.'

'No. I don't think so. What did she say?'

Jane looked at Sam's tense face and raised her hands to it. Sam jerked his head away.

'She didn't say anything that made sense. Nothing. It was all shit.'

'No. What did she tell you about me?'

Jane shook her head. There was going to be no escaping it. She had thought for a moment back there that if she tried, if she acted as though nothing had happened — but no.

'She didn't tell me anything,' she said quietly. The woman's grip had lifted but she was aware of her presence, more engulfing than ever before. 'Only that you were looking for me.' She laughed rather wildly. 'And you'd more or less told me that already.'

'One scotch,' murmured Eddie's voice behind her. Jane picked up her glass without looking at him.

'She fed you some whisky already,' said Sam. He watched her hands on the glass; he didn't seem able to look at her face. 'I can smell it. Whisky to comfort and sustain you, Janey. But none for me. Because of what I've done.'

'And what's that?' whispered Jane.

'I've brought you back here. I came to get you, you know. I came to find you and bring you back. To go through it again.'

'It. What do you mean?'

'You know, Jane. The same thing that Miss Archer and Willie and Haydn Phillips went through.'

Jane swallowed, feeling suddenly queasy.

'You *knew* about that?' she said. 'You knew about that all along, when you came to see me?'

Sam nodded.

'I didn't know the details, I didn't know too much about Phillips at all. But I knew that it happened. I knew from Willie it had to happen – has to happen – every generation.'

Sam shook his head, his eyes screwed up as if he was trying to ward off a bright light.

'I didn't believe it, not really. Not in itself. But they did, the people before me: my great-grandparents, grandparents, Willie. And the belief itself lives, you know, it's a thing. And it's inside of me, bred strong.

'So when your letter came, I set out to get you. Because you should never have gotten away, it wasn't fair. I wanted to bring you back, do you know why?'

Sam lifted his head and looked her full in the face. Pain and desire were laid bare in his eyes.

'For me. Because I never stopped wanting you. Not a day since you've been away. Not an hour of a day.'

Jane was silent. She couldn't speak. She had been expecting something else. She had been so infected by Miss Archer's fear that she had been ready to hear Sam confess all kinds of sinister things. But after all, it was this. She could have laughed with the relief of it.

But she didn't; instead she gazed at Sam and as she did so, felt other, deeper emotions begin to move inside her. She sat motionless on her stool, feeling the protective layers being peeled away inside her, revealing the simple, long-hidden truth.

'I – never – ' she said slowly. She stopped. It was so hard to speak, like dipping her arms into a pool and bringing up one heavy stone after another, pulling them through the water to the surface. She spoke painfully, without knowing what was coming. 'I never – ' she began again, 'stopped – wanting – you either.'

413

Sam shut his eyes. When he opened them she saw shame there as well as pain.

'Look what I've done,' he said desperately. 'I've brought you back, I reckoned I could control it, use it, but I can't. I should never have brought you back, never. Not with me being who I am, not with Gwyn doing what he does.'

Gwyn: the syllable was like a door opening in Jane's head. She saw him with unsettling clarity – Gwyn her husband and lover, whose eyes burned with a secretive light, Gwyn whom they'd left bent almost double over the bedside table, writing like a man possessed.

'Gwyn. Oh God, Gwyn,' Jane said slowly. 'He's making it happen, isn't he? He's making it, he's writing it. Like Miss Archer said. Does he know?'

Sam's hands clenched into fists.

'I don't know. Do you know what he's writing? He said you dream it.'

'I have dreams, but I can't remember them. When I wake I only have impressions and feelings – and fear, now. What about you?'

He shook his head.

'I don't know anything but the birds.'

'What shall we do?'

'I don't know,' Sam repeated. 'I didn't reckon on this. I didn't reckon on any of it. I only reckoned – you.' He said the word on a long, fierce note. Gradually, as he went on looking at her, the other emotions vanished from his eyes and she could see only longing. 'Come to me,' he said humbly. 'Help me make sense of this.'

'Yes,' said Jane. And suddenly, recklessly, she slid off her stool and threw herself into his arms.

They ran almost all the way to the reservation. Across Toller, behind the power station, up the long straight road. When they could see the trailers, and feel the wind rushing into their faces and stinging them, Jane laughed. On the outskirts of the reservation a group of young people were gathered round two boys on bikes. They turned and stared at Sam and Jane as they rushed by.

The evening air was full of vibrations: things coming together, sliding into place, moving past them and ahead of them. Jane didn't know if they were running with it or away from it; she only knew that she and Sam wouldn't, couldn't stop now.

'God,' she gasped, as they entered the reservation, 'this place has changed.'

'Better, huh?'

'Much.'

The dreary grid of houses Jane remembered was painted and planted with yards. And it had sprouted two new enclaves: houses with simple gables and porches, where bikes were tied to railings and pick-ups and saloons stood in driveways. The trailers that remained were in better condition than before and conifers had been planted to the north-east of them as windbreaks.

'The centre's over there,' said Sam, pointing to a brick and wood building, all sloping roofs and lighted windows, that stood between them and the lake-shore. But his hand was pulling her steadily in the other direction, to the line of trailers that curled into the middle of the reservation. 'See that one there, with the orange door? That's mine.'

'But isn't that —?'

'Willie's old trailer. Yes. He moved into one of the new houses. I'm on the list for one of them too — my name came up twice already. I only took the trailer on out of sentiment, to please him but now I'm kind of fond of it. Does it bother you?'

Jane pulled on his arm to make him stop. They were midway between the trailers and the houses and she turned towards the houses.

'Which house does Willie have?'

'That one, three from the end. He's on the porch working on his engine. Do you see him?'

She did. There was Willie; he had seen them too. The familiar large silhouette was straightening up, gazing back through the gathering darkness at them. They had used to hide from it, and run; she could still hear Sam's gasp of fear across the years. Now it put a different fear in her. She looked at the dark outline, defying it.

'I see him.'

Jane turned back to Sam and reached up for him. His mouth

met hers, importunate, and she revelled in the coldness of his skin, the heat of his tongue, and wrapped her legs around his, pulling him against her. She burrowed her hands beneath his coat and sweater and shirt, greedy for his flesh.

'Fuck him,' she said passionately.

'Fuck them all,' said Sam.

She kissed the sides of his smiling mouth, again and again, and spoke with an exultant fury she hadn't allowed herself to feel in twelve years.

'Fuck me. I want you to fuck me.'

'I intend to.'

Jane didn't realise she'd been asleep until Sam's trembling woke her. She raised herself on her elbow and looked around. The overhead light was on, filling the trailer with brightness and making black squares of the windows. Discarded clothes ran out in a trail from their makeshift bed of cushions, here on the floor.

She wound the tablecloth more tightly around the two of them.

'Ssh baby,' she said. 'You're dreaming.'

'No, not dreaming. What's that?'

'It's just the wind, taking the door. You know how it does.'

'No, no.' Sam's big body curled up like an embryo, butting Jane's breasts with his head. 'I'm sorry,' he muttered. 'I'm sorry.'

'I'm not sorry. I'm never going to be sorry about that.'

She got her hands under Sam's chin and turned his face up to hers. His eyes were wide, the pupils shrunk with fear.

'Janey,' he said, 'I've just seen it.'

'It was a dream.'

'It doesn't matter,' Sam said. He shook his head sadly. 'I told you that in my dreams the birds have been coming closer. This time it was right here – at the window, like the m-martin at the school. But huge.'

He was shaking violently now.

'It's all right,' said Jane fiercely.

'It isn't. You didn't see it. It's huge, goddamn huge. It filled the window.'

Sam shuddered and licked his lips; they were damp with sweat.

Jane relinquished her hold and rolled away from him, out from beneath the tablecloth. She knelt naked on the floor and lifted her face to the ceiling. The cold struck her limbs, and travelled along her skin into her nipples and vagina.

Her mind was clear, at last. Making love with Sam had empowered her. She was the strong one now: Sam was frightened of the Dark Bird, of Gwyn's poems, of what he'd done in bringing Jane back.

But she no longer felt fear. She wasn't going to run away any more. What had happened in this trailer had been a good thing; the best thing she'd done since she married Gwyn. It had released a long pent up energy inside her and given her back her fierceness.

It was time. There was nowhere to run now. Whatever the woman was afraid of, she and Jane would face it together.

'Gwyn will be coming soon,' she said, with absolute certainty. 'Ssh.' She leaned over and stroked Sam's forehead. 'It'll be all right.'

'It won't,' said Sam. 'It won't. Forgive me for bringing you back. It won't be all right – Gwyn's coming and he'll be bringing the Bird with him.'

'I know,' said Jane, looking up at the window and the purple dark beyond. Gwyn was out there, hurrying through the dark towards her, bringing his strange burden. She felt – not calm, certainly not at peace, but strong. She was nerved up, the blood tingling her veins, like a soldier before a battle. 'I know,' she said again. 'I'm glad. I'm ready.'

34

Even in the darkness I can see the Hill. It rises in the middle distance, a deepening of the night between here and the tref. The Bird People are walking back to their homes, passing round the foot of the Hill. I can't see them: they carry no torches. They'll be back tomorrow, with the sun.

Our fires are being stoked up for the night. Since the departure of the Bird People, there's a steady bustling of noise and movement in our camp – the people arranging themselves for sleep.

At the edges of my sight I can see them, fussing and organising, arguing. But my eyes are drawn to the Hill. I'm frightened to look away in case, when I do, it's still there, like a stain on my vision; like when you've been looking at the sun.

I feel that as long as I keep looking, I'll be stopping something terrible. I'll be keeping something else from getting in.

'Standing guard, my lady?'

Madoc's footsteps halt, an arm's length away from me.

'A brave sentry,' he says. 'But I think it's too much for you, alone.'

My eyes are still on the Hill.

'Why?' I say, keeping my voice light. 'Do you fear a danger, my lord?'

'There's always danger. From far away, from close to home. You must know that by now.'

'I do. And I don't know how to guard against it.'

'I do,' says Madoc. 'There's only one way, we must stand together. We must always stand together.' He's speaking quickly as if he doesn't want to be overheard. I turn in surprise to look at him: his eyes are hectic, fervent like a lover's. 'We mustn't let circumstances separate us. Whatever happens. You see that, Ceinwen, don't you? You understand.'

'I don't want any separation,' I say, having to snatch my breath.

'There won't be any. Give me your hand, Ceinwen.'

His hand is hard around mine, like a pledge there's no release from.

'Look at them, my lady. The kindred and the people of six princedoms. They belong to us. We've brought them this far and soon we'll have our people on our own land. They belong to us and you and I, we belong to each other. Do you remember?'

'I remember.'

'You're mine. Say it.'

'I'm yours.'

'And I'm yours, my lady. Forever.'

This is so unexpected, this renewing of our pledge, so unmistakable, the passion and force in his voice. In his face. I can't think; I can only feel: relief, confusion, puzzlement, love.

We stand looking at the people, congregating in the big shelter.

'Leave your sentry duty and come to bed,' says Madoc.

There's where our bed will be – near the front of the shelter as usual, where Madoc can be easily roused. The hide curtain is rolled up on the ground, waiting to be hung from the roof.

Unfolding hides and brychans all around our space are the kindred, and standing next to Marged, looking modestly towards our rolled curtain, is Ko-ka.

The scheming little bitch. My hand stiffens in Madoc's.

'What's the matter, my lady?' he says teasingly.

'Ko-ka is waiting for you.'

'She'll have a long wait.'

'You're not going to open Mah-jo-pah's gift to you? After all, Madoc, she's very beautiful.'

Madoc laughs.

'She's no danger to you, my love. She doesn't have what you have, what makes you my love.'

'Oh. What's that?'

'You're playing games. You know very well.'

'No,' I start to say, and then something warns me not to.

There's something wrong here, something I'm not understanding. Careful, Ceinwen, be careful. I let a smile steal over my face. It was the right thing to do – Madoc sees it and thinks I've understood. His strong hand flexes on mine, his fingers stroke my wrist.

'You see, you are playing with me,' he says, 'my lover. My ambitious lady. My partner in power.'

Madoc catches my other hand too and brings both of them together, placing them over his heart. There's young he looks, like a boy kissing his girl after the harvest supper, like the young prince who used to race his horses in front of me, and dream.

But these words he's murmuring, these are no boy's love words. 'I need your ambition, Ceinwen. I need your passion for power. We're hunters, you and I. We go after our quarry together and we kill. Because I'm the arrow and you, my lady, you're the bow. A supple, fine, lethal bow.'

No. No. I try to speak but fear stops me and then Madoc's mouth is on mine, and his hands are soft and forceful along my back, stroking me, bending me to his will.

A little while ago, the hide curtain came down on top of us. Madoc lay above me within its heavy, musty folds and laughed. I laughed too. We haven't hung the hide back up, but we've pulled it away from our faces and made a cocoon of it. It's so stiff and badly tanned that it stands up easily.

'Madoc,' I say, into his chest, 'tonight, during the feast, why were you staring at me?'

'Ah, when you were talking to Rokai?'

'You know who Rokai is?'

'Of course. I asked. I wondered who had put such an anxious look on your face, and Mah-jo-pah told me.'

I press my body against his, getting rid of all the distance between us.

'You know about Rokai and Glesig?'

Madoc closes his arms round me.

'Yes. I wouldn't have picked her out as the one, would you? But after I'd watched her for a little, I could see it.'

'See what?'

'What made Glesig love her so much. She looks – noble. In their way, not ours. Don't you think, Ceinwen?'

'I think she looks in love.'

There's a little tremor goes through me as I say that. Madoc moves his head to try and look at my face.

'Hmm. With our friend Glesig, you mean? Still?'

'Yes. She still loves him, just like he still loves her.'

'Oh I know he still loves her.'

'She told me he stole the dreamstone.'

Madoc chuckles.

'Yes, I wondered if she had. Is that what made you look so alarmed? And tragic? Your face, Ceinwen, you know, I've never seen you look like that.'

I rub my cheek against his chest, smoothing away the memory of those feelings.

'Ah Ceinwen,' says Madoc. 'My love. What's worrying you?'

'That Glesig stole the stone. It means nothing's what I thought it was.'

'Listen, Ceinwen.' Madoc caresses me intently, drawing my body the length of his. His skin is warm against mine, his stomach hard. The thin, strong cord around his waist chafes gently against me, pulled by the weight of the stone in its leather pouch. 'Do you feel that?' he says.

I nod.

'That stone was freely given to me,' he says. 'By you. And I'm using it for the good of our people. For the glory of new Gwynedd. You should be very proud.'

The sun's scarcely up but Madoc is already away, gone into the tref with an escort of twenty men. It is bitter cold, like the blades of knives, and we are huddling round the cook pots, all trying to get a bit of heat from the steam.

I help Ko-ka to a bowlful of the stew. Very gracious I am to her this morning. The faces of our women are twisting this way and that, watching what I do. They all thought I'd be out of Madoc's bed last night, you see, and the lovely Ko-ka in my place.

Wenlyn smiled and gave me a low bow this morning, acknowledging my victory. It makes me a bit uneasy, that everyone seems to have taken it for granted that Ko-ka would oust me. I hadn't realised they all expected it. There's so much talk going on in this camp behind my back, so many things people no longer say to me. Still, I won.

Wenlyn's gone with Madoc into the tref: a very official looking party they made, fully armed and wearing their kindred and lordship symbols. Gone to negotiate the peace, and our settlement.

I give myself a small bowlful of the stew – the everlasting shaggy bull meat, of course, and mixed with the long salty grains the Bird People brought us last night. These grow wild here and are harvested in the summer; I've never tasted anything like them before, they smell of the marsh.

I make myself finish the stew, though I can hardly swallow it. It's important to be strong, there's a lot to do.

I fill my bowl again, almost up to the brim this time, and put a handful of dried fruits in my purse. I take a piece of wood from the edge of the fire and kindle it in the embers, to make a torch. Walking carefully, so as not to spill the stew, I leave the big shelter and walk between the groups of men to the small shelters.

Dawyl is scowling and rubbing his arms: he's just come on to watch after his cold night's sleep. He pretends not to see me until I'm right next to him.

'Stand aside,' I say. 'I've brought the prisoner his breakfast.'

'He's had his breakfast,' says Dawyl, then he falters and mumbles 'my lady.'

'A piece of old bread,' I say. 'That's not how the princes of Gwynedd treat their noble prisoners, Dawyl. Yes, you didn't know that, did you? You'd better watch how you treat Glesig from now on.'

Dawyl looks uncertainly round for someone who can confirm or deny this, but the other guard is gaping just as much.

'Madoc ap Owain is treating with Glesig's kindred now,' I say. 'Let me through at once. And bring some wood for a fire.'

I'm good at bluffing, of course I am. I've had plenty of practice: hesitantly but almost respectfully Dawyl steps aside.

As soon as I'm inside I draw the flap back across the entrance, to give us privacy. My torch glows in the darkness, showing me Glesig lying, still bound and gagged, on his side. I put down the bowl, prop the torch between some stones, and go to him.

Duw, he stinks. He's been lying here in his own filth.

I take his shoulders and try to straighten him up.

'Glesig,' I say. 'Help me. Sit up. I've brought you food, and in a minute I'll make a fire in here for you. Sit up so I can untie you.'

His eyes blink listlessly at me but he slowly braces himself against the floor and helps me lift him into a sitting position.

I struggle to untie the leather gag: its knots are tight and resist, but I manage to get them undone. It loosens and falls around his throat.

'Glesig. Are you all right? Can you speak?'

He licks his lips, staring at the ground, and for a second I'm afraid he'll cry out.

'Don't shout,' I say. 'Please don't shout. None of your people are in the camp now, it would only make more trouble.'

'Please untie my hands,' he says, and his deep voice crackles like straw.

I can't untie the cords around his wrist: I have to take out my knife and cut them. Glesig eases his hands free; his arms are stiff and he brings them apart slowly.

He levers himself away from the fouled patch of ground.

'I'm dirty,' he says bitterly.

'I'll get them to bring you water. Look, here's a rag, you can clean your hands on this. I've brought you some food, stew, with your country's grain in it.'

Glesig shakes his head.

'I'm not hungry.'

'You must eat it. You've got to get strong again. We've got things to do.'

Glesig begins to eat, obediently, but he doesn't ask me any questions. As he chews the first mouthful, he recognises the taste of the grain and shuts his eyes.

'You didn't prepare this.'

'Not alone, your countrywomen helped us. Your people were here last night.'

'I know. I heard their voices.'

'I talked to Rokai.'

Glesig puts the bowl of food down.

'She wanted to know if you were with us. She wanted to know if you still had the stone.'

'What did you say?'

'She knows Madoc's got it. She was very upset, I thought she'd faint. She loves you.'

'Is she still Mah-jo-pah's wife?'

'Yes. Glesig, why didn't you tell me about it?'

He puts his hands up to support his head; it's as if he's too heavy to hold himself up.

'It wasn't a thing to tell. It was dishonourable.'

'You told Madoc.'

'Madoc and I are two men. He made me his brother. We loved each other.'

I hug my knees tightly. It's true, I remember them coming across the bailey in Dreugyllt, Madoc's arm round Glesig. I remember them sitting head to head at the long table, their charts spread out.

'You and Madoc. Oh Glesig, what happened to change that?'

Glesig gives a smile, like an exhausted ghost of his old sardonic self.

'Brothers fight.'

'Over what?'

He looks at me.

'You didn't tell him,' I whisper.

'No.'

'Neither did I. He can't have been sure. But it wasn't just that, Glesig, it started before that.'

'No, it wasn't just that. We're very different, Madoc and I. We stand between one another and the sun.'

'What do you mean?'

'We cast a shadow on each other. His light puts out mine. Mine won't allow his to shine. When we arrived on the southern shore, that was when we felt it. So we began to struggle.'

'Yes, I saw. I thought – I don't know what.'

'You should never have given him the stone.'

I look at Glesig, and I can see him as he was on the battlefield that day, bleeding and broken. I can see my hands, working quickly within the folds of his tunic to cut out the sacred stone. I'm so ashamed.

'I know I shouldn't. Forgive me.'

Glesig shrugs.

'It's not for me to forgive. Any more than you can forgive me for stealing it from the Hill. You and I, we're not very different, great lady.'

'No. I understood that last night.'

There's a scuffle outside the door, making us jump. My heart pounds like hammers in a forge. Is it Madoc, back so soon? But it's Dawyl's voice that speaks, unwillingly respectful.

'I've got the wood here, my lady.'

'Leave it there. I'll come out and fetch it in a minute. Now bring some water as well, for washing.'

I can hear him swearing under his breath as he stamps away. He says something to the other guard. It sounds like 'Don't leave the bitch.'

'I daren't stay much longer,' I say. 'I'm frightened. Madoc's so strong now, all full of power and plans. And I never know what they are. I think I can persuade him to let you go, but not if he finds me here.'

'Untie my feet,' says Glesig, 'and let me go. I've got to be with my people.'

'You wouldn't get ten yards. And I can't let you go to turn them against Madoc. He's my lord, I love him. He's leading us to a new country.'

'Do you remember what I said about the dreamstone?' says Glesig. 'It increases the desires of the heart. And you know what Madoc's greatest desire is, don't you? Power. The urge to be great. Ambition. The dreamstone is making his heart burn up with pride and longing.'

'That's no failing in a prince, is it?' I say. 'But I swear I'll help you and Rokai, somehow.'

Glesig looks at me wordlessly.

'You do love her, don't you? Duw, Glesig, you do want her to be your wife still?'

Longing comes into his face then, a longing which is immediately quenched by disbelief.

'It's not possible. I'm dishonoured.'

'We'll see. I must go.' I get to my feet and bend over him, my face close to his. I take it in my hands and kiss him on the mouth, the kiss of friendship.

Outside the day is so bright it hurts my eyes. I nod at Dawyl, who is carrying a pail of water towards the shelter.

'Good. Be sure you treat him well and leave off his gag and wrist ties. And make up a fire for him.'

All the faces are turning towards me as I walk away from Glesig's shelter. I don't bother about them. I must make amends, I must find a way.

What's happening over there in the tref?

Between here and there the Hill stands, drenched in cold light, its crown of tree trunks black against the sky.

'Is my hair still up?'

'Yes, madam. It looks lovely.'

'And the holly leaves? Are they in place?'

Marged checks the holly leaves stuck into my hide cloak. We found them, faded but still green, in what's left of the herb sacks, and we've worked their stems into the hide to make a pretend garland round my throat. It's to celebrate Madoc's return and the triumphant peace he's negotiated.

The two brothers of the Hellynt kindred, Iorwerth and Dafydd, came back to the camp hours ago and told us to prepare for a big celebration. It's to start tonight, they said, and continue tomorrow. Madoc has been all day with Mah-jo-pah and the other elders, in Mah-jo-pah's house and in the holy hall, settling the terms of the alliance. He has done well. Shortly after noon, the Bird People and Madoc's people were known to be at peace with one another. But the discussions have gone on for hours since, and messengers have been going between the camp and the tref exchanging gifts and information.

A complicated process, this peace. The whole camp is alive with excitement and speculation. Rumours go sweeping round, and people are looking sideways at me, falling silent when I come near. Some of them have curiosity in their eyes, some have smiles. They'll be sucking up to me now, see, wondering how to get on the good side of Madoc's princess.

I'm standing here before the banked up fire, near our last two casks of wine which we're preparing to open. Everyone else is gathered around me, watching the men return. They're coming past the foot of the Hill now, barely visible in the dusk. But even across this distance and in this shadowy light, we can see that they're triumphant. The little kindred banners flutter from their spears, and they're singing one of the Gwynedd songs. Their voices, all taking different parts, sound strange floating across this flat plain.

I touch the holly leaves, and lift my fingertips to my neck. It's bared for Madoc and if there were a head-dress left intact in the camp, I'd be wearing that too. I want to honour him and please him, and put him in a mood to grant my request.

'Look at his face,' says Marged in awe as the men approach. 'He looks like one of the old kings.'

And it's true, he does. His face is blazing with strength and happiness, but not in the old impetuous way. Madoc looks more solid than before, more fixed. So this is what you meant by greatness, Madoc. I can see you've got it now.

Madoc stops a little way away from me and his eyes meet mine, smiling.

'Kindred of Gwynedd, Dyfed, Deheubarth, Clochran, Morgannwyg and Gwent. We have made an alliance with the people of this country. We are at peace to build our new nation.'

A noise like a hum comes from the people around us, swelling, growing heavy and golden like the sound of a swarm of bees.

'My lord,' I say, and hold my hands out.

Madoc raises his voice.

'Tonight we'll feast alone, and tomorrow at dawn we'll meet the Bird People on the sacred Hill – '

The hum of the people dies down and slowly, I sink into a curtsey.

' – where I will seal our peace with my marriage to the Bird People's most highborn daughter, Rokai.'

The hum surges back, builds, sweeps higher and higher and topples into a babble of noise, cheering and laughing and calling out.

'God bless Madoc!'
'Madoc ap Owain ap Gruffydd.'
'Madoc, prince of Ynys Llyr!'
'Madoc and Rokai!'
'Madoc and Rokai!'
'Madoc and Rokai!'

I'm on my knees on the ground, staring up into his face but he's not looking at me. He's smiling at the people.

The noise batters in my head like sea.

'Madoc!' I say, holding my hand out to him, but he doesn't take it. Instead he nods to Wenlyn, who's at his side. Wenlyn comes to help me up, as if Madoc's too great for me now, and in his face I see pity.

There, this is a joke. Isn't it? Cruel, he thinks Madoc is, to play this trick on me.

I need Wenlyn's hand to help me struggle to my feet – my balance is gone. Wenlyn's hand is cool and long-fingered, it feels very different from Madoc's. There's laughter coming from the people; their faces turn and laugh at me.

I cross the small distance to Madoc, leaning on Wenlyn's arm. Any minute now, his face will soften. There, see, he's looking at me, his blue-green eyes clear like the lake beyond Cynfael.

'My lord,' I say, 'you've won a great triumph for us all.'

Madoc's eyes are soft and cruel. I try not to gasp.

'I have a request, my lord,' I say. 'A proposal to put to you, an idea . . . I must talk to you about it urgently.'

I've shaken Wenlyn's arm away from me and reach out to Madoc. The noise of cheering and shouting has died and in the middle of all these people there's only a poisonous, listening silence. Now Madoc is walking me out of it: his hand grips my arm and walks me away, through the people, past their faces – inquisitive, excited, some even sorry – to the open ground.

'Madoc,' I keep saying. I'm saying it in different tones. 'Madoc. Madoc . . .'

'Things are changing now, Ceinwen. You'll have to accept that.'

'This marriage,' I say. I'm concentrating very hard, trying to find my way around it, trying not to scream. 'What does it mean?'

'It means marriage. It means Rokai becomes my wife; the prince of the new Gwynedd is married to the daughter of the Bird People's greatest warrior. Rokai's father killed forty-nine Ridge people before he died. It's like marrying the Princess Gwenllian. Our children will found a new dynasty.'

I don't know if the shudder's in my mind or my body, but Madoc's grip tightens on me, so he must feel it.

'Your children. Your . . .' Now the trembling's started, it won't stop. My arms are shaking and the words can hardly come out of my mouth. 'What about our children?'

'We have no children. You haven't given me any.'

'But I will. When we're settled. I did – Madoc, I did have a child starting, when we left Dreugyllt. When the horses got loose on the crossing, I lost him.'

'Did you? You didn't tell me.' Madoc looks curious, as if I've offered him something unusual to eat. 'I'd like to have sons with you, Ceinwen. Well, perhaps we still will then.'

'Madoc?'

The hope rains down on me, making me weak.

'Why not? Of course, I'll have to find a way to stop the sons of different mothers fighting. I'm not repeating my father's mistakes.'

His face is thoughtful and content. And brutal. I know now that there's no saving me. Madoc's decided; he has been a while now. That's what all those looks and whispers have been about, among the kindred.

And somewhere in me I must have known too, because I'm not surprised. And I'm not struggling to believe it. I just don't understand why.

'Why?' I say. It comes out ugly and raw. 'I've given you everything. I showed you how to cast your net over the seas. We belong to one another.'

'There are different ways of belonging, Ceinwen. We'll always belong to one another. But I have to marry for our nation.'

'You're married to me.'

'Not in the eyes of anyone but ourselves. So it needn't change. Rokai will be the first woman in the new nation, but you'll live with us. Or close by.'

'Along with your other wives.'

'It's the custom of the country. A good one, it saves all the trouble the priests force on us at home, with excommunicating and disinheriting. It's like the old law of Hywel.'

'But there's always a first wife. And I'm your first wife.'

'Not any more. It's not possible.'

'I love you, Madoc. You belong to me.'

'And I love you. But take care, my lady. You've no right to use that tone with me.'

'I've every right.' His fingers are digging into me, bruising my arm, and he doesn't even know it. Just like that very first night in Cynfael, when we watched the skill sticks and he was silently fighting for me. I feel sick, in my stomach and in my heart. Sick all the way through.

In the creeping darkness, the land is outlined hard and definite. I see the people one by one, standing looking at us. I grasp Madoc's hand and prise his fingers off my arm. It takes all my strength but I don't waver. As I force his fingers up, one by one, he looks a little surprised.

'You traitor,' I say and the fury flows into my voice, lifting and lilting it. 'You filthy, low cheat. You'll never, ever rest again, as long as you live.'

And I spit on his cloak and walk away, and he doesn't move. He doesn't strike me, doesn't come after me, doesn't shout for anyone to stop me. Of course he doesn't; he doesn't dare.

I walk on and on, the poisoned blood coursing through my body; past the staring crowd, past the big empty shelter, round the back of the camp to the small shelters.

'Get out of my way,' I say to the guard, a half-free man I don't know. He doesn't move. 'Get out of my way, God rot you.'

He's looking round, probably for Dawyl, who should be with him.

I take my knife out of my belt and grab his hair.

'I'll kill you, you scum.'

'Ceinwen Maelgwyn, don't! I'm a Morgannwg man, we're kin.'

I look into his horrified eyes: yes, he looks a bit like my Da.

I bring the knife down fast, cutting his cheek from eye to chin. He gasps and staggers.

I push my way into the shelter.

Glesig is on his feet, staring at me. They've tied his hands again.

'Madoc is marrying Rokai,' I say clearly as I bend down and cut the ropes around his feet. 'He's betrayed both of us. Turn round, give me your wrists. You're free, come on.'

I push Glesig towards the doorway: he stumbles a bit, I don't think he's taken in what I said. Outside, people are appearing from the front of the camp, surging forward but hesitantly, stopping and starting. My half-free kinsman is kneeling on the earth, holding his bleeding face.

'It's your blood that saved your life,' I say to him. 'Be proud of it. It's not dirtied with high birth.'

As Glesig comes out behind me, the people shout. Among them I can see the astonished faces of some of the Bird People hostages, and I can see Madoc, running round the corner of the big shelter and stopping.

He and Glesig look at each other across the dark ground. It's a second, but it lasts and lasts. Then Glesig says something in his own language, some word I don't understand, and he seizes my hand and we run across the frozen earth, stumbling, jumping, cutting our feet on stones and ice, running away from the camp, towards the Hill, and no one follows us.

35

Gwyn tripped over a bag in the shadows and then stumbled against the end of the bed. It was so dark beyond the little circle of light on the table. He steered his way round half-recognisable shapes until he reached the door, and felt for the light switch. It clicked beneath his fingers and the overhead light filled the room.

He felt exultant and dazed. He had no idea how long he'd been working: he glanced at his watch. Bloody hell – it was nearly six o'clock. He'd worked through all day. Well, no, he'd had that sleep at some point: he couldn't remember when, he hadn't checked the time.

And look what he'd written. A piece of intricate, iron-hard poetry, tightly disciplined, forcing the images and the action to interlock, to twist and turn and run off on each other's energy until they exploded into that last scene.

No, not exploded: imploded. That was what it felt like: a build up of pressure in his head and his heart that had become greater and greater until it caved in, letting the energy flood back on itself.

He felt dazed and exhilarated. But he also felt frightened. Something had happened with this last poem that was different from all the others. It had gone further. Gwyn wasn't sure what he meant by that, but he knew it was true. The other poems he had always wanted to hug to himself and gloat over; this one he didn't. This one he admired and feared. It wasn't his. It had escaped from him.

Jane. Where was Jane? Suddenly Gwyn wanted to show her

the poem. Coming back to himself in this empty hotel room was a shock. Slowly and reluctantly, like a child realising he'd done something wrong, he admitted that he'd been dishonest with her. After the evening at Sam's, things should have got better – he had told her he'd help her, that there'd be no more shutting her out. And instead, he'd been more secretive and antagonistic than ever.

It struck him now that he'd been cruel. And it struck him, with a horrible cold edge, that she'd been gone a long time. She'd been gone too long, and with Sam.

Could they have been at Miss Archer's all this time? Surely not. They must have reached her house at eleven at the latest, and why hadn't they called him here? Weren't they wondering where he was?

Gwyn stared around the bedroom with its two beds with checked counterpanes, the two used cups by the coffee jug, the two towels hung over the heated rail to dry. There was nothing to suggest that three and not two people belonged in this room, and everything that was here had been used not by him but by Jane and Sam. The only evidence of Gwyn was the paper on the bedside table, and the unpacked bag next to it. It was like being a ghost in his own life.

Gwyn sat down on the edge of the bed and stared at the sheets of paper, covered with his handwriting. The strokes of ink, running on line after line, looked sinister. He tried to remember what had been going through his mind while he wrote, but he couldn't: his body had been here, writing, but his soul had been – where?

Gwyn could feel it coming from a long way off. He struggled to armour himself; he tried to be rational and to laugh it away. But he was already scrambling the papers into his coat pocket, and rushing round the room, picking up Jane's discarded jumper and her sponge bag and her hairbrush, jamming them anyhow into her bag. He couldn't stay here any longer and he couldn't bear the thought of bringing Jane back here tonight. He couldn't stay in this room or this hotel or this town. He'd find her and take them both away, before anything happened.

The terror swept down on him as he bent over her bag. He pushed the last items into it and, humming the 'Cwm Rhondda' to try and keep his breathing steady, he hoisted a bag under each arm and half ran to the door of the cabin.

The woman at reception was annoyed and insisted on sending her husband to check the room while Gwyn paid.

'So what's wrong with it?' she said for the third time as he signed the bill. 'What makes you change your mind like that? We won't be getting anyone else in for that cabin at this time of the evening. You said you'd stay two days.'

'No we didn't,' said Gwyn. 'We said tonight. And I'm paying you, aren't I?'

'You bet you are. You surely don't think you can come into our cabin and use the facilities and leave without paying? We don't do things like that in this country.'

'I need to find someone's address,' said Gwyn. 'Do you have a telephone directory you can lend me?'

'This isn't an information bureau. Hey, what about your wife? Are you walking out on your wife? Is that what this is?'

'I'm trying to find my wife, for God's sake. That's why I need this address. That's where she went this morning. Please,' he said, speaking with exaggerated politeness, 'would you be so very kind as to lend me your telephone directory or tell me where I can find one? It will save us both a lot of trouble.'

The woman reluctantly brought out a thick book from beneath the desk.

'Look in it right here,' she said, as if she suspected Gwyn of running off with it.

Archer, As, Bs, Cs . . . what was the woman's first name? Jacqueline? Penelope? Something like that. Jennifer. Yes, a J; here were the Js . . . Gwyn got the correct change out of the hostile but by now rather curious woman and went to the telephone kiosk on the other side of the lobby.

The first J Archer was Jock. But the second was a woman, with a well enunciated, rather rasping voice. As soon as Gwyn asked if she was Miss Jennifer Archer there was a silence.

'Gwyn Thomas,' the voice said eventually. 'I know you by your accent.'

'Miss Archer,' said Gwyn. 'Is Jane with you?'

'No. She hasn't been here for some time – not since midday.'

Was it Gwyn's imagination or did the voice sound uneasy? 'Where are you, Gwyn?'

'I'm at the Rebelle Hotel.'

'Have you been there all day?'

'Yes, but I'm leaving now. And I want to find Jane. Where's she gone? Is she with Sam?'

'I imagine so,' said Miss Archer. 'No. I – I know so. They were going to meet in a bar called Eddie's, on Toller Street. But that was early afternoon, so they might be back at the reservation now. Gwyn, would you come to see me? I can drive you to the reservation afterwards.'

'No,' said Gwyn flatly. 'I won't. I've got to find Jane. What did you tell her? What do you know about this?'

'Please come and see me. Or let me drive over to you. We can talk on the way to the reservation.'

'No!' Gwyn didn't know why, but the fear had him so strongly now that it was making him shake. 'Tell me now. If you know something, tell me, it's the least you can do. There's no time.'

'I've been thinking and thinking all afternoon, ever since she left. I don't know if I could have stopped it. I truly do not, Gwyn.'

'What happened to Haydn Phillips?'

'He told Madoc's story, just like you're doing. But he wasn't as strong as you, Gwyn.'

'You don't even know me.'

'I know what Jane says about you. And I've read some of your poems. Mr Jenkins must be very proud of you. He recognised that you'd be the one, you see, just as I recognised it in Jane.'

Gwyn felt the sky begin to crumple and rain down on him.

'You know Goff? Miss Archer, you and Goff have known each other all along?'

'Oh no, not *all* along. We exchanged letters years ago, when Haydn went back to Wales, and then Mr Jenkins wrote to me when Haydn died. Mr Jenkins wasn't involved, Gwyn. He was only an onlooker, someone who tried to assist Haydn after it had happened. He came to know the story through Haydn's side of it and I told him then that it happens every generation, that there'd be another one. I shouldn't have told him anything, I know, but it was such a relief to be believed and not to be judged.

We promised each other we'd try and stop it next time, if we saw it coming; if we thought we knew who it might be.'

'And you did.'

'I tried – a little. Perhaps not enough.'

'That's more than Goff did,' said Gwyn bitterly. 'Wasn't it? I suppose he wrote and kept you informed, did he? Of the experiment?'

'No,' said Miss Archer. 'We never wrote to one another again. Except for a month ago, just after you and Jane had returned from Wales. I received a letter from Mr Jenkins then, out of the blue, after such a long time. He said that he believed you were the one after all, and that he'd tried to prepare you. He asked me to help you if I could.'

'But you can't.'

'I can't tell you anything you don't already know. Except that, Gwyn, each time there's a choice. Choose well.'

'Choose what?' Gwyn shouted desperately but the line had gone dead.

Get a grip on yourself, mon, thought Gwyn to himself. But it was hard to stay calm while you were running. He tried to force his pace to slow, but whenever he got down to a walk he would lengthen his stride and speed up until he found he was running again.

His brain couldn't make sense of what was happening. He didn't believe in this sentimental occult stuff. The surface, rational part of his brain was wrangling with Miss Archer and Goff and Sam as he rushed through the dark streets, rehearsing arguments, telling them why they were wrong and sloppy-minded to think what they did. But a lower, deeper part of his brain knew. He was not in control any more – oh Christ, had he ever been? And there was danger in it, for him and for Jane.

The way through the Commercial District seemed much longer than Gwyn remembered from this morning. But then, he was running blind; he hadn't bothered to stop and orientate himself before he left the hotel. He had turned several times in the direction he thought would lead to the reservation, but he was still in the grid of office and warehouse-lined streets. There was a man loading some boxes into a car on the corner of a side street;

Gwyn jogged across and got directions: left up Second Avenue and then bear right at the top, keep going till you see the lights.

Second Avenue took him out of the Commercial District and across the edge of a windswept, semi-derelict street. There were kids gathered outside a monstrous blue and yellow legoland building, and some drunks either going into or coming out of a bar – he couldn't tell which. The street sign caught his eye: Toller Street. This was where Jane had misspent her adolescence. He took the right hand fork of the road and walked steadily away from Toller Street, along an ill-lit carriageway. The sharp air grazing his face told him that the lake was near and the collection of lights ahead in the blackness must be the reservation.

Gwyn felt ashamed of his fear. These were people, after all, like himself. Very like himself, if you believed Goff's theory. He tried for an ironic chuckle as he looked around, fortifying himself: he was standing on a tarmac road, in the middle of grass, just like any road leading into a Welsh village. But he couldn't imagine anything less like his home country than the line of trailers ahead of him and the blocks of tongue-and-groove houses to the right, and the openness, the naked exposure that he felt, standing here on this land.

Sam lived in a trailer, he knew that much. He just had to ask which one. A pang of pure cowardice kept him from moving as the possibilities of what he might find crowded his mind. Then he forced himself to walk on towards the line of caravans. He hesitated by the first: he could hear loud radio music and several voices coming from within. His nerve failed him and he walked on again; the second trailer was dark. He moved back on to the tarmac road and then, further ahead, in a pool of light cast from an oblong window, he saw a man. He was big and grey-haired, wearing a heavy jacket over something bulky. He stood stooped forward, his arms wrapped round each other, as if he'd been there a long time and was trying to keep warm. His head was turned towards Gwyn and, though Gwyn couldn't see his features, he suddenly knew that this was Willie.

The older man stood watching as he walked up the line of trailers and only finally, when Gwyn was in the shadow of the next trailer down, did he step out of the light to meet him.

They looked at one another, close together in the darkness.

Willie was Goff's age or older but a much fitter man. Age had hardly shrunk him at all and his bulky shoulders and arms spoke of strength, and possible violence.

Gwyn gazed up into the unforgiving face. This man might once have been as handsome as Sam but now his features were set hard; disappointment and the long exertion of his will had taken all the mobility out of them.

'I'm Gwyn.' He spoke quietly, to stop his words from carrying into the lighted trailer.

Willie didn't reply; there was only the faintest twitch of his eyelids, that might have meant surprise or scorn.

'I've come for Jane.'

The older man shook his head.

'You can't have her,' he said, and to Gwyn's surprise his voice was just like any other elderly, mid-western male's. 'You can go in there but you can't bring her back out.'

'What the hell do you mean?'

'You're just like them all,' said Willie, his voice clipped with contempt. 'You think you're in control, don't you?'

'No,' said Gwyn. 'Not any more than you are.'

'But we are,' said Willie. 'Shame on Sam, didn't he tell you? This time we are.'

'Oh yes? How's that?'

Willie dug his hands deep into his pockets.

'Go on in,' he said. 'Get along, you – what are you this time? A poet? – go on in Mr Poet and get better acquainted with your creation.'

Gwyn had never heard anything like the emotion in Willie's last words: it was hatred, but pure, almost transcendent, a hatred which had been felt for so long that it was like the oxygen in Willie's lungs or the sun on his face. It made Gwyn's pulse die.

Willie stepped aside, leaving the way clear for Gwyn to reach the door of the lighted trailer. And he didn't look at him again; instead he resumed watching the trailer itself, as if he were settling in for the night.

Gwyn had to force himself to walk through Willie's body space; his flesh seemed to shrink into itself as he did so. He didn't know if he was frightened of the man or of himself or of what he was about to find. He shook his head desperately, then jumped up the trailer steps in one leap and banged loudly and urgently on the door.

It was Jane who opened it.

Everything was wrong: Gwyn knew it as soon as he stepped into the trailer. He had expected trouble, but not this kind; not the yellow lamplight and the warm reds and oranges of the cushions and Sam in a big dark jumper with the sleeves pushed up, and Jane leaning against the kitchenette cupboard, perfectly at home, pouring him a bourbon. The trailer wasn't the drab metal box he'd had in mind; it was cosy and there was intimacy here.

Jane's face was softened and she met his eyes over the glass with a look that made him afraid: it was a deep, strong look, full of complicated things. She seemed to have made up her mind to tell him something; oh God, he didn't think there'd be any prizes for guessing what.

'We've been waiting for you,' Jane was saying. 'Come on, take this. You're behind.'

'You can say that again,' said Gwyn. 'I reckon I've always been way behind you two.'

'What do you mean?'

'Oh, save it.'

Gwyn shook his head wearily and shrugged, letting the bags fall to the floor. Jane focused on them for the first time.

'What are they doing here?'

'I've checked us out.'

'Sweetheart, why?'

Jane was frowning but her confidence was undimmed. Gwyn looked across to the bench seat by the table where Sam sat. He was toying with his glass and his wrists and forearms, exposed in the lamplight, looked vulnerable. He was watching Jane and Gwyn closely and making no effort to disguise it.

Gwyn rubbed his hand across his eyes, a child's gesture. He was tired and momentarily bewildered. There was something in Sam's expression he couldn't place. A pain was gathering in his heart, stopping him from thinking clearly. What was it Willie had said?

He gestured the glass away.

'I'd close the curtain if I were you,' he said to Sam.

Sam gazed at him unwelcomingly. 'Meaning?'

'Meaning your favourite uncle's outside, looking in.'

Sam couldn't contain a nervous start. His glance flickered to the window, then to Jane and now Gwyn saw that it was a febrile glance. Jane shook her head at Sam reassuringly, lovingly even. The pressure on Gwyn's heart increased.

'He can't have been there long,' Jane said. 'He wasn't out there when I looked before.'

'Maybe not,' said Sam. 'All the same . . .' He got up quickly, took two strides across the trailer and yanked the curtains closed.

He looked, thought Gwyn, half hunted and half sly. But who was the slyness for – Willie outside or Gwyn inside? Or Jane? But he didn't want to think about Sam and Jane. Belatedly, Gwyn lurched towards the glass which Jane had now put down on the cupboard, and slugged the bourbon.

Jane flinched, though at what he couldn't tell.

'What's the matter?' he asked. 'Things not going as planned?'

'I don't have anything planned,' said Jane steadfastly. 'Do you?'

'Do I?' Gwyn stared at her. He laughed, an incredulous, high sound. 'That's a good one. I'm Mr Way Behind, remember? Sam's the boy for planning, aren't you Sam?'

'If you're going to pick a fight,' said Sam, 'sit down and do it.' But his cheekbones were stained red and his voice shook.

'Scared, are we?' said Gwyn. 'Or just excited?'

'Gwyn,' said Jane suddenly. 'Why did you check us out of the hotel?'

Gwyn looked at her, vibrant in front of him.

Because we're in danger and we've got to get out.

He might have said it but he didn't. He couldn't. The sight of Jane glowing with this new sureness in Sam's company killed the words even before they rose into his throat.

Everything was wrong. There was danger here, he could feel it all around them. The warmly lit oblong trailer pulsed with it. But jealousy was closing on his heart and he kept silent.

With the silence came anger: a lovely pure, clarifying anger that flooded through him and washed clean his bewildered eyes.

So, finally, at long last, it had come to this: Jane standing in front of him, with her lover within arm's reach, and dishonesty in her face.

Jane was a liar. Well, that wasn't so surprising, was it? It wasn't an hour ago that he'd learned that Goff, his old teacher and protector, had all along been withholding the truth. And of course, he'd always suspected Sam was a liar.

The funny thing was, of course, that the victim of lies – once his eyes were opened – knew more than the deceivers. In bits and pieces maybe, and not for very long, but at this moment Gwyn knew that his bitter understanding put him ahead.

'Let's play a game,' he said, looking straight into Jane's eyes. 'Let's play poker. Truth poker.'

Jane's confidence had gone now. She tried to smile.

'You've got cards here Sam, haven't you?' Gwyn insisted, still looking at Jane.

'Sure,' said Sam. On the edge of his vision, Gwyn saw him move to a drawer and fetch them.

'And you can play poker?'

'I can play.'

'And I'm sure you taught Jane, back in your glory days. Well my wife, what do you say?'

Jane was reaching out for him anxiously. 'Go sit down, sweetheart.'

'What, sit while my lady's standing? What's the matter?' Gwyn added as Jane stood motionless, suddenly very white. 'Got no time for old fashioned courtesy, have you? Or is it being called a lady that upsets you?'

'Shut up, Gwyn, you're acting crazy.'

Jane spoke stiffly, as if she couldn't work her mouth.

'Oh, I don't think so,' said Gwyn politely. He was coasting on his anger now, perversely enjoying himself. 'Have you and Sam got any objection to the truth?'

'No. Of course not.'

'What about you, my brother in arms?'

Sam was sitting back down, shuffling a pack of cards, his eyes moving from Jane to Gwyn. His face was as bright and clear as a child's.

'I'm all for the truth,' he said. 'At last.'

'Well, good.' Gwyn smiled, putting his hand on Jane's back. 'Let's gather round this table, then, settle ourselves – here you are, my lady, be seated – and I'll explain the game. We used to play this in my old school, we called it bluff poker back then. We deal three cards a person, one face up, two down, and we bet on what we've got. No pick up. The betting just goes on our existing hands. We used to bet cigarettes; now we'll bet questions and answers, shall we? Oh look, he's bringing us the bottle too. Thanks, brother. Cut the cards, Jane. That's right. So, three handed poker with the stakes being the truth. The value of the questions, and the answers, goes up in tens. You deal, Sam, my brother in arms, you deal.'

Jane sat back against the bench seat cushion and held her cards close to her. On her right Sam was relaxed, studying his cards with his elbows on the table. Opposite her, Gwyn had glanced once at his hand and stacked the cards face down on the table, his hand covering them. His eyes gleamed at her and she couldn't tell if they were teasing or malicious.

Jane was struggling to hold on to her equilibrium. The strength she had felt earlier, the certainty of knowing who she was, had been shattered by Gwyn suddenly calling her 'my lady'. The words and the way he spoke them reminded her not just of the poems but of things beyond conscious recall, things she knew she lived through in her dreams.

She had thought she and the woman were reconciled. But now she wasn't sure. Gwyn had walked in here, watched her through narrowed eyes, and now seemed to be diverting the flow of her energy into a course of his own devising.

She was aware of the woman's fear again, clawing at the edges of her mind. She drew on her new strength to keep it out, but she could still feel it, tearing away little strips of her composure, ripping at her courage.

She moved her left arm convulsively; it knocked against the side of the kitchenette cupboard. Gwyn had seated her carefully, she realised: to leave her seat she would have to climb past first Sam, then him.

'Study your cards, Jane cariad,' said Gwyn.

Jane looked at her hand. She had a three, a Jack and a five, all different suits. She'd been dealt a low hand, one that couldn't possibly win, and there would be no pick up to come. Yet she had to bet. This was poker without chance, Jane realised; a static

442

battle of wills. She didn't know why she'd agreed to it, except that there hadn't seemed any option.

'Your call, Gwyn,' said Sam.

'Fifty dollar question,' said Gwyn immediately and looked at Jane.

Jane stared down at her cards. Gwyn was playing high. Of course he was; there were some things he badly wanted to ask. OK, then, let him win, as quickly as possible, and ask his first question. She knew what it would be anyway; all she had to do was decide whether or not to confess the answer.

'I'm out,' she said.

Gwyn raised his eyebrows. 'So easily? Giving in can be dangerous, you know.'

'I'll raise you,' said Sam. 'A hundred.'

Gwyn hesitated. He hadn't glanced at his cards again after the first time. He looked instead at Sam; Jane thought he was trying to gauge Sam's intentions. Sam returned his look steadily.

'A hundred and fifty,' said Gwyn.

'Two hundred,' said Sam.

Gwyn smiled.

'I'll see you.'

Sam put down his hand: three aces. Jane choked on her bourbon. Knowing Sam's skills, she had wondered whether he'd cheat, but she hadn't expected him to be so blatant.

Gwyn removed his hand from his cards and flipped them over, showing three twos. He gave a twisted smile.

'A bit insulting,' he said. 'Am I supposed to let you get away with that?'

'My game,' said Sam.

'You cheated.'

'Prove it.'

The atmosphere in the trailer was suddenly dangerous. It occurred to Jane that when Gwyn was angry, fear chilled her but seemed not to touch Sam. But when Sam was angry, suddenly all three of them teetered on a knife edge of violence.

Gwyn looked at Jane; his eyes were hot and hard.

'Ask your question,' he said bitterly.

Sam scooped up the cards and riffled them in a lazy cascade;

they fluttered back down to the table top with a gentle flap – flap – flap.

'My question is, Gwyn Thomas, Poet . . . what did you write today?'

Jane gripped her hands together under the table.

'Not that!' she said impetuously. They both looked at her: Sam sharply, Gwyn with suspicion.

'What's the matter?' he said. 'Afraid of what you'll hear?'

'Yes.'

'That's interesting. Who are you afraid *for*, though? Yourself? Brother-in-your-arms here? Surely not for your husband?'

Jane held his stare, trying to get through to him. 'For all of us.'

'Oh balls,' said Gwyn. 'I think you're having second thoughts about what you've done. Well, it's too late now, my lady.'

'Why do you keep calling me that?' Jane's cry was unexpectedly loud in the still trailer.

'Sorry, his lady. No, you're not really his lady, though, are you? You're not anyone's. You're for yourself.' He turned to Sam. 'Sorry to disappoint you, brother-in-her-arms, but that's the way it is. I've realised that now. And that's why I'll tell you what happens in today's instalment. Are you both sitting comfortably? Then I'll begin.

'Today, my good friend Madoc, having taken the measure of his wife, decides that his future lies elsewhere. He becomes betrothed to a rather lovely young woman from the Bird People – his Indian pal's old sweetheart in fact.'

A shudder ran through Jane's body, so deep she felt her bones would splinter. Was it herself or the woman? She couldn't tell; she could only feel the terrible, bone deep pain.

Through the misery, she saw Gwyn smiling at Sam. Sam sat unmoving for a minute, then he picked up the cards again and handed them to Gwyn to shuffle and deal.

Jane picked up her new cards with numb hands. She stared at them for several seconds, then, as the cards began to tremble in her fingers, she realised that she couldn't just sit here and let events overtake her. She had promised to fight and she would; she had to try and win this hand and stay on top of things.

444

Two eights and a three: not a great hand, but she could win with it. If Sam didn't cheat.

She began the betting cautiously; Sam pushed it up; Gwyn matched Sam. She went up again; Sam matched.

It was at this point that Jane saw Sam realise she was playing in earnest. She felt his eyes on her, appraising, and she searched his face, trying to discover his emotions. Was he frightened; was that why he was forcing the pace? Was he fighting Gwyn for her? Or was he fighting her?

She didn't know; she couldn't tell any of it, and it was a horrible, disorienting realisation.

Jane called on the tenth bet: all three of them looked down at the cards as they showed. She had won.

She raised her eyes to Sam, then to Gwyn. They were both motionless, hardly breathing, waiting for her question. Help me, she prayed to the woman, help me ask the right one.

She gazed at Gwyn's shuttered face. She couldn't bear to ask about Madoc; she couldn't bear to ask a question about Gwyn himself. Do you still love me? It was rising from her heart to her lips, but she couldn't part them and speak. She didn't dare, for fear of the answer.

Looking from Gwyn to Sam, concentrating hard, she thought of the birds. They were what lay at the heart of all this; they were what made Sam so afraid, and what crowded Gwyn's poems though he denied it, and shadowed her own dreams. Even as she thought of them now, she could feel the terrified woman shrink further. She turned to Gwyn.

'What do the birds mean in your poems?'

There was a long silence, during which Gwyn gazed into Jane's eyes and through them, seeing things she couldn't, and didn't want to see.

He gave a little half smile finally, tinged with surprise.

'They mean – ' he said, and his voice, suddenly lower, sent a thrill through Jane ' – destruction.'

No, thought Jane, pushing the answer away even as she struggled to understand it. No, please God, no. But she knew it was right: inside her mind she could feel the woman tensing, crouching, trying to hide herself in the shadows.

Gwyn sat opposite her, with that awful look of surprise and satisfaction on his face.

'Yep,' he said, 'that's it, mon. Destruction; the power to destroy.' His voice became conversational. 'You've got to have it, you know, I've always known that. You've got to have it and you've got to be willing to use it, otherwise the buggers grind you down.'

Watching him, Jane wondered how she could have missed it until now. She had been so stupid – she'd put it down to being a writer, to his passion for his work. But it wasn't just that: there was a streak of ruthlessness in Gwyn. He'd had to fight for what he wanted, always, Goff had told her that much. But what Goff hadn't added was what she now realised: when Gwyn fought, he won.

Why hadn't Goff warned her of that? Loyalty to Gwyn? Love for him? Yes, both of those, of course; but also, perhaps, because he didn't want to face what Gwyn was capable of.

'Goff.' She didn't realise she'd said his name aloud until she saw Sam's face turn to her, and Gwyn's eyes focus on hers once more, sharp and shiny. 'Goff,' she said again. Gwyn's eyelashes swept down and he chuckled softly.

'Dear, dear,' he said in a very Welsh accent.

'Gwyn, what really happened between you and Goff?' Jane's voice was shaking. 'What's the truth in that story about you and him? Why did you leave his house?'

Gwyn pushed out his lower lip.

'What the hell would you know?' he said defiantly. 'You don't know what it was like living with him, being sucked dry by him. Every bloody day, every bloody night, the old stories, the old songs, the old poets, Christ, he nearly sent me off my head. And not a word of praise, or even acknowledgement, for anything that came from me. Nothing – I couldn't do anything right for him unless it was words he put in my mouth; he wouldn't let me live, Jane, he didn't think I was worth anything on my own . . .'

Gwyn's voice had changed from defiance to pain, a raw pain that filled Jane with pity.

'I didn't mean the rumours to go that far. I just thought it would help me get away. I just wanted him off my back.'

Since he'd begun talking about Goff, Gwyn hadn't looked up

from the table. Jane gazed at his bent head and felt the weight of his guilt, tasted the old shame.

'And you never told them it was you who started the rumours all along.'

'I tried! I did try! I told everyone it wasn't true, I even said I might have accidentally given the wrong impression. It was just too late.'

Gwyn's voice had gone high like a little boy's. Now he wrenched his head up and glared at Jane and Sam, and they both saw that his eyes were red and shining with tears.

'Oh, what the fuck do either of *you* know?' he said despairingly. 'We're all liars and traitors, the lot of us. You, my bloody wife, you've spent the whole afternoon fucking your old boyfriend here. And God knows how many times you've done it before, and what you've told him about me. And you, my brother my enemy, I expect you think she loves you? But she hasn't been in touch much over the last twelve years, has she? And she didn't waste much time between meeting me and marrying me. And you, cariad,' – he jerked his head back to Jane – 'I bet you don't know the reason he's brought you back. I bet he hasn't told you what he and Willie have cooked up between them?'

Jane looked at Sam. He was listening carefully, leaning forward on his elbows.

'What do you mean?'

'Ask Sam. Ask the uncle's nephew. Do you know what Willie's doing out there? I couldn't work it out at first, but now I see: he's standing guard on you. Sam's got you here and you've got me here and Willie's making sure we stay. Do you know what he said to me as I came in? He said "Shame on Sam, hasn't he told you? We're in control this time."'

Jane watched Gwyn's furious, tear-stained face, and Sam's relaxed one. Her thoughts were slow to come; it was difficult to concentrate with the claws piercing deep into her mind, scratching, gouging.

'Sam?'

Sam began collecting the cards. 'So we don't play any more' he said.

Surely, thought Jane, Sam wouldn't hurt me. But after w she'd just learnt about Gwyn, she wasn't sure of anything.

'Sam, look at me.'

He did so, easily. But Jane saw that his eyes were no longer clear.

'Oh Jesus,' she whispered. Then she struggled to get her voice back to normal; someone had to be reasonable, someone had to resist this vortex of fear and suspicion which seemed to be sucking them all in. 'Listen Sam,' she said. 'I want to know what's happening. Before Gwyn came, you said – you said he'd bring the dark bird in. You said it would be the end. What did you mean?'

Sam shuffled the cards quickly, skilfully, but didn't answer.

'Miss Archer!' said Jane, fighting down panic. 'That's it, I should have listened to her. She said it, this morning. She said you have to tell me the truth. But you didn't, did you? Why not?'

'You didn't ask, till now,' said Sam, biting his lip. 'I guess you had other things on your mind.'

Jane couldn't look at Gwyn. 'Well, I'm asking now.'

Sam's hand continued to shuffle the cards, his long fingers moving compulsively around the deck.

'I'm sorry,' he said at length. 'I didn't mean to hurt you. In spite of Willie, I never held you responsible. And when the birds began to come, I didn't look for you straight off. I tried to keep away.

'But it was too strong for me. And Willie said it was my duty, as keeper of the story, to find you.'

'Keeper of the story,' whispered Jane. 'That's what Miss Archer called you this morning. What does it mean?'

'Just that I know the secret story. About – the woman. There are keepers of the story every generation but if you believe what Willie says, then – I'm the last.'

Jane clenched her teeth and dug her elbows into her sides trying to ignore the sudden accelerated scrabble of fear. She didn't know the significance of what Sam had said, but Gwyn's head was up, like an alert dog's, his tear tracks gleaming faintly.

'Good God, mon,' he murmured. 'The last keeper. The last keeper of the First Man's story. The Last Man.'

'That's what they say.'

'Who says? I don't understand,' said Jane sharply.

'I told you the story of the First Man and Woman,' said Sam. began tearing at the edges of the topmost card. 'You know that they sent the Dark Bird away, and that things have been wrong ever since. The story says that things will never be right again for the Mandans till the spirit of the Bird is restored, and restored by a White Mandan.

'Like Jennifer told you, someone tries to set it right in each generation, and it never, never works. But the keepers of the story have always said that one day the spirit will be restored. The First Man and Woman sent the Bird away; they say that the one who brings its spirit back will be called the Last Man.

'Our nation has run right out, Jane,' Sam went on quietly. 'You know that. Remember those discussion classes we had at school on the poor old dying out American Indian tribes? We always knew there were only a few of us left with any Mandan blood at all. There are kids being born now with Mandan blood, sure; even here on the reservation. But not White Mandan, that's all gone. I'm the last White Mandan – the Last Man.' Slowly, he met her eyes. 'I don't know,' his voice was scarcely audible, 'I never knew if I believed it, but now, since I saw that thing outside the window . . .'

Scratch, scratch, scratch. Scrabble scrabble. The claws were scoring her mind now, eroding it faster and deeper, mazing it with fear. The Last Man. She could see it now, as she looked at Sam's lean face, watching the play of muscles and bone under his skin. The Last Man. That was what Miss Archer had tried, confusedly, to warn her about. That was what Sam had meant when he said, 'I'm sorry for what I've done.'

As if she were watching a film, she saw Gwyn take the cards from Sam's hands and put them down on the table. He was gazing at Sam intently and when he finally spoke, his voice was avid.

'Why have you brought Jane here? Tell me what you want with her.'

'You know what I want,' said Sam. 'I don't pretend otherwi But it's something else that's brought her back here, not me.'

Gwyn thought for a while, his eyes on the bourbon bottle. he nodded. 'We've come this far . . .' he said.

He and Sam exchanged a long look. In Sam's face dre flicted with longing; Gwyn's cheeks grew slowly flushed a he turned towards Jane he was breathing fast.

'Come on, cariad,' he said softly. 'You know what we have to do, don't you?'

Jane shrank into her chair.

'What do you mean?'

'We have to go on and find out what happens.'

'No. We can't – it's too dangerous!'

'We can't avoid it. And I don't want to. Besides, I think you owe Sam and me a favour each, don't you?'

'No.' Jane's voice was cracked. 'Sam, tell him how the birds scare you. You said if he brought the Bird in it would be the end . . . oh no, please. What's he doing?'

Across the table Gwyn was unfolding a wad of paper from his breast pocket, a wad of closely written paper. They were his poems; all of them, folded in together. He had come to the trailer carrying them next to his heart. He set about turning the sheets till he found a blank side and then he took out a pen. He glanced up and Jane saw that although his face had softened, it wasn't with love or forgiveness; instead, his eyes were rapt in the familiar, mesmerised way. And yet as she stared in horror, he stretched his left hand across the table and pressed it inconsequentially against her cheek.

'Don't look like that, cariad,' he said. 'You do see, don't you? I have to write the poems, so that you can dream them. Because it's only when you dream them that things move on. And things must move on because there's a lot waiting to happen. Old Sam here has to have his last chance. And I have to complete my work. You do see that.'

'Gwyn, I love you.'

'There's no time for that now, cariad.'

Jane could hardly bear to look at his preoccupied face, alight with a tenderness which had nothing to do with her. He brushed away her avowal impatiently.

'Sssh Jane,' he said. 'You really mustn't hold me up. She's got ᵈot to do, and she's got to move fast.'

'Who?'

'e. Madoc's woman. My narrator.'

' put her hands up to her head. Now there was no escape,
ᵉ to shelter or hide. Sam moved on to the bench seat and
ᵐs tightly round her.

'No, no, no,' she whispered.

'I'm here with you,' said Sam. 'I'll keep you safe. Gwyn's right – we can't avoid it, we have to go on.'

'Of course we do,' said Gwyn, his head bent to the page. 'No Jane, don't say anything. Don't come between a man and his work. There's nothing more important than a man's work, didn't you know that? No, you probably didn't. There you've been, getting in on my poems, and Sam's special secret. Coming between Sam and me, keeping us apart when we could have been working together. I tell you, you shouldn't have done that. But there – I needn't tell you. You'll find out for yourself now.'

36

There's dark, the wood is – terribly dark. We can hardly see where to walk: I'm stumbling with my arms stretched out in front of me feeling my way against bark, twigs, something soft and fine in the air – a spider's web. And I can hear nothing but the sobbing of my breath and Glesig's and the rolling sounds the stones make under our feet.

I can't think. My breast is bursting but I can't stop to breathe: if I stop, the pain just goes deeper.

Oh Duw, why is there no noise? It was comforting when I thought they might be chasing us. Then I wanted to get away. Then my chest and my head burned to escape.

But there's nobody following us in here. There's no one coming after us. There's just the two of us, in the stillness.

My breath is coming in huge gasps. It fills my ears: good, no room to speak. No room to think.

'Ceinwen, give me your hand.'

Glesig is turned towards me, panting. I can't see his face properly.

'No. I don't need it.'

'Where are you going?'

'On.'

'lease, Ceinwen, take my hand. I want you to.'

an against a tree. Reluctantly, I stretch out my left hand

l Glesig's touch.

ne's coming,' says Glesig. He sobs the words; his whole

body's heaving, trying to get breath. Being tied up has made him weak. 'There's no need to run.'

'I know.'

'Madoc didn't try and stop us. He's let us go.'

Glesig sounds quite wondering, as if Madoc's been very good to us. Doesn't he realise?

'Madoc doesn't want us any more,' I tell him. 'He's finished with us.'

But Glesig goes on talking, as if he hasn't heard.

'He's set me free,' he says wonderingly. 'Free to go with you.'

'He doesn't *want* us any more,' I repeat furiously. I can feel my face crumpling up like a leaf being burned in the fire. I grit my teeth and press down and down, but I can't stop myself trembling.

'No, he wants Rokai,' says Glesig. 'My Rokai. He wants to show that he's beaten me, he's taking revenge.'

'What for?'

'Because he loves us.'

I laugh, a loud, mad laugh.

'There's funny. I thought he only loved power. Isn't that why he's marrying Rokai?'

'No. He doesn't need to marry anyone. He has all the power he needs over my people by holding the dreamstone. No one will touch him because of the curse on taking it by force – and while he holds it he can do what he likes with them.'

The curse; I shut my eyes wearily – I don't want to have to look at this truth which I can now see.

'He took it from me, knowing I'd stolen it from you,' I whisper. 'He wouldn't take it from you himself because he knew about the curse. But he accepted it from me and said not one word of warning.'

Glesig's hand tightens on mine and I can feel the weals Madoc's cords have left on them.

'Don't blame him too much. The stone has maddened him, it' made him cruel to the people he loves.'

'Cruel! Dear God, cruel would be to beat me and humil: me, the way he did on the swamp river. It's more than cru let your woman do what you don't dare!'

'I think he dared,' says Glesig quietly. 'If he had to. B

gave him a way of avenging himself on you. He's a jealous, passionate man, Ceinwen; he suspected you and he wanted to break you.'

'And now he wants to make me into his slave. Duw, how he must hate me.'

'Yes, he hates you. And he loves you too. And that's our chance. It's our hope, Ceinwen. We must plan on that.'

His words trickle through to me slowly. I lift my head and stare at him. Glesig's eyes meet mine in the dark, bright with defiance.

'What kind of plan? There's nothing we can do against him.'

'There is. We must get the stone.'

'Sweet grey mother, listen to him! Get the stone? How?'

'If we get the stone, we can restore it to its place. It belongs here, in this wood, by the sacred spring. It's been gone so long – ' For a second Glesig's voice is ashamed, then he goes on urgently: 'We must get it. Madoc means to use the stone against my people, you know he does. There'll be no limit to what he'll do – he's gone past caring. We must get it away from him.'

'We can't! He's surrounded by men at arms. If we go back there we'll be killed. And even if we could get it – I know Madoc. He'd marry Rokai tomorrow anyway.'

'But he wouldn't have the stone. Ceinwen, if Rokai is the wife of the man who uses the dreamstone that way, she'll be damned. All her children will be damned. The destroying will carry down the generations and never stop and when she dies, she'll never rest.'

'I see,' I say. 'You want me to save Rokai, is that it?'

'Yes. And me. And you. We both stole the stone Ceinwen. We're both cursed till it's back in its place.'

I press my hands to my forehead; I feel dizzy with all this.

'Well, Glesig. Have you got a plan, then? How are we going to get this stone?'

Glesig reaches out and begins to play with a piece of my hair. His eyes are shamed.

'There's one chance. He loves you. He hates you and he loves

re's something in his voice that makes me stare at him.

'Duw, you still love him as well. How can you, after all he's done to you?'

Glesig shrugs.

'The three of us have always been dangerous for each other.'

'Go on.'

Glesig stares at my hair and twines it round his fingers.

'It's – for you to do. If you go back to the camp, I believe Madoc will take you in. If you go back and pretend to repent. He'll punish you but I don't believe he'll kill you.'

Staring, I am; staring at Glesig's bent head and his hand, twisting this way, fanning out the strands of my hair.

'You want me,' I say slowly, 'to go back down there tonight.'

'Yes,' says Glesig simply.

'You want me to ask Madoc's pardon. Throw myself on his mercy. And find some way to get the dreamstone away from him.'

'He'll want to sleep with you tonight.' Glesig raises his head and looks straight at me now. 'He'll want that, to confirm his power and his triumph. That will be your chance.'

Am I mad to hope? After all that's happened to me, and brought me here to this great danger, am I crazed to dream of lying in Madoc's arms again?

'If I get the stone away, where will I take it?'

'Bring it here. I'll wait for you. We'll go to the top of the Hill together, to the sacred place. They'll come in the morning – you're right, Madoc will still come. And so will my people. And we'll be there waiting for them, with the stone.'

I watch him thoughtfully. The shamed look is still on him but he's hopeful too. He drops my hair and clasps my hands in his.

'Ceinwen, you do see, don't you? If we hold the stone tomorrow, everything will be changed. We'll be honoured people. We'll be able to ask for things and have them. The marriage will no have to go ahead.'

I laugh, trying to still my heart.

'What, no marriage at all?' I say mockingly.

Glesig smiles.

'You're shaking, great lady.'

'I'm frightened, Glesig.'

The feast is already well advanced. They lost no time, then. The big fire is blazing, throwing a bright glow over the people who are gathered in a loose circle around it. Some of them are dancing; others are listening to the women playing the crwths or to the story-tellers. I can see Madoc, with the high kindred in horseshoe shape around him: standing in the crescent is a man — I think it's Iolo, the Conwy bard. Hard at work all day he's been making up tonight's praise poem. He'll have had to add a new element at the last moment: Our New Princess.

They haven't seen me yet. I know where the look-outs are and I've kept away from them, coming down the Hill in the darkest parts, where neither moonlight nor firelight reaches. I don't want them to see me until I'm on them. Madoc might have given orders for me to be taken on sight, tied up and hidden away like Glesig was. Or even killed: I don't know what he's capable of doing, any more.

I'm off the Hill now, on a level with the camp. I can't get from here to the fire unseen. The only thing to do is to try and pass as one of the serf women. I must hide my hair. If I pull my cloak up over my head to make a hood like the serf women wear and hold the rest of the cloak out in front of me like an apron — yes, that will do, and over there is brushwood, which I can pile on to my apron cloak, and bend my face over it, labouring along.

Now, walk fast but not too fast to the edge of the camp . . . the look-out has seen me, he's watching. I can't tell who it is from here and I don't dare lift my face.

'What are you doing over there?' he shouts, as I come within earshot.

'Collecting wood, what do you think?' I call back, making my voice hoarse.

'Well, tell someone you're going next time.'

He's a young man, one of the serfs himself, from Gwent I think. He peers at me as I go past, but the piled up branches hide everything but my eyes. All the same, he looks hard and hesitates. A smile crosses his face but he says nothing and I walk on, past the other look-out who nods at me, and to the edge of the people. Quickly now, working my way through them without . I have to get through so many, all in my way, feasting and drinking the last of the wine. Several of the groups have an ik-ho-map-kee going round, the people sucking in the smoke through the narrow tube.

'Watch it,' a woman says angrily as I drop wood on her.

I'm near Madoc's group now. Through my bundle of wood I can see Marged standing next to Ko-ka, and Elen further up and then the men, seated on the ground – Morddyn, Rhos, Gran and the Hellynt brothers. And in the middle of them is Madoc, with Wenlyn on one side of him and little blonde Heledd on the other. Madoc's looking up at the bard – his eyes are fixed on him, dark and bright, as he listens to the poem of his triumphs.

I bend down, shake the wood on to the ground and unfasten my cloak from my head. Now, when I stand up again, they will see me. What am I going to do? How am I going to manage this? My legs have carried me here but I haven't made any decision yet, haven't worked out what my first words will be.

I straighten up and look around. There's odd – no one is looking at me. They're all talking to each other or eating or listening to the bard. For a second, but it feels like much longer, I stand here in the middle of them unseen, then I begin to move through them, around the end of the group, and while the kindred's heads are beginning to snap round, stare and exclaim, I step into the firelight.

Iolo the bard is in front of me, his back turned to me, and all around me people's faces gaze. Iolo's stream of words falters and he turns to see what everyone's looking at. Now his verse stops in mid flow. In the group furthest away, there's still noise and music but here in the heart of Madoc's celebration there's dead quiet.

Madoc has seen me. He doesn't move, doesn't jump up or raise a hand. He sits quietly, looking past the stumbling Iolo, now trying to get out of the way, to me.

I was going to bow or kneel. I was going to put my face down on the earth and pretend submission. But I can't. I know in thi' moment that I will never do that. I look into Madoc's upturr' face and I see that he doesn't expect it either. He is watching waiting. There's recognition in his eyes and satisfaction: he k I have come back here not with penitence but a challeng'

I walk through the watching faces to him. When I'm i feet away from him I stop. He's still sitting, and so a'

They'd rise if he let them, but I see his hand move quickly to tell them to stay down. Stand up Madoc; I am willing you to stand up for me. This one last time, meet me as an equal: if not your princess, your well-matched enemy.

But he doesn't stand. He runs his eyes curiously over my face and then he brushes at Heledd's skirt as if she was a fly annoying him.

'Get out,' he says. 'Can't you see that your lady's back.'

Heledd goes pale; for all that she enjoys being favoured by him, she's still frightened of him. She pulls herself to her feet and darts backwards into the crowd.

'Sit with me, Ceinwen,' says Madoc. His voice is smooth and triumphant. 'Take your place. It is yours still, for tonight.'

As I move forward, turning in the empty space and gathering my cloak, I see Wenlyn staring at me. For once he looks shocked. I turn my face away from him and gaze out at the kindred.

'And it will be my place tomorrow, my lord,' I say, as I sink to Madoc's side.

'Really, how's that?'

'You'll see,' I say. 'I'll be beside you tomorrow, Madoc, never fear.'

'I know you will,' he says. 'Where else would you go? Go on,' he says to the bard, who's hovering on the edge of the firelight. 'Go on with your song. This is a feast, man! Let's have some food and wine for my lady. Quick, pass it to her so she can drink our health.'

Marged is here, handing me the cup. I don't smile at her; I need to keep all my strength for Madoc.

'To our nation, my lady. To the marriage that will found it and to the greatness of New Gwynedd.'

'To our greatness.'

The wine tastes good, though it's been watered down many ∼mes now.

∼Tell me, Ceinwen,' says Madoc under the sound of the bard's ∼what have you done with Glesig?'

∼hing. I left him to himself.'

∼shouldn't have freed him. The high kindred were very ∼ I had to restrain them from following you both and ∼'

'Why did you?'

'Glesig's no threat to us now. You must have realised that — we've got what he stole. He's nothing but an outcast to his own people. A despised one.'

'Well then, why should the kindred bother to kill him — or me?'

'They don't think as far ahead as I do. They never have, that's why I'm their prince still, despite everything. But they're loyal in victory, Ceinwen. They didn't like it that you defied me.'

'Why didn't you let them kill us then?'

Madoc smiles teasingly.

'Because I knew you'd come back. I told them so. I knew you'd realise you had nowhere to go and that your best chance lay back here, with me. We're practical people, you and I.'

'You're right again, then. What a clever man you are, as well as a great one.'

'Mmm. All the same, a show of strength wouldn't do any harm. I can't let them think you can do what you like.'

Madoc takes hold of my shoulder and pulls me off balance. Then, holding me at arm's length, he lifts his right hand and starts to hit my face, hard and repeatedly, knocking my head from side to side. Through the pain and the stunning jolts I can see his eyes laughing.

It lasts a long time and when it stops, I am too dizzy and sick to see. The ground and the silent faces are whirling in a mist and then, and as I try to find something solid to hold on to, a hand is held out. It is his hand, lifting me up and pulling me back into my place by his side.

'My lady Ceinwen is forgiven,' Madoc says gravely. 'Carry on with the song. You see, my love,' he adds in a murmur, 'now they're satisfied. And I can sleep with you tonight. And we'll celebrate the New Gwynedd that's about to be born.'

Dear God Madoc, what have you become? I see it now, feasting blazes on and on into the night and you're still o my cheek, bruised by your hand, and giving me win your marriage with another woman. You're not a ma you're a warrior prince, a deal maker, a leader. You

459

by your ambition. No, you're not a man – you're more like a boy, made mad by his own strength.

How they lurch at me, these faces I know well. Little Marged, Wenlyn, stern old Morddyn. They come out of the firelight and vanish again. Will this feast never be over?

Each time Madoc strokes my face, it hurts. But I still lean into his touch.

'My love,' says Madoc. 'God, you're beautiful. You'll always be beautiful, won't you?'

'Will you always want me?'

'Of course. You were my first love. I've brought you a long way, haven't I Ceinwen?'

'You have. Do you know the first time we made love inside a curtain like this?'

'No, when? Ah yes, touch me like that.'

'In Caer Llion, in the Red House.'

'Mother of God . . . mmm, what? Caer Llion? Oh my love, I want you so much tonight. Oh. Oh Ceinwen. I swear . . . fucking you . . . I swear . . .'

He's asleep. Lying in my arms he is, his face buried into my neck like a baby. And smiling too. He's deep asleep, I know from the little noises he's making in his throat. He doesn't wake as I slip my arm from beneath him and grope for my clothes. He nestles deeper into the brychan as I find my knife and draw it out, and as I carefully warm the blade between my thighs, until it's as warm as sleeping flesh.

He stirs as I slide my left arm over his waist and lift the leather pouch away from his stomach. Gently, gently, I guide the tip of the knife blade into the stitching along the top of the pouch and slit it open. Now the knife comes back, slowly, making sure not ⌐ touch his skin.

‧This is the part where I must be skilled and quick. I take from ⌐olds of my skirt the pebble I brought down from the Hill. ⌐g it clenched in my fist, I pass my right hand back over ⌐ to join my left hand, which holds his pouch. Then I ⌐lf against him as if cuddling in sleep, and while I rub ⌐ with my head my hands work to slip the dreamstone ⌐ch and tuck the pebble in its place. Slowly I replace the pouch against his stomach, slowly, slowly withdraw my closed fist across his body, and then my hand is out of the brychan and sliding under my dress, hiding the dreamstone.

The palm of my hand burns as if it's been stung by nettles. My heart is galloping, but Madoc doesn't wake. I wait. I lie here, with Madoc's head on my shoulder, and force myself to wait a little longer.

He's turned away from me at last. I get up from the brychan, tuck it around him, and climb so, so carefully into my dress. I put on my cloak. Last, I stoop and pick up the dreamstone from the ground.

I thought that at this moment I might waver but instead I find that I am smiling. I feel my way to the flap of the curtain and inch out.

As I expected, many of the people are awake. Almost all the small fires dotted through the shelter have people huddled round them, and here at the shelter mouth, there's work going on. Women are preparing rather sad garlands of winter leaves and twigs, and rubbing up the cups and plates and trinkets that will be given as marriage gifts in a few hours. Men are mending bows and spears and polishing swords.

They all look at me as I come out from within the curtain. I join the nearest fire, my arms hugging my body as though for warmth.

'I can't sleep any more,' I say. Dawyl is among the men; he half smiles to himself in satisfaction at seeing me humbled. I put my head down, to hide the anger in my eyes, and walk off, around the side of the shelter and then out into the darkness, where no one can see.

With every step I take away from the camp, I feel stronger and more confident. I've left them far behind, so even if they've started looking for me now, it's too late. They won't find me in tim The moon is low in the sky now, soon the darkness will be to fade in the east.

I'm at the foot of the Hill. I have come straight here; it's easy to find my path even in the dark. The dreamstone where it wants to go.

The dreamstone lies quietly in my right hand. It doesn't burn my palm any longer and it's not heavy. It's easy to climb the Hill this time; my feet find their own way and I'm not out of breath.

The unhappiness has gone too, thank God. Instead I feel a power that's like the flight of seagulls over the ocean – it wheels in the great space of my mind, soars into the white and sets me free. Ah Madoc, you will be so surprised.

Ahead is the wood and the place where I left Glesig. I slow down as I walk towards it.

'Who's there?'

'It's me: Ceinwen.'

'Have you got it?' Glesig's voice is tiny, choked with hope and dread. Then suddenly he sighs. 'It's here. Oh Ceinwen, you did it.'

I find that I'm smiling and trembling together.

'Yes. I have it. It's in my hand. Do you want to feel it?'

'Yes. Yes. Give it –' Suddenly he breaks off. When he speaks again, his voice is a funny mix of humble and triumphant. 'No, I won't hold it. You keep it until tomorrow.'

'You don't want even to touch it?'

'Tomorrow. I'd like to give it back to Mah-jo-pah tomorrow, to put in its place. But you hold it till then.'

'Let's go to the spring now. We haven't got much time, it'll be getting light soon.'

'I know my way well. Follow me, great lady.'

I have one hand in Glesig's; my other is curled around the dreamstone. I'm carrying the perfect stone to its home, to the place where soon I'll be looking into Madoc's eyes again. But with such a difference. Tomorrow we will be equal, at last.

37

Jane lifted her head from the table and looked around the trailer. It looked like the aftermath of a disaster: Sam lay hunched on the bench seat; Gwyn was slumped over his poem, his head cradled on his arms. They were still asleep; how long had it been? The light shone brightly, the curtains were closed, giving no clue to the hour, but Jane's watch said six forty. They had been here all night.

Jane could remember everything: all the dreams back from the very beginning. She knew that the others would remember too, when they woke. Glesig, Madoc, Ceinwen: they had broken through the barriers which had kept them and now they were here, with Sam, Gwyn, Jane. But who was really here? She, sitting here stiff and frightened, was Jane, but what of the other two? When they opened their eyes, who would be looking out of them?

Move. That wasn't Jane, that was someone else. The unknown woman, now known to Jane as well as she knew her own heartbeat – Ceinwen. Move.

The urgency made it impossible for her to sit still. She had to get up, to get away from these two sleeping men and the trailer, go somewhere. There was more to do and she had to get away from these two to do it.

Cautiously, Jane flexed her legs and climbed on to the s● She stepped over Sam's sleeping body, carefully, carefully. steadied herself as she reached the floor. She looked do● Gwyn's head on the newly handwritten sheets. The writ● peculiarly neat.

Gwyn and Madoc; she had discovered last night how ruthless Gwyn could be. What was going on inside that tousled head, looking so vulnerable on his folded arms, like a tired child's?

No time. Go.

Jane crept quickly to the bedroom, slipped on her coat and let herself out of the trailer.

In the blue half-light she could see easily. The reservation was waking up: lights shone in the windows of several trailers and a woman was feeding cats on the porch of her house. Jane walked swiftly down the line of trailers and across the open ground. She didn't stop to think where she was going; she let instinct take her. Without hesitating she made for the south-western corner of the reservation and the dirt track which ran south to White Dove.

The man stepped into her path as she reached the track. He had been waiting by the fence. His face was patched with cold and his large bulk moved stiffly.

'Not this time,' he said.

Jane looked up into the inclement eyes.

'Let me by, Willie.'

'You don't get by me, lady. You don't go there on your own.'

Jane moved impatiently to go round him, wondering even as she did so that she dared defy him.

'I said no,' Willie began and went to grab her. But she put her hand up to ward him off and he fell back. She turned and looked at him as she hurried past; he was staring after her with a startled expression.

Hurry. Quick. The dirt track was long and the air so cold that it hurt her lungs to run. The blue colour was leaving the air as she ran, thinning to grey and then to misty white. What was so urgent she didn't know, but she knew she had to get there.

Now she was past the edges of Middle Renoxia, past the sports pitches, and the bigger, smarter houses of White Dove were nestling on the lower slopes of White Dove Hill. The dirt track, which had once led all the way up to the wood, now stopped is side of a high fence. Beyond it, a shopping mall had been t. Jane took to the streets of White Dove, passing between ouses, alive now with the bustle of children getting ready ool and husbands leaving for their offices. She hurried, zing, until the houses gave way to the wood.

The well worn path led her through the bare trees and the swathes of thorny undergrowth, across the patch of ground where the kids made huts every year, to the circle of tall old trunks which hid White Dove Pool.

It was more exposed than Jane remembered: she could see into it from several yards off. But as she stepped into the clearing, she felt the hush. She moved forward to the edge of the pool. It was frozen in patches but between the ice the dark water rippled gently in the wind. Here and there she thought she caught reflections of the sky.

Now that she was here, Jane didn't know what to do. Ceinwen was silent; the urgency had changed to a tense attentiveness.

She was waiting, but for what?

'You came.'

She jumped sideways. She hadn't heard any footfalls; Sam had materialised out of nowhere. She scanned his face: it had a stunned, oppressed look. Jane took her hands out of her pockets and tried to keep the terror from showing in her eyes.

'Don't do that,' said Sam. 'Don't pull away from me like that. You don't have to be afraid of me.'

Jane remembered how he had held her last night, pinioning her to the bench seat and forcing her to listen to Gwyn, yet rocking her gently at the same time. Her comforter and her gaoler.

'What are you going to do to me?' Her voice was reedy with fear.

'Shit Jane, I don't want to hurt you. I love you.'

'How can you? If you feel the way about – her – that you said you did, how can you love me?'

Sam shivered.

'I don't know,' he said painfully. 'Confusing, huh?'

He was breathing heavily though he tried to disguise it and Jane noticed that his sheepskin was lopsided: he had fastened it on the wrong buttons.

'You followed me? I suppose Willie told you.'

Sam said nothing.

'Did you dream, Sam?'

He nodded, glancing at her and she saw a play of emotion his face: awe, misery, anger and, she thought, somethin calculation.

'I waited,' he said, 'I waited while you were with him.'

Jane couldn't tell if he was speaking as Glesig or himself. She watched him watching her.

'Paradoxical, isn't he?' he added. 'Different dimensions, same problems.'

The sense of urgency tugged at her again. She didn't know any longer if she were afraid of Sam's motives, or of his recriminations or of her own churned feelings.

'Sam, what have you come here for?'

'What have *I* come here for? Oh help yourself to my past, why don't you? The Last Man wants to be present at the last act if it's all right with you.'

Jane looked away, feeling sudden shame.

'Janey, why don't you look at me?'

Jane could feel Sam stepping towards her, so close that she sensed the warmth of his body just behind her.

'Get away from me, Sam.'

'No. I want to know why you can't look at me. I have to know.'

Jane shut her eyes, as if that could banish the sense of his closeness.

'It's because you don't dare, isn't it?' Sam said. His voice had lost some of its tightness; he sounded stronger now, like the Sam of yesterday afternoon. 'Isn't it?' he said, and she felt a light, faint touch on her hair. 'It's too strong for you. That's it, isn't it Janey?'

'Yes,' she whispered.

'We're a part of each other and you know it.'

'Yes.'

Sam's hands were hard on her shoulders, pulling her round to face him. In her mind Jane felt the woman resist and with all her strength, she seized Sam's wrists and held him off.

'No! I'm not coming back!'

Sam stared at her, a smile touching his face.

'What?'

'I'm not coming back to you. It's not going to happen.'

'What do you mean?'

she watched, Sam's smile began to go into reverse.

married to Gwyn and I love him.'

'You love me, too.'

'Yes, I love you. But not like I love Gwyn.'

Sam's face was suddenly without colour.

'I don't understand. We belong together.'

'Not like that.'

'You – are the other half of me,' he said unevenly. 'I can't live without you. You – match me.'

Jane felt a sharp, distant grief, like an echo of a feeling.

'I know I do. I can't live without you either. But not to live with you, not like your wife – '

'No,' said Sam. 'No, it's not true. We're in the story together. It's not true.'

But it was true. Jane had half-known it when she was waiting for Gwyn to arrive last night; now nothing had ever been clearer or made more sense.

'We are in the story together. We do belong to each other. But we'll always love other people and we need to be with them. You made a life without me, Sam. You have Dee Ann.' The crazy thing was that when she said it, it hurt. Sam heard it and his eyes darted over her face.

'You're jealous. You're jealous of Dee Ann.'

'Yes, I'm jealous. You're right, we are the other half of each other. I love you Sam, like I love myself. Like Ceinwen and Glesig love each other.'

'Don't quote them at me!' Sam jerked her towards him. 'Don't you use those names to suit yourself. They mean nothing to you.'

'They do. I care about them, as much as you do.'

'Jesus fucking Christ, Jane, I don't give a shit about them! I only care about you.'

Sam was clinging to her like someone about to fall. His face was ugly with defiance.

'That isn't true,' said Jane uncertainly.

'It is true. It is, it is. Janey, I've waited for you so long, I've felt like half of me was missing all these years, and finally I found you again. And Janey, I will not let you go.'

Sam was holding Jane's arms so tightly she couldn't move. uncurled her cold hands and stroked the sweater stretched on his chest. From beneath the mixture of grief and lo could feel the urgency returning. There was no time for

Sam was holding her back, stopping her from doing what had to be done. It was a strange sensation, as if the chambers of her heart had begun to war with each other. She pulled restlessly against Sam and felt his hand lift from her arm and move to her hair. He wound his fingers into it and pulled, tipping her head backwards. And as she looked helplessly up into his face, the fear came racing back.

Gwyn ran along the dirt track, stumbling in his panic. Block after block of oblong Renoxia houses stretched out to his left; beyond the sports pitches to his right he could hear the roar of a distant highway. Why had he been the last to wake? How much time had he lost?

The moment of waking was still with him – the silence of the empty trailer, the knowledge of what he'd done, and the shadowy emotions, which were his and not his, still coiling inside him making his tongue taste of blood.

Jane was in danger. He'd known it instantly and known too that it was his fault. Everything was his fault. He'd come to America bringing it with him.

No, that was idiotic, it had already been here, here was where it started for Christ's sake . . . oh for Christ's sake, how much further?

That's it, boy, don't think too much; don't think about what you know now, it's too dangerous. Too close by half. That rage goes too deep and that appetite. Christ, you can be cruel. Look what you did yesterday, mon, look how you skewered her. But look what she did. The same as Ceinwen. No, don't think about it. You'll go bloody mad.

There were bigger houses on the left now, gabled American things with gardens that would be leafy in summer. And they were built on a slope; yes, this was it. The Hill. Follow the streets.

Gwyn saw the fringe of trees ahead quite suddenly, at the end of a curving street. His footsteps stopped slapping the road and began to make shushing noises on the fallen leaves. He ran as ⸱ as he could up the wooded hill, jumping briars, blindly ⸱ing on and up, gasping to ease the stitch in his side. The ⸱ levelled out; he was on the summit. Somewhere here, ⸱ere near – and then between the trunks of the trees ahead, he saw figures. They were standing very close together, almost embracing. He stopped on the edge of the clearing, suddenly wary of going on. Jane and Sam were on the banks of the pool in a peculiar pose; Sam seemed to be cradling her head. No, he wasn't cradling it; he was holding it back – he had her by the hair.

Yet she wasn't struggling. Jane had her hands on his chest and was listening to something he said. As Gwyn watched, Sam let go of her hair and covered her hands with his. He had his head bent, staring down into her eyes.

Why didn't Jane move away? Why was she standing there, gazing up at Sam like a statue? There was something horrible in the tilt of her head, the nakedness of her throat.

Gwyn knew the danger was almost on them now, yet he hesitated in the shelter of the trees, irresolute.

'Take off my ring.'

Sam had flattened all the emotion from his voice.

'Why?' Jane tried for a matter of fact tone but the word trembled.

'You gave it to me and I've worn it ever since, for love. But that's over now. You took your love back, didn't you, great lady?'

'Don't call me that.'

'Come on. It's my name for you, remember. OK, if you won't, I will.' Sam released her hands and quickly tugged off the cheap, gold-plated ring; without looking, he tossed it sideways and it fell with a tiny splash into the pool. 'So, it's gone. Like everything else, like Willie said it would. Now it's your turn.'

A heart was beating faster and faster inside Jane.

'What for?'

'To give me something, Jane. Not just to take.' Sam stepped back from her and stood hunched, hugging himself. He was staring at the ground and Jane could see his mouth working as he tried to school his face. He took a deep, shaky breath.

'It seems to me that I've lost out every way,' he said. 'I've lost you. I've lost my chance to be the last Mandan hero. I've lost Willie's respect. We've come this far – will you at least help me see it through?'

Jane's lips were cold with dread. 'What do you mean?'

469

'Will you take me back – like you took us last night, and show me what happened to the stone?'

Sam looked briefly into Jane's eyes and the pain in his face made her ashamed.

Silently, digging her nails into her palms to control her fear, she nodded.

A sudden movement on the edge of the clearing made Jane turn her head. Gwyn was trying to walk towards them but he seemed to be having difficulty moving his legs. Sam moved swiftly towards Jane.

'Will you do it?' he asked urgently. 'Don't you think you owe me that, at least?'

'Yes,' said Jane. 'I do.'

As soon as she spoke, it began. Gwyn was still walking towards her but she no longer saw him; both he and Sam had faded to shadows and as she watched, the clearing itself began to change. The trees became thicker around the edge, and the undergrowth denser. The sky above grew hard, casting a white light on the grass. Where the pool had been there was now only grass and a silver trickle of springwater.

Jane was alone in the clearing. It was almost daybreak; it was time. Already, she could hear the sound of voices some way off and feel the vibrations of feet travelling over the ground. She turned away and gazed through the tangle of winter branches, her eyes straining eagerly, apprehensively, to see who was coming.

38

They're coming. I can hear them coming. Between the great trees that stand guard round this patch of earth, through the thickets of undergrowth that cluster between them, I feel their approach. The earth thrums with their footsteps. On the end of the heavy branches, the twigs quiver.

Now I can hear their voices. The wind carries them up over the brow of the hill. Chanting, they are, and singing. There's Gwynedd singing, taken in parts, and there's also the strange high chanting of the Bird People. They are coming from different directions.

So white it is here: in these last moments as darkness lifts, the frost glistens on the branches and the ground. It gleams on the bare trunks. And even beyond them, in the wood, there's no shadow, only whiteness.

Around my feet the heavy dew has frozen on to the edges of my shoes. Only the spring is alive, where it trickles out of the cleft in the ground. It runs just a few feet across the clearing, spreads out over the moss and shimmers into ice crystals.

I'm alone here. Glesig wouldn't come into the clearing with me. He says he doesn't have the right. He's hiding, out there in the bushes, waiting to see them approach. I can feel him near. I can feel his fear and his hope.

The voices are louder and I can hear the swishing of people making paths through the undergrowth. They are nearly here. Now they must have seen each other — I can hear shouts greeting, in Glesig's language and, yes, in our own — cried awkwardly, it is, in the back-of-the-throat way of the Bird People. The nations are making friends.

So Madoc is going ahead with it. Of course he is, I never doubted him. He's come to the sacred place to seal a bargain he knows he can't keep. To marry Rokai.

Oh no, Madoc. Never.

Between the trees, the first ones I see are the Bird People: the men are dancing with their spears, the women are chanting and carrying gifts. They stand five, ten deep around the clearing, and now on the other side I can see our own people peering between the trunks, Madoc's men at arms spread out among the women of the kindred, the half-free and serfs jostling behind them.

The clamour of voices breaks as the people see me: but they are seeing me in waves, and as one part of the crowd falls silent or shouts an alarm, others are chattering or starting a new song, or pushing each other out of the way. I stand by the spring, facing the two huge trees which form a gateway into the clearing and although I should feel afraid, I don't.

The banner, dark green holly leaves on a tattered blue background, shows against the icy branches. And a mass of dark feathers, half covered with beautiful beaded swaddling, hovers next to it. Beneath these standards, Madoc and his new ally Mah-jo-pah lead their high kindreds into the clearing.

Madoc looks wild; his face is very pale and set into hard lines. His eyes narrow when he sees me, but he's not surprised: he turns and says something quickly to Mah-jo-pah and they move forward, their men at arms and elders and high women behind them. There's no Rokai; I would look for her but I can't turn away from Madoc. His eyes are green-blue like they were the day we met above Cynfael but they have something deeper in them now. Madoc ap Owain ap Gruffydd is looking at me with enmity, with respect; after so long, he's finally seeing me clearly.

Look well Madoc. My heart is as red as my lips; red like holly berries on the snow. You want me; but how much? You see my love, this is the time of reckoning.

Madoc and Mah-jo-pah stop a few paces away, on the other of the spring. Mah-jo-pah is dressed in splendid robes; they're painted with dyes and decorated with swirls of feathers. He looks terrible and fierce and I feel a twist of fear which isn't mine: it belongs to Glesig. Ssh Glesig, don't distract me; Mah-jo-pah is speaking.

Very chilling he is too, as he turns to Madoc and says, 'Why is this woman in our sacred place? This is an insult. It is a blasphemy.'

Behind him, the other elders are blank-faced, their eyes half closed. But the standard bearers and the people around the edges of the clearing are murmuring and gesturing with a muffled anger.

I lift my head just like a great lady.

'I am here to honour the spirit of this place,' I say to Mah-jo-pah. 'I have come to give my blessing to this marriage. As First Woman of Gwynedd, I must pass my gifts to the new wife.'

There's astonished Mah-jo-pah looks. He's staring at me hard. His face is intent; his body doesn't move a muscle. He is listening. He can feel something.

He's realising that there's something new about me, and something gone from Madoc. He's sensing the stone on me, just like Glesig did.

'Is the wife such an important person in this nation?' he says slowly. His eyes move down from my face to my hands, which I'm holding cupped together in front of my breast.

The dreamstone nestles in there, beneath my fingers.

'She is,' I say.

Mah-jo-pah looks sharply from me to Madoc. Madoc half smiles then bows his head slightly, as if to acknowledge my new power.

'As you can see,' he says, 'she is.'

Mah-jo-pah nods slowly.

'I can see,' he says thoughtfully.

All the time, he's looking at me. Duw, it feels good.

He raises his voice.

'Bring Rokai,' he commands.

Between the trees on Mah-jo-pah's left, the line of warriors parts and the women come spilling out into the clearing. They are half dancing, half trotting, and all of them suddenly chattering in their jay-like voices. Duw what a terrible noise! It batters my ears like hailstones.

In the middle of them, swaying at waist level, is Rokai. She's sitting in a litter of woven canes and rushes with a canopy of red-dyed canes over her head. She looks set-faced and wretched and very, very beautiful. As she's helped down from the litter, she looks straight into my eyes.

I smile at her, though it nearly kills me. Little Rokai; so high born, so desirable to Madoc.

Madoc is watching me curiously to see what I'll do now. Go on, he seems to be saying; make your move.

'Glesig!' I call clearly. 'Glesig.'

The Bird People don't understand at once. The name isn't quite right; only Rokai gasps and clenches her fists in her skirt.

He comes from the side of our own people: I thought he would. The crowd shifts and ripples and gives way and then walking out of it, big and wary, but with his head up, comes Glesig.

As they recognise him, a strange noise comes from the Bird People – like an animal snarling, an evil noise that comes low down in their throats.

Glesig reaches the spring and squats down in front of Mah-jo-pah, raising his arms above his head and clenching his hands.

Mah-jo-pah stares at him, his face dark with outrage, and then, looking at me, says, 'He doesn't belong to us. He is a criminal.'

'No,' I say. 'He's not a criminal any more. He has brought you back the dreamstone.' And slowly I unclasp my hands to show the little stone lying in my palm.

The growling stops instantly, on a sigh. There's an absolute quiet from the Bird People and absolute stillness, as they stare longingly. But our own people are muttering now, shaking their heads and asking one another what on earth is going on.

'Make them be quiet,' I say to Madoc. I say it abruptly and dismissively, like he's spoken to me, too often. He gazes at me, not surprised or resentful but drinking in my strength. He raises his hand to quieten the people, without taking his eyes off me.

'Get up, Glesig,' I say.

Glesig stands up. Like everyone else, his eyes go first to the dreamstone, and he too breathes out, long and deep. But then his eyes fly to me, and from me to Rokai. For the first time since I laid eyes on him in Dreugyllt, Glesig looks proud.

I look at Madoc. He pushes his lower lip out at me gently,

mockingly; asking what I'm going to do with all this. After his first stare at the dreamstone, he doesn't look at it again: all his concentration is on me.

'My lord,' I say, too softly -- I meant to go on being hard and commanding, but an invitation creeps into my voice. 'Come to me.'

Madoc makes a sideways ceremonial movement with his knife, taking leave of Mah-jo-pah, and crosses the empty ground. He's coming straight towards me and would step heedlessly into the spring if I didn't say quickly, in Welsh, 'Don't step on the holy water.' He turns his stride just in time.

'You're sharp-eyed, my lady,' he says as he reaches me.

'It's not like you to forget other people's laws. Especially not in a holy place. On an occasion like this.'

'I was distracted.' His breathing is well controlled but his nostrils are flared with the effort. 'I had a dream last night that you were in bed with me, as my wife.'

Rokai and her women stand silently to one side, bewildered. Madoc and I are speaking the soft language of home and our words mean nothing to them. I look at the faces of our own people, on the other side of the clearing: their eyes are fixed on us uncomprehendingly.

'I am your wife,' I say. 'We became husband and wife at the ladyrock, the sacred place of my village. You're not free to take another, my lord.'

'You stole from me.' Madoc is standing an arm's length away, gazing at my face as if it's a chart he's trying to read or a coast he's seeing for the first time. 'You lay underneath me and then you stole from me.'

'I only took back what I gave you. And I had no right to give it to you. It belongs here, in the possession of the Bird People.'

'You think so do you, Ceinwen? Well my lady, shall I tell you what you'll be doing when you hand over this stone to them? You'll take away our nation's hopes of peace, leaving our people naked, easy prey for any attacks or aggression. Sweet Chris' don't they deserve better than that?'

I hesitate. Madoc's face is alive with passion; despite the louses of wind and cold on his skin, he looks very young sees my indecision and he goes on, talking quickly and furi

'You thought I'd forgotten that you were the one. But I hadn't. Cast your net over the seas: you said that. You told me to go and be great and I've done so. I've brought us here, with our new nation. I'm a great man now and I've made you a great woman. Be a great woman. Don't betray your people.'

I look across at our kindred, in their ill-fitting animal hide clothes, covered with the remains of the linens and silks they brought from home. Behind them are the half-free and serfs, promised a better life here in Ynys Llyr – their own land and the right to bear arms. What Madoc says is true. How do I know that Glesig's people will honour their alliance once we've returned the dreamstone? How can I be sure?

'The kindred hate me,' I say. 'You didn't know that, Madoc. You've been too busy making politics. I kept them in order and they hate me for it.'

'They won't hate you now.' Madoc is gazing at me hectically, like he did the night of the skill sticks. 'I'll kill anyone who doesn't show you respect. You're my wife. My queen. Their queen.'

'What about your new marriage?'

Madoc shrugs. 'What about it? She's nothing. You'll always be queen over me and our people.'

I'm moving towards him: slowly, very slowly, the dreamstone's head, its graceful wings, are floating towards him.

'No! Don't listen, he's lying!'

Glesig's shout tears through the air and wrenches my head around. I see the anguish on his face and I hear myself say 'Glesig' and then I see Madoc turning, very slowly and deliberately, like a wildcat that hears the rustle of its prey.

'Glesig Dog,' he says, and it's as if the words were bile in his mouth. 'Here's your friend Glesig, coming back like a dog to his vomit.'

There's a weight on my heart that stops me speaking. I want to reach for Madoc but he's looking at me, and oh sweet Christ, with a look of such violence.

'Madoc,' I say at last. 'Tell me the truth. Do you love me? Do love our people?'

s laugh is low and maddened.

u don't understand anything,' he says. 'You don't understand what it is to be a prince. What good does love do our people? They need power – and I can get it for them. In battle, in trade, power over our neighbours on the land – give me that stone.'

I shake my head, my breath coming in spurts.

'It will be a dishonourable power.'

'There is nothing dishonourable in being stronger than your enemies.'

'You'll be stronger by false means – by stealing their sacred stone. That's unworthy of you, my lord.'

Madoc's face is twisted with rage.

'I should kill you for saying that. You know nothing about being great. You know nothing about princeship or loyalty.'

'No?' My voice is shaking now, terribly, uncontrollably. 'No? Let me tell you what I know about loyalty. You've hit me and humiliated me. You've lied to me. You've gone your own way and left me to justify you and your deeds to your own people. I have been loyal to you through everything.'

Madoc is staring at me intently, his eyes glittering.

'Oh, you liar,' he says quietly. The words sound like endearments on his tongue, spoken in our language of home. 'Do you think I don't know? You betrayed me with that Dog. With my own prisoner.'

At last he has said it. I look at this furious young prince and suddenly I no longer need to struggle for breath. When I speak, my voice is steady.

'Once,' I say, just as quietly as he. 'I went with him once, when I could get no comfort or truth from you. Is that worse than all the things you've done to me, my lord?'

Madoc steps towards me. His face is anguished, like that of a boy in pain.

'Much worse,' he says. 'How could anything be worse than betraying me like that?'

'Haven't I atoned?' I will not step backwards. I let Madoc come so very close to me, almost touching, and the fear is welcome: it overflows this terrible pain I'm feeling. I look into Madoc's violet eyes and I see the rage and madness in them. 'My lord, haven't I atoned?'

'Do you think,' he whispers, 'that there can ever be atonement for betraying me? Me, Madoc ap Owain ap Gruffydd? And with my own slave?'

He reaches out to me, very gently, and winds his hand in my hair. And gradually he starts pulling my hair backwards, forcing me down.

'Do you know what they call you in the kindred?' he asks. 'They call you a village whore.'

That word. That word in his mouth; I close my eyes.

'Madoc,' I say. 'I'm your wife.'

'Not any more,' says Madoc softly. 'Loving you has been my curse, Ceinwen.'

My legs buckle; I fall on to my knees.

'Leave her!' The voice comes from a long way off: it's Glesig. Beneath Madoc's raised arm I can see that he is trying to move forward, but Mah-jo-pah's hand is out, restraining him.

'Let them be,' he says. 'The dreamstone will find its own destiny.'

'Glesig wants to interfere,' says Madoc. He draws his hand out from my hair, watching the long dark strands slide over his fingers. 'My foster brother the dog,' he says sadly. 'Oh Ceinwen, why did you have to do it?'

Now the fear was gone and there's nothing left but this great, heart-cracking pain.

'Madoc,' I say, 'I love you. How have we come to this?'

'Because you're a traitor.'

'Kill me then,' I say, and I mean it; yes, Madoc, I mean it.

'I will,' he says. 'I'll have to kill you. You've let me down, you deserve it. But first, give me the stone.'

I look down to where it lies in my hand. And I know I must not.

'No! Kill me, Madoc. But leave them the stone. It's made you mad.'

'Give it to me.'

'Never.'

Madoc bends down over me and his eyes blot out the sky.

'Kill me,' I whisper, 'and I'll be with you for ever. Till Morgannwg and Gwynedd die.'

Madoc smiles: a blinded, tender smile.

'And longer.'

His hands are round my throat at last, touching me again, and this time they are hard and strong, like iron.

'Let her go!'

It's Glesig's voice, shouting. There's a thudding of feet, a flashing of limbs, then Glesig is clinging to Madoc's back, people are running from all sides and the violence explodes on us all . . .

Men are falling under spears and knives and arrows, women are crushed and stabbed. The fighting is so bloody and furious that there's no chance of running, and no path out. A young Gwent serf is trampled and pierced through the back with a spear. Koka's long silver-grey hair is tangled with a man's legs and brown with blood. And in the middle of the choked clearing, Madoc and Glesig are rolling over and over, struggling like lovers. Glesig is half-blinded with the blood pouring from Madoc's shoulder; he splutters like a man swimming. Madoc's teeth are gritted and as he forces Glesig's head back with his knife, he looks up at me for an instant and through the storm of bodies and blood, he says my name.

I didn't mean this. Sweet God, I didn't mean this. Not this death, this terror. I was wrong. I'm trying to fight my way to Madoc, stumbling through the thrashing bodies, dodging blades, but he's gone, he and Glesig have vanished under a pile of dying people, and I'm being dragged off my feet and squeezed away from him, knocked further and further back, until a blow hits my shoulder and throws me into the air and out of the clearing, and I smash down on my side, skid dizzily and then half run and half crawl in the wrong direction, not towards Madoc but away from him, leaving the fighting further and further behind as I scrabble my way down the Hill.

He is dead. Madoc is gone; I know it in every inch of me. It is black dark and the fighting is long since over. All afternoon, in the failing light, they have been carrying the dead down from the clearing. There are more of them left than us: I've counted seventeen of our people still living. They must have made s kind of peace: no one harries them as they go back and forth, bringing down the dead.

I saw Glesig's body being brought down by his own people. They didn't take it to their tref – they dropped it at the foot of the Hill, half-way between the tref and our camp. I haven't seen Madoc's body. It could have been any of those that have been carried down since it got too dark to see. But I don't need to see him; I can feel he's gone.

I have been hidden in this thicket, at the foot of the Hill, for so long. I can't get my arms and legs to move, they're stiff and have no strength in them. Not enough to kneel, not enough to bend my knees and pray.

In my left hand, so cold it's chilling my flesh, is the dreamstone. If I could drop it I would, but I can't seem to open my fingers. They grip on the stone, stuck to it by the cold that keeps deepening. And all I can see is Madoc's face with the knowledge of death on it, speaking my name.

It is night-time now. Fires are burning in the camp and up in the tref: funeral fires. And a party of survivors, Glesig's people and ours, is crossing the slopes of the Hill, picking over the ground, searching by torchlight.

They are searching for the stone. But I won't let them have it. I can't. Madoc died for this stone and I love Madoc more than I can love any god of theirs. Or any God at all.

Oh my lord, I wanted you to kill me but instead I've killed you. I keep seeing your face, calling me without words. What was in your heart at that moment? Did you know that I loved you? When I bring you the stone, will you know?

I'm leaving the shelter of this thicket. I'm coming out into the night to find you, and lie with you. Oh, but this night is so big. Now I'm standing here in the open dark, there's nothing between me and the sky: the vast sky, full of eyes.

I take one step, two. But now a shout is breaking through the dark, then another, and lights are travelling across the plain towards me. They've seen me. The Bird People are coming for the dreamstone and for me.

Madoc, don't leave me alone here. Call me, bring me to you. y love, the fear is closing up my eyes. I'm running to you but n't see you, I can't find you. Madoc, where are you?

39

Jane had stopped speaking; she was crouching on the edge of the pool, her face grey-white like the frost and her eyes looked at Gwyn but didn't see him.

I can't see you. Her mouth shaped the words. *I can't find you.* She turned her head, searching the corners of the clearing. There was a terrible sadness in her eyes.

Gwyn wanted to move to her but couldn't. He wanted to go to her and hold her, cover her eyes with his hands and say 'I love you', but he couldn't.

His limbs felt like rock, dead and rooted into the ground. He didn't know how to rationalise what had just happened. Under his hands he had felt the flesh of Ceinwen's throat, Glesig's fierce, struggling sinews, the dense iron of his sword. Through the frenzy, as he'd grappled and fought, he had known a sick, deadly rage shot through with love. And other things – intimations of an incredible beauty that came like memories: the southern shore of Ynys Llyr where they had landed, Ceinwen's face in the dawn in Caer Llion, her hair heavy around her shoulders; racing his horses with Glesig at Dreugyllt while Ceinwen looks on, laughing. Then there had come the unbearable pain which oddly enough was quite bearable, and then nothing – nothing at all. Just an aching loneliness and the distant sound of Ceinwen's voice, calling him.

Dear God, thought Gwyn, they were here and Madoc wa me. But he knew that at the same time he'd still been G watching Jane talk, watching Sam grow stiller and stiller listened. And now Madoc was gone and Ceinwen was gone; the enraging, poisoning presence of Glesig was gone. But somehow they were all still here. There was a huge weight of guilt which linked him with Madoc. His own cruelties and treacheries crowded in on him now: the secret, relentless enmities he had pursued against Goff, Jane, even Sam.

Gwyn blinked his heavy lids, trying to clear his vision. He saw that Sam was moving, walking heavily round the pond to Jane. He was almost as haggard as she, his good-looking face suddenly ugly. He squatted down in front of Jane and took hold of her coat lapels. In a gentle monotone he began to question her.

'Jane. Where is it? Jane. Where's the stone? What did she do with the stone?'

Jane focused on him but her expression didn't change.

'It's in my heart,' she said. And she gave a little sideways smile.

Sam looked at her, very still.

'What are you saying?'

'In my heart,' Jane repeated. She looked past Sam, around the clearing. Gwyn's blood went thin as her eyes met his then moved restlessly by, unseeing. 'It hurts,' she whispered.

'Jane,' Sam lifted his hand to her face and guided her gaze tenderly back to him. 'Why do you keep it, if it hurts you?'

'It's for him.' Jane looked straight at Sam for a second, sudden hope in her face. Then it faded. 'No,' she muttered, 'not you. I must give it to him. I must – give it – ' Her words trailed off as she twisted out of Sam's hold and moved unevenly across the clearing, peering into the trees. There was something unbearably sad in the slow, hopeful turning of her head.

'What's she doing?' Gwyn heard his own voice full of dread.

'She's looking for you,' said Sam slowly.

'But I'm here. Jane! I'm here!'

'She can't hear you. Don't you see? She's gone away from us. She's where Ceinwen is.'

ʼane was lost in the mist. She took careful steps, stumbling on ʼe hard ground. She couldn't remember who she was or what was doing here; she only had a sense of great loneliness. grey mist wrapped round her as she stumbled towards the bodied voice. It was calling her from a long way off, yet it

482

was familiar. She moved towards it and as it grew clearer, the mist seemed to be changing in front of her – becoming darker and coalescing into a form: a man, hurrying towards her, his dark curled hair, his broad shoulders, his wide apart, down turned eyes all pulling at her memory and her heart.

It was him. It was Madoc. She reached out her hand to him but as he ran towards her, his face changed. It twisted with pain; she saw deep lines sear his cheeks and forehead and blood ran out of his mouth. Through the sweat that clung to his lashes, his eyes glittered with a terrible despair.

'No!' The howl tore out of her throat, making her double up. She covered her head with her hands and turned blindly, scrabbling desperately back into the refuge of the dark.

Jane swayed in front of Gwyn, her arms up, shielding her head. Her moaning seemed to go on and on. Gwyn, his hands frozen half-way towards her, looked dumbly at Sam.

'It's me,' he said hoarsely. 'She's terrified of me.'

'She's falling!' said Sam. 'Gwyn – for Christ's sake, go to her!'

Gwyn shook his head. 'I can't,' he whispered.

There was a rush at the edge of his vision and Sam pushed him, roughly, against Jane. Instinctively, Gwyn's arms went out and he held her; the blood flowed back into his sinews and he took her weight, knelt down and lowered her gently on to his lap.

'Why – ?' He looked up at Sam, bewildered. 'Why are you bringing us together – I thought . . .'

Sam lifted his eyes from Jane's white face and met Gwyn's eyes.

'I finally understood some things,' he said quietly. 'She belongs with you.'

'But I've hurt her,' said Gwyn. He stared down at Jane, as she lay with closed eyes, scarcely breathing, across his lap. 'Jane, Jane. Oh cariad, can you hear me? Sam, she's ice cold.'

'I'll build a fire.' Sam was already moving across the clearing, rooting for dry sticks. 'Keep talking to her. Rub her hands and face.'

Leaning over Jane, Gwyn tried clumsily to chafe her fro~ face.

483

'It should be you holding her, not me,' he said in a stifled voice. 'I've got Madoc in me, I tried to kill her. It was you who saved her.'

'No.' Sam now had an armful of sticks and, with trembling hands, was building them into a pile a few feet away. 'Gwyn, it's you Jane's looking for. She loves you. You know that, don't you?'

Gwyn bowed his head: he did, now.

'I'm sorry,' he said. 'For everything. For Madoc. What can I do?'

Sam was striking matches, three at a time, and touching them to the twigs and dead leaves. Shielding them with his hands, he coaxed some sparks into a flame.

'I swear I never wanted to hurt her,' Sam said, and Gwyn realised that he was struggling against panic. 'I wish I could tell you what to do but I don't know. I only know you have to choose.'

Gwyn shook his head in despair. In his arms Jane's lips had bleached to the same grey as her skin; her pulse was slowing.

'Choose what?'

'I don't know. Miss Archer said it to me, several times, but I never understood.'

Gwyn stared into the smoking, sputtering fire. Choose. The word chimed with something in his mind, some memory from his conversation with Miss Archer yesterday. He saw again the lobby of the hotel, the wood-look plastic surround to the telephone, the calendar hanging above it. Yes, Miss Archer had said something similar to him, at the end. Oh Christ, what was it? Yes, that was it. She's said: you have a choice. Choose well, Gwyn. But what in God's name did she mean?

Choose. What was it that he had the power to choose? Madoc had had power to choose many things but Gwyn was a nobody, a writer.

Yes, of course, he was a writer. Gradually, through the fear that held his mind immobile, an idea came. He was a poet. He could choose what to write: he could choose how the poems went.

Every generation people found new ways of playing out the old story. Haydn Phillips had painted it; Gwyn had written it. he didn't have to write it the same, did he? He was free to choose a different way. A different ending. Could that be it, thought Gwyn; if I can find another poem, make another ending . . . Here, now, for always.

'Sam. Sam, listen – '

Above his fire, now beginning to burn brightly, Sam stared mutely at him.

'I'll give you another ending. I'll write you a better one, for you and for her.' He bent eagerly down and touched his cheek to Jane's cold one. He could only just hear her breathing now. 'My love,' he whispered. 'Ceinwen. Madoc loves you. He'll make you his queen. Listen – '

Stumblingly, too fast for it to be natural, he began to snatch at words and rhythms. Ceinwen was in the clearing; the woman he loved more than power, more than kingship, more than life, was waiting for him. He, Madoc, went across and knelt by her; he saw what she held in her hands. He knew then he had been wrong. He told her, asked her, to give it back to the Bird People. No – to Glesig himself, his brother . . .

Nothing's happening, thought Gwyn. He could hear his voice sounding horribly insincere, galloping off with itself, and in his arms Jane felt somehow lighter as if she were slipping away from him.

He met Sam's eyes.

'It's not working.'

'For Christ's sake, Gwyn, tell it from her point of view!'

Gwyn dug his nails into his palms in anguish. Yet again, even now, he was blundering, getting himself in the way of everything. Of course: Jane would only hear if it were the woman's voice. Gwyn's voice didn't matter now, nor did Sam's: it was Ceinwen, not Madoc, who needed a new ending.

Gwyn began speaking again. He spoke uncertainly but fast, groping for the right cadences and images, cobbling together the things that might sound like Ceinwen and he heard his words hitting the air like a madman's. Worse than mad, they sounded dissembling, vainglorious and silly. Why couldn't he get Ceinwen's voice now? He threw words after words, phrase after phrase, but all he heard was a stupid, dishonest man pretending to be a woman. It was an insult to her and to Jane. Frantically, he laid Jane's head down across his lap and wrenched the wad of poems out of his breast pocket. His fingers fumbled them, crumpling the sheets down, as his eyes raced along the lines of verse which he'd written with such confidence.

Whatever had been in them had gone. They were all wrong. They were a sham, a disguise. They were nothing but words, his words and no one else's.

At first Gwyn didn't realise he was crying. It was only when he heard himself sobbing between the futile phrases that he understood.

He looked down at Jane: at her exhausted eyes, her high-bridged nose, the shadows under her cheekbones. It seemed to Gwyn that he had never seen her more clearly. She was someone he hardly knew, and he was only just beginning to love her properly. He raised a hand to wipe his eyes and the sheets of paper flapped mockingly in his face.

'I hate you!' he shouted. Sam stared at him. 'I hate them!' Gwyn repeated despairingly. 'I hate them, I should never have written them. Take them, burn them, oh Jesus, get rid of them!'

He was tearing at the poems, ripping the lines across and down, shredding them, and in a last incoherent gesture, he threw them into Sam's fire. The flames leapt at them and they burned fiercely, brightly, exploding into the heat.

Beneath Gwyn's hands, Jane gave a little fluttering shudder. Gwyn pressed his lips to her forehead: it was damp.

'Sam,' he tried to say but he had no voice.

The sound was like the rushing of the wind: it travelled through the darkness and made Jane raise her head. She put her hand to her heart: she hadn't wanted to be roused; she had sought refuge in the dark. But now the soughing noise was disturbing her, making forgetfulness impossible. She waited for the pain to return.

Yet no pain came; instead the darkness was suddenly, softly alive.

The woman's presence was all around Jane, breathing in her breast, looking through her eyes. There was sadness in it and suffering, but also something pure, which ran through her like a blade.

Listen. Ceinwen was moving towards the sound, taking Jane

'Gwyn burned his poems,' said Sam. Jane caught her breath.

'Your poems?' She reached up to Gwyn and touched the rough, damp stubble on his cheeks. 'You destroyed your work?'

Gwyn traced her tired eyes with his fingers.

'I chose. I chose love. And Sam chose forgiveness. That's when you came back to us.'

'But where's the stone?'

'Oh Jane.' Gwyn's hand, stroking her cheeks, was very gentle. 'Don't you see, there was no real stone any longer. It was the guilt Madoc made Ceinwen carry – the guilt they all made her carry, for all those years. But you don't need to carry it any more.'

'No. There is a stone.' Jane couldn't tell if it were she or Ceinwen speaking so fervently. 'We took it and kept it, too long. And now it's lost, so how can we ever give it back?'

'I don't think we need it now.' Sam was staring towards the his face intent. 'Look. They started to come when Gwyn his poems.'

trees around the clearing were thick with birds. There were hundreds of them, perching in silent lines on the branches. watched, still more flew in and settled among the flock, making a soft susurration like the rushing of wind. small, dark birds, swallow-tailed, and in their shades of black, blue and purple.

id Sam. 'My name bird.'

m Jane to Gwyn and, slowly, Gwyn raised his

d Ceinwen, passionate and low. *And you, my you at last.* But Jane herself was silent, for turning her face up to him and his mouth vingly, on hers.

ing, her face lifted to the sun. Then all a great cloud and the hill echoed with

with her. *Come.* She was pulling at her now, drawing her where she was afraid to follow. *Madoc is near.*

No, Jane tried to say, but she could not resist. Ceinwen swept her on and already the darkness was thinning.

The soughing noise grew louder until it seemed to envelop them. And through it, very close to her, spoke a voice Jane knew.

'Jane. Cariad. Jane, can you hear me?'

Slowly she opened her eyes. She was in Gwyn's arms and he was crying. He looked dirty and loving and there were tears pouring down his cheeks.

He gazed down at her and Ceinwen sighed, a passionate ing sigh. But Madoc's eyes were green-blue, Jane sai Gwyn. But Ceinwen still smiled.

'My love,' said Gwyn. 'Oh my love, are you b right?'

Jane shivered and put her hand to her h

'Are you still hurting?' Gwyn asked.

'No.' Jane's lips were dry. 'There's missing.'

'The stone,' said Gwyn. 'The

Jane shook her head.

'But I couldn't see you,' where, but I was so lo you?'

Gwyn smiled, r

'I found you

'Sam?' Th turn anx small. fac j

s
his
mome.

'Sam,'
'Don't say
'But I don't

'Gwyn burned his poems,' said Sam. Jane caught her breath.

'Your poems?' She reached up to Gwyn and touched the rough, damp stubble on his cheeks. 'You destroyed your work?'

Gwyn traced her tired eyes with his fingers.

'I chose. I chose love. And Sam chose forgiveness. That's when you came back to us.'

'But where's the stone?'

'Oh Jane.' Gwyn's hand, stroking her cheeks, was very gentle. 'Don't you see, there was no real stone any longer. It was the guilt Madoc made Ceinwen carry – the guilt they all made her carry, for all those years. But you don't need to carry it any more.'

'No. There is a stone.' Jane couldn't tell if it were she or Ceinwen speaking so fervently. 'We took it and kept it, too long. And now it's lost, so how can we ever give it back?'

'I don't think we need it now.' Sam was staring towards the sky, his face intent. 'Look. They started to come when Gwyn burned his poems.'

The trees around the clearing were thick with birds. There were scores, hundreds of them, perching in silent lines on the branches. As they watched, still more flew in and settled among the flock, their wings making a soft susurration like the rushing of wind.

They were small, dark birds, swallow-tailed, and in their feathers gleamed shades of black, blue and purple.

'Martins,' said Sam. 'My name bird.'

He looked from Jane to Gwyn and, slowly, Gwyn raised his hand in a salute.

Oh my lord, said Ceinwen, passionate and low. *And you, my friend. I've found you at last.* But Jane herself was silent, for Gwyn's hands were turning her face up to him and his mouth came down fiercely, lovingly, on hers.

A young girl was laughing, her face lifted to the sun. Then all the birds rose together in a great cloud and the hill echoed with their wild noise.

with her. *Come.* She was pulling at her now, drawing her where she was afraid to follow. *Madoc is near.*

No, Jane tried to say, but she could not resist. Ceinwen swept her on and already the darkness was thinning.

The soughing noise grew louder until it seemed to envelop them. And through it, very close to her, spoke a voice Jane knew.

'Jane. Cariad. Jane, can you hear me?'

Slowly she opened her eyes. She was in Gwyn's arms and he was crying. He looked dirty and loving and there were tears pouring down his cheeks.

He gazed down at her and Ceinwen sighed, a passionate, longing sigh. But Madoc's eyes were green-blue, Jane said. This is Gwyn. But Ceinwen still smiled.

'My love,' said Gwyn. 'Oh my love, are you back? Are you all right?'

Jane shivered and put her hand to her heart.

'Are you still hurting?' Gwyn asked.

'No.' Jane's lips were dry. 'There's no pain. But – something's missing.'

'The stone,' said Gwyn. 'The stone's gone. You gave it to me.'

Jane shook her head.

'But I couldn't see you,' she whispered. 'I looked for you everywhere, but I was so lost. Oh Gwyn, for so long. How did I find you?'

Gwyn smiled, rubbing his eyes.

'I found you. With Sam's help.'

'Sam?' There was a flurry within Jane and she felt Ceinwen turn anxiously, pulling away from Gwyn's embrace. Across the small, crackling fire, Jane and Ceinwen looked together into Sam's face. At at the sight of it, Ceinwen sighed again – but this time it was a gentle sound.

'Hallo, my friend,' said Sam.

Jane stared, bewildered: Sam looked sad but also somehow stronger, more complete. She waited for reproach to come into his eyes but he only held her gaze, very straight, and in those moments she realised he was letting her go.

'Sam,' she said, but he shook his head.

'Don't say it. There's no need.'

'But I don't understand. What happened?'